HIS FIRST LOVE

HAMMOND FAMILY FARM ROMANCE

LIZ ISAACSON

AEJ
CREATIVE WORKS

ISBN-13: 978-1-953506-31-3

CHAPTER 1

Hunter Hammond sat down on the bench, the beautiful organ music filling the chapel, and rested his forearms on his knees. His head bowed, he tried to clear his mind and push all the achiness from his muscles.

He closed his eyes and prayed, letting his thoughts move wherever they were wont to go.

"You okay, Hunt?" his dad whispered from down the pew, and Hunter just nodded. He simply wanted to sit for a minute. Ponder, and try to rejuvenate before he started full-time at Hammond Manufacturing Company in the morning.

Am I in the right place, Lord? he asked, and the answer came instantly.ff

Tingles ran down his shoulders and into his fingers, sliding down his spine and all the way to his toes.

Yes, he was in the right place.

Exhaling the last of the tension out of his back, he raised

his head and looked up to the pulpit. He'd missed coming to church here for the past seven years as he'd been off at MIT, learning and working and trying anything he thought he wanted to try.

He'd earned his master's degree in Bioinformatics, which blended computer science with genetics, molecular biology, math, database creation, and operating systems. He loved computers almost as much as he loved crossword puzzles, and as he'd progressed through high school, he'd realized how very good at math and science he was.

The horses and goats on the family farm where he'd grown up and worked until he'd left for college hadn't cared about his skills with numbers and formulas, but MIT had. He'd earned a full scholarship there that he only came close to losing once.

He glanced down the row, over the tops of three children's heads. His half-siblings. Really, they felt like his full siblings, and he grinned at the youngest of them, Deacon, a cute five-year-old that finally looked like a Hammond.

"Hunt, look," the little boy said, and Hunter pulled the dark-haired child onto his lap to look at what he'd been writing.

"It's your name," he whispered. "Remember, we have to talk quiet at church."

"Shh," Deacon whispered back. "How do you spell your name, Hunter?"

Hunter started to spell it for him, pleased when Deacon knew all the letters and got them all about lined up in a row.

"Good job, buddy," he whispered, pressing a kiss to the boy's head.

"Good morning, friends," a man said, and Hunter looked up to the pulpit again, where Pastor Benson stood. He'd definitely aged since Hunter had attended church here for the last time, and he had plenty of gray hair now, with wrinkled laugh lines around his eyes.

Hunter loved Pastor Benson—and not just as a pastor. He'd spent a lot of time at the Bensons' house, as he'd dated their oldest daughter for years.

His father hadn't been pleased with Hunter and Molly's relationship. Looking back, Hunter could see his dad's point of view, and he knew that twelve was way too young to start dating.

At the same time, he'd been devastated when Molly had finally ended things between them completely the week before his sophomore year started. Hunter had disappeared for a while that year, and he'd discovered his tenacity and talent for science and math while he hunkered down and tried to figure out who he was.

"We have a lot of visitors today," Pastor Benson said. "It's nice to see all the young people home from college." He beamed out at the congregation, and added, "Let's stand and sing hymn forty-two."

Hunter set Deacon on his feet and picked up a hymn book as he stood too. He didn't count himself as one of the "young people home from college." He was twenty-five years old and had been living in Massachusetts for years now. He'd graduated a year ago but stayed back East to finish a project he'd founded during his collegiate career.

He'd gotten his two billion dollars on his twenty-first birthday, and he'd done something with it already. Now, he was set to start at HMC in the biometric lab, and his voice scratched on the first note. He recognized the nerves, though his dad had been telling him not to worry. Everyone at HMC knew him; he'd be fine.

Hunter sang the hymn, using the music and the message to once again relieve his rising anxiety. He'd been seeing a therapist for over a decade, and he was glad to be back in the Denver area so he could see Lucy in person. She'd been amazing over the past several years, and he'd been able to do video counseling with her to keep himself mentally strong.

He glanced down as Deacon stepped on his foot, and found his next oldest sibling trying to wrench the pen away from the five-year-old. "Tucker," Hunter said quietly, and the seven-year-old looked up at him. Hunter shook his head and nodded his cowboy hat toward the front.

Tucker was the middle child of Dad and Elise, and he looked like it. He was half dark and half light, with blonde hair that came from Elise and brown eyes that came from Dad. Beside him stood Jane, a ten-year-old that, at first glance, looked like Dad hadn't had any part in her creation. She had Elise's blue eyes and blonde hair, though if Hunter looked further than surface colors, he'd find the Hammond chin and nose on Jane's face.

She looked at him and smiled, and Hunt smiled back.

He'd loved these kids as he'd grown up. He'd left for MIT only a week after Tucker had been born, and he'd come home to hold Deacon for a whole weekend before he had to return to Massachusetts.

The song ended, and Hunter sat down. He reached over and took the pen from Tucker and gave it back to Deacon. Tucker glared at him, and Hunt reached into his breast pocket and pulled out another pen.

He lifted his eyebrows at Tucker, who softened and nodded. Hunter looked at Deacon, his message clear. Tucker leaned over and said, "Sorry, Deac," and Hunter handed Tucker the pen.

When he looked up, he met his father's eyes, and Hunter saw so much of himself in his dad. Gray Hammond had grayed too, but he still radiated power from his broad shoulders and strength from his eyes. Dad had been a corporate lawyer for the first twelve years of Hunter's life, and he'd been his absolute best friend forever.

Hunter hated disappointing him, and he'd worked as hard as he knew how to make sure he upheld the Hammond legacy and made something of the money his father had given him. Extreme gratitude flowed through him as he continued to hold his father's gaze, and finally Dad grinned and whispered, "We need to go fishing."

Hunter nodded, his chest tight. He missed fishing with his father terribly. He missed hugging Elise. He missed laying on the floor while the littles crawled all over him, trying-but-not-really-trying to get away from him as he tickled them.

He'd missed Ivory Peaks and his life here with a force he hadn't even recognized until now.

You're back, he told himself as Pastor Benson got behind the mic again and began his sermon.

Hunter refused to look around and find the rest of the Benson family. He and Molly had managed to stay friends through the rest of high school, but Hunter hadn't kept in touch with her over the past several years. She'd earned some money to a university in Denver, and as far as he knew, she'd gone, graduated, gotten married, moved on.

Hunter had tried to do that too. He'd taken his uncles' advice and kissed a lot of girls. Uncle Colton had said there was nothing wrong with kissing, and after a rocky start, Hunter found he sure did like it.

His senior year, he took a different girl to every available school dance, and he'd kissed them all. In college, he asked out anyone who caught his eye, and he kissed all of those women too. He'd met a girl named Abby, and he'd started to fall for her. They'd dated for a year before he finally had to accept that they were on two different paths.

His had always been coming back to Colorado and Ivory Peaks. Always. He loved the farm with every cell in his body, and he loved his grandparents more than that. He knew he'd use his degree at the family company, and he'd known Abby had her own family obligations.

When she'd finished her bachelor's degree at MIT, she'd returned to New York to work in that family business, and they'd broken up.

Hunter could still hear her voice sometimes, if he held

very still and blocked out all other noise. He missed her too, but it had been a couple of years since that relationship had ended, and he'd once again taken some time to find himself before he asked anyone else out.

For the past year, he'd dated only casually, and that had been enough for him.

Looking down the row of children to his dad, he thought he might like to get started on a family earlier than Dad had. He'd just turned fifty-five, and he had a five-year-old. Elise was much younger than Dad, but they'd stopped with three kids, because Dad didn't want to be eighty when they graduated from high school.

The sermon ended, and Hunter started helping Deacon and Tucker to pack up their notebooks, books, and pens. "Come on, guys," he said. "You can ride with me if you don't dawdle."

"Can I, Dad?" Tucker asked, spinning to their father. "Hunt says we can ride with him."

"Are you going back to the farm?" Dad asked, handing Jane something she'd dropped. "I thought you might stay for the luncheon."

Hunter shook his head, unable to come up with a reason why he'd do that. Why did Dad think he would?

Deacon slipped his hand into Hunter's. "I'm ready, Hunt. No dawdling."

"Good boy," Hunter said, smiling down at a carbon copy of himself. In that moment, he realized that Deacon could be his son. If he'd met someone and fallen in love and they'd had a baby when he was just twenty years old....

Hunter looked up and away from the thought. “I’ll take the boys,” he said. “Maybe I’ll stop by the store and get ice cream on the way out.”

“We have plenty of ice cream,” Elise said with a smile as she leaned around Dad. Hunter loved her too, because she’d first loved him when he was an awkward and unsure teenager. She’d loved his father through everything imaginable, and that made her a saint in Hunter’s eyes.

“Grandma made a cake last night,” Dad said. “Trust me, we have everything you could want.”

Hunter paused as others moved up the aisle in front of him. “Is it for me, Dad?”

“Of course,” Dad said with a healthy grin. “Grandma and Grandpa can’t wait to see you again.”

Hunter hadn’t stayed at the farm last night, because he hadn’t quite been in town yet. He’d driven in that morning, just in time for church. Everything he owned was either in the back of his truck or on its way from Massachusetts.

“I don’t need a big welcome home party,” he said, his mood darkening. He didn’t really like having the spotlight on him, and he gave his father a glare.

“It’s Grandma,” Dad said. “What am I supposed to tell her? That she can’t make a cake for her favorite grandson?”

Hunter softened then. “Where are they?” He eased into the flow of people moving toward the doors at the back, his hand still gripping Deacon’s.

Dad moved into the aisle with him, and they stood at the exact same height, shoulder to shoulder. “They don’t get to church much anymore,” he said. “Not since Grandpa’s fall.”

Hunter nodded, his teeth automatically clenching together. He hadn't been here for that; he hadn't had availability to come visit. Regret laced through him as he moved slowly toward the door.

In the foyer, the crowd dispersed a little, and Hunter had more breathing room. "I'm over this way," he said to Deacon, tugging on the boy's hand to get him to go left. "You comin', Tucker?"

"Yeah." Tucker hurried over to Hunter while Dad and Elise and Jane went right. He dropped his bag, and Hunter paused to wait for him to pick it up.

"I still think we should get ice cream," he said to Deacon. "Do you think Grandma got butter pecan?"

"She got vanilla," Deacon said, looking up at him. "And cookies and cream, and that gross bubble gum kind that Jane loves."

"Hmm." Hunter looked up, thinking they definitely needed more ice cream, and everything around him fell away.

Molly stood fifteen feet in front of him, next to her mother. She still had that gorgeous smile framing white teeth. Her reddish-brownish-blonde hair had always struck Hunter right behind the heart, as had her bright green eyes.

Hers met his dark ones, and he saw the moment she recognized him. Those eyes widened, and she lifted one hand to cover her mouth, which had opened slightly.

Her mother said something to her, but Molly didn't react. Hunter knew exactly what was going on, because everything around him was muted too. Just gone, because there was Molly, and she was all he'd ever wanted or needed.

Hunter realized in that moment that he'd never gotten over her. He may have kissed other girls, but he'd only ever wanted to kiss her.

She blinked, leaned toward her mother, and said something to her.

Her mother's eyes flew to Hunter, and he managed to lift one hand in a half-hearted wave.

"Hunt," Deacon said, and all kinds of chatter and noise met his ears as his senses returned.

"Yeah?" Hunter glanced down at the boy for a fraction of a second. "What?" He looked back to where Molly had been, but she'd moved.

No! his heart cried out. He had to find her and talk to her. He had to know if she was seeing someone or if she might be available to be his again.

"Tucker's gone," Deacon said, and that got Hunter to focus.

"What?" He turned around, expecting Tucker to still be collecting his bag from the floor. He wasn't there. He wasn't anywhere behind Hunter. "Where did he go?" He scanned the front doors, but bright sunlight poured into the building, blinding him.

"Hello, Hunter," Molly said, and Hunter felt like he was being whiplashed all over the place. He swung around again, and she stood in front of him now, definitely older than the girl he'd first crushed on, but still just as beautiful. She smiled and tucked her hair, just as she'd done in the past.

He remembered when *he'd* tucked it for her, and then kissed her. He'd done that many times, and he wished he could think of something else. Anything else.

"Hey, Molly," he said. "I, uh, sort of have a problem."

Her smile faltered, and she glanced at Deacon. "You do?"

"Yeah," Deacon said with plenty of five-year-old sass. "He lost our brother."

CHAPTER 2

Molly Benson had felt an incredible energy when she'd arrived at church that morning. She hadn't known what it was, and her father's sermon, while great, hadn't been the source of Molly's excitement that day the way she'd expected it to be.

Now, she stood face-to-face with Hunter Hammond, having been drawn across the foyer toward him by some unseen magnetic force. *He* was the reason for the renewed energy at church today, and Molly wished the Lord had given her some hint that the boy she'd shared her first kiss with would be standing in front of her that morning.

He wasn't a boy anymore, that was for sure.

In fact, he'd bulked up and grown another four inches during the last three years of high school, and Molly had regretted breaking up with him more than anything else in her life.

At least until she met and married Tyrone Hensen.

Trepidation moved through her, and she told herself it was because Hunter's brother was lost, not because she'd already been divorced before she'd turned twenty-five.

"What's his name?" she asked, glancing around for another miniature of Hunter Hammond.

"Tucker," Hunter said, and he raised his voice and called the name again. He looked at Deacon. "Did you see if he went outside?"

There were three entrances to the foyer, one on each slanted side of the front of the church. Molly's mother and father stood next to the one on the right, as that one led to the parking lot most patrons used. The crowd had thinned enough now that Molly could look over her shoulder and meet her mother's eye.

She managed to convey that she needed help, and her mother started toward her. "We can split up," she said. "My mother will have seen him if he used the west door."

Mama arrived, and she said, "Hunter Hammond. How are you?" in the most pleasant voice. She stretched up and hugged Hunter, and Molly was jealous of her mother. Ridiculous, but oh, so true.

Hunter smiled, and such a gesture should be illegal because of what it did to Molly's pulse. "Real good, ma'am."

"He's lost Tucker," Molly said as they parted. "Did you see him go out the west door?"

"No." Molly's mother sobered and looked from Molly to Hunter to his little brother. "Let's check out front."

"I'll take Deacon out the east door." Hunter moved that way, and Molly couldn't seem to get her feet to work.

"Mols," Mama said, and Molly jolted back to attention. She didn't have time to stare after the handsome man Hunter had become. As she followed her mom out the front doors, she wondered if Hunter had felt any of the electricity she had. Had he simply moved on? Was he married? What was he doing now? Where was he living?

He might not even be back in town for good, Molly told herself. *Don't go getting your hopes up.*

There were a hundred different things that could keep Molly from reconnecting with Hunter, and her mind started to list all of them as a defense mechanism.

She heard Hunter calling for Tucker around the corner, and her mother did the same thing. A little boy came around the corner to their left, and Mama said, "There you are, Tucker Hammond." She moved down the steps, holding tightly to the handrail, Molly noticed. Her mother was getting older, and while she still possessed every ounce of charm and sophistication she always had, her last round of fighting off her uterine cancer had taken a lot from her. Molly's divorce hadn't helped anything, and pure regret moved through her as she followed Mama.

"Your brother is looking for you, baby," Mama said, scooping the child into her arms.

"I'll get Hunter," Molly said as she looked at Tucker. He definitely had the same brown eyes as his brother and father, and coupled with that light hair, Molly thought he'd break more hearts than Hunter had.

After she'd broken up with him, he'd dated plenty of other girls. A different one every weekend. Sometimes he'd taken Laurel Phillips to a football game on Friday night and Teri Childs to a movie on Saturday night.

He didn't stay with any one girl at all, and Molly had told herself over and over that he was doing what she'd said they should. Meet and go out with a lot of different people. Then they'd know who they really liked.

Hunter had told her for about a year that he liked *her*, and that he didn't need to take anyone else to dinner to know it. And yet, when she'd finally ended their four-year relationship, that was exactly what he'd done.

She pushed the high school memories out of her mind as she went around the corner. "Hunter," she called to the tall man on the edge of the cement, looking out over the cemetery and the woods behind that.

He turned toward her, his anxiety plain to see. She gestured for him to come to her, saying, "Mama found him. He's okay."

Relief painted over his handsome features, and he strode toward Molly, his youngest brother in his arms. Time slowed for Molly. All sound disappeared. All she could see was Hunter Hammond in that cowboy hat, a boy who looked just like him on his hip, and her entire future with him right in front of her. Just out of reach.

"Thanks, Molly," he said as he passed, not slowing down for even a moment. Time sped again, and Molly spun around as the scent of Hunter's cologne lingered in her nose. My, he knew how to put together an arsenal against a woman, didn't he?

The dark slacks, white shirt, and trendy tie. The cowboy

hat. The good looks—superior looks. Molly had never met a man as handsome as Hunter. No woman had. He was just that gorgeous.

And the cologne too?

It was almost like he knew he wasn't playing fair.

She ducked around the corner too, just in time to see him take Tucker from Mama, now carrying both boys in his arms. He pressed his forehead to Tucker's, his mouth moving. Molly was too far away to hear what they were saying, but the soft, adoring look on Mama's face said enough.

She loved Hunter too.

She always had; it had been the Pastor who'd warned Molly about getting too serious with a boy too young. To her knowledge, Hunter's father hadn't been very keen on their relationship either.

Molly approached slowly, smiling at her mother. Mama linked her arm through Molly's and said, "I have to go check on Dad. We'll see you at the house for lunch?"

"Yes," Molly said, glancing at her quickly. She couldn't keep her eyes off Hunter, and she really wanted to invite him to lunch too.

Mama left, and Hunter set both boys on the ground beside him. He adjusted his hands in theirs and looked at her. With the crisis over, he seemed calm, confident, and perfectly collected.

"Thanks for your help," he said, that smile appearing again.

Neither of them moved. Molly finally reached up and

tucked her hair behind her ear, her voice stuck somewhere down inside her chest.

"Do you live with your parents?" Hunter asked.

Molly raised her eyes to his. "No, I have my own place."

"So you live here." This time, it wasn't a question.

"Yes," she said. "You? Just visiting?" He'd gone to college at MIT. Like, the actual MIT, where only geniuses and future Nobel Peace Prize winners went to get educated.

"I'm starting at HMC tomorrow," he said, the smile faltering. "I'm literally moving back today."

"To the farm?"

"For now," he said. "I'll probably get a place in the city. It's too far to commute for long."

She nodded, every cell in her body buzzing with the words *Hunter Hammond is back in Ivory Peaks. Hunter Hammond is back!*

"Do you want to come to lunch at my house?" she blurted out before she could think too hard about it.

His eyes widened a little bit, and he looked down at his two brothers. "Hey, you guys," he said, dropping into a crouch. "Will you go wait for me on the steps? I just need to talk to Molly alone for one second."

"All right," Deacon said, and he took Tucker's hand. The two of them walked away while Hunter straightened. He kept his eyes on them until they'd sat on the bottom step, and then for another few seconds.

When he finally looked at her, a storm rolled across his face. Molly wanted to recall the invitation, but it was too late. She wasn't sure what was going through his mind, because Hunter had never said a whole lot. He'd felt deeply, but he'd gone to therapy to learn how to do that. For a long time, he'd told her he'd simply existed behind a barrier made of frosted glass.

He softened and lifted one hand toward her, sliding his fingertips along the side of her face and tucking her hair behind her ear again. It took all of Molly's will power to stay still and not lean into those hands she'd known so well.

"I want to, Molly," he said as his hand dropped back to his side. "But I literally rolled into town ten minutes before church started. I haven't seen my grandparents yet, or really talked to my parents. So I really shouldn't."

"Okay," she said, her voice a bit ragged. She cleared her throat. "It's okay. You go have fun with your family."

He nodded, and Molly wished with every birthday candle on the planet that he'd ask her out for another time. She'd clear any schedule she had to in order to be there.

He didn't though. Instead, he just nodded, ducked his head so his cowboy hat concealed most of his face, and said, "Deacon, Tuck, let's go."

The little boys came toward them, and Hunter looked up at her as they took his hands. "See you around, Molly." He started toward the small parking lot, and Molly turned as he went by and watched him take the boys to a large, gray truck that had a white trailer attached to it.

It was exactly the kind of vehicle someone as masculine and male as Hunter would drive, and he lifted Deacon into the backseat while the child laughed. Molly smiled too, because wow. Hunter Hammond interacting with children was another low blow to her feelings for him. She'd seen him hold his sister when she was a baby, and she'd suspected then that he'd be a caring and attentive father. To actually *see* his concern for his brothers only cemented that.

He closed the door and turned back to her. Embarrassment leapt to Molly's face, and she ducked away from him, hurrying toward the steps that led back inside. She'd made her feelings for him known. She didn't need to add further humiliation to her already burning life.

Inside, she met her mother as she came down the hallway that led to Dad's office. "He's going to be a few minutes," she said. "That means at least an hour. Can I ride with you? Or were you planning to go home and then come to the house for lunch?"

"I can take you," Molly said. They went out the west doors and around to the back of the church, where Dad always parked. Only a few spots were available, and usually the family took them.

Ingrid's car was gone already, which meant all of Molly's younger siblings had already left. She clicked the button on her fob to unlock her car, and the vehicle beeped. Molly's neck felt so tense, and after she got behind the wheel, she pushed out her breath and rolled her shoulders.

"Is Hunter coming for lunch?" Mama asked.

"No," Molly said miserably. Too miserably. Her mother's gaze on the side of her face felt too heavy to bear, and Molly quickly started the car and put it in reverse.

"You invited him, though, didn't you?"

"Yes, Mama," Molly said. Her mom didn't ask another

question, and that drove Molly crazy. She knew this tactic, because she'd grown up with it. She'd seen her mother fall silent when talking to Ingrid about her prom date, and when asking Lyra if her boyfriend was going to propose soon. Eventually, they all broke and spilled way more than necessary, and definitely more than they would've said if their mother had simply kept questioning them.

Molly wasn't going to give in this time. Her parents only lived eight minutes away from the church, and she flexed her fingers on the steering wheel as she approached the first red light. The blocks passed, and Molly started to congratulate herself as she made the final turn onto the street where she'd grown up.

"Molly," her mother said as she pulled into the driveway beside Ingrid's sporty red hatchback. "Did you at least get his number?"

"No, Mama," Molly said, putting her plain white sedan in park. "He doesn't want me anymore." She looked at her mother then, her eyes wide and all of her hurt feelings streaming from her.

"You don't know that." Mama reached over and brushed Molly's hair off her shoulder.

"He didn't ask me out," Molly said. "He didn't even say if he was seeing someone."

"He wasn't wearing a wedding ring," Mama said. "There's still time, Mols."

"No." Molly shook her head. "He won't want me once he finds out I've been married."

"Molly," her mother started, but Molly opened her door

and got out of the car. She didn't want to hear how she was good enough for another man, and that a divorce was not the end of the world.

It felt like the end of the world, like the biggest failure of Molly's life, and she didn't want to hear anything her mom might say.

Thankfully, inside the house, all three of her sisters stood in the kitchen, each of them seemingly trying to talk over each other.

The youngest, Kara, had just graduated from high school. In just a few months, she'd go off to school in the city. Ingrid would return to college for her last year, and Lyra would go back to Utah, where she went to school in Salt Lake City.

Mama and Dad would be empty nesters for the first time, and Molly would keep getting up and going to school every day, teaching the second graders in her class how to read and how to be kind to one another.

She just needed to make it through this summer. Somehow.

Without much to do to fill her time, Molly had been working around the church, helping her father with some of the annual cleaning he did.

She needed more to do. Another job. Something worthwhile to donate her time to. A hobby. A class to learn something new.

"Molly," Ingrid said, smiling as she caught sight of her. "Get in here and tell Lyra that there is *no way* Harry Styles is as cute as Niall Horen." She grabbed onto Molly's hand, blissfully unaware of Molly's encounter with Hunter, and dragged her into the kitchen.

Molly said, "Okay, I can entertain some arguments on both sides." She put a smile on her face, and it wasn't long before her blues got eradicated by the laughter and loud voices of her sisters. She'd always been able to rely on them to cheer her up and take her side, and Molly loved them powerfully.

At the same time, she couldn't spend the rest of her life with her sisters, and when her father came home and they all sat down to dinner, Molly could see an empty spot at their table specifically for Hunter.

She looked away and closed her eyes for the prayer. Once her father finished that, he looked at Lyra and said, "I hear Rick is coming by tonight."

Molly's hand froze as she reached for her fork. In fact, only her father continued to move at all. All the females in the room had frozen.

"Daddy?" Lyra asked.

Her father put a bite of meatloaf in his mouth, his bright eyes dancing. As he swallowed, a smile lifted the corners of his mouth. "He came to see me after church, Lyra."

"Quinn," Mama said, almost breathless herself. "Did he ask you for your blessing?"

Dad shrugged one shoulder and said, "Maybe."

Chaos erupted at the table, with Lyra bursting into tears and Mama praising the Lord that the proposal was finally going to happen. Ingrid talked about how she could record the whole thing, and Kara kept agreeing with everyone else.

Molly was happy for her sister. Of course she was. Her parents and sisters had acted with the same level of excitement when she'd gotten engaged too. She didn't want to ruin anything for Lyra, and no one knew about Hunter's return to Ivory Peaks. So she painted a smile on her face, and said, "I'll help you with your hair, Lyra. Doesn't Rick like it when you curl it?"

CHAPTER 3

"We don't need to tell anyone about Tucker getting lost for a few seconds," Hunter said as he turned onto the dirt lane that led back to the farm. "Okay, guys?"

"Okay," both boys said from the back seat. Hunter didn't think for a second he could actually keep it a secret. He'd have to have a reason for why he was twenty minutes behind everyone coming home from church, and he wasn't going to bring up Molly's name.

At the same time, why couldn't he bring up Molly? Perhaps his father and Elise could help him understand the knot of feelings in his chest.

No, he told himself. *You pay a therapist for that.* He'd call Lucy in the morning and find out if she had any appointments that week. He could zip down the street during the day if he had to.

He pulled to a stop in front of the farmhouse he'd grown

to love over the years. He'd definitely had moments where he hated living here, and moments where he'd loved it. Now that he hadn't been here for a while, only the fond memories seemed to be coming through.

He killed the engine about the time his grandfather walked out the front door, and Hunter jumped from the truck then. "Grandpa," he called, feeling very much like the little boy he'd been when his dad would bring him out to visit his grandparents.

Hunter helped the little boys down from the back seat first, and then he hurried toward the front porch and up the steps. "Grandpa," he said again, taking the older man into his arms. "Oh, it's so good to see you." He loved his grandfather so much, as the man had spent a lot of time with Hunter out here on the farm. They'd had many talks over the years, and so much of who Hunter wanted to be existed inside his grandpa.

"Oh, my boy," Grandpa said, and he pulled away and ran his hands down the sides of Hunter's face, a soft, loving smile on his face. "I think you're taller than last time you were here."

Hunter chuckled and shook his head. "Nope. I think you're shorter, Gramps."

"That makes you taller, doesn't it?" Grandpa turned and started toward the front door, which Tucker and Deacon had left open. "Come see Grandma. She's been fretting about you for an hour."

Grandpa limped into the house, and Hunter followed

slowly behind him, holding the door open and then closing it softly behind him. "He's here, Bev."

Hunter grinned as his grandmother hurried into the foyer to greet him. He let her fuss over him and cry when she saw how "grown up" he was. He accepted the new book of crossword puzzles and the bottle of lemonade she kept in her fridge specifically for him, and he felt like he'd come home.

At the same time, he knew he couldn't stay at the farm forever. His thoughts wandered as he wondered where he'd end up, and by the time Grandma and Elise served lunch, Hunter's nerves had returned in full force.

He sat next to his father, realizing he was just as big as the man now. Maybe five or ten pounds heavier, as Hunter shared a lot of interests with his dad, but one of them was not running marathons.

The conversation flowed around him, mainly focusing on his siblings and what they'd be doing now that school was out for the summer. They usually went to Coral Canyon for the summer, and as Hunter ate and listened, he realized his move back to Ivory Peaks had delayed them from returning to their summer home in the mountains.

"You guys can go," he said. "I'm fine here."

"I wanted to be here," Dad said.

"*We* wanted to be here," Elise corrected him, shooting a look at Dad. "Coral Canyon isn't going anywhere, Hunt. We wanted to see you and find out how your first week at HMC goes." She gave him a warm smile, and Hunter's heart expanded with love for her. She'd always been interested in what he was interested in, even when she didn't understand some of the terms he used.

She'd patiently ask him questions until he could explain what he was doing at school, and why he liked it. She didn't know it, but it was something Elise had said about taking advantage of educational opportunities that had spurred Hunter into asking his uncle about his work with veterans.

Uncle Cy and Uncle Ames had been a huge help for Hunter, who'd then started an educational foundation specifically for injured veterans and cops to get special training through MIT when they couldn't go back into the military or on the force. The idea was that they could then get educated in something technological and continue to be good, contributing citizens for their communities.

He was still the founder and CEO of the foundation, but only in name. He'd turned over all the day-to-day operations to William Hyde, his best friend from MIT, who still lived and worked in the Cambridge area.

"Plus, your father wants to go fishing with you," Elise said, shooting a knowing look at Dad.

"I want to go fishing too," Deacon piped up. "I got a new pole, Hunt, and it's awesome."

"Is that right?" Hunter asked. He knew his father took his other sons fishing, and he was suddenly envious of all the years they had ahead of them. Time to talk and discuss real life things. Time with Dad, when he wasn't stressed or worried. Time to be themselves and be accepted by Dad.

Hunter had loved going fishing with his father, even

when some of the discussions hadn't been particularly pleasant.

"Just Hunt and I are going this afternoon," Dad said, looking at the younger boys. "I need you guys to stay here and help your mother with the peas."

"Da-ad," Tucker whined. "I helped with the peas all day yesterday."

"It was an hour, not all day," Dad said. "Don't argue with me, or you won't get to come fishing tomorrow either." He gave Tucker a stern look, and the little boy began to pout as he pushed his fried potatoes around on his plate.

Hunter wanted to tell his dad that it was okay if the little boys came, but Dad met his eye and shook his head. It wasn't about him or even them. It was about Hunter, and he nodded.

Lucy had taught him that it was okay to have things be about him sometimes. This was just one of those times.

"Okay," Elise said. "Who learned something new at church today?" She looked around at everyone. "Grandma and Grandpa would probably like to hear what Pastor Benson said." She smiled at them warmly, and Hunter didn't miss the way they smiled back at her.

Elise possessed a special kind of charm, and Hunter wanted a woman like her for his wife. Someone with pure kindness inside them, and someone who loved the Lord, loved him, and loved the family they could build together before they even started.

She supported Dad through anything and everything he wanted, but he did the same for her. Since Deacon's birth,

Elise had restarted her lawn care business, and she ran it from right there at the farm, in addition to everything else she was responsible for.

Hunter couldn't help thinking about Molly Benson and the way his heart had practically screamed at him to make sure she didn't get away from him for a second time. He wasn't sure what that meant. He hadn't asked for her number or tried to set anything else up with her after she'd invited him to lunch at her parents' house.

The truth was, Hunter wanted to go, but he knew he couldn't. He also didn't want to reconnect with Molly with her parents nearby. He wanted to see her when they could be alone, talk about anything, and he could hold her hand and kiss her if he felt like he should.

His heart pounded in his chest, right there at the dinner table with his family. He'd made a mistake by not getting her number or asking her to dinner for tomorrow night. Like a bolt of lightning, he thought of Uncle Wes, and how he'd talked to his wife, Bree, on the phone for a while before he'd even met her.

Shoulda gotten her number, Hunter told himself. *You've got to get her number.*

He anticipated being very busy for the next few weeks. Even if it wasn't busy in the labs at HMC, he'd be tired in the evenings, and he couldn't think of anything better than talking to Molly only moments before he went to sleep.

"Hunt?"

"Hmm?" He looked up at the sound of his name.

"Are you done?" Dad reached his hand toward him, and

Hunter looked down the table, realizing that everyone had finished and gotten up except for him.

"Oh, yeah, thanks," he said, lifting his plate toward his father. Dad took it, something sharp in his eyes. Hunter looked away, because he didn't need to have this conversation right now. They could talk about Molly once they got out on the lake.

He wiped the table for Elise and sat on the couch with all the siblings while they begged him to look up the videos and things they liked on his phone. His father was very strict with electronics, and Hunter wasn't surprised that none of them had a phone or a tablet. They'd be lucky if they got either of those things before they became teenagers, and Hunt sure did like holding Deacon on his lap while Jane pressed into his right side and Tucker into his left as they watched a video about a tiny man making tiny food.

"There's this channel called DIY crafts," Jane said. "Look that one up, Hunt."

He typed in what she'd said and showed it to her. "Which one is the best?" With the little boys, she'd get one video on this channel, so she better pick the best one.

"DIY Halloween," she said. "You have to scroll down... right there." She settled into his side to watch it, and Hunt could admit he liked the six-minute video about making Halloween treat buckets, costumes, and doing gory makeup.

"All right," Dad said a while later. "You kids go help Momma. Hunt, I've got our stuff loaded for fishing."

"All right." Hunt groaned as he got up from the couch,

the other kids grumbling about having to do any gardening on the Sabbath, and he tucked his phone in his back pocket.

"You're going to spoil them with that thing," Dad said, but he wore a smile.

"Don't worry," Hunt said. "I won't show them stuff all the time."

They didn't say much on the way to the lake, and Hunt carried the boat while his dad carried the poles and tackle box. As he launched the boat with his dad in it, he realized that they'd traded positions. It had always been Dad carrying the boat and pushing them out once Hunter had gotten in with their gear.

He rowed too, something his dad had normally done. Hunter's mind churned, and he didn't know where to start the conversation. Had his dad felt like this too?

"Nervous about tomorrow?" Dad asked after they'd reached a quiet spot and thrown their lines in.

"Yes," Hunter admitted. He watched the water where his line disappeared, but it stayed absolutely still.

"I know you don't want me to say you'll be fine," Dad said. "So I won't. It's perfectly normal to be nervous about starting a new job."

"Thanks," Hunter murmured.

"Are you going to get a place in the city?"

"I was thinking so, yes," Hunter said, looking up to meet his dad's eye. "I can't commute from out here. It's over an hour each way."

Dad nodded, his dark eyes still as sharp as ever, despite

the gray hair. "No, you can't. The company owns several condos. You might ask Laura if there are any available."

"You don't think I should just buy my own place?"

"That's up to you," he said. "You could be at HMC for a long time. Buying might be better than renting."

"Yeah." Hunter didn't have any other big dreams. He just wanted to live a simple, quiet life. "I like the farm, Dad."

"I know you do."

"You'll let me buy it when you and Elise don't want it anymore, right?" He looked straight into his father's eyes, hoping he could see the earnestness which ran through Hunter's veins.

He didn't seem surprised at all. A smile crossed his face. "If you want it right now, Hunt, you can have it."

"I don't need it right now," Hunter said. "I don't know what I want my whole life to look like. I just don't want you to sell it to Jane or Tucker."

Dad nodded. "They're not my second family, Hunt."

"I know that, Dad." Hunter sighed. "That's not what I meant at all."

"Okay," Dad said his voice pitching up. "I just don't want you to think I love them more than you."

"I don't think that." Hunter looked away, because yes, sometimes over the past decade, he *had* felt like that. Lucy said those feelings were normal, and Hunt hadn't tried to hide them. He hadn't embraced them either, because he knew they weren't true. Human beings were simply complicated, and that was why he talked to someone else about how he felt.

Several minutes went by while he tried to untangle his thoughts enough to mention Molly.

"Have you seen or talked to your mother lately?" Dad asked.

"No," Hunter said, his voice hard. He hadn't told his father everything that had happened surrounding Sheila, and he didn't want to get into it right now either. He needed to schedule an appointment once a week with Lucy, he knew that. One session to deal with his feelings surrounding his new job. One session to deal with his mother. One for Molly. One for his dad....

"Okay," Dad said.

Hunter reached up and took off his cowboy hat, ran his hand through his hair, and reseated his hat. "Dad, I ran into Molly Benson after church today."

Dad's eyebrows shot straight up. "You did?"

"Yeah." Hunter couldn't help smiling.

"Oh, boy," Dad said with a chuckle. "I've seen that look on your face before."

"I still like her," Hunter said. "Is that stupid? I mean, who still likes a girl a decade after she broke up with him?"

Dad shook his head and reeled in the rest of his line. He cast it back out, something contemplative in his expression. "Hunter, you're twenty-five years old now. If you like that *woman,* call her and ask her out. Maybe she still likes you too."

He nodded, a new fire starting in his blood. "She asked me to lunch with her family today."

"There you go. You know she's single, and she's interested."

"I thought you didn't like Molly."

"Hunt." Dad sighed and met his gaze. "I just didn't want the two of you to get too wrapped up with each other as kids. You met her when you were eleven. *Eleven,* Hunter. Jane is going to be eleven this year."

"I know, Dad."

"I was worried about you," he said. "Limiting yourself. Tying yourself to someone when you hadn't really even explored the world, or your possibilities, or other girls."

"I've kissed a lot of other girls now," Hunter said.

"Hunter," his dad admonished, a smile growing on his face. "Really?"

Hunter shrugged. "Uncle Wes told me I should."

"You're kidding." Dad looked like he'd been hit with a brick, the smile disintegrating as fast as it had appeared.

"I wasn't supposed to tell you that."

"I'm going to have a talk with Uncle Wes."

Hunter burst out laughing. "Dad," he said between the chuckles. "This was before Jane was born. You don't need to have a talk with him."

"I'm going to tell his kids to kiss a lot of girls," Dad said, still not even smiling.

Hunter shook his head. "I better text him and warn him that you're on the warpath."

"Oh, I'm not on the warpath." Dad's face cracked into a smile then, and when Hunter met his eyes again, they laughed together. Once he sobered, Dad said, "But define 'a lot' of girls, Hunt...."

Hunter just smiled, feeling grateful for this moment. For his father, and for the fishing boat that always brought them together. "A lot, Dad."

"You don't even know how many," Dad said, slight disgust in his voice. "You went out a lot the last few years of high school."

"Almost all of them," Hunter said. "It was innocent, Dad. I didn't do anything wrong."

"You loved Abby, though," Dad said, turning things serious again.

"Yeah." Hunter looked out over the water and turned his reel a few times. "Yeah, I did love her."

"Okay." Dad took a deep breath and blew it out. "You know what it feels like to fall in love. You know you like Molly. What are you going to do about it?"

"I didn't get her number or anything," Hunter said, dropping his eyes to the bottom of the boat. "I didn't ask her out. I just said I couldn't come to lunch." He looked up. "What would you do? Do you know where she works or anything like that?"

"No," Dad said. "But I know who her father is, and that he's our pastor."

A smile filled Hunter's whole soul, because he could easily get Molly's number. He just had to call her father to do it.

CHAPTER 4

Molly had barely set a bowl of cat food on the floor when her phone rang. Gypsy darted between her legs and started eating as if she'd been starved for days. Molly's other pet, a well-behaved miniature schnauzer, had already been fed, so Gypsy was probably perturbed she'd been attended to second, the spoiled thing.

Her father's picture sat on the screen, and Molly swiped on the call. "Hey, Daddy." She'd left the house where she'd grown up an hour ago, after Lyra's boyfriend had become her fiancé. She'd contained the tears to her car on the drive home, and she'd been dry-eyed for a half-hour now, so her voice was fairly normal.

"Molly, I just got off the phone with someone who called for you," he said.

She frowned. "For me?" She hadn't lived with her parents for years now. Who would be calling her childhood home looking for her?

"Yes," Dad said.

"Who?"

"Hunter Hammond."

Molly sucked in a breath, her vision turning all the way dark for a moment. "What?"

"He called to get your number, and I wasn't sure if I should give it to him. You didn't mention him at lunch today."

"Mama...." Molly's voice trailed off, because she couldn't think straight enough to form an explanation.

"He left his number," Dad said. "He said it was all right if I gave it to you. Do you want it?"

"Yes," Molly blurted out. "Yes, I want it."

Her dad let a few seconds of silence go by, and Molly heard his displeasure in the gap. He recited the number, and Molly spun away from the laundry room where she fed her pets and hurried into her kitchen to get a pen.

"Say it again, Daddy," she said. "I didn't have anything to write with."

He repeated it, and Molly looked at the numbers on her shopping list like they were worth their weight in gold.

They were *Hunter Hammond's* phone number, so they were.

"Molly," her father started.

"Daddy," she said. "I'm not fourteen anymore. I'm twenty-five, and I've graduated from college, have a good job, and have been married. If I want to call Hunter Hammond and date him and kiss him, I'm going to."

Her father sighed. "I suppose you're right."

"Why don't you like him?" she asked.

"I *do* like him," her father said. "He's a good kid. He's just—"

"He's not a kid," Molly said. She pictured Hunter in that cowboy hat today, both of his little brothers in his arms. He was definitely not a kid. "Neither am I."

"You're right." Her father drew in an audible breath over the line. "You're right, Molly. I apologize."

"Thank you," she said quietly. "And thanks for calling to give me his number."

"Love you, Mols."

"Love you too, Dad." The call ended, and Molly stood there gazing down at the numbers on the shopping list. She should've asked how long ago Hunter had called. Then she wouldn't come across as desperate when she called him back.

"You asked him to your family lunch today," she muttered to herself. "Nothing more desperate than that."

She picked up the pad and ripped off the top sheet that had eggs, milk, coconut oil, and Hunter's number on it. She folded it and put it in the pocket of her sweats, which she'd changed into the moment she'd arrived at home.

She didn't need to call him right now. It was barely eight o'clock, and surely he'd be awake for a while longer. Determined to wait an hour, she set an alarm on her phone and turned to the kitchen. She could make bread while she waited for the alarm to go off. That would free her mind to think about what she'd say to him too.

Hey, Hunter. My dad called and gave me your number.

So far, so good.

She got out the yeast, the flour, and the salt. She heated milk and butter, added sugar and yeast, and breathed in the sharp smell of it as it bloomed. She mixed half white flour with half wheat, added a dash of honey, and kneaded in salt with everything else. Her hands could make bread without any direct instruction from her brain, as she'd been baking with her mother for years now.

Molly didn't come up with anything witty or intelligent to say to Hunter while she put the dough together. She rubbed olive oil over the top of the ball of kneaded dough and draped a tea towel over the bowl.

She faced her phone, knowing an hour hadn't gone by. One needed to for the dough to rise properly, and another after she shaped it into the pans. Molly realized she'd be up late tonight to get the bread baked.

Maybe she could pass the time by calling Hunter....

"Dear Lord," she prayed, bending her head back to look up at the ceiling. "Help me say the right things."

Still nothing came into her mind, but she'd have fresh bread in a couple of hours, and she had absolutely nothing on her schedule for tomorrow. Hunter had always liked to eat, and Molly could easily offer to bring him lunch somewhere.

She picked up her phone and paced out of her kitchen, beyond glad she'd sold the house where she and Tyrone had only lived for eight months. He'd told her she could keep it in one of his rare shows of compassion, but she hadn't wanted it. She'd have to go through getting his name off the mortgage, and she'd already had to do so much to separate her life from his.

Selling the house had been the easiest thing to do, and Molly had done it.

She'd bought a smaller place—only two bedrooms—closer to her parents, but still an easy drive to her elementary school. It took her forty minutes to get into the city, where Hunter said he'd be working, but she had the time.

All she had was time.

"Just do it," she whispered to herself. "Be brave, Molly. Brave like you were when you finally told Tyrone you were leaving." Something strange and wonderful bloomed inside her, and she felt herself physically straighten and strengthen.

She paused, because she absolutely could not call Hunter and walk at the same time. In fact, she should get over to the couch to make this call. She did, perching right on the edge of it. Saltine, the cute little cream-colored schnauzer she'd fallen in love with the moment she'd walked into the dog adoption event, curled into her hip. He only weighed sixteen pounds, and she loved the comforting weight against her.

Comfort eased through her, showing on her face in the form of a smile. "Hey, my little friend." She stroked the dog, watching Gypsy stalk into the kitchen, her nose up in the air. She could smell the yeast, and that darn cat would do her best to get something to eat off the counter before the night was up.

She jumped up onto the island, and Molly said, "Hey, get down."

The cat looked over her shoulder, clearly unperturbed by Molly's command. She'd suddenly gone deaf, because she just tippy-toed her way across the island for a good ten seconds before she finally did what Molly said.

She shook her head and looked at Saltine. "I'm going to call Hunter now. I am." She took a deep breath. "You'll stay right here by me while I do?"

Saltine looked up at her with his beautiful dark eyes that seemed to say, *I'll stay right here. Don't worry. You've got this.*

Molly took another breath and looked at her phone. She withdrew the paper where she'd written down Hunter's number, and she programmed it into her phone. Nice and normal too, just Hunter Hammond. When she was a teenager, she'd given everyone a funky little name in her phone, and she smiled as she remembered that her best friend had been MacAdams, though her name was Macey Adams.

With the number in her phone, she had no reason not to call Hunter. Her heart raced, and she quickly got the job done, much like she had to do when she needed to call a parent and let them know their child had been naughty at school that day. She hated those calls more than anything, and she found herself jumping to her feet as the line rang.

"Hello?" Hunter's voice came through the line deep and luxurious and like falling onto a bed covered in blankets fresh from the dryer.

Molly smiled to herself as his voice dripped through her

whole body.

"Are you there?" he asked, and Molly cleared her throat.

"Hunter," she said. "It's Molly Benson."

"Molly," he said easily, as if the sight of her didn't make his heart beat any differently than it normally did. "Your dad must've called you."

"He did," she said with a light laugh. She told herself to calm down. This was *Hunter*, and she knew him.

You knew him a decade ago, she told herself. *He's not the same as he was then.*

"Listen," she said, thinking that at his core, Hunter probably was the same as he'd been as a teenager. Good, and kind, and hardworking. He left Ivory Peaks every summer, even when he didn't want to. He worked his grandparents' farm every morning and every evening, no matter what else was going on.

"I'm listening," Hunter said, plenty of teasing in his voice.

"I'm really struggling," Molly admitted.

"How about I start?" he asked. "I called your parents' house to see if you were there. I know you said you didn't live with them, but I figured it bein' the Sabbath and all."

"Mm hm." She paced in front of the island, the night beyond the back door still plenty light. Maybe she could drive out to the farm tonight.

"I was hoping to get your number no matter what," he said. "I'm, well, I'm wondering if you'd like to go out with me. Get dinner or something. Catch up. That kind of thing."

Warmth moved through Molly's whole body. She wanted

to go out with him more than anything. "I think I'd like that," she said, smiling with her entire face.

He chuckled and blew out his breath. "Whew. That was hard."

"Was it?"

"You couldn't even talk." He laughed again, and Molly joined him.

"Yes, well, some of us have grown into a tall, dark, handsome, muscled man."

"Yeah, and some of us have grown into a beautiful woman."

The silence between them said so much, and Molly wanted to dive into it and swim around for a while.

"I have to start work at the family company tomorrow," he said. "What are you doing?"

"Nothing," she said. "I teach second grade, and we're out for the summer."

"Wow, that's nice," he said. "And look at you, being a teacher. Did you ever tell me you wanted to be a teacher?" He was very careful not to say *when we were dating*, and Molly noticed.

She wasn't even sure if what they'd done counted as dating. They'd barely been twelve the first time he'd held her hand, and though they were inseparable for a few years, and they kissed each other, she'd broken up with him right before their sophomore year. They'd practically had their entire high school careers to themselves.

"I doubt it," she said. "I didn't start thinking about teaching until my junior or senior year."

"Do you like it?" he asked.

"Yes," she said. "I just finished my second year, and I've had some hairy times, but yes. I like it." She didn't want to be a career teacher though. Molly already knew that. She taught, because she was twenty-five years old, and she needed a job that could support her. She didn't want to live with roommates or her parents, and she'd gone to school for four years to get a degree.

What she really wanted was to be a wife and mother. She wanted to raise a house full of children, the way her parents had. She wanted to teach her girls how to braid their hair and how to bake bread, the way her mother had taught her. She had no idea what to do with boys, but if she got any, she felt certain the Lord wouldn't let her lead them too far astray.

"...right now?" he asked.

"I'm sorry," she said. "I think I lost you for a second." Really, she'd disappeared inside her own head.

"Oh, can you hear me?"

"Yes, I can now."

"I said I was on my way to town to get ice cream. Grams has a whole freezer of it, but not the kind I like. I wondered what you were doing right now, and if you'd like to come along for a ride."

"Sure," she said, looking down at the sweat pants she currently had on. Those would have to go. She should probably burn them anyway, as they were from her senior year of high school and bore plenty of evidence of all they'd been through.

"Great," Hunter said. "What's your address?"

Molly rattled it off for him, and the next thing she knew, he said, "Oh, I'm right around the corner from you. This says three minutes."

"Three minutes?" Molly couldn't leave the house in three minutes. She needed at least ten to be presentable for Hunter. "I better get changed."

"I'm sure what you're wearing would be fine," he said.

"I'm sure you're wrong," she said, already moving toward the hall that led to her bedroom. "Don't come to the door, okay? I'll come out when I'm ready."

"Two minutes," Hunter teased, and Molly grinned. "Don't hang up, okay? Just…you can put me on speaker while you change."

She smiled as she entered her bedroom. She did lower the phone from her ear and put him on speaker. Once he'd gotten his cell phone, he'd call her from the barn and say similar things.

I don't care what you talk about, Molly. Just talk to me while I feed the horses.

And she would. She'd loved talking to Hunter, because he never judged her. He never told her she should've done something different.

He will now, she thought. He didn't have the same innocence as children did. She hesitated. If she went out with Hunter, she'd have to tell him everything.

"I drove from Big Springs this morning," he said with a yawn. "Before that, I stayed in Chicago."

"How far is it from here to Cambridge?" she asked,

deciding on the spot to go for it. Hunter would find out everything about her past anyway. He was a smart, resourceful man, and Ivory Peaks wasn't that big.

Technically, Molly didn't live in Ivory Peaks anymore, but plenty of people knew her story who did.

"Thirty hours," he said. "I drove it in three days."

"Wow," she said, stepping out of her sweat pants and leaving them in a puddle on the floor. She wasn't the neatest housekeeper, and if she hurried, she wouldn't have to let Hunter into her house. She didn't believe for a moment that he'd sit out in his truck and wait for her.

That would be something Tyrone would do; Hunter would come to the door, despite what she'd told him to do.

She hurried into her closet and scanned while Hunter told her about his drive across most of America. When the doorbell rang, he said, "That's me."

"I'm coming," she said, reaching for the closest pair of pants. They were black jeans, and she quickly leaned against the wall to pull them on. "Skinny jeans," she muttered, and Hunter chuckled.

"Oh, I hear a cat," he said. "Do you have a cat, Molly?"

"Yes, and she's not nice," Molly said. "So I'd tread carefully if I were you."

"I'll sit on this mighty fine front porch," he said. "You've always wanted a front porch."

"That one's too small," she said, yanking on the jeans to get them over her ankles. She shimmied into them and stripped off her lounge T-shirt. She grabbed a blouse in green and gray, because with her reddish hair, she looked good in green. Purple, too, but she didn't have time to hunt for her paisley print right now.

Hunter was waiting.

"Too small?" Hunter repeated. "You've got a table and chairs out here."

"I never use them," she said, searching now for shoes. "They're too small too."

"They are?"

"You sit in one of those chairs, Hunt, and I'll pay you twenty bucks if you don't fall right out." There was no way the tall, broad-shouldered cowboy could perch on that delicate porch furniture. Even when Molly had bought them, she'd known she'd never use them. She'd almost been bucked right out, and she was half the width of Hunter.

She grabbed a pair of sandals, reminding herself it was summer, and she wouldn't have cold feet. A moment later, she retrieved the phone from the shelf and strode down the hall.

On the other end of the line, Hunter yelped, and a terrible crash nearly deafened her. Despite her best efforts not to, she let out a string of laughter, covering up anything Hunter might have said.

She glanced around, wondering what she was forgetting. Nothing came to mind, and Molly reached for her purse and headed for the front door. Somewhere along the way, her footsteps slowed, and before she knew it, she'd stopped a few paces from the exit.

Hunter waited on the other side of that door, and Molly could barely breathe.

CHAPTER 5

Hunter couldn't think of anything to say, and Molly had gone quiet too. He'd fallen right off the tiny, doll-sized chair on her front porch, and his ego wasn't the only thing bruised. His knee smarted, as did his tailbone, and he stood at the top of her stairs, waiting.

She didn't come out, and Hunter looked down at his phone. He was lucky he hadn't cracked it when he'd fallen, as he'd thrown it in his attempt to catch himself.

His voice had dried right up, and he half-wished he hadn't asked to see Molly that evening. He really just wanted his butter pecan ice cream and a soft bed to sleep in. After all, he had to get up at five-thirty to help his father with the farm chores, get ready for work, and make the journey from farm to city.

His stomach swooped, and no amount of fishing or Elise's caramel corn had soothed him. Nothing was going to be the same after tomorrow, and Hunter wanted to enjoy tonight.

He should tell Molly that he needed to get back to the farm, and he'd call her another time to set up a date. He had no idea what he'd been thinking earlier this afternoon. He didn't have time to start a relationship right now. He was starting a new job—a high-stress job at the family company. He had to find somewhere to live and move there. He couldn't take on a woman and attending to her, trying to show her how great he was in the early stages of a relationship.

"What am I doing here?" he asked himself.

"Getting ice cream." Molly stepped to his side as he flinched at the sound of her voice. "Sorry," she said. "Did I startle you?"

"Yeah, a little." He looked at her, and while his stomach stayed tight, he no longer wanted to go home alone. He still had way too much to do to take on a girlfriend, but perhaps the two of them wouldn't want to see each other after this anyway.

When his eyes met hers, Hunter knew he'd want to see her again. *We can go slow*, he thought. He probably should go slow with Molly anyway, because he couldn't make lifelong decisions based on what he'd known about this person over a decade ago.

"What's your favorite flavor of ice cream?" she asked.

"Butter pecan." His throat caught on the last syllable, and he cleared the stickiness away. "Yours?"

"I'm a traditionalist," she said with a pretty smile. "Chocolate."

He nodded and indicated her steps. "Should we go?" He started down the steps, and she came with him. He went to her side of the truck and opened the passenger door for her. She climbed up and in, and Hunter couldn't help noticing the skin-tight jeans she wore, along with that lovely blouse that brought out the red in her hair.

"You look really nice," he said, leaning into the doorway and smiling at her.

"Thank you, Hunter." She tucked her hair, and Hunter wondered if he needed to sleep for the next few weeks. Once he got things figured out at work, he'd have more time for Molly, and if he could give up sleeping, he could start a relationship now and do everything else.

He nodded, tapped the door, and stepped back to close it. Once behind the wheel, he aimed the truck toward the grocery store. His mind ran with things to say or ask, but he couldn't seem to grasp onto one for long enough to speak.

"Did you like MIT?" she asked.

He glanced over at her. How did he sum up six years of school? "Yes," he said. He supposed that would do. "What did you end up doing?"

"I stayed here," she said, looking out her window at the neighborhood. "Got my teaching degree. What did you major in?"

"Bioinformatics," he said.

"What?"

No one had ever heard of bioinformatics before, and

Hunter gave her a small smile. "It's a branch of computer science that extends into some biology subjects, as well as some business systems."

"I have no idea what that means." She laughed, and the mood in the truck lightened.

"It means I use computer science and information to understand biology."

"That doesn't help."

Hunter smiled, but he didn't want to explain what he'd learned over the past six years. It was hard to distill down into one sentence. "We aim to answer questions about biology—about genetics, DNA, proteins, that kind of stuff—with patterns and sequences we can see in the data."

"Sounds complicated."

"It is," he said. "I have a master's degree, and it was six years of highly technical mathematics, biology, genetics, and computer science classes."

"So no analyzing novels."

Hunter chuckled and shook his head. "No, ma'am."

"I teach seven-year-olds about weather and how to add and subtract."

Hunter glanced at her. "Maybe one of your students will make a break-through in science one day."

Molly just looked at him, and Hunter's awkwardness grew. They reached the grocery store, and as they walked in, he asked, "Do you just have the one cat?"

"I have a dog too," she said. "He's really sweet. You'd like him." She stepped closer to him as someone started to back out of their parking space. He reached over and grabbed onto her arm to tug her further out of the way.

"Whoa," he called, and the car slammed on the brakes.

His heart skipped with her skin touching his, and Hunter quickly dropped her arm once she was out of danger. His fingers tingled, and he wasn't sure what that meant.

"How big is this dog?" he asked. "I have rules about that."

"Rules?"

They reached the entrance, and the doors slid open. Hunter wanted to take her hand in his again, and he started stewing about how to do that without being too grabby and too obvious. He felt like he hadn't had to work this hard to impress a woman in a long time, but he also wasn't worried about what a woman might know about him from before.

With other women, there was no before. There was just right now, and the date, and he didn't have to reveal anything he didn't want to.

Molly knew more about him than anyone besides his family members, and Hunter wondered if this was a good idea. He'd have to overcome things she'd once known about him that had changed.

"Listen," he said as they walked past the baked goods to get to the freezer cases. "I think we should—I mean, if you want to do this, I think we should start with a blank slate."

Molly glanced up at him. "A blank slate?"

"Yeah," he said, his hands starting to sweat. "I'm not the same person I was when we were eleven or twelve."

"Oh, I see."

"Are you?"

"Not at all," she said, nodding him toward the correct aisle.

Hunter turned and started scanning the cases. He needed a lot of butter pecan ice cream to get him through the next week. "What do you think?"

"I think we can try," she said. "I don't know how to turn off my memories."

"Right," he said. "But you—I mean, you can't make judgments based on who I was then. You have to go on right now." He spotted the butter pecan and practically dove for the door. "Could we at least try that?"

"Sure," she said, pacing past him to the next door down.

With their preferred ice cream flavors in hand, Hunter led the way toward the picnic supplies and picked up a bag of bowls and a box of plastic spoons. He grinned at Molly when he caught her gaping at him, and he lifted the spoons. "I thought we could find somewhere to overlook the city and sit on the tailgate to eat our ice cream."

"I don't see why you need a bowl," she said with a smile.

"Good point." He put the bowls back and they headed for the check stand. Twenty minutes later, he pulled up to Hawk's Overlook and swung the truck around before backing in. The conversation had been easier on the way up the mountain road, and Hunter wasn't sure why.

He got out of the truck and went around to the tailgate. After lowering it, he swung their ice cream into the middle of the gate and turned to help Molly up.

With his hands on her waist, he said, "Jump," and she

pushed off the ground. She giggled as he set her on the tailgate, and Hunter couldn't remove his hands from her body. He stayed right where he stood, one of her knees pressing against his hip.

Their eyes met, and all Hunter could think about was kissing her. If it was any other woman, he'd have smiled and leaned a little closer. He'd have asked if he could kiss her, and if she'd said yes—he'd never had a woman tell him no—he'd kiss her right here, right now.

Forty-five minutes into their first date.

Wait, he thought. *Is this a date?*

Would Molly think it was?

Her fingers touched his collar, and Hunter's blood started to boil right inside his veins. He ducked his head instead of leaning closer, using every ounce of his self-control not to speak the question in his mind.

"The ice cream's going to melt," Molly said, her voice quiet and like music to his soul.

He backed up, and the temperature cooled. He worked not to clear his throat, and he managed to stay silent as he swung himself up onto the tailgate too. She got their quarts out of the plastic bag, and she ripped open the box of spoons. After handing one to him, she said, "You know, I thought you were going to kiss me."

"I was thinking about it," he admitted without looking at her.

"I know," she said. "You've looked at me like that before."

Hunter didn't know what to say, so he simply opened his

ice cream and took out a spoonful of semi-melted butter pecan from the edge. The sweetness and creaminess made his whole body rejoice, and Hunter looked down at the city. "I love this spot. I've really missed this."

"No mountains in Massachusetts," Molly said.

"Definitely nothing like this."

They ate in silence for a few minutes, and then she said, "I didn't mean to make you uncomfortable."

"It's fine," he said. He scooped another bite, but he didn't put the ice cream in his mouth. "I suppose it's unrealistic for me to think we can do anything with a clean slate."

"We were best friends for a lot of years," she said. "You were my first boyfriend, Hunter. We were together for a long time."

"I'm aware," he said, and he didn't think there was a day that had passed where he hadn't thought of her, at least while he'd been in Colorado.

"I would've kissed you," she said.

"I think that's the problem," he said. "I'm acting on nothing more than memories and hormones." He shook his head, unsure of how to put his feelings into words. "I think you are too, and that's exactly what I *don't* want this relationship to be." He tore his eyes from the city and took his bite of ice cream.

When he finally got up the courage to look at Molly, she gave him a small smile and nodded. "You're right, Hunter."

He drew in a deep breath and reached for her hand. "I would like to hold your hand, if you don't mind."

"I don't mind." She tucked her ice cream back into the plastic bag and set it on her other side so she could scoot closer to him. With her fingers intertwined with his, she leaned her head against his bicep, and they watched the sun paint the last of its rays over the city of Denver.

"I have a very early morning," Hunter said, though he didn't want to break this evening.

"Let's go," she said, hopping off the tailgate.

Hunter took her home, and he had no idea what the week ahead held for him. At her door, he drew her into a hug and told her exactly that. "So can I call you when I know more?"

"Sure," she said. "You have my number now."

"Yes, I do." He smiled at her, leaned down, and pressed his lips to her cheek. "Thanks for coming along last minute, Molly." He walked away, his cowboy boots thumping on the steps as he went down them. He was proud of himself for controlling his hormones, and an increased measure of hope filled him that he and Molly could have a second chance at recreating their first love.

THE NEXT MORNING, HUNTER ARRIVED AT THE huge, thirty-seven-story building in downtown Denver by eight-thirty. His appointment with Laura wasn't until nine, and she was going to go over all of his options for living and getting paid. Once that was done, he had a meeting with human resources to finalize all of his hiring paperwork, and then his lab manager was set to meet him for lunch in the company cafeteria.

"You can do this," he told himself, but he didn't get out of his truck. He thought of Uncle Wes, who'd been the CEO before Laura. He'd lived in one of those company-owned condos, and he'd come to this building hundreds of times.

He thought of Uncle Colton, who'd worked on the Human Genome Project and inspired Hunter in his own career in genetics and biology. He'd worked in the labs here too, and he'd survived.

His own father had come here every day—and a lot of weekends—to deal with everything legal for this massive company.

Hunter picked up his phone and tapped to call his uncle.

"Hunt," Uncle Wes said, his voice normal and not gravelly, which meant Hunter hadn't woken him. "Getting ready for your first day?"

"Yes," Hunter said, his throat closing on him.

After a few beats of silence, Uncle Wes said, "Hunter, this is just like going to that animatronics class. You didn't want to do it, but you did. And you didn't hate it."

Hunter smiled at the memory. He'd sat outside on a bench to make that call to his uncle, and Wes had asked him all kinds of questions until Hunter had identified why he didn't want to take the class.

"Robots are creepy," he'd told Uncle Wes. And they were, but he hadn't hated the class. He simply wasn't interested in robotics, especially with puppets involved.

"I don't want to have a life I hate," Hunter said, thinking of the farm and how much he'd love that life.

"You don't have to work at HMC," Uncle Wes said. "I think you'll like it, though. They haven't had anyone in their labs with your skill set, ever."

"Then there won't be anything for me to do." He didn't want to analyze the qualities of plastic—what had put the Hammond name on the map. His great-great-grandfather had invented the most common type of plastic used around the world, and that was what had funded Hunter's extremely comfortable life. It had funded his father's too, and it would fund his son's, and his grandson's, and on and on.

There was plenty of money in the Hammond family, that was for sure.

"There will be plenty for you to do," Uncle Wes said. "You get to make up what you do, Hunt. Not only that, but *you* can take this company into a brand-new direction. *You* can open up brand-new fields for the company to explore. It's going to be *amazing*."

Hunter basked in his uncle's words, because for some reason, when Uncle Wes said something, it got through Hunter's thick skull better than when Dad said them.

"Uncle Colton is here," Uncle Wes said. "Tell 'im, Colt."

"Hunter," Uncle Colton said. "Your first day!" He sounded like Hunter had just invented a cure for cancer. "You're going to have a great day. I want you to call me afterward and tell me all about it."

Hunter nodded, though his uncles couldn't see him. "I

wish I was coming up to Coral Canyon next week with everyone," he said. "I miss you guys."

"We miss you too," Uncle Colton said. "You'll come for the Fourth, right?"

"Yes," Hunter said. "I can't miss another Fourth of July in Coral Canyon."

"Oh, we are going to par-tay," Uncle Colton said.

"Okay," Uncle Wes said with plenty of disgust. "You're too old to say stuff like that."

"Whatever," Uncle Colton argued. "You're just mad because Michael said I'm more fun than you."

"He just meant because you have quads, and you let him drive them. Which," Uncle Wes said with plenty of emphasis. "Is illegal, Colt. There's a reason I told him no."

Hunter could listen to his uncles bicker all day long. He grinned at their back and forth, actually a little jealous he didn't have any siblings closer to him in age. He didn't have anyone in his family terribly close to his age. No one he'd run around and played with as a child. He was an island in the Hammond family, and he'd often felt like it, especially once all of his cousins started being born.

Uncle Colt had adopted a little girl, and Kate had just turned eighteen. Michael, Wes's son, came next, and he was twelve. There were plenty of cousins after that, as the twins, the youngest of Hunter's uncles, both had four kids.

They all lived in Coral Canyon, and Hunter knew Elise would like to move up there. Her friends were there, and all the cousins. The only thing tethering them here was the farm. Once Hunter took it over, he knew his Dad and Elise would move.

"Anyway," Colton said with plenty of emphasis. "You're going to do great, Hunter. Try not to worry about it."

"I'm trying," Hunter said. "Uncle Colt?"

"Yeah?"

"What if…?" Hunter paused to organize his words. "What if this doesn't suit me?"

"Then you quit," he and Uncle Wes said together. Hunter could just see the two of them, their eyes meeting, and entire conversations being had.

"Hunter, if this isn't what you want to do, you'll know," Uncle Wes said. "You quit. You can still be a Hammond."

"Yeah, Uncle Ames and Uncle Cy never worked at HMC," Uncle Colton said.

Hunter thought of the farm, and the chores he'd helped with that morning. There was nothing like cold, crisp air in the Rocky Mountains, with half-frozen dew on the blade of grass, and animals awakening from their slumber to get fed and watered for the day.

"Okay," Hunter said. "Thanks, you guys. I better go."

"Good luck," Wes said.

"Call me later," Colton added.

Hunter hung up, but he didn't get out of the truck. Instead, he dialed Lucy's office to get an appointment for that week. He had so much to work through, and after today, he felt sure he'd have even more.

CHAPTER 6

Molly woke the next morning because Gypsy's voice couldn't be ignored. The fussy cat was hungry again, and Molly groaned as she got out of bed and went to feed the gray monster. With that done, she went into the second bedroom of her house and stretched, lifted barbells in a few exercises she'd paid a personal trainer to learn, and leashed Saltine for a walk.

She went around the neighborhood loop, which was really a horseshoe-shaped route that took her about twenty-five minutes.

With all that done, she put out fresh water for her pets and returned to the kitchen to make coffee.

"Oh, my goodness, the bread." She'd completely forgotten about the bread, and the yeasty smell of it hit her straight in the nose. How had she missed that?

Probably because Hunter was still on her mind, and he occupied every brain cell, leaving none for her nose.

The dough had risen, and risen, and risen, and now a gloppy, nearly foaming mess sat on the counter surrounding the bowl. Molly made a face as she scooped up the first globs of dough, and she seriously doubted she should be putting it down her disposal.

The house and everything in it wasn't new by any means, and she could just see a plumber visit in her future.

School had been out for a week, and Molly's rule for herself during the summer was to work on a project every day. Last week, she'd trimmed back her roses one day, helped at the church another, and cleaned out two cupboards on a third.

Today, she was going to tackle her closet, which would require her to pick up her clothes. She kept her house decently clean where people could see it, but no one came into her bedroom. Molly certainly didn't care if she had to step over a pair of shoes to get to the bathroom. She generally disliked housework though, and sometimes even her living room and kitchen could get a little crusty.

She put a cozy mystery on her audiobook app and got to work. While a PI investigated the murder of an accountant, Molly got her closet cleaned out. With three bags to donate to Goodwill, she vacuumed the carpet in her walk-in and went back into the kitchen for lunch.

She thought of Hunter and what he might be eating for lunch. "Dear Lord," she prayed. "Please bless him to have a good first day at HMC."

He'd asked her if they could start with a clean slate, but she didn't know how to do that. She could see the worry and doubt right on his face when they'd talked about his job last night. It wasn't even hard. She'd seen the look in his eye when he'd helped her onto the tailgate, and she'd counted to exactly twelve before he'd moved the conversation to Hawk Overlook and how much he liked going there.

He was as predictable as the sun rising, and Molly found that so attractive. She loved routines and schedules, and yes, predictability.

Of course he'd changed, but so much of him was the same too.

He didn't call that night, and Molly didn't dare call him. *He's busy,* she told herself. *He just started a new job and moved back all in twenty-four hours.*

Hunter didn't call or even text the next day or evening either. Or on Wednesday, Thursday, or Friday. At this rate, Molly was going to have an immaculately clean house, with every cupboard, closet, and shelf sparkling and organized by the end of June.

Now that so much time had gone by, Molly felt too foolish to call Hunter. Besides that, he'd said he'd call her. He'd said he'd be busy this week as he started at HMC, and she didn't want to pressure him or cause him any undue stress.

The moment she had that thought, anger bloomed inside her. She hadn't wanted Tyrone to be uncomfortable either. Ever. She'd have done anything to make him happy, and she knew now that she couldn't bend forever without breaking.

She shouldn't have to, either.

"He probably hasn't given you two seconds of thought,"

she said to herself as she unpotted a snake plant, or mother-in-law's tongue, and moved it to a bigger pot. Her project for the day was cleaning up her houseplants and making sure they were ready for another year of thriving growth.

She needed time to figure out how to trust herself again anyway. With everything that had happened in the last year, Molly didn't even know which way was up anymore. She needed more time on her knees, more time with her parents, and more time to find her center.

She didn't want to spend Friday night with her plants, her uptight cat, or Saltine, as cute as he was. When she finished her project for the day, she tapped out a message to her two best friends from school, Diana Drivers and Roxanne Woods.

Need a girl's night. What are you two up to tonight?

Diana would be all over girl's night if she was available. She had twin five-year-olds that drove her to the brink of madness most days. Her words, not Molly's. Anytime Diana could get out of the house without them, she did.

Roxy would be harder to convince. She didn't like noise and crowds, and even in Ivory Peaks, on a Friday night, they'd encounter both at any restaurant they went to. Not only that, but Roxy had just gotten engaged, and she was in that disgustingly happy stage that unfortunately included the fact that she couldn't do anything alone anymore.

I can't, Diana said. *It's Jason's birthday tomorrow, and we're going out with his parents tonight.* She'd added a skull and crossbones emoji. Molly couldn't help smiling though she saw her fun evening with her friends disappearing right in front of her eyes.

Diana was the glue of the group. If she didn't come to girl's night, they wouldn't have one.

Andrew and I are shopping for a cake maker, Roxy said. *I think we've almost narrowed it down to three.*

That's great, Molly sent. *Maybe another time. Have fun at dinner, D!*

The weekend slipped away, and before Molly knew it, she was faced with another Monday morning. Another stretch and lift session. Another walk with Saltine. When she got home, she decided to start another batch of bread.

This time, though, she was going to finish it and take it to Hunter. If he didn't want to start another relationship with her, he should have to say it to her face. "Or say anything at all," she said with quite the vehemence in her voice.

Once the dough was covered and rising—and she wouldn't forget about it this time—she pulled out her phone and texted Hunter. *I made some fresh bread today. Do you have a minute for me to drop it off? I can just leave it in your office or whatever.*

She read over the words again and then again, hoping they wouldn't come off as passive-aggressive. She also didn't want to leave the bread in his office. "Or whatever," she muttered, jamming her thumb against the screen to erase that last sentence.

She wanted to see him, and she wondered if it would be easier to just say that.

"I made some bread as an excuse to come see you today. Will you or won't you take two minutes to say hello?" She shook her head and erased the text completely. Maybe she should just show up at HMC. It was a public building. She could get inside and have someone page Hunter for her.

Oh, he wouldn't like that, and Molly found herself smiling. Actually smiling. If they were starting with a blank slate, how could she possibly know he hated the spotlight? That paging him would embarrass him not bring him closer to her? That showing up unannounced, even with homemade bread, was akin to causing a natural disaster?

He'd said he'd call, and he hadn't. It was time for Molly to take the situation into her own hands and give everything a shake. Once it all fell out, then she'd know what she had to play with.

MOLLY STOOD IN FRONT OF A PRETTY BRUNETTE wearing light pink gloss on her full lips. Hunter had to walk past her every day, and Molly's heart did a small cartwheel inside her chest.

"Yes, there's someone here for Mister Hammond." She grinned the whole time, and she cocked her head slightly as whoever she'd called spoke on the other end of the line. "Yes, ma'am. I'll let her know." She replaced the receiver in the cradle and looked up at Molly. "Mister Hammond will be a few minutes. If you don't mind waiting, you can have a seat over there." She indicated the space behind and to Molly's left.

"Thank you," Molly said, taming her voice into something as professional as the receptionist's. She turned away, wondering why she hadn't thought to go full-out with her makeup.

She'd only swiped on a little bit of mascara and then some clear Chapstick in the car as she navigated to the downtown Denver area. Her lips tingled with the eucalyptus flavor even now. She'd walked two blocks in clear June weather with the large loaf of bread in a brown bag.

As she sat down, she shifted the bread from under her arm to her lap, and she settled her purse next to her on the couch. She knew how to waste plenty of time with the apps on her phone, but today, none of them could hold her attention for longer than a few seconds.

What would Hunter think when he saw her? They hadn't spoken or seen each other in over a week. Was she being too forward?

Molly managed to kill a few minutes by looking at the available dogs on the town's pet classified board, and before she knew it, Hunter said, "Molly?"

She jerked her attention away from the cute little white Westie she'd been looking at. Her eyes landed on Hunter, and half of her body wanted to get up while the other half went numb. The man seriously could not look any better.

Not a single thread sat out of place. He wore a black pair of slacks, a pressed white shirt, and a tie in purple, yellow, and blue. Gold. Gold, not yellow. The man never wore yellow, that was for sure. It was always gold when it came to Hunter.

She hadn't expected to see him in his cowboy hat, but it hadn't gone anywhere. He wore a different one now than he had last Sunday. This one was dark as night and it went well with the slacks and shiny shoes. His footwear made her stare, because she'd expected to find the cowboy boots he'd had on last week.

"What are you doing here?" Hunter took another step toward her, and Molly got her whole body to cooperate.

She stood up and thrust the paper bag toward him. "I made bread, and I thought maybe you'd like a loaf."

He looked down at the bag and then back to her eyes. He didn't smile, and he seemed so perplexed. She felt the exact same way. Hunter belonged on a horse or a farm, and while she'd seen him in church clothes before, there was something different about him being in this high-rise and not a chapel.

"It's...lunchtime," she said, shaking the bread so the bag rustled. If he didn't take it, she'd tuck it back under her arm and scurry away, her tail tucked between her legs too.

He took the brown bag from her. "And you thought I'd have lunchmeat and cheese with me? Maybe a bottle of mayo." He grinned then, his dark eyes shining like the stars. "All I was missing is the bread." He lifted the bagged bread a few inches, his smile fading. "Thank you."

Her chest constricted, and she suddenly needed to get away. "I don't...sorry to bother you." She twisted and picked up her purse. "I hope I didn't interrupt anything important."

She nodded without truly looking at him and stepped away from him and the couch and the perfectly perky secretary listening in.

She jabbed at the elevator button, dangerously close to tears. *Please, please,* she prayed, looking up at the numbers above the doors.

"Molly," he said behind her.

She didn't turn around. "It's fine, Hunter," she said. "I don't need you to say anything else." He'd said so much with the silence over the past week. She wasn't sure why she'd needed to come here and make sure his non-contact had meant what she'd feared.

At the same time, she knew exactly why. She didn't trust her own feelings, and she needed to have proof of everything before she could make a final decision. If she'd been more careful with Tyrone, she never would've dated him for a year. She never would've married him.

"You don't need to go."

"Oh, yes, I do."

Hunter stepped next to her, his nearness too much for her. She shifted away from him, because the cool, crisp scent of his cologne hadn't been dulled by the few hours he'd been at work. It was like he'd spritzed himself with the stuff that made her swoon on his way up from the lab.

Annoyance sang through her, and she just wanted to leave with as much dignity as she could. She hadn't seen Hunter in years. She could avoid him now that they lived in the same city.

"I meant to call," he said quietly.

"I don't need an explanation," she said, sending him a glare. She'd never stood up to Tyrone, and she could easily see herself folding for Hunter too. That so wasn't going to happen. "Though, you know what, *Mister* Hammond? You said you'd call me, and you didn't." She scanned him from head to toe, committing his good looks to memory.

She couldn't believe she was going to walk away from him, but she respected herself enough to do it. She *had* to do it.

The elevator dinged, thankfully. She edged away from him again, and said, "I realize you've had a lot going on, and I tried to give you the time and space you needed to do it. I don't know what the last eight days have been like for you, but I'm trying to think of a reason why you couldn't have simply sent me a text."

"Molly." Hunter watched her get on the elevator.

"How long does it take to type and send, 'I'm so sorry, Molly, but I'm still swamped at the moment. Hoping I can take you to dinner when things calm down.'?" She cocked her head. While she could go on and on—the teacher inside her really liked to lecture, and everyone needed to watch out once she got started—the doors started to close, separating her from Hunter.

Her heartbeat hopped, skipped, and jumped all the way back to the lobby, down the two blocks, and even once she'd reached the safety of her car.

There, she pulled out her phone to call Ingrid. "Should've called her to begin with." Molly hadn't mentioned Hunter to anyone but Mama, and as far as she knew, no one else knew he and Molly had gone on a quick ice cream date last week.

"Mols," Ingrid said. "I have five minutes before my lunch is up."

"Oh, I forgot you had a job."

"Some of us have to work in the summer, Molly." Ingrid laughed, and Molly wished it didn't make her feel worse.

"I know. I'm sorry."

"Hey, I was just kidding," Ingrid said, sobering quickly. "What's wrong?"

Molly pressed her eyes closed and took a moment to calm herself down. She didn't want to cry on the phone with her sister. "I think I just made a big mistake."

"I don't want to rush you, but four minutes."

"Okay." Molly told her the situation in a couple of sentences. "I shouldn't have shown up here, right?"

"I'd love it if a hot guy showed up with homemade bread at my work," Ingrid said. But Hunter had made fun of her for doing it. He'd joked about having everything but the bread to make a sandwich. Molly pressed her teeth together as her eyes filled with tears.

"That's because you love bread."

Ingrid giggled. "Who doesn't love bread? Maybe he was just shocked."

"Oh, I think he was shocked all right." Molly started her car, because it was too hot to sit in it without air blowing. "Plus, I'm not a hot guy, and it's obvious he doesn't want to perpetuate a relationship. I should've known from the week of silence." She backed out of her parking spot and tapped the Bluetooth button. "I'm going to lose you for a second."

The car beeped as it connected the call, and Ingrid was saying, "…see what happens next.

"I think I'll block his number," Molly said. "I don't need to humiliate myself again."

"Molly, you've liked Hunter for so long. Do you really want to block his number?"

She came to a stop so pedestrians could cross in front of her. Oh, how she hated the city. It took forever to get anywhere, and everyone and everything was so loud. "No," she finally admitted. "I'm pretty sure I just blew it with him, though. I didn't let him explain anything, and I just walked away."

"That's actually not bad," Ingrid said. "He'll feel unsettled and like he needs to close this…or reopen it."

"Maybe."

"I have to go," Ingrid said. "I'm sorry, Mols. Want me to bring burgers tonight?"

"And all the fries," she said, finally turning onto a one-way street that would take her to the freeway that would get her away from the downtown madhouse.

"You got it," Ingrid said, and she ended the call in the next moment.

She stopped by the grocery store once she'd made it back to Ivory Peaks, because she had an entire afternoon ahead of her, and she needed potato chips to wallow in her humiliation. She got the dill pickle flavored ones, the sour cream and cheddar flavor, and the plain, ridged kind.

No, she wouldn't eat three bags of potato chips in one day, but the week was young.

Back in her car, she took a moment to open the classifieds again. This time, she didn't start looking for another dog. She went to the associated dating app, her thumb hovering over the button.

She'd never used a dating app, because her marriage had only ended thirteen months ago. She hadn't ever wanted to date again, because she didn't want to explain to anyone that yes, she'd been married before. No, she couldn't hack it.

She felt damaged on the inside, but on the outside, no one could see the scrapes, dings, dents, and gashes. But once they found out she'd been married and divorced before age twenty-four, they'd know.

Hunter would know.

"This is for the best," she said to herself. She didn't tap on the dating app either, and she set her phone in the cup holder and continued toward her house. She'd already taken Saltine for a walk, but she could take him again. She could take a kickboxing class on the fitness channel on her smart TV. Heck, she could take a nap if she wanted to.

Molly turned the corner, and her house came into view, the third one down the street on the right.

A huge gray truck sat in her driveway, and Molly hit the brakes. "Hunter," whispered from her mouth.

CHAPTER 7

Hunter stared at the text he'd sent Molly a half an hour ago, only a few minutes after she'd left in that dang elevator.

I'm so sorry, Molly. Things have gotten away from me this week. I'd of course love to see you again once I get my life together.

According to his phone, she hadn't even seen it.

Frustration and feelings of failure filled him, and he looked up from the text she hadn't seen. He'd met with Lucy on Thursday after work, and that wasn't the only thing he'd had to do after his long commute to HMC and then back to the farm.

He felt torn in a dozen directions, and tonight, he needed to go out to the farm again to make sure Matt Whettstein and his family had arrived and moved in safely. Dad and Elise and the littles had left for Coral Canyon that morning, and Hunter had spent the entirety of the Sabbath with them.

The weight of the world settled on his shoulders, and while he'd thought of Molly every day for the past week, he hadn't found ten seconds to text her.

His thumbs flew across the screen, and he typed, *That took me ten seconds. I really am sorry. Please call me.*

He erased the last sentence, because Molly wouldn't call him. He wouldn't if he'd said the things she had to a woman. Even with the messages he'd sent, if he was Molly, he'd just text back.

He'd moved out of the farmhouse on Saturday, and that had been a hard and busy day. He'd spent the beginning of the week looking at the company condos, then apartments and houses in the downtown area. He didn't want to wait to buy something, because the two-hour commute was terrible, and he'd ended up taking a condo in the building right next to HMC. He could ride an elevator down to the ground level, walk half a block, and take another elevator up to the sixth floor, where his lab was.

He sent the text and leaned his head back against the rest. "I don't know what else to do," he said. "Tell me what to do." He did like Molly—he'd always liked Molly. He remembered keenly the way his heart and mind had screamed at him last Sunday to make sure she didn't get away from him again.

Yet he hadn't texted…. "Why didn't I text her?"

His phone rang, and he straightened. His boss had said he could take the afternoon off, no problem, and Hunter was sure she'd only done so because of his last name. He expected to see Laura's name on the screen, ready to lecture him for using his family name to get a few hours off.

Instead, Molly's name sat there.

Stunned, and with his heart pounding and his fingers shaking, he swiped on the call. "Hey," he said, actually leaning closer to the screen in the middle of his dashboard, though that made no sense. The truck used its speakers when he was connected to a call via Bluetooth.

"You're taking up my whole driveway," she said. "I need to be able to get to my garage."

He swung his attention over his shoulder, and sure enough, her dark blue sedan sat several car lengths down the street. "Sorry," he said. "I'll move."

"Great," she said, and it sounded like she might hang up.

"Did you get my texts?"

"Just now," she said, her voice softening.

Hunter didn't want to move until he knew he could stay. "Do you have a few minutes to talk?"

"I have all day," she said.

"I just need a few minutes," he promised, smiling. Hunter flipped his truck into reverse and backed out of her driveway. He eased up next to the curb and glanced at the perfectly baked bread on the seat beside him. He had said thank you when he'd taken it, but he didn't think Molly had appreciated the teasing.

He picked up the bread and got out of his truck as Molly pulled into her driveway. She went all the way into the garage as Hunter went up her walkway, but he paused before entering her garage.

She got out with a grocery bag and faced him.

"I'm so sorry," he said, because he knew that an apology could go a long way. He didn't know how to explain everything that had happened that had kept him silent. "I—there's been so much going on, and I should've called you and told you about it every night." He just said whatever came into his mind. "Could I do that? Call you every night and keep you up-to-date?"

"You do what you want, Hunter." She turned away from him and went up the few steps to the door that led into the house. At the top, she turned back to him. "You can come in, if you'd like."

Hunter hurried after her, barely catching the door as it started to swing closed behind her. A little white dog came running toward him, barking for all he was worth.

"Stop it, Saltine," Molly said, and the dog scurried away from him and after her as she went into the kitchen. A gray cat sat on the counter and stared at him with baleful eyes. "Get off the counter, Gypsy." She tapped the cat on the back, and it yowled in response. The feline gave her a sour look, but she did hop down to the ground. She held her tail high as she stalked into the living room. She jumped up onto the TV stand, then the mantel, and then to the very top shelf of the bookcase in the corner. She perched there and zeroed in on Hunter again.

"Don't mind her," Molly said, removing three bags of potato chips from the sack. Hunter's stomach roared, because he still hadn't eaten lunch.

"Would you mind if I made a sandwich?" he asked. "I

had this gorgeous woman bring me a loaf of homemade bread, and I haven't eaten lunch yet."

Her eyes met his, and Hunter's pulse sounded like thunder in his ears. Finally, Molly's stoic face cracked into a smile, and she ducked her head. "Turkey or ham?"

"Both," he said, moving toward her. He joined her in the kitchen, and while it wasn't terribly small, it wasn't big either. He felt entirely too close to her, especially since she'd stepped away from him in front of the elevator at HMC.

She got out lettuce, tomatoes, avocados, and pickles too, and before he knew it, he'd assembled a ham and turkey sandwich with all the trimmings—and so had she. She led the way over to the dining room table, and they sat down together.

Before Hunter could put anything in his mouth, he looked at her again. "I really am sorry."

She nodded. "I heard you." She took a bite of her sandwich and looked at him, her eyes clearly telling him to start talking.

So he did. He told her about his first day at HMC, and how Laura had greeted him as an equal. She'd given him a tour of the whole building, he'd signed paperwork, and he'd met his boss in Lab Six.

"I was doing farm chores in the morning, and in the evening, and looking at apartments and condos and houses." He wiped his mouth and reached for a bottle of water she'd retrieved from the fridge and set in front of him. "I met with my therapist."

He watched her closely, but Molly didn't flinch at all. "You know I see a therapist, right?"

"I do now," she said.

"I've been seeing Lucy for a decade."

That brought her eyes to his, where they locked. "Hunter."

He wasn't sure what she was asking, but he felt like she should know this. "I'm going to have times where I need to talk to someone. That's just how my life is."

"I can support that."

"Can you?" he challenged. "Because I do it so I can be the best, most whole person I can be. I'm broken otherwise. You should know that, Molly. I'm…I need the help."

Molly just looked at him, and he wished she would say something. Maybe reassure him that he wasn't broken. He wasn't sure.

She said nothing, though, and Hunter went back to his sandwich. He finished it and brushed the bread crumbs from his fingers. "Then my uncle in Wyoming called, because he knows about my charitable foundation in Cambridge, and he wondered if I'd heard of equine therapy. I have a ton of connections with veterans and retired police officers, and that's who Uncle Ames thinks I should focus on with equine therapy too. So we've been on the phone for hours, talking about a new foundation, and I've been really excited about it."

She nodded, and when she got up, he did too. They moved over to the couch, where her little dog jumped between them, circling and leaning into Molly's thigh.

"Then I moved on Saturday, which was exhausting, as I now live on the fifteenth floor in this condo the company owns. My parents left for Coral Canyon this morning, so I spent all day with them and the kids yesterday. Tonight, I have to go out to the farm and make sure our caretaker has arrived and has everything he needs."

Hunter experienced a moment of pure exhaustion, and the sigh that came out of his mouth expressed it.

"I'm sorry," Molly said. "Now I feel like a complete idiot."

"Don't," he said. "You didn't know any of this, and that's my fault." He couldn't believe he'd forgotten about Uncle Wes's tactic of talking to his girl in the evenings, though they were miles apart. "I've been thinking about you, if that's any consolation."

"A tiny one," she said.

Hunter smiled and looked down at the shoes he hated. He honestly wasn't sure how long he'd last at HMC. Everything about it felt just a little bit wrong, and working with Uncle Ames on an equine therapy operation for veterans and retired policemen had ignited a new energy in his blood Hunter had needed to make it through the first week at his new job.

An idea burst into his head as if the Good Lord himself had drawn back a curtain and flooded his mind with light. "I need help with the new foundation," he said. "It's way more work than I can do while I'm also working in Lab Six. Would you—you're not working this summer. Maybe you'd like to help me with it." He looked at her eagerly. "I'll pay you."

Molly just stared at him. After a few seconds, she asked, "How much?"

"However much a program director earns," he said. "I can look it up."

She cocked her head to the side, and Hunter knew exactly what she was going to ask. "How are you going to do that?"

"You know I have money," he said matter-of-factly. He distinctly remembered the other kids almost making fun of him for being rich. Molly had been on the group text.

"Do I?" she asked.

Hunter took a deep breath. He'd never had to explain anything to anyone at Cambridge. So many of the students there came from money, and he was just another one of them.

"My family has a lot of money," he said slowly. "We have a family legacy or tradition or whatever you want to call it, where each child gets two billion dollars when they turn twenty-one years old. We're expected to do something good with it. Something to give back to the community, or the world, or something to increase the money we've been given."

Molly choked and lifted her hand to cover her mouth as she started to cough. "I'm sorry," she said through her fingers. "I thought you said two *billion* dollars."

"I did."

Those pretty green eyes were so wide, and Hunter hated

that. He didn't want his worth to be tied to the numbers in his bank account. He never had, and he reverted back to his thirteen-year-old self who had felt two inches tall when the other kids told him how rich he was.

"I started an educational fund in Cambridge," he said. "My best friend still lives there and he runs the foundation for vets and retired cops. I'm going to start another one here. If you think you can help me with a lot of the organizational stuff, I'd love to work with you on it."

Molly lowered her hand and her eyes went back to normal. "You know what to do, obviously. If I can help, I will."

"I'll pay you," he said again.

"Okay," she agreed. "You work out what that salary will be." She stood and moved back into the kitchen. "Chips?"

Hunter got to his feet too and tracked her as she opened the sour cream and cheddar chips. "No, thanks," he said. "Molly."

She looked up and popped a chip into her mouth.

Hunter gathered together all of his bravery and courage, though he still had to clear his throat to say, "I want to work with you on this, but I have an ulterior motive."

Her eyebrows went up, and she swallowed. "What's that?"

"To spend more time with you," he said, grinning. "I'll get to see you, and bring you dinner, and hang out with you and this stalker cat who hasn't looked away from me once." He indicated Gypsy, still staring at him from atop the bookshelf.

Molly burst out laughing, and that made so much happiness stream through Hunter. He couldn't help chuckling with her, and he finally shook his head. "What do you think? Will you work with me on this, but also let me hold your hand and maybe kiss you after one of our meetings?"

Hunter shifted his feet, plenty of disbelief streaming through him that he'd just asked Molly if he could "maybe kiss" her.

She lifted her sparkling emerald eyes to his, and nodded.

"HEY, MATT." HUNTER LAUGHED AS HE WENT UP the last of the steps and shook the older man's hand. He wasn't quite as old as Dad, but he was probably fifteen years older than Hunter.

Matt grinned, chuckled, and shook his hand too. "Hey, Hunt. You're looking good."

Hunter looked down at his white shirt and tie. "Yeah, I'm in the office these days. Well, the lab."

"That's what your dad said." Matt looked out over the front yard. "The farm looks great."

"How was the drive?"

"Good," he said, moving over to the railing on the porch and leaning against it. "Brittany slept most of the way, so I can't complain."

"Oh, you've got the kids this summer?" Hunter glanced toward the front door. The homestead here at the farm wasn't exactly childproof, and Hunter struggled to remember how old Matt's children were.

Matt removed his ivory cowboy hat and ran his hand through his dark hair. His skin glowed with a healthy tan, as he probably spent eighty percent of his time working outside. He was tall and lean, but strong and one of the best men Hunter had seen work with horses and goats. It was almost like he spoke the same language as the animals he cared for, and Dad was very lucky to get someone like him to come take care of the farm every summer.

"Yeah, I have them," he said. "Their mother...." He cleared his throat and didn't continue. Though Hunter's curiosity pricked at him, he didn't press the question.

"How old are the kids?" he asked. "I can't remember."

"Brittany is eight," Matt said, his voice almost back to normal. "Keith is almost fourteen."

"That's right," Hunter said, leaning on the railing next to Matt. "I thought he was close to my cousin's age. Michael?" Hunter looked at Matt, his eyebrows up.

"Of course." Matt smiled and put his cowboy hat back on his head. "Wes has brought him down a time or two when I've been here."

Hunter nodded and looked out over the yard too. "I'm so glad you're here."

"You're welcome any time," Matt said. "Obviously."

"I'll be out on weekends," Hunter said, the words just coming out of his mouth. "I have a place in the city, but I love the farm."

"I know you do." Matt grinned at him and turned back to

the house. "We're just going to be in the homestead tonight. We've only been here for twenty minutes, and Keith said if we don't eat soon, he's going on strike."

Hunter followed Matt into the farmhouse. "What does that mean?"

"I have no idea," Matt said over his shoulder. "But I put some spaghetti on to cook. You hungry?"

"I'm always hungry," Hunter said, and that was true. His sandwich with Molly had been consumed hours ago, and he'd eaten a protein bar on the drive from her house to the farm. They'd started brainstorming names for his equine therapy center, and he had a healthy list of horse-related terminology.

Horses, hooves, saddles, manes, galloping. There were dozens of choices, and Hunter wanted to collaborate with Uncle Ames too. He'd put the idea in Hunter's head, and he trusted his uncle explicitly. Uncle Ames owned a police dog academy in Coral Canyon, so he knew how to deal with animals, and he knew what it took to set up a huge facility.

Hunter's foundation in Cambridge was housed in a single office on the MIT campus, and Hunter made a mental note to call Will that night too, just to check in. Will graduated a year ahead of Hunter, and he'd immediately taken a job with the university. He was exceptional with numbers, and MIT needed the best professors they could get.

Hunter had somehow convinced him to work with him on the educational fund, and they'd both poured everything they had into The Next Step, the foundation that funded tuition at MIT for retired or injured military and police men and women.

Matt popped the top on a jar of spaghetti sauce, and he poured it into the pot the spaghetti had just come out of. "Britt," he called. "Find Keith and tell him dinner's ready."

Hunter sat at the counter and watched Matt get out forks and plates. He put the pasta back in the pot and used a pair of tongs to stir it all together. Hunter knew how to put together a simple meal, and he could make almost anything into a sandwich, and so many things could be mixed into scrambled eggs.

His phone rang as a dark-haired girl skipped out the back door and yelled, "Keith! Dad says dinner's ready."

"It's my dad," Hunter said, getting to his feet. "I want to eat, but don't wait for me."

Matt waved that he'd heard, and Hunter answered the phone. "Did you make it okay?"

"Yeah, of course," Dad said. "Did Matt arrive?"

"He sure did." Hunter went back out onto the front porch and sat on the top step. "He's got his kids this summer. He couldn't say why."

"His wife went into a treatment program," Dad said. "And she's his ex-wife now. He just told me they got divorced in the spring."

Hunter's heart grew heavy. "I'm glad I didn't push that."

"He'll talk about it," Dad said. "He probably just needed a minute."

"Probably." Hunter understood that feeling. He'd often needed minutes and hours and days to work through how he felt about his mother leaving him, and even now, he had moments of doubt that he was a worthwhile human being.

He never told his father that, though, because Dad would be devastated. He'd worked so hard to provide a good life for Hunter—and he had. He absolutely had. Hunter had been surrounded by people who loved him, and he had no reason to feel the way he did.

And yet, he did. There was something powerful between mothers and their children, and he didn't understand it. Lucy said he didn't have to understand it. He just had to deal with the emotions when they came.

"How's the house?" Hunter asked.

"Feels like it's been shut up for eight months," Dad said. "Elise is spraying all kinds of fruity things, and we've got all the windows open."

"I wish I could be there."

"We're having dinner at Colton's tonight. They'll all wish you were here."

"Maybe I should come," Hunter said. "I could fly up this weekend." He could talk to Uncle Ames, and they could talk more about starting the foundation in Colorado, with the main center here in Ivory Peaks—maybe even right here at the farm—and the possibility of expanding to Coral Canyon.

Uncle Ames owned a big parcel of land, and he wasn't using all of it for his police dog academy, and he was thinking of expanding his operation to include equine therapy. He didn't have contacts with veterans, but he worked with a lot of police departments around the country. They weren't retired or injured officers, but he could easily find that information through his contacts.

"You can if you'd like," Dad said. "Don't feel any pressure, Hunt. Everyone knows what it's like to be fresh from college and starting a new job. Trust me on that."

"Dad, how big is the farm?"

"Oh, let's see." Dad sighed a long breath and added, "Gotta be about thirty acres. I know Grandpa got the county records when I bought it from him. He might still have it in that office of his."

"He doesn't throw anything away," Hunter agreed. "I'll ask him about it."

"Why?" Dad asked.

"I'm thinking of starting a foundation for equine therapy."

Dad whistled through his teeth. "Wow, Hunt."

"I actually think I'd benefit from it," Hunter said, his voice very quiet. "There's a long way to go, and I don't really know everything I need to know to start something like this. But I've been talking to Uncle Ames, and we both have contacts, and there's a ton of information online."

Dad let several beats of silence go by, and Hunter tensed. "You know, Hunt, you don't have to do more than you've done. You used your money for the right thing, and you've satisfied the criteria of receiving your money."

"It's not about the money, Dad. I like helping people. I like horses, and I love the farm." He closed his mouth before he said too much. He'd only been working at HMC for a week. He wasn't going to quit even though he didn't love the work.

He'd thought about it, though.

"I know you do, Hunter," Dad said just as Hunter had confessed that he'd benefit from the equine therapy. "I've always known you'd work that farm. You have the hay in your blood."

Hunter nodded, but his voice was too tight to say much.

"How are things with Molly?" Dad asked, and Hunter shook his head.

"Worse than they are at HMC," Hunter said dryly. "If you can believe that."

Dad started laughing, and that broke apart all the uncertainty in Hunter's chest. He joined his father, and he told him about his foolish silence with Molly, and her showing up at the office, and his afternoon off eating sandwiches and going on a walk with her and her tiny little dog.

"How little?" Dad asked.

"Little," Hunter said. "She said he's only sixteen pounds."

"Oh, boy," Dad said again, and they laughed together again. Hunter felt better every time he talked to his father, and he got back to his feet, an ache in his back from leaning over the counter in the lab.

Before he went back inside, he took ten seconds to text Molly. *Thanks for a great afternoon. Can I take you to dinner on Wednesday evening?*

CHAPTER 8

"That's all he said," Molly said as she scooped out another chocolate chip cookie dough ball. She didn't put it on the tray but deposited it right into her palm. She took a bite of it and looked at Ingrid.

Her sister had darker hair than Molly, and it didn't have any of the red from Mama. Molly had always wanted less red in her hair, but she liked that she and her mother looked so much alike. Lyra and Kara also had lighter brown hair with some red in it, and Ingrid always felt like the black sheep.

She definitely belonged to Daddy, though, and together, the six of them made a good family.

"I can't believe you didn't ask more questions," Ingrid said, scooping cookies onto the sheet instead of eating the dough. "That's so not like you."

"It's Hunter," Mama said, a knowing glint in her eye. "She just goes along with him."

"No," Molly said, the teasing quality in the kitchen disappearing. "No, I don't."

Ingrid exchanged a glance with Mama. "I'm sure she didn't mean anything by it. Just that you knew Hunter from before, and so you trust him."

Molly popped the second half of her cookie dough ball into her mouth, regretting her damper on the cookie-making. "I'm sorry," she said. "That was a little bit too violent of a reaction."

"I'm sure he'll have an amazing date planned," Mama said, turning away from the island.

"Mama," Molly said. "I'm sorry."

"I know you are." She turned back and smiled at Molly. "You are a smart woman, Molly."

She shook her head, because she didn't want to have this conversation. After picking up her scoop, she started making more cookie dough balls. "I'm going to freeze this sheet."

"Good idea," Ingrid said. "Then you can eat them all day tomorrow while you fret about your date with Hunter." She shot Molly a playful look, but Molly didn't deny that she'd worry about her dinner date.

"Molly, I don't think you should bottle up how you feel," Mama said, stepping back to the counter. "It's obvious that you still don't trust yourself to make decisions when it comes to men, and that you're second-guessing yourself with everything when it comes to Hunter."

Molly froze and looked at her mother. They didn't have a problem saying true things to one another, but she'd never seen her mother look so earnest. She shook her head, but she couldn't verbally deny what her mother had said. "What do you want me to do?"

"Go talk to someone."

Molly thought of what Hunter had said on Monday. He'd been going to therapy for a decade, which meant he'd gone as a teenager. She wasn't sure if he'd started before or after she'd ended their relationship, and she didn't want to know.

"I'll think about it," she said, and that was more than she'd ever given Mama before. "For the record, I think you're wrong. I trust myself to make decisions just fine, and I'm not second-guessing anything. I made bread and took it to the man's office yesterday. It was embarrassing and humiliating, and when he didn't react in such a way that indicated he wanted to go out with me, I stood right up to him."

Her heartbeat fluttered just thinking about what she'd said to him. She drew in a deep breath. "He asked me out, and I said yes. When I asked him where we were going to dinner so I could dress appropriately, he said it was a surprise. That isn't me second-guessing anything. That isn't me not trusting myself to make a decision." She shot Ingrid a look. "What's wrong with wanting it to be a romantic surprise?"

"Nothing," Ingrid said. "You just...don't like surprises." She glanced over Molly's shoulder as Lyra came into the kitchen. She wore her work uniform and she laughed into the phone pressed to her ear.

Molly watched her for a moment, but she didn't even

look at the three of them in the kitchen. She dropped her purse on the buffet and went down the steps to the basement, where her bedroom was.

"She's going to be the death of me," Mama muttered.

"Did I act like that?" Molly asked, turning back to her sister and mother.

"A little," Mama said, but Ingrid shook her head.

"Not even close."

The three of them looked at one another, and then they all burst out in laughter. Molly needed this afternoon with her family, and gladness filled her that she'd come over and brought her extra chocolate chips.

"She's so young," Mama said. "I hope she'll finish school." She turned back to the sink as her voice broke on the last word. "I'm sure things will work out."

Molly and Ingrid exchanged a glance, and Ingrid went right back to scooping. "Don't worry, Mama. I'm not going to get married until I'm at least thirty-five. I'm going to finish school, and then get a Master's degree."

Mama twisted back and smiled at Ingrid. "I'm sure you will, sweetie."

Ingrid beamed at Molly, who let her feelings stream through her. She wondered if her mother had ever gotten choked up over her engagement with Tyrone, and she decided to do what her mother said and let things out instead of keeping it bottled up.

"Mama, did you ever worry about me and Tyrone?"

Her mother's shoulders stiffened, and Molly had her answer. "A little," Mama said.

"Did you think he wasn't good for me?"

"We don't need to talk about this," Mama said.

"You're the one who said I shouldn't keep things bottled up," Molly said. "I'm just asking."

Mama turned around, her eyes flashing dangerously. She leaned against the counter behind her and folded her arms. "Yes," she said. "I worried about you and Tyrone. Mothers have an extraordinary way of seeing things their children can't. I didn't think he was a perfect match for you, but I trusted in the Lord, and I believe He leads us—each of us—where we need to be. So I let you make your choices and your decisions, and now here you are."

Her chest heaved, and Molly had frozen somewhere near the beginning of her speech.

"Mama," Ingrid said. "She was just asking."

Molly blinked at her mother, seeing her for so much more than she ever had before. She'd always loved her mother and trusted her advice. She'd always believed her mother, and she knew her mom had incredible faith. She'd leaned on that faith during the divorce and every day since, and Molly's eyes filled with tears.

She dropped the scoop and rounded Ingrid and the counter to take Mama into a hug. "I love you, Mama," she whispered.

Her mother clung tightly to her. "I wish I could've saved you this pain and disappointment." She gently pushed Molly away but kept her grip on her shoulders. Her dark green eyes shone as she searched Molly's face. "Here you are, my darling. And it's right where you're supposed to be. You've learned so much about yourself and what kind of husband you want, and you *know* now. You need to stop beating yourself up for what happened."

Molly nodded, her tears spilling down her cheeks. "I'm trying. It's just so *hard*." She should've known. She should've seen Tyrone for the abusive man he was. They'd dated for longer than they were married, and she hadn't seen it.

Why hadn't she seen it? Why hadn't the Lord shown her what He'd allowed her mother to see?

Like sunlight bursting through a thicket of trees, Molly knew. She'd had to learn for herself. She'd had to experience the heartache and the misery to know the good and the joy. She'd had to tread along this awful path so she'd know better in the future.

"How am I going to tell Hunter?" she asked.

Mama's hands fell from her shoulders, and she wiped at her eyes. "When the time is right, you'll tell him."

"He won't want me."

"Why wouldn't he?" Ingrid asked as Molly passed behind her to return to her scooping position. "Lots of people get married more than once."

Molly couldn't explain why she felt the way she did. Hunter existed on a plane she could barely see, let alone reach. He deserved the best kind of woman out there, not one who'd made mistakes and been with another man and come up short time and time again.

He'd want a woman who was his equal, and Molly feared she'd never be that kind of woman.

She finished scooping her dough balls, covered them tightly with aluminum foil, and took them out to the freezer in the garage. She stayed to help clean up, and she sat at the table with Mama and Lyra as they got out the wedding binder and did a little bit of work on planning for her sister's big day.

She gathered all the frozen dough into a plastic bag before she hugged everyone in her family good-night, and she drove back to her place alone. Gypsy cried at her for food, and Saltine licked her hand as she refilled his water bowl.

Through it all, Molly couldn't stop thinking about Hunter and whether she should tell him about her failed marriage tomorrow or keep it quiet a little longer. If she didn't tell him, she could see him again. If she did, he might end things between them.

She finished taking care of her pets and wandered down the hall to her bedroom. She stepped out of her jeans and shoes and into a silky pair of pajamas in a deep blue. They looked amazing with her hair too, and Molly had definitely learned to play to the strengths in her red hair.

Going to bed early, she texted to Hunter once she'd climbed into bed. *You sure you can't give me a hint about the restaurant tomorrow night?*

Wear close-toed shoes, he sent back with a smiley face. *Are you feeling all right? It's barely eight.*

Just an emotional afternoon at my mother's, she sent to him. *But the good news is, I got frozen cookie dough out of it.*

Save me some, he said, and his next text contained a heart. *See you tomorrow at five-thirty.*

She let her phone drop to her chest without responding. "Five-thirty is early for dinner," she mused. Where could he be taking her?

The man had plenty of money, and he obviously knew how to spend it. Did he own a private jet? Would he whisk her off to LA or New York City for a fancy dinner with plenty of dessert?

A smile touched her mouth as her fantasies took flight, and Molly let her eyes drift closed with beautiful thoughts of Hunter running through her mind.

THE FOLLOWING AFTERNOON, MOLLY POPPED another frozen cookie dough ball into her mouth, knowing she'd regret it. She'd eaten four already, and an ache had settled in her teeth. Her stomach tightened, and her solution was to eat something else to try to get it to quiet.

"Me-oooww," Gypsy sang from her perch on top of the bookcase, and Molly looked up to her.

"I can't calm down," she said. "He's going to be here any minute." She looked down at the black denim skirt she'd chosen. Perhaps a skirt was too dressy. Maybe she should just run and change really quickly.

She'd already done that three times, and she'd left her bed covered with a huge amount of discarded clothes. She apparently didn't own anything suitable for a date with

Hunter Hammond, and she lamented the fact that she'd left getting dressed to four o'clock. Had she chosen her outfit earlier in the day, she would've realized the dilemma and had time to run to her favorite boutique to find something better than what she currently owned.

Saltine lifted his head from the couch and both he and Gypsy turned toward the door. Hunter had arrived.

He jumped down from the couch, and so keyed up were Molly's nerves that she forgot to shush him as he ran toward the front door, barking at it before anyone had even touched it.

Gypsy added her yowling voice to the fray, and Molly simply stared at the door.

A moment later, the doorbell rang. Hunter knocked a couple of times too, and called, "Molly, it's just me."

Just me.

Just Hunter.

She knew him, and she liked him. They'd always been so comfortable together, even as awkward teenagers. Those two words thawed her, and she darted around the couch and picked up Saltine, shushing him.

"It's just Hunter," she said as she opened the door with her free hand. "Stop being such a nuisance."

Sure enough, Hunter stood on her front porch wearing a magnificent pair of jeans, a red and white plaid shirt, that sexy cowboy hat—this one in a light brown—and the boots she was more accustomed to seeing on his feet.

He held out a box with the words Sugar Lane on the front. "I'm sure you don't need these, because you ate all the cookie dough, didn't you?" he teased, his smile big and genuine.

"No," she said, returning that grin and taking the box. Three large oatmeal chocolate chip cookies sat inside, and her heart warmed.

Her favorite cookies, from her favorite place. The sweet gesture brought a smile to her soul, and she looked up at Hunter, who'd tucked his hands in his front pockets. "Thank you."

"You like those, right?"

"They're my favorite." She stepped into his personal space and pressed a kiss to his cheek. His hand landed lightly on her hip, but they separated quickly, a slight awkwardness between them.

"I saved you some cookie dough. Come see for yourself." She stepped back out of the doorway to make room for Hunter. He entered her house, his eyes going straight to Gypsy on the bookcase.

"Does that cat ever get down from there?"

Gypsy meowed at him, which was better than her yowl, and Molly closed the front door. The weather in Ivory Peaks had been warming up, and there was no sense in cooling the outdoors.

"When she's hungry," Molly said. "Then she really lets me know what I'm doing all wrong."

Hunter chuckled. "I bet she does." He threw one more glance at the cat before he led the way to the sheet pan of frozen cookie dough. "May I?"

"Of course." Molly set Saltine on the floor, and the dog

immediately ran to Hunter and started sniffing. He jumped up on Hunter's knees, and Molly worried that Hunter wouldn't appreciate that.

He popped a whole cookie dough ball into his mouth and crouched down. He scrubbed Saltine's face and back with his big hands, and Molly found herself a little bit jealous of her pup. She wanted to hold those hands in hers and feel them run down the side of her face. She wanted them to flow down her shoulders as Hunter kissed her, and she wanted one of them to knot in her hair as he held her in place and let her know what hid in his mind.

She cleared her throat, and Hunter straightened to a standing position. "That was amazing," he said. "You Bensons always were good in the kitchen." He reached for another bite of cookie dough. "I finished that bread this morning too. Amazing." His dark eyes seemed to harbor a bright light in them, and Molly couldn't look away as he put the cookie dough in his mouth.

"Already?" she asked, setting the cookies on the counter beside the tray of dough. "The whole loaf?"

He nodded while he chewed his treat. After he swallowed, he said, "I make sandwiches for breakfast, lunch, and dinner."

Molly laughed, because that lined up so perfectly with what she knew and remembered about Hunter. "I can make you some more," she said.

He shook his head though. "No, I don't think you'll have time."

"I won't?"

He edged closer to her, and Molly held her ground on the corner of the island. His hand reached for hers slowly, and Molly inhaled just as his skin touched hers. Pure fire ignited between them, and Molly had never felt anything so hot.

"I've got a contract for you to sign," he said. "I've talked to my uncle again, and he knows someone who knows someone in Texas who started an equine therapy facility. He's going to put us in touch with them. You're going to be so busy with this, you'll wish you never agreed to it."

Molly could get lost in the rolling lilt of his voice. "Maybe I won't sign your contract then." She grinned at him, so pleased when he returned it.

He stood a head taller than her now, and he easily spanned twice her width. He possessed a charm and charisma that spoke directly to her spirit, and Molly found herself leaning toward him.

He leaned toward her too, and her pulse took flight, the beats so close together, it was almost like the hum of a hummingbird's wings.

He paused, seeming to figure out what he was doing. He straightened. "We've got a schedule," Hunter said, his voice a bit lower than normal. "Come on, sweetheart. We don't want to be late, or the food will be cold."

"It will?"

He glanced down the length of her body and said. "Shoot. I should've told you no skirts."

"No skirts? Hunter." She shook her head. "I know you want it to be a surprise, but the gig is up. Where are we going that won't allow me to wear a skirt?" She held up one foot. "I wore the closed-toed shoes."

"We have to ride a horse to get there," he said, his eyes sliding down her legs. "I mean, I guess you could ride a horse in that. Just seems like it might hike up quite a...bit." The last word was barely made of anything but air.

He flushed and released her hand. "Up to you." He took a couple of steps away from her and reached for another cookie dough ball.

"I'll be so fast changing," she said, already moving toward the mouth of the hallway.

Twenty minutes later, Hunter turned onto the road that led to his family farm. Molly had been here many times in the past, and it sure hadn't changed much. "You have such a beautiful farm," she said.

"It is great, isn't it?" Hunter gazed out the windshield at the farm. "I do love it here."

"And dinner is out here?"

He cut her a glance out of the corner of his eye. "Yep."

Molly grinned and let him drive back to the stables. She let him help her onto a beautiful golden-colored horse, and she let him lead her through the evening sunshine to a stand of trees on the other side of the farm.

The conversation with him was easy and light, and when they swung down from their horses, Hunter took her hand and led her to a table in the shade of a huge live oak. Two chairs sat at the table, and a pale cream cloth covered it.

Two plates sat there, covered by two silver domes, and a vase of vibrant red roses dominated the center of the table.

A waiter appeared from behind a tree of all things and filled their glasses with a light pink lemonade.

"It's ready, sir," he said. "Let me know if you need anything else."

"Thank you," Hunter said.

Molly gripped his hand and watched the man in the dark suit glide back behind the tree. "You billionaires really know how to pull out all the stops, don't you?"

He laughed, lifted her knuckles to his lips, and said, "Let's eat, sweetheart. I'm starving."

CHAPTER 9

Hunter sat in front of the computer and typed in a couple of new parameters. "Is it ready?" he asked, looking past the monitor to a ginger-haired man named Joel Mittany.

At least twenty years older than Hunter, Joel kept his eyes on his handheld tablet for a moment before turning to him. "Yes. Did you get that last number?"

"Seven-point-seven-four-five." Hunter read it from the screen. They'd been in the lab for an hour, trying to get the x-ray machine calibrated properly before they set in the crystals. Hunter had used x-ray crystallography extensively at MIT, and he'd been training the other scientists here at HMC for a couple of weeks now.

This maiden voyage had to go well, and everyone else would be here in fifteen minutes.

"Let's fire it up," Joel said with a smile. He came to Hunter's side, and they both looked at the screen.

"Double-check me," Hunter said, standing to give Joel room to see the screen.

The other man took the stool Hunter had been on, and he studied the computer screen, glancing at his tablet every few seconds. "You got it, Hunt." He looked up and stood up, his eyes harboring as much anxiety as Hunter felt in his soul. "All we can do is try it."

Hunter nodded, because truer words had never been spoken. No one was going to die if the calibration still wasn't right. He wasn't performing heart surgery. He simply wanted this demonstration to go well.

They only had a limited time to take everyone from their other tasks in Lab Six, and Hunter—as the very youngest and newest member of the team—wanted to make a good impression.

Everyone had been extremely nice to him upon his arrival. He suspected his last name had a whole lot to do with that, and he wanted—*needed*—to prove that he absolutely deserved to be there. He knew his stuff. He was extremely good at problem solving, thinking of new solutions, and using the complicated, scientific equipment to get results.

Then, he could use computers and programs to analyze those results. That was what Bioinformatics was, and Hunter loved it with his whole soul.

"Okay," he said, thinking of his conversation with his aunt. He and Laura had met a couple more times since his first day at HMC, and they'd decided to take the company more toward developing new drugs with the knowledge and skills Hunter had acquired at HMC. The possibilities with Bioinformatics could take them in other directions too—waste cleanup, developing stronger strains of crops, improvements in agriculture, and even alternate energy sources.

But there was more money in medicine and pharmaceuticals. Uncle Wes had started HMC in that direction, but when he'd left, his vision had fizzled. Not only that, but they'd never had anyone with a degree like the one Hunter held. No one had ever worked for HMC with his level of training, in this innovated field of science.

"You start it," Joel said, nodding his encouragement at Hunter.

His heart pounded hard and stopped for a moment. He breathed, and his pulse raced forward again. Reaching down, he met Joel's eye. "If this doesn't work, we only have time for one more calibration."

"I think this is it."

Hunter pushed the button, and the two men looked first toward the leaded glass that separated them from the two rotating generators. Both men wore protective eyewear and coats, as the room was cooled to sixty-five degrees Fahrenheit at all times.

The scene in front of them looked straight out of a science fiction movie, and Hunter heard the water recirculating coolers kick in. They kept the generators from overheating on the other side of the protective glass, and they were extremely noisy. Located on the opposite side from where Joel and Hunter stood, the recirculating coolers only produced a healthy hum in the control room.

"There it is," Joel said, and Hunter switched his gaze to the computer screen in front of them. "Put it on the wall."

Hunter tapped to transfer the data coming in from the small computer screen to the computerized wall panels.

The detectors embedded in the wall behind the x-ray generators picked up the locations of the rays after they were scattered by the crystal. Hunter and Joel had put in a known substance—a controlled test where they knew what the pattern should be—to test the calibration of the generators.

"That's aspirin, all right," Joel said, the key elements being highlighted by the computer system.

Hunter grinned, his relief off the charts. "Perfect," he said. "Let's get the first demo set up." He switched off the projection and powered down the generators. They'd need a few minutes before they could be fired up again anyway, and Hunter wanted today's lesson to be a smash hit.

"Which one do you want to do first?" Joel said, looking at his tablet. "I have two possibilities in my notes, but I didn't differentiate which was first." He looked at Hunter for guidance, and a swell of pride filled his chest.

"What do you think?" he asked. He'd learned over the years of watching his father and uncles that asking others what they thought made them feel important and useful. It didn't really matter which demo was first, so why not let Joel choose?

"I say we go for the easiest one first," he said. "Show

them that it's not hard to read. Then we can put in the mutated sample and see if they can find the plot points."

"Good idea," Hunter said. "I checked that sample we got from Beyer-Maines too. It's been growing really well in the cool storage. I think the crystal is big enough to map, and we could do that this afternoon after the demos. Then, we'll have the data and we can start trying to figure out what that bacteria contains."

Joel nodded and tapped his tablet with the electronic pen. "Hunter...do you really think we can develop a new drug by working backward from a bacteria or virus?"

"One hundred percent," Hunter said, looking up in surprise. He studied Joel's face, wondering where the question had come from. "Didn't you do that at Sullen's?"

"Not by analyzing the proteins and makeup of actual diseases," he said. "It was more trial and error. We knew this drug inhibited that protein, and while it wasn't a perfect fix, it usually worked." He shrugged one shoulder, though he still wore a look of concern. "If it didn't, or the side effects were too drastic, we tweaked."

"Tweaked." Hunter couldn't believe medications had been made like that in the past. "This tells us exactly what we have." He gestured to the complicated set-up behind the protective glass. The equipment back there cost millions of dollars, and Hunter respected that greatly. "We can take a person's DNA and their blood, and we can actually develop a medicine that's personalized *to them,* based on their individual susceptibility to specific drugs."

"It's incredible, isn't it?" Joel asked. "I've just never seen the data points come out like this. *I* barely know what I'm looking at."

"The experiment—the actual blasting of the x-rays through the crystals is only the very beginning," Hunter said. "It's only the biology. Then we have to analyze that data. If we can't read it, we can send it to a couple of other labs."

Hunter really didn't want to do that; he'd done well at MIT on the data analysis end of things, even going so far as to write his own programs to find the information he needed hidden in the graphs and charts. He'd earned a scholarly distinction because of it, and his heart started kicking out those extra beats again.

He really did love science and computers.

Behind him, the door opened, and Hunter cleared his throat. "Can you do the intro, please?" he asked Joel in a quieter voice.

"Of course." Joel clapped his hand on Hunter's shoulder as he passed him. He indicated the chairs they'd set up earlier that morning, and Hunter was more than happy to be the faceless man behind the screen while Joel led the demo. When he had to, he stood up and explained something, using the most basic terminology possible so that everyone could understand.

The machines performed flawlessly, and by the time lunch came, Hunter's smile spread across his whole face, and his mood had reached the stars. The group of men and women left the control room together, all of them chattering and in good spirits.

Several people stayed close to Hunter, continuing to ask him questions about what else could be analyzed with x-ray crystallography and how the data would then be read and interpreted.

Finally, everyone dispersed in the company cafeteria, and Hunter stood with the two people he'd become closest to over the past couple of weeks. Larry Lucas had picked up a bowl of soup and a grilled cheese sandwich, and Cassie Rogers had selected a salad and two pieces of pie.

He grinned at her tray. "Going for dessert first, I see."

"After that?" She shook her head and smiled. "We should all be eating pie."

"Not a big warm fruit fan," Hunter said.

"There's chocolate." Cassie grinned at him and went first to find a table for the three of them. He followed the blonde to a table by the windows and sat next to her. She groaned as she sat, and Hunter glanced at her.

"You okay?" he asked.

She gave him a quick look and then glanced across the table to where Larry had settled. He sported dark hair the color of tar, with bushy eyebrows in the same vein. He liked to go running and boating around the Denver area in his free time, so he had tan skin and could probably climb a million stairs without getting winded.

He looked curiously at Cassie too.

Her blue eyes met Hunter's again, and he shook his head. "You don't have to tell me."

"It's okay," she said. "I groaned like I was about to die."

She smiled at him and Larry and leaned in a little bit. "I haven't told anyone yet, so please keep it to yourselves."

Hunter nodded along with Larry, who'd already taken a bite of his sandwich. The tension in Hunter's body wouldn't allow him to start eating the pizza slice he'd picked up.

"Terry and I are expecting another baby." Cassie grinned at the two men and straightened. "There. You're the first people I've told besides our families."

"That's great," Hunter said, smiling at her. All the negative energy bled out of him as he picked up his pizza.

"Yes, congrats, Cassie," Larry said. "That makes three for you guys?"

She nodded, her expression growing serious. "I hope I can handle more kids than adults."

Larry chuckled, though he didn't have any kids yet. He was dating a woman fairly seriously—at least that was what he'd told Hunter. He hadn't mentioned Molly to anyone at work, other than the secretary who'd called him upstairs a week ago. Even then, all he'd said was *thanks for letting me know my friend was here.*

He thought about her as he took a bite of his food and chewed. They'd been on a few pretty amazing dates lately, and he caught himself smiling. The horseback riding with the catered dinner. Hunter had taken her to a concert in the park on Friday, and they'd gotten dinner from a food truck. He'd held her hand as they meandered around, talking, and then eventually getting ice cream.

He'd gone out to the farm on Saturday, and he'd stopped by her place on the way back to the city. She'd fed him dinner, and they'd walked her dog together. More hand-holding. He made sure to text her every single day, and he'd called last night just to talk.

"I can't believe you eat cheese pizza," Larry said, breaking into Hunter's thoughts. "You're smiling like a loon. What's going on with you?"

"Nothing." Hunter quickly shoved the last of his pizza in his mouth, but the bite was too big.

"Oh, boy," Cassie said, the teasing in her voice amped up. "You hit a nerve, Larry."

Hunter shook his head as his friends laughed. He nearly choked on the bread in his mouth, though, so he couldn't really refute what she'd said.

"Seems like it," Larry said. "Who puts that much pizza in their mouth if nothing is going on?"

"I think it's got to be a woman," Cassie said, forking in her last bite of pie.

Hunter's face heated, and he knew it would turn a deep red soon enough. He continued to chew, almost wishing he could spit out the pizza there was so much. He ducked his head, using his cowboy hat to hide his face a little.

"Come on, Hunt," Larry said. "I told you all about Delia."

"You've been dating Delia for three years," Cassie said. "You need to man-up and marry that girl."

"Who says I haven't tried?" Larry shot back, and Hunter watched their non-verbal exchange from under the brim of his hat.

"Larry," Cassie said, her voice much softer now. "I didn't know that…did she say no?"

Larry shook his head. "I haven't asked officially." He cut a glance at Hunter, their eyes meeting for a moment. "I keep asking her about marriage. A wedding. If she wants to go ring shopping so I'll know what she likes." He surveyed the two of them opposite him. "She…doesn't seem interested."

Hunter finally swallowed his pizza. "What does she say?" Larry had turned thirty-one last fall, but Hunter had no idea how old Delia was.

"She says she wants to open her salon first," Larry said. "Or she'll say she can't go shopping because her sister needs her to babysit."

Cassie put her fork down, which meant things were about to get serious. "Larry," she said calmly. "No woman I know would choose babysitting for their sister over diamond shopping with the man they love."

"So you're saying she doesn't love him?" Hunter asked, really wanting to know. "Maybe she's just not ready. Not everyone is ready at the same time."

Cassie looked at him, then back to Larry. She shook her head slowly. "Not if you've been dating for three years." She reached across the table and covered Larry's hand with one of hers. "I'm sorry, Larry. It's just my opinion."

Larry nodded, though he looked supremely uncomfortable. "It's nothing my mother and my brother haven't said to me." He flashed a pained smile and focused on his soup. "I just don't know how to break up with her."

"Because you love her," Hunter said, once again thinking

of Molly. He'd loved her with a fifteen-year-old's version of love.

Larry nodded but kept his face down. "So, Hunter, who's got you stuffing your face with pizza so you don't have to talk about her?"

Hunter opened his mouth to say, "No one," but a woman approached their table and said, "Hunter Hammond?"

He looked up at Laura's assistant, instantly annoyed she'd phrased his name as a question. He knew her, as he'd been up to his aunt's office several times now.

"Hello, Tilly," he said in a cool voice.

"Miss Vaughn would like you to come see her this afternoon."

"Just whenever?" Hunter asked, thinking of the experiments he and Joel had scheduled.

"Right now, if possible." Tilly flashed him a tight smile. "I'm to escort you up if you can spare a few minutes."

Hunter looked at his tray, which still held his cookies and potato salad.

"I'll clean it up for you, Hunt," Larry said.

"Yeah," Cassie said. "The boss is calling." She gave him a knowing smile, but Hunter didn't know what she knew.

He grabbed his cookies, stood, and said, "Sure, you can escort me up to see Miss Vaughn."

CHAPTER 10

"You're kidding." Molly took the folder Hunter handed her, but she didn't open it. Hunter slouched on her couch and closed his eyes. He still wore his slacks, but his light blue shirt peeked through the open collar of a white lab coat. The tie around his throat had been loosened, and she could just imagine him pulling at it as he rode the elevator down to the parking garage beneath his building.

She hadn't been to his condo downtown yet, but she hoped to be able to see it soon. Hunter had admitted to not being much use in the kitchen, but he'd survived on his own in Cambridge, so he must be able to put together some semblance of a meal.

"Hunter," she said, striding toward him, the folder gripped in her fingers. "What did she say?"

He opened his eyes, and he looked so tired. Those dark depths threatened to swallow her, though, the same way they always had. It had been his eyes that had first captured her in sixth grade, the first year they'd been at the junior high together.

She'd known him before that, of course. His dad had brought Hunter to church week after week, faithfully. They'd been in Sunday school classes together. Molly had always thought Hunter was cute.

Now, he was downright handsome. Sexy, even.

He gave her a small smile, drawing her attention to his mouth. "She said she's been running HMC for over a decade, and she's looking to retire."

Molly perched on the edge of the loveseat kitty-corner to the couch he sat on. Her heartbeat thumped in the vein in her neck so violently she could feel it move her skin.

"She said she thinks I'd do a really good job as CEO." He let his eyes drift closed again. "I told her I was twenty-five years old."

Molly wanted to let him rest, as he so obviously needed to. Her pulse wouldn't let her stay silent, though. "Hunter, do you want to be CEO?"

"No," he said. "Not only am I only twenty-five years old, but we did an amazing experiment in the lab today, and that's what I like doing." He sighed and sat up, running his hands up his face and dislodging his cowboy hat as he moved his fingers into his hair. "In fact, it was the first thing I've done in Lab Six that I've enjoyed."

He lowered his hands, and he wore a new look on his face Molly had seen a time or two. He talked about the crystals they'd grown with a novel bacteria in it they'd gotten from a hospital in Maryland, and the new focus in Lab Six was figuring out how to develop a drug to combat the bacteria they'd shot x-rays through.

Hunter came alive when he spoke about the science, the computer programs needed to analyze the data they'd collected, and future experiments he hoped to do.

After a few minutes, he hung his head. "Sorry, I'll stop talking now."

Molly had settled back into the love seat while he'd been talking. "I like listening to you talk about your job."

"You do?" He lifted his eyes to hers, something sparking in his expression.

"Yes." She smiled at him. "You seem to really love it."

"I'm just barely into it." He searched her face. "How am I supposed to run the whole blasted company?" He shook his head. "I can't do it. I can't even get myself over to the grocery store to get milk, and I've been out for three days."

Molly laughed and stood up. "You can take mine, Hunt."

He joined her in the kitchen and slid his hand along her waist. Molly tensed instantly, and Hunter dropped his hand. "Sorry," he murmured, stepping away from the fridge and around the island, where he took a seat on one of the barstools. "Do you want to go to dinner?"

Molly turned from the fridge without taking out the gallon of milk she planned to give him. She held onto the handle with both hands and pressed her back into her fists and the door. "Hunter, I…." She cleared her throat, nervous when he wouldn't look away from her. He existed in a universe she would never get to, and he had no idea that he did. He didn't think he could run his family's company, but Molly could see him in the corner office, handling everything with the same perfect precision he had his crossword puzzles, the way he'd kissed her as a teenager, and the straight A's he'd gotten the last three years at MIT.

Yes, she'd asked, and he'd finally told her.

She didn't think he'd be happy in the corner office, despite the two walls of windows and the beautiful view of downtown Denver and the Rocky Mountains. Hunter was a doer, not an overseer. He'd stayed in Massachusetts for an extra year to run his educational foundation. His name might still be on it while he wasn't there, but he spoke to his friend about it several times a week.

"Molly?" he asked.

She blinked and opened her mouth, desperate for the Lord to fill it with the right words. "I've been married," she blurted out. "Before. I'm divorced now, but I was... married...before."

His eyes widened, and Molly wanted to flee. She gripped the door handle to keep herself in position. "I wanted you to know."

"You look like you're about to throw up," he said, cocking his head to the side.

"I feel like I'm about to throw up." Molly emitted a nearly-hysterical giggle, tears springing to her eyes.

"Molly." Hunter got up and came toward her, such a huge presence in her house. "What's wrong?" He didn't hesitate as he gathered her right into the safe circle of his arms.

Molly's eyes closed as she melted into his strength, taking in a deep breath of the scent of his lab coat, his skin, and his cologne. He reminded her of the clearest summer day, with a hint of something clinical and something musky.

Hunter held her right against his chest, his heartbeat steady and calm. Molly wanted that strength in her life, and she gripped the back of his coat in her fists.

"Why are you so upset?" he whispered.

"I don't want you to think badly of me," she said just as quietly. "You mean so much to me, and I just...don't want you to think I'm one big failure."

"I would never think that."

Molly gave a tight shake of her head, not daring to move too much in case Hunter released her. His warmth sank right into her skin, then her soul, and she knew then that she liked him far more than she ever had as a teen.

"You know what I do when I feel like this?" He ran one hand up her back and into her hair. He pulled away slightly and looked down at her, stroking her hair back off the side of her face.

Molly couldn't look him in the eyes. "What?" Her embarrassment streamed through her, and not just for what she'd said. She released him and quickly wiped her eyes. He didn't back up and give her a single inch of breathing room.

"I pray for help," he whispered. "Do you want me to pray with you?"

Molly marveled at the strength inside this good man. He may only be twenty-five, but Hunter possessed a maturity well beyond his years. She nodded. "Would you?"

"Of course." He took her hands in his and ducked his head. Molly let her burning eyes close again, getting some relief just from that.

"Dear Lord," Hunter said, his voice deep and quiet. "We acknowledge Thy hand in our lives. We thank Thee for a beautiful place to live, and that both Molly and I have good, comfortable homes." He shifted his feet. "Lord, life is hard sometimes, and we need Thy help. Please bless Molly to feel of Thy love for her, and to know that she is valuable and beautiful and...good."

He paused for a moment, and Molly pressed with everything in her to keep the tears in. They quivered right on the edge of her eyelids, because hearing him pray for her was the sweetest thing anyone had ever done for her.

"Don't let her mind twist the truth into the wrong thing. She is kind, smart, and worthy of being loved."

Molly gave up trying not to cry and let her tears flow down her face.

"Bless her family, and mine, and help me to have a clear mind to know what to do about my work. Amen." Hunter retreated quickly then, and Molly hastened to wipe her face.

"Excuse me," she whispered, stepping quickly out of the kitchen and down the hall to her bedroom. She closed the door quietly behind her and moved over to the bed. She drew in a shuddering breath and looked up at the ceiling.

"Am I kind, smart, and worthy of being loved?" She almost didn't want God to tell her. "Am I good?"

A sweet, peaceful feeling flowed over her, causing a shiver to move over her shoulders and down her back. She got up and went back into the kitchen to find Hunter holding Saltine in his arms as he tried to coax Gypsy down from the bookcase.

He turned as he heard her footsteps, and he quickly bent to put the little dog on the floor. "Molly, I'm sorry. I—"

"Don't be sorry." She hurried to him and wrapped her arms around the back of his neck. "That was beautiful, and I just needed a minute to compose myself." She pressed her forehead to the knot on his tie and took a breath. "I hate crying, and I especially feel like a fool for doing it in front of you."

"You can do anything in front of me," he whispered, his mouth right at her ear. "Okay, Molly?" He pulled back, and this time, she had the courage to look at him. "We get to be ourselves with each other. We get to feel what we authentically feel. We don't have to hide from one another."

She nodded. "I'd like that."

He gave her a small smile and let the moment drag out. "Dinner?" he asked again.

"Yes," she said. "Let's go to dinner and talk more about this CEO thing."

"Not that," he said, releasing her and moving over to the kitchen counter to pick up the folder. "Anything but that, okay?" He faced her. "Instead, I was thinking you and I need to talk about going to Coral Canyon for the Fourth of July."

Molly nearly fell down as she stumbled over her own feet. She met Hunter's dazzling eyes and asked, "Together?"

He smiled and shook his head slightly as if he didn't quite believe she had to ask. "Yes. Together. Me and you, we're…." He ducked his head in that adorable way he'd done since he was eleven years old. "Together. Right?" He looked straight at her again, and Molly's whole soul rejoiced.

"Yes," she said, smiling too. "We're together."

He laughed and reached for her hand. She gladly put hers in his and let him lead her out the front door. "What are we going to do in Coral Canyon?" she asked.

"Oh, just about everything," Hunter said, opening the door of his truck for her. "Talk to Uncle Ames about the equine therapy. See my cousins and aunts and uncles. Go to a parade and watch fireworks. Eat a lot of ice cream. Remember that ice cream shop on Beverly Street?"

Molly laughed as she climbed up on the runner. "I remember."

"I want to go there every day," he said, leaning into the door. "Talk to my dad and Uncle Wes about me being the CEO." He sobered and reached out to cradle Molly's face. "Make sure everyone important to me knows we're together."

Molly leaned into his touch, her smile blooming across her face. "I think I can pencil in the trip," she said.

Hunter laughed, stepped back, and closed the door. Molly watched him walk around the front of the truck, feeling herself start to fall in love with him all over again.

THAT NIGHT, AFTER HUNTER HAD DROPPED HER off after dinner, after Molly had fed a grumpy Gypsy and soaked in a hot bath, Molly knelt beside her bed.

She closed her eyes and tried to vocalize what she was feeling. The intense gratitude for the revelations of that day. The joy she felt at being with Hunter Hammond again. The relief that she hadn't ruined everything by choosing the wrong man to marry. That she wasn't damaged. That she was worthy of being loved.

Everything stuck in her throat, so she just stayed on her knees and let her feelings stream from her, hoping the Lord would accept the prayer in her heart, even if she couldn't vocalize it.

CHAPTER 11

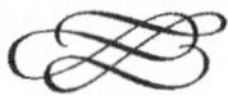

Hunter started laughing as he pulled up to the house where he'd stayed during the summer months. The littles had decorated it with a huge banner that said, WELCOME HOME HUNTER.

"Look, they even got you in there," he said, pointing as if Molly couldn't see the twenty-foot sign that spanned nearly the whole front porch. Underneath his name, in a different color of paint, sat AND MOLLY.

Molly laughed too, going, "Oh," as the three kids came running out of the house and underneath the banner.

Hunter quickly put the rental car in park and got out of it, laughing as he jogged toward Tucker and Deacon, who both led Jane. He scooped up both little boys and shifted them so he could press Jane into a hug as she wrapped her arms around his waist.

"You're here," they started to chant. "You're here. You're here. You're here."

"I'm here," Hunter said, laughing through the words. "Who did the sign?"

"All of us," Deacon said. "I spelled your name, Hunt."

"It's great," he said, setting Tucker on the ground. "You added the part for Molly, right, Jane?"

"Yes," she said, grinning up at Hunter. "Dad didn't tell us she was coming until a couple of days ago."

"That's because I didn't tell him until a couple of days ago." Hunter ran his hand along her silken hair. "Thank you, Jane." He turned toward the car, where Molly stood. He gestured for her to come on over, and she did. "You guys, this is my girlfriend, Molly Benson." He grinned at her and moved Deacon to his left arm so he could hold Molly's hand with his right.

"Mols, these are the littles. Jane's the oldest. Then Tucker. Then Deacon."

"It's so great to meet you," Molly said, her smile genuine and kind. "Let's see…Tucker, you're in second grade, right?"

"I finished second grade," Tucker said.

"Molly teaches second grade," Hunter said.

"I'm going to start kindergarten this year," Deacon said.

"Is that so?" Molly asked. "Do you know how to read already?" She glanced at Hunter. "I bet you do. You Hammonds are all so smart."

"Momma's teaching me," Deacon said.

A dog barked, and Hunter turned to find Hutch standing at the top of the porch steps. He was an old dog now, and he'd always been silver, so the only way Hunter knew was because he hadn't nearly been knocked down by the overeager goldendoodle.

Hutch barked again, and Hunter set Deacon on his feet and went up the steps. "Hey, my friend." He scrubbed the pup behind the ears and along his shoulders. "Can't go down the steps, huh? It's okay. I'll come to you."

Footsteps came up behind him, and soon enough, everyone joined him on the porch.

"There they are," Dad said, and Hunter straightened, his heart leaping at the sight of his parents. He surged toward Dad and Elise, engulfing them both into a hug at the same time. They both laughed, but a tight pinch in Hunter's chest prevented him from joining in.

Dad and Elise both held him tight, seeming to know that he needed them to do exactly that, and several long seconds later, he stepped back. He expected Dad to ask him what was going on, but it was Elise who linked her arm through his and said, "Introduce me to your Molly."

"You've met her before."

"Not for a long time," Elise whispered. "Be a gentleman, Hunt."

He turned back to Molly, who was still surrounded by the littles. They all talked to her at the same time, and Molly glowed with their attention. He wondered if she wanted a lot of kids, because looking at her, Hunter suddenly did. A lot of them—as long as they were hers too.

He wasn't sure what that meant, and he quickly dismissed the thought. "Molly, this is Elise." He smiled at her. "My mom. And you remember my father, Gray."

"Of course," Molly said as Elise's arm in Hunter's tightened. He'd never called her his mother before, and they both knew it. He wasn't even sure where the introduction had come from today either. It was just there, and it was just right.

"Nice to see you both again." Molly glanced at him, somehow sensing that something bigger than her meeting his parents was happening.

Elise stepped forward and hugged her, and even Dad gave her a quick embrace. They both looked at Hunter again, and he saw the searching questions in their eyes. He had so much to talk to them about, and he didn't want to let any of it come out.

It has to all come out, he told himself, but so much happiness filled this space and this moment, and he didn't want to ruin it. So when Jane said, "Hunt, come have a piece of the cake I made with Mom," he allowed himself to be swept inside with the children, as if he were still one of them and didn't have to engage in difficult adult conversations.

THAT EVENING, HUNTER HELPED CLEAR THE table, very aware when Elise said, "Tucker, you and Deacon take Hutch out. Jane, go get your skirt to show Molly."

Dad joined Hunter at the sink. "Uncle Colt wants to host dinner at his place tomorrow."

"That's fine," Hunter said. "We don't have plans other

than going to Uncle Ames's place, but that's in the morning."

"Elise and I would like to talk to you."

Hunter nodded, because they needed to talk. "It's going to take longer than just taking out a dog or getting a skirt."

Dad nodded and patted Hunter's upper arm. "We know." He indicated that Hunter should leave the dishes and go with him. Hunter followed his father, glancing at Molly, who nodded. She'd handle the kids, and Hunter sure did appreciate that.

He detoured over to her. "I think we're just going to be on the back deck. You can come out." Anything he had to say, she should get to hear.

"I don't mind entertaining the kids," she said. "You have some important things to talk about with your parents."

Hunter gazed down at her, wanting to kiss her very much. He leaned down, hoping his eyes could convey what he wanted even if he couldn't do it. He swept his lips along her cheek and whispered, "Thanks, Mols."

"Molly, look at this skirt I made," Jane said, and Hunter stepped away as she turned toward his younger sister.

He joined Elise and Dad on the deck, where they both sat on a bench built into the railing. He groaned as he sat next to his father, and he wished he had the folder Aunt Laura had given him last week. He wished he had something to do with his hands, but he didn't.

Focusing on his cowboy boots, he said, "I hope I didn't make you feel uncomfortable by calling you my mother," Hunter said.

"Of course not," Elise said, her voice pitching up at the end. Hunter didn't dare look at her, because his own emotions spiraled through him. "It's all I've ever wanted to be, Hunt," she continued. "I'm honored to be your mother."

Hunter nodded, a smile moving through him that barely touched his face.

"Hunter," Dad said, all the prompting he needed to say. He often added a lot more, but tonight, he didn't.

Hunter straightened, not ashamed of what he'd done or what had happened. "Wow, it's hot even here." He chuckled and lifted his cowboy hat to wipe the sweat off his brow. "Maybe that's just because you two are grilling me." He grinned at his father, who managed a smile though his eyes held concern.

Hunter looked past him to Elise, and when their eyes met, Hunter couldn't stay still. He got to his feet and stepped over to hug her. There was so much to say, and yet, he couldn't get any of it out. She held him as tightly as he did her, and Hunter supposed they could communicate with touch as easily as with voices.

"Momma, Tucker won't let me hold the leash," Deacon called from the yard, and Hunter released Elise.

"I got it," Dad said, and he stood up to go take care of the boys. He got them to stop arguing, and he sent them inside with the promise that Molly would turn on a movie and make them popcorn.

As he approached the bench again, Hunter said, "I stopped talking to Sheila a few years ago." He cleared his throat, wondering how often Dad spoke to her, if he did at all. Based on what had happened with Hunter, he suspected they never talked. "She's always used me, and I've always known it. I couldn't seem to let her go, though, because." He stopped and shrugged, studying his hands. "She's my mother."

Dad patted his leg and Elise laced her arm through his.

"It took me a while to realize that a mother is not just the person who gives life once." He looked at Elise. "She is the one who gives life continually. She is the one who sacrifices for the ones she loves, day after day. She is the one who loves her children unconditionally, and never asks for glory though she deserves it, and loves her kids' dad even when he's not perfect." Hunter's voice grew quieter and quieter with each word, but they all held pure power. "A mother shows her kids how to be like her just by living the right way, and she shows her sons the need to find someone just like her to be their wife and the mother of their children."

He smiled fondly at Elise, who had tears falling down her face. "You *are* my mother, and I apologize that it has taken me so long to realize it."

"Oh, Hunter." Elise gripped him and hugged him hard. "I love you so much."

"I know you do." He held her tight. "I love you too." They separated, and Hunter drew in a steadying breath, sure his father would want more information.

He let several silent moments go by before he asked, "What happened with Sheila?"

Hunter cleared his throat, but he could talk about this.

Enough time had passed, and Lucy had advised him to talk to his parents about this so he could remove it from his heart and mind. "She knows the family traditions, Dad. She knew I'd get a bunch of money when I turned twenty-one, and she was right there, wanting some of it."

"I'm so sorry," he said. "I should've anticipated that."

"I dealt with it." Hunter gazed out over the back lawn, where he'd once thrown a ball for Hutch while Jane cried after she'd caught her fingers in the cupboard door.

"What happened?" Dad asked.

"You're not going to do anything, are you?" Hunter looked at his father, and the look in his eye gave the answer. No, his father wasn't going to do anything. Hunter could still feel the summer sun and taste the salty air down in Florida, where Sheila lived. Hunter hadn't quite known what to expect when he'd gone, but he should've. Foolishness filled him as rapidly now as it had as he'd flown home on the red-eye.

"It doesn't matter what happened," he said. "Sometimes we need a push to do what we've known all along. Sometimes it hurts a little more when we get that push than if we'd just taken the step ourselves." He wondered if that would be the same for the job at HMC. Would he get shoved into it? Or should he take the first step and just accept it?

"I hate that she pushed you," Dad said darkly.

"There's something else." Hunter took a big breath and held it for a moment. He didn't want to talk about Sheila anymore, or ever again, with his parents. "Laura offered to start training me to be the CEO of HMC, starting on January first of next year."

The words felt like bombs coming out of his mouth, and he really didn't like the way the silence permeated the summer night in front of him. "I'd like to talk to you and Uncle Wes about it while I'm here. Get all the angles. Examine everything."

"Hunter," Dad said, his voice full of shock. "CEO? You're twenty-five."

"That's exactly how I felt," he said. "I don't think I breathed for twenty-four straight hours." He chuckled and looked at his father. "You don't think I can do it."

"Of course I think you can do it," Dad said instantly. "The real question is whether you think you *should* do it, and whether or not you *want* to do it."

"Sometimes—"

"Hunter," Elise interrupted. "In this case, both have to be true. You need to want to do this job, *and* you need to think you should do the job."

Hunter looked at her, because she rarely spoke up and offered advice. Hunter had always gone to Dad for that. They talked about important things while in a fishing boat, with God's glorious nature around them. This felt so odd to be talking about such life-changing things on a backyard deck, of all places.

"She's right," Dad said, his voice distinct and powerful. "You don't owe HMC anything. This is not a duty-bound thing. If you want this job, you take it. If you don't, you don't."

Hunter wasn't sure what he'd expected them to say. He wasn't sure what Uncle Wes would say either. He wanted to hear it all. He needed time to mull it all over, flip it around, examine it, and come to a conclusion.

"I'm not sure I went to MIT for six years to be CEO," he said. "I studied biology, math, and computer science. Nothing with business."

"You're smart," Elise said. "Who goes to MIT on a full scholarship for *six* years?"

Hunter smiled at her, because he knew he'd done something exceptional. He didn't like to be told he was exceptional, but every once in a while, he did need to be reminded of it.

"I want to start an equine therapy branch of my foundation," he said.

Dad smiled at him. "Then do that."

"I want the farm."

"Buy it from us," Dad said.

"We actually started working on something I'm interested in at HMC."

"Keep doing that," Elise said.

Hunter nodded, letting his thoughts flow through his mind without trying to examine them. Dad and Elise gave him a few minutes of silence.

Then Elise said, "That Molly Benson sure is beautiful. How are things going with her now?"

Hunter couldn't contain his smile, and he didn't even try. Elise giggled too, and she said, "I see that smile."

"Yeah, well, she makes me smile."

"Hold onto that," Dad said. "Real tight, Hunter." He stood up and extended his hand toward his wife. "Come on, sweetheart. I think we've grilled Hunt enough for one night."

Elise stood and put her hand in Dad's. She paused and looked down at him. "Love you, son."

Hunter basked in the warmth of her love, and he touched his fingers to the brim of his cowboy hat, the highest level of respect he knew how to give her.

"Real tight," Dad said as they walked away. They reached the back door, and Dad turned back to him. "Real tight, Hunter."

"I got it, Dad," Hunter said, shaking his head. "Maybe you could send her out here so I can hold her *real tight*."

Dad grinned and said, "I'll do that."

CHAPTER 12

Molly couldn't take in the scene in front of her fast enough. The sheer number of dogs in the field overwhelmed her instantly, and the fact that one man controlled them and commanded them made her jaw drop.

"That's my uncle," Hunter said, lifting his hand in a wave as the man in the center of at least forty dogs did.

"This is incredible," Molly said, trying to find another landmark to latch onto. She kept coming back to the mob of large dogs, the majority of them German shepherds or close to that size, because they were so impressive.

"He's had this facility for oh, I don't know. Eight years."

Molly gasped as she saw a smaller figure out in the field with the dogs. "Oh, my goodness." Her hand in Hunter's tightened. "There's a child out there."

Hunter chuckled and put his foot up on the bottom rung

of the fence. "That's my cousin, Chris. He's Ames's oldest, and he's named after my grandfather." Hunter wore the family pride right in his voice.

"He's barely taller than those dogs," Molly said, her heart still pounding. "How old is he?"

"Five or six," Hunter said. "I think six. I think he just turned six this past spring." He glanced at Molly and grinned. "He's got a twin, Lars. Uncle Ames said they wanted to mail me a piece of birthday cake, and neither of them would let it go. So my uncle finally said he'd take the cake and mail it. He called me while he ate it around the side of the garage." Hunter laughed, and Molly really liked how close he was with his family. Not just his core family either, but all of these uncles and cousins.

Her heart jumped again, because they had dinner plans with another of his uncles that evening, and apparently all five of the Hammond brothers would be there. Molly's memory strained around the edges, because she'd attended a couple of big family dinners with Hunter the one summer she'd come to Coral Canyon with his family.

They'd come for Ames's wedding, in fact.

The man in the field whistled, and all the dogs dropped to the ground. He said something to the six-year-old, who opened a gate. The dogs closest to it started inside, and soon enough, all the dogs had been penned and contained.

From there, she watched them walk through little doorways cut into the side of a building, where they could obviously go to rest or find a patch of shade. Plenty of them stayed outside too, and Ames said something to his son before turning toward Hunter and Molly.

He jogged the last few steps, laughing by the time he reached Hunter. He took Hunter into a tight hug, and Molly stood back and watched the love between the two of them. "Look how tall you are," Ames said, gripping Hunter's shoulders and standing back.

He did stand about three inches taller than his uncle, and he had to be over six feet. "It's the cowboy hat," Hunter said, taking it off.

It wasn't the cowboy hat, and Ames Hammond said so. His gaze shot to Molly, and his smile didn't slip a single bit. "Hello, Molly."

"Hello, sir." She extended her hand for him to shake, but he took it and pulled her in for a hug.

"Don't sir me," he said, chuckling. "I already feel really old with Hunter here showing me how grown up he is." He stepped back and grinned at her.

"How old are you now, Uncle Ames?" Hunter asked innocently, but one look at his face showed he knew exactly what he was asking.

"Fifty-three," Ames said, lifting his cowboy hat too. "Good news is I still have all my hair." He slicked it back with his free hand. "At least you know we have good genes for that, Molly."

She laughed with him, her thoughts racing ahead twenty-five years to when she and Hunter would be fifty years old. Ames had just said she wouldn't have to worry about Hunter being bald then, as if she'd still be in Hunter's life.

Warmth filled her, and she met Hunter's eye. He was thinking something along the same lines as her, she was fairly sure, but he hadn't even kissed her yet. Her body temperature increased as she thought about kissing him, and her blood burned with desire.

"You definitely have the land for an equine therapy unit," Hunter said. "Maybe not as much as I've got at Ivory Peaks, but enough." He surveyed the land, and Molly found herself doing the same.

She could see Ames out in a field, in complete control of a whole herd of horses. She could easily see Hunter out there too. She wasn't sure what he'd talked about with his parents last night, as he hadn't said much about it, but she hoped he was getting the advice and help he needed to make a decision about being the CEO at HMC.

Molly had no doubt he could do it. The job just didn't seem like it fit him at all.

They started walking down the dirt lane that led between two fields, one of which held plenty of equipment. It looked like an obstacle course, and Molly wondered how that helped the dogs become good police dogs.

"Molly's going to help me with it," Hunter said, and she turned back to the conversation.

"You two should go meet with a man named Pete Marshall," Ames said. "He started an equine therapy unit at a ranch in Three Rivers. Built it from the ground up."

"Non-profit?" Hunter asked.

Ames shook his head. “No, they’re for-profit, but they’re funded with a lot of grants. He knows how to get the national sponsorships and endorsements, and he’d have some good leads for counselors, trainers, and horses.”

“Sounds like we need to meet him,” Hunter said, pulling out his phone and starting to tap on the screen. “What did you say his name was?”

“Pete Marshall,” Molly and Ames said together.

“Where’s Three Rivers?” Molly asked, leaning out to see past Hunter to Ames.

“Texas,” Ames said, and Molly’s eyebrows lifted.

“Wow,” she said. “Texas. If we do end up going there, I’ll have traveled more this summer than I ever have.”

Hunter smiled in her direction, not truly meeting her eyes. “We should go to Texas,” he said. “It’ll be hotter than the surface of the sun, though.” He finished typing his note to himself and tucked his phone away. “You’ll send me his number?”

“Comin’ your way.” Ames used his device to get that done, and then he said, “I’ve got some good contacts with police units around the country. The bigger ones, obviously, as that’s who usually takes my dogs. Cy’s got a ton of contacts in the world of veterans. He said he’d talk to you at dinner tonight.”

“Great,” Hunter said. “We’re just gathering contacts and as much information as we can right now.” He took Molly’s hand in his again, squeezing as he did. “It might be too much for me to take on.”

She noted how he'd said "we" initially, and then finished with "me."

"How are things at HMC?" Ames asked.

"Good," Hunter said, his voice so full of false nonchalance that even Molly looked at him.

Ames watched him for a couple of steps and then turned his attention back to the fields and fences in front of him. "You know, I used to feel like I'd missed something by not working there."

"Mm," Hunter said, and Molly just kept her ears open. She didn't work inside a business setting, and she wasn't sure what the climate would even be like.

"I felt like maybe I wasn't a good enough Hammond or like I wasn't living up to some sort of family expectation."

Molly wanted to jump in and say that Hunter had a master's degree in some pretty amazing stuff, and he could literally work anywhere. It didn't have to be HMC, and in fact, she wasn't even sure he'd stay there very long. The man adored the farm, and Molly wouldn't be surprised if he ended up there, feeding the goats and raising horses, growing hay and selling cattle.

She kept her mouth shut, because she and Hunter had only been back together for just over a month now, and she really couldn't say what was going on inside his head. He said very little of what he actually had in his mind, and while Molly knew he'd been shocked by his visit to Laura's office, he also carried a great sense of family duty.

"You were a great cop," Hunter said.

"Like I'm sure you're a great scientist." Ames really knew how to drive home a point, Molly would give him that.

"I *am* a good scientist," Hunter said. "My therapist says to vocalize things out loud when they're true, even when I feel like waving them off."

"Good for you," Ames said, grinning. "We all need to do that more. I wonder what I would say."

"You're amazing with those dogs," Molly said. "Watching you…wow."

"I *am* amazing with dogs," Ames said, and Hunter nodded.

"You've got it Uncle Ames." They laughed together, and even Molly smiled.

"What about you, Molly? What would you say?" Ames asked.

Molly's mind blanked. "Oh, I don't know. Nothing much."

"Not true," Hunter said. "Molly's amazing in the kitchen. She's a good cook and an amazing baker."

"I *am* a good cook and an amazing baker," she said, playing their game. It sure did feel good to say that out loud, and she realized the wisdom in Hunter's therapist. Normally, she'd just say something like, "Nah, I'm not that good," or "There are so many people who are good cooks."

Pride filled her at her own talents and strengths, and she didn't recognize them nearly as often as she should. She wanted to change that, and she determined to have a self-recognition minute every single day to remind herself of what she was good at.

MOLLY SAT AT A COMPUTER IN THE FRONT OFFICE of Hunter's uncle's house, clicking her way around a website that boasted a ton of riding classes for kids, therapy sessions, and pictures of people and horses.

She'd contained her search to equine therapy centers in the Denver area, and there were already four surrounding the city. That didn't mean there wasn't a need for another one, but Molly wanted theirs—hers? Hunter's?—to be a little bit different.

Molly leaned closer to the computer screen and noted that all the people riding during therapy were adults. She clicked on the tab for more information about their therapy sessions, and sure enough, this center only offered counseling and riding services for those over the age of eighteen.

She checked the next center, then the next, and finally the last.

She pulled the pad of paper toward her and wrote a single word on it.

"Mols," Hunter said, and she spun around in the swivel chair. "Dinner's ready, and everyone's here."

"Coming." She got up and crossed the office toward him. He waited for her, easily sliding his hand along her waist to the small of her back. She fit so naturally in his arms, and the air around them sparked with a healthy charge.

"Thank you for coming here with me," he said. "I know my family is big and loud, and I promise we're not going to spend every day with all of them."

"Yes, you are," one of his uncles said as he walked by. "All of us. All the time."

Hunter chuckled as his uncle went by, calling, "My kids are coming. Prepare yourself, Hunt. I've been telling them you're here all day."

"You need to prepare yourself for his kids?"

"That's Uncle Cy, and yes, his kids are crazy." He leaned closer on the last word, whispering it into her hair. Molly closed her eyes and slid her hands along the collar of his shirt. She'd just touched the skin on his neck when a little girl shrieked and a very solid body slammed into Hunter, causing Molly to stumble too.

Hunter only laughed as he released her and swung the little girl up and into his arms. She had a shock of nearly white-blonde hair, and she said, "Hunty, I bringed you an apple pie."

"You did?" he asked, smiling up at her for all he was worth. Molly loved watching him interact with little children, and though these were his cousins, Molly suspected he was brilliant with all kids, and the note she'd scratched out to herself held even more meaning now.

"Let's go, let's go," someone yelled from the direction of the kitchen, and Hunter turned that way with his cousin.

Molly turned back and retraced her steps to the desk, where she tore off the top piece of paper from the pad there.

She looked at the few notes she'd written, her eyes landing on the last one.

KIDS, she'd written in all capital letters. A tingle rang down her spine, and Molly felt the hand of the Lord gently guiding her to exactly where she needed to go.

Hunter needed to specialize in and open an equine therapy center that only served children.

CHAPTER 13

Matthew Whettstein sat and listened to the entire proposal Molly Benson had put together. She had every T crossed and every I dotted, and she was an excellent presenter. When she finished, she closed the blue binder she'd gone through, and placed her hands on it.

"What do you think?"

Matt looked up at her, not quite sure what to say. "What do I think?" He shook his head, in a complete state of awe. "I think that was the most amazing thing I've ever heard."

"You think so?" Molly's face lit up. "Be real, Matt."

"I am being real." He stood up and walked into the kitchen. "Water? You have to be parched after that speech."

Molly had been coming around the farm a lot for the past month or so. She'd found the deed from the county that showed the property lines, and she'd asked Matt to work with her on the proposal for a children's equine therapy center. He hadn't seen Hunter much, but he knew Molly was working with Hunter on the project.

She'd been doing all the research, designing all the blueprints, and gathering all the applications and information. She'd gone to Three Rivers, Texas, to visit an equine therapy unit there, and she'd come back with pages of notes.

Hunter had been quite busy downtown, at least according to his texts, and Matt had been helping Molly with anything she needed around the farm, as she designed the space for the new program, based on things she'd learned from the cowboy in Texas. She'd stayed for dinner a time or two, and Matt could admit he missed having a female presence in his life.

He told himself as he pulled a couple of bottles of water out of the fridge that he did have a female presence in his life—his daughter, Brittany.

"You know," Molly said as Matt put the bottle on the table in front of her. "I was thinking of bringing a cake out for Keith."

Matt sat down where he'd been a moment ago. "You don't need to do that."

"He'll be fourteen, right?" Molly asked. "Even fourteen-year-olds like cake, and I'm a really good baker." She gave him a kind smile, and Matt's soul sucked it right up.

Life had not been kind to him lately, and he could use as much joy and happiness as he could get.

Keith could too, he thought, though he'd already turned her down. "All right," he said. "He does love chocolate cake."

"My specialty is chocolate cake," she said. "Saturday? I'll make sure Hunter comes, and once I have a name for this thing, I think we might be ready to present it to him." She looked down at the blue binder, her brow furrowing.

"Saturday's fine," Matt said. "I'll talk to Hunter's grandparents. They love birthday parties."

Molly smiled and nodded, her thoughts clearly starting to wander.

"You can tell Hunter about everything in that binder now," Matt said. "You two could come up with a name together." He watched Molly, but she never gave away anything about her and Hunter's relationship.

Matt remembered the two of them going out years ago, as kids, and he thought back to when he was fifteen. He hadn't dated anyone in high school, because girls scared him. He'd grown up and gone to farrier school, only to drop out before he'd finished because his father had fallen and broken his hip.

He'd needed help with his small operation, and Matt had worked that until Daddy had died. A sense of sadness filled him, and it was amazing to Matt how easily the darkness and depression could sink into his soul. It seemed to take ten times as much light to drive that darkness back out, and he hated that.

An image of his girlfriend in Sugar Pond flashed through his mind, and he could just remember her soft, wavy blonde hair, her freckled cheeks, and those pink lips.

He'd married someone else, and while he wished he and his two kids had been enough of a pull for Janice to make the necessary changes in her life, in the end, they hadn't been. He'd spent many nights on his knees, begging the Lord on behalf of his wife. Begging that she wouldn't return to the bottle.

In the end, she always did, and Matt had finally had to make a decision to take the kids and leave. It was his job to protect them, especially with Britt's condition, and he couldn't be home all the time to make sure Janice didn't say or do something to damage the children.

Molly said something he didn't catch, but Matt nodded anyway. The back door of the cabin opened, and Matt turned that way to find Keith entering the cabin. He wore a surly look, as he had ever since they'd returned to the Hammond family farm in Ivory Peaks at the beginning of June.

Matt knew it was hard on his son to leave Sugar Pond every summer and come live hundreds of miles away from his friends or anyone else he knew. He hadn't had the heart to tell his son that this year, they wouldn't be returning to Sugar Pond at all. That he'd sold the house when Janice had checked herself into yet another recovery program. That he couldn't bear to keep living the lie that she'd get better and they'd repair their marriage, and someday, they'd have another baby and a stable family life.

Keith refused to cut his hair, and it curled out from beneath the cowboy hat he wore. "I got the barrels moved, Dad."

"Good boy," Matt said, forgetting that Keith hated being called a boy. His birthday was on Friday, and Matt supposed he was leaving boyhood behind.

"See you Saturday," Molly said, and she waved to Keith and then Matt as she headed for the front door.

"Yep, 'bye," Matt called after her. Once the door closed, he turned back to his son. "Did you see Britt out there?"

"She's getting the eggs," Keith said, standing at the sink and washing his hands. "What's for dinner? Anything?"

"I was getting to it," Matt said, though he didn't know what to make for dinner. They'd been through everything in his skillset, including frozen pizza, hot dogs, spaghetti, macaroni and cheese, corndogs, peanut butter and jelly sandwiches, and cold cereal.

He couldn't remember the last time he'd fed his kids a vegetable, and a fresh wave of guilt hit him in the stomach.

"Which means you haven't even thought about it," Keith said, rolling his eyes. "I can make French toast."

Matt nodded. He just needed to get away for a few minutes. "I need to go check on Chris and Bev." He ducked his head so his son wouldn't detect the little white lie, and he hurried out of the cabin the same way his son had come in.

Outside, Matt sucked at the air, the panic threatening to drag him under something dark and dangerous, where he'd never get free again.

"Dear God," he moaned. "I can't break down like this. Please, help me." He managed to make it to the small shed behind the cabin, and he pressed his back into the wood, feeling the very real solidness of it. He breathed in, his head spinning. He breathed out, his eyes closing.

He breathed in. He breathed out.

He'd left Janice in Salt Lake City four months ago. Their divorce had been final the day before that. His heart might never heal, but the cuts and scrapes up and down Keith's arms were gone now.

They both remembered everything that had led them back to Ivory Peaks, though, and Matt sometimes wished the human brain couldn't hold so many memories.

"Just get through this minute," he whispered, something a very good friend had told him once. "Breathe in, one second. Breathe out, that's two." He continued to focus on the sound of his own soft voice, the hardness of the wooden shed behind him, and the numbers until he calmed completely.

He drew in another deep breath then, and said, "Thank you, Lord. Now, please give me the strength to show my kids what it takes to move on from heartbreak and find a new version of happiness."

Even if it was just for them, though Matt desperately wanted to find a way to move past this splintering in his life and into a new place where he could feel joy again. He wasn't sure if that was possible or not, but he wasn't going to stop praying for it.

A FEW DAYS LATER, MATT HELPED BRITT UP THE steps to the main farmhouse, where Keith's birthday party would be held. The moment he touched the top step, he knew Molly had been baking for a while. The scent of chocolate and caramel hung in the air, and his mouth actually watered.

"Watch your step going through the door," he said, glancing over his shoulder to make sure Keith hadn't made a run for it. He hadn't, and the boy even gave Matt a smile. Matt returned it, glad he'd agreed to let Molly bake his son a cake.

"Dad, look at all the ba-ba-ba-lloons," Britt said.

Matt turned back to her. He stepped right up to a huge blue, orange, and white balloon arch, and he grinned at it. "Wow," he said. "I don't even know how to do this."

"Mom did," Keith said, and that made the smile slip right off of Matt's face. Keith hadn't spoken with the disdain or sarcasm he had in the past, and he smiled at Matt as he passed him and went under the arch.

"Happy birthday," Molly singsonged as she greeted the children. Matt passed under the arch too, and he accepted a hug from the strawberry blonde woman who'd somehow carved herself into all of their lives in only several short weeks.

"Fourteen," she said to Keith. "What are you going to do this year?"

"Uh, I don't know," Keith said. "Go to school?"

"No," Molly said with a scoff. "You've got to have a plan for every year." She glanced at him as she moved back into the expansive kitchen. Not only did a beautiful chocolate cake sit there, but an entire cupcake tier in the shape of a tree, all filled with gorgeously decorated cupcakes.

"Are these red velvet?" Matt asked, drawing closer.

"With cream cheese frosting and silver sparkles," Molly said. "I call them my stardust cupcakes." She gave him a grin and turned back to the stove. "I'm still waiting for your fourteenth-year bucket list."

Keith exchanged a glance with Matt, who inclined his head. He'd sure like to hear what his son wanted to do this year, because then maybe he could make it happen for him. Right now, the only gift he had for his son was the video game he'd been asking for since it had come out in March.

Money wasn't the issue for Matt. He simply didn't want Keith sitting in front of a screen all the time. The brain needed time to itself, where it wasn't fed with music, sound, video, flashing lights, or games.

"I honestly don't know, Molly," Keith said. "What do you think I should do this year?'

"Well," Molly said. "When I was fourteen, I made a goal to sew a dress."

"That sounds boring."

Matt cleared his throat, and Keith quickly added, "No offense."

Molly laughed, and even Matt smiled. "None taken." She turned, the handles of tall pot gripped in both of her hands. "Is there something you want to do? I wanted to wear something I'd made, and I set a goal for that to be a dress. I had to try four times before I got one I wouldn't be embarrassed wearing." She grinned at him over the pot, which she tapped. "When I turned fifteen, I told my mother I wanted to learn to make the most delicious pot of spaghetti in the whole world. Lucky for you, my family let me experiment on them for three hundred and sixty-five whole days, and I mastered it."

"Wow," Britt said as she came up beside Matt.

"I heard it's your favorite food," Molly said just as Hunter came in the back door of the farmhouse, holding onto his grandmother's arm and closely followed by his grandfather.

"The party's here," he said, grinning around at everyone. Matt sure did like this farm, and he loved Ivory Peaks, and while he hadn't intended to stay here once this summer assignment ended, now he thought he certainly would.

Gray and Elise would return, and they had children his Britt could play with. Matt needed the support now that Janice was gone, and he reached over and pushed Britt's hair off her shoulder. The girl looked so much like her mother with those light green eyes and her sandy hair.

"I think I'd like to build something this year," Keith said, glancing at Matt again. "Maybe something simple like a table or something." He turned fully toward Matt. "Are tables hard, Dad?"

"Not too bad," Matt said. "It's big, but the cuts are straight and long. You could start with a shelf."

"I could," Keith said. "But I think I'd like to do a table."

"That sounds great," Molly said, twisting with a pan of garlic bread in her hand this time. "I'm sure your dad could help you with that. He's great with wood."

Matt was great with wood, but he didn't thank her for saying so. He watched his son, and Keith graced him with a small smile.

"Yeah, a table," Keith said. "For our new house."

Matt's stomach swooped, because Keith shouldn't be thinking they needed a new house. Hunter arrived and clapped his hands together loudly. "Garlic bread is my all-time favorite kind of bread. Are we ready? I'm starving."

"He's always starving," Molly said, rolling her eyes. "We have to sing *Happy Birthday* first." She indicated the cake and started lighting the candles.

Once she finished, everyone looked to her, and she lifted her hand as if they were seated in church, about to sing the opening hymn.

The song started, and Matt joined his voice to the others in the room, putting his arm around his daughter. He looked around, and this felt like a family affair. The food all laid out in a perfect display. The glowing cake and star-dusted cupcakes. The people and the love that permeated this place.

That was one of the things he loved best about this farm —Matt had always felt like he was loved here, and like there was a place for him here. Perhaps after Gray and Elise returned, he could simply stay on and work the farm. Gray had asked him to several times over the years, and this time, Matt determined he'd say yes if the offer came.

The song finished, and everyone whooped and clapped, Matt included. His heart lifted with a bit of joy over his son's fourteenth birthday, and he nudged Britt to go in front of him to get her food. With her tics, she sometimes needed a bit of help carrying things.

He always assigned her to get the eggs, because if she practiced, she could overcome her physical limitations. He thought of the equine therapy program Molly had presented to him, and he believed Britt would benefit from it greatly. Sometimes the other kids at school made fun of her, and while Britt held her head high and did her best not to let their words hurt her, the truth was, sometimes they did.

Sometimes words *really* hurt.

Matt noticed Hunter looking toward the front door, and then Molly. He turned that way too, and the woman standing there stole the air right out of his lungs.

He'd pictured this woman in his mind only a few days ago. The soft, wavy blonde hair, her freckled cheeks, and those pink lips. The hair had been pulled up into a ponytail. He could barely see the freckles on her face beneath her blush, but the lips were the same.

Those lips.

Those eyes—loads of green, with a hint of blue. Matt knew her, or at least a version of this woman from two decades ago.

"Gloria?" he whispered at the same time she said, "I'm sorry." She glanced around at everyone staring at her, her eyes skipping right past Matt as if she didn't see him standing there at all. "I thought I had an interview this afternoon, but it looks like y'all are havin' a party."

CHAPTER 14

Gloria Munson had knocked. She had. Twice. No one had come, and she'd heard the singing wafting out of the open window, much the same way the scent of marinara and garlic bread had.

A tall, broad, dark-haired man came toward her, his hand extended. "I'm so sorry. I'm Hunter Hammond, and I forgot to cancel with you."

Gloria kept her eyes on him, because it sure was easier than looking at Matthew Whettstein. What in the world was he doing here?

What rotten luck, she thought as she painted a smile on her lips and shook Hunter's hand. When she'd heard the birthday singing, she would've left and texted him had she not needed the job quite so badly.

As it was, she'd stood just inside the mouth of the doorway and listened to everyone sing for someone named

Keith. By the glowing smile on a lanky teen's face, Gloria assumed him to be Keith.

"I'm sorry," she said as she released Hunter's hand. "I can go." She hated the words as they came out of her mouth, and she wished she could take them back. "Actually, if we could still do the interview today, that would be ideal for me. I have another interview in Silver Lake tomorrow morning, and another in Golden in the afternoon."

Her smile shook, and she let it drop. Gloria leaned closer to Hunter, as everyone else in the house seemed transfixed by her sudden appearance at their family party. "I need a job quite badly."

Hunter nodded, his smile kind and his eyes wiser than his age. "Why don't you stay for dinner?"

"No," she said firmly, though she hadn't eaten since breakfast. "No, it's fine." She reached into her back pocket. "I know it's not super neat, but I have my résumé right here." She started to unfold the piece of paper she'd already used twice that day.

She hadn't liked either man she'd interviewed with earlier that day nearly as much as Hunter Hammond—or this farm. The land here possessed something she could feel deep down in her core.

It reminded her of her father's farm, and Gloria sucked in a tight breath.

Hunter took the paper from her, and she held the air in her lungs for too long, too long.

He looked up at her, something curious in the dark glint of his eyes. He was an extremely attractive man, for women who liked the dark, tall, serious type. Gloria preferred a man with a bit more color in his hair, and eyes that didn't look so bottomless, who could make her laugh and hold her when she cried and bring her a cup of coffee exactly the way she liked it.

Hunter stepped back and Matt appeared only a few feet behind him. Gloria's heart squeezed inside her chest, almost as if it didn't want to let go of any more beats. She couldn't hold it back though, and her pulse raced forward as their eyes met.

"Matthew," she said, unsure why she'd chosen to use his full name when they'd been so familiar before. She blinked and their year-long relationship flitted through her mind. She could see everything, feel everything, remember everything.

"Gloria." Matt glanced at Hunter as he stepped past him, and Gloria knew everyone was still watching. Still, Matt didn't hesitate as he closed the distance between them and hugged her.

She tried not to sink into the warmth of that embrace, but it was impossible. Gloria thought she'd have done it to anyone who hugged her, because it had been so long since someone had. So, so long.

Her eyes squeezed closed, and she tried to hold her emotions back just as tightly.

"What in the world are you doing here?" He stepped back and searched her face. "You know you're in Colorado, right?"

A laugh mostly comprised of air burst from her mouth,

and she ducked her head and nodded. She reached up and wiped her face quickly, feeling a little bit of wetness there. *How embarrassing,* she thought, and she drew her shoulders back and the air into her lungs, cinching everything tight again.

A pretty redhead stepped next to Hunter and took his hand, saying, "Hunt, should we pray so we can eat? Everything's getting cold."

"Yes," Hunter said. "Come on, Gloria. You can stay. You obviously know Matt. This here's Molly." They turned, and he indicated the two kids in the room. "Matt's kids, Keith—the birthday boy—and Brittany. And my grandparents, Chris and Bev Hammond."

Gloria's smile faltered at "Matt's kids," but she quickly hitched it back into place. "Nice to meet you," she said to Molly, nodding to the kids after. She shook both Chris's and Bev's hands, noting their pleasant smiles. Everyone exuded a welcoming spirit, and Gloria relaxed a little.

"I'll say grace," Hunter said, turning back to the food spread across the countertop and swiping off his cowboy hat.

Matt did the same, bowing his head and pressing that hat right over his heart. With everyone else's eyes closed, Gloria took a sneak peek at Matt, getting all those colors in his hair—brown, auburn, red, black, and even gray. She remembered laying in his arms as they laughed about how he had so many different colors of hair, seemingly every strand a unique shade.

Overall, his hair came across as a beautiful chestnut brown, and in the sunlight, it could shine like gold.

Hunter said her name in the prayer, and she quickly closed her eyes and listened. "...safely. Bless this food and all those who made it, and bless Keith Whettstein that his fifteenth year on this good Earth will be the best one yet. In fact, bless all here in this company that this next year will bring us good fortune, clear vision for the future, and increased faith in Thee. Amen."

Gloria couldn't even repeat the amen, as stunned as she was by the power and faith in Hunter's voice. She wished she'd been paying attention when he'd prayed for her, because whatever he'd said would surely come true.

She really wanted good fortune, clear vision for the future, and increased faith in the Lord. Yet...she'd never thought to pray for those things. Her needs were so immediate that Gloria spent so much time and energy just trying to figure out where she'd sleep that night and if she'd feel safe enough to actually drift off.

"You have pretty hair," a small-person voice said, and Gloria looked down at Matt's daughter, Brittany.

"Thank you," she said, taking in the girl's light green eyes and barely brown hair. Her mother must've been fair, because she hardly looked like Matt at all. "I like yours too." She reached up and trailed the very tips of her fingers down the braid in Brittany's hair. "Do you braid it yourself?"

She grinned and giggled. "No. Da-da-daddy does it."

"He does?" Gloria looked up and found Matt watching them. "That's great." *Surprising* would be a better word, as

Matt had barely been able to use a can opener the last time she'd known him.

These hands are so clunky, he'd joked, and she'd taken the can opener to get the job done. She couldn't remember what they'd been making, but they'd been at her house, and she'd had something bubbling on the stove she'd needed the can of food to finish.

"Corn chowder," she said right out loud. Heat filled her face as Molly and Matt both looked at her. "Sorry."

"It's actually spaghetti," Molly said, tilting her plate as if Gloria had never eaten pasta and sauce before. She exchanged a glance with Matt, leaned in close to him and said something Gloria couldn't quite catch.

Matt's eyes crinkled as he smiled and shook his head. Molly laughed lightly and stepped away from the counter, making room for Gloria to get a plate. She picked one up and handed it to Brittany, nodding for the little girl to go ahead of her.

"How old are you?" she asked.

"Eight," Brittany said, struggling to reach into the tall pot and get herself some spaghetti. Gloria reached for the tongs and she put some noodles on the girl's plate. "Thanks." She smiled up at Gloria with precious childhood innocence, and Gloria actually envied her.

She didn't have to worry about bills, where her next meal would come from, or if she should get back in her truck and figure out a way to return to Montana.

"Let me," Matt said, reaching for the girl's plate.

"I g-g-got it, Daddy."

"Okay." He took his daughter's plate anyway and held it for her. "Put your salad on here." She did, placing the biggest piece of garlic bread left in the last empty spot on her plate. He took the plate over to the table for her and everything, and Gloria wasn't sure what that was about.

Not your business, she told herself as she kept her head down and served herself plenty of spaghetti, green salad, and garlic bread. Her stomach roared in an audible growl, and Matt, who'd returned to the buffet for silverware, chuckled.

Their eyes met, and instant flames licked through Gloria's chest. Did he feel anything when he looked at her? He'd obviously moved on with his life after the demise of their relationship. Gotten married. Had two kids.

No wife here with him, though. The thought stole through Gloria's mind, almost a thief stealing the barrier she needed between her and a man as handsome as Matt.

Questions filled Matt's eyes, and Gloria had plenty for him too.

Laughter erupted at the table to their right, and Gloria looked that way. She had time for one question, and the rest could wait until they could be alone together. She shivered at the very idea.

"Do you work here?" she asked.

"Yes." Matt picked up a couple of forks and two cups of lemonade. "I'm the foreman for the farm during the summer. Her owners go to Wyoming for the summer." He flashed her a devastating smile that crashed through her the way it always had.

Crazy how time could erase so much but not the pain of losing her father—at least not yet—and not the intense attraction between her and Matthew Whettstein.

Gloria took her plate over to the table, where only one spot waited. She smiled at Hunter's grandparents and took the empty seat next to Hunter, because she hoped they could at least talk about the job while they ate.

"So you know Matt," Hunter said, tracking him as he returned to the table too. He passed one fork and one cup of lemonade to his daughter and sat down next to her. Gloria had to look past everyone at the table to meet his eye, so she focused on Hunter instead.

"Yes," Gloria said. "We go back, oh, what? At least twenty years."

"Wow," Hunter said, genuinely surprised.

"He's barely twenty years old," Matt quipped, and Hunter chuckled. So they had a friendly relationship too. Gloria looked back and forth between the two of them, wondering what the relationship actually was.

"I thought you said you were the foreman," she said to Matt, twirling her first forkful of spaghetti. "That the owners went to Wyoming." She looked at Hunter. "But you're interviewing for jobs."

"My dad owns the farm," Hunter said. "My parents go to Wyoming every summer. Used to drag me along and everything." He grinned around at everyone at the table. "Matt takes care of everything here for us."

"I sense a but," Gloria said, watching everyone carefully.

"But this year, Hunter's starting an equine therapy center." Matt took a bite of his garlic bread.

"No," Hunter said a little too quickly. He shot a glance at Matt and then met Molly's eyes before returning his attention to Gloria.

"Yes," Molly said before he could speak. "That's the goal, Hunt."

"Right, but we're not there yet," he said. "I just bought a few horses."

"He bought seventeen new horses," Matt said in a deadpan.

Hunter had the decency to look a bit sheepish. "I do love horses, and these have worked in a therapy program before. It seemed like the Lord opening the way for me. Maybe a little early, but I couldn't just ignore it."

Gloria nodded, finished her bite of pasta, and said, "Equine therapy. That's amazing. So I'd work with the horses?"

"You said you're good with them," Hunter said.

She had no idea what he'd done with her résumé, and she'd need to get that back before she left. She only had the one and no way to print another.

"I am," she said. "My father owned a ranch in Montana, and I worked there my whole life." She shot a glance at Matt, begging him to stay quiet. In the end, when she looked at Hunter again, she couldn't fib to him, even if it was a tiny, white lie.

"Well, almost my whole life. I did a little stint at a ranch in Sugar Pond for a couple of years." She nodded to Matt. "That's where I met Matt."

"Right," Hunter said, looking between them again. "You're from Sugar Pond."

Matt just nodded, and Gloria took a peek at his kids. His son definitely came from him, and he had the quiet, brooding look down pat. He'd probably break a lot of hearts, the way Matt had, and Gloria found herself smiling at him.

"I know everything about running a cattle ranch," Gloria said. "Particularly horse care, as I was primarily responsible for their care."

"She's got a veterinary technician certificate," Matt said.

"Right," Hunter said. "I read that." He ate, and Gloria settled into the rhythm of it too. Molly kept the conversation with the children going, and Matt contributed plenty too.

Gloria didn't want the meal to end, though she definitely needed time to figure out where she could park her truck that night. It only took ten minutes to set up the tent over the bed of the truck, and another ten to get her airbed inflated and made for the night.

Twenty minutes. She wanted to do all of that long before dark, and one glance at the clock on the stove told her she had hours to spare. Though the beginning of August lingered just around the corner, the sun still didn't go down until at least nine or nine-thirty.

It was barely six o'clock right now.

"Cake," Molly announced, and she got up from the table,

collected everyone's plates, and took them to the kitchen sink.

Matt joined her in the kitchen while she sliced the cake and put the individual pieces on smaller dessert plates. He put a fork on each one and started delivering them to the table, two at a time.

"Happy birthday, bud," he said, placing the first piece in front of his son.

"Thanks, Dad." His son smiled for maybe the first time that evening, and soon enough everyone had chocolate cake. Molly brought a plate of red velvet cupcakes to the table, and asked if anyone wanted milk, coffee, or hot chocolate.

Gloria would kill for a cup of coffee, and thankfully, Hunter said, "Coffee, please, sweetheart." They smiled at one another, and their feelings for each other were pure and sweet. *Beautiful*, Gloria thought, and she wondered how long they'd been together. Neither of them wore a ring on their left hand, and she noticed Matt didn't either.

The cake and cupcakes disappeared amidst chatter and laughter, and Gloria relaxed in this cool house with plenty of spirit.

"What are you going to name the equine therapy center?" Chris asked.

Hunter leaned back in his chair, his eyes fixed on Molly. "We don't know."

"It's going to be exclusively for children," Molly said. "I have a list of ideas, actually. Maybe you could all vote." Her eyebrows went up, and she jumped to her feet in the next moment. "Let me get my binder."

Hunter chuckled as she bustled away. "Her and that binder." He wasn't making fun of her though. His fondness for her rode on the air, and his smile said it all when she returned with a blue binder. She stayed standing as she opened it and started reading off the names.

"A Helping Hoof." She looked up, her eyes bright. "Shooting Star. Go North. Stable Strides. Silver Spur. Ride Tall."

The list went on and on, and none of them sounded quite right, even though Matt, Bev, and Hunter all voiced their like of this one or that one.

Molly finally finished, and she sat down. "None of these are right. I can tell just by looking at you guys." She sighed and looked at her list again.

Gloria's pulse started to hammer beneath her ribs. She'd eaten more tonight than she had in a long time, but she really wanted another cupcake. She reached for one nonchalantly, and said, "What about something like…Pony Power?" She peeled back the silver wrapping on the red velvet cupcake, keeping all of her focus there as if the task was akin to heart surgery.

"That sounds like something kids would like." She glanced at Brittany. "Kids like ponies."

"I *love* ponies," Brittany said, grinning at her.

"Pony Power," Hunter said, saying it as if he were testing how it rolled across his tongue. "I really like that." He looked at Molly, who stared at Gloria with wide eyes.

"Pony Power is the one," Matt said, and even Chris and Bev agreed.

"I think it's great," Keith said, and getting a teenager to agree to something felt like a miracle to Gloria.

"It's perfect," Molly said, her voice touched with awe. "Gloria, you're a genius."

She shook her head, a lick of embarrassment flowing through her. "No, I just—it just popped into my head."

"You better hire her, Hunt," Molly said, getting up. She retrieved a pencil from a nearby table stacked with puzzle books and returned to the table. "Pony Power. Genius." She wrote the words at the top of the paper in her binder.

"Don't lose my pencil," Hunter said. "I've been using that one on my crossword puzzles since my sixteenth birthday."

Molly looked at the pencil, then Hunter. "Really? Why?"

He gently took it from her. "Elise gave it to me. Look. It's from her and Dad's trip to Alaska. It's...." He ground his voice through his throat. "Important to me."

Molly nodded and took the pencil from him and back to the table.

The mood had definitely shifted, but when Hunter turned and looked at her, Gloria found the same confidence on his face he'd possessed all along. Something was softer about him now, though, that she hadn't seen before.

"If you want the job, Gloria," he said. "It's yours. With Molly's and Matt's approval, I'm not sure how I could say no." He smiled at her, and the easiness of it caused her to marvel.

"I want it," she said.

"Great." Hunter stood up and picked up the dessert

plates. "I'll let Matt show you where your cabin is." He nodded to the other man. "Right now, I need more cake."

Gloria finished her cupcake and got up when Matt did.

"You kids stay here with Molly, Chris, and Bev." He met their eyes, a silent question between them. All three of them nodded, and Matt looked at Gloria. "I won't be long. Just have to take Gloria to her cabin." He nodded toward the back door, and Gloria smiled around at everyone.

"Thank you so much for inviting me to stay," she said. "It was wonderful. Happy birthday, Keith." She nodded and turned to follow Matt, the thought of being alone with him suddenly more terrifying than exciting.

CHAPTER 15

Hunter stood with his elbows up on the top rung of the fence. He could remember when he couldn't do that, when he'd had to stand on the bottom rung to even see over the top. Now, though, he stood tall enough to see over almost any fence or door here at the farm, and as he breathed in the last of the truly hot summer air, Hunter felt more at peace than he had since Laura's offer.

He hadn't made a decision on it yet. He hadn't spoken to Molly about it again. He and Dad talked a couple of times a week, and Hunter had asked Uncle Wes to call him again that night.

School would start in a few weeks for Molly, and today might be the last weekday he got to see her out at the farm. She'd been working with Matt and Gloria for the past several days as they assessed the horses he'd bought, as the construction crew Matt had hired came to build the stables they needed to house the horses, and as the work for the program continued to move forward.

He wished he'd been able to go to Three Rivers with Molly, but she'd taken a ton of pictures, and she'd worked with Matt to get a layout for their program here at the farm. Hunt really liked listening to her talk about it, because she seemed to have as much passion for the equine therapy project as he did. Gloria and Matt had been at her side every step of the way, and that eased some of Hunter's guilt about his long hours in the lab at HMC.

All three of them stood out in the pasture Hunter was currently watching over, and he saw Molly peel off and go north, back toward the farmhouse.

Matt and Gloria continued to meander through the pasture, their hatted heads and the distance between them and Hunter making it impossible for him to see their faces. It was obvious to anyone with eyes that they liked each other. Matt didn't reach for her hand though, and she never strayed too close to him with any one step.

They definitely had a history, though, and Hunter wanted to know what it was. He trusted Matt with every fiber of his being, and he didn't want to lose either of them. Gloria really did possess a special kind of talent with horses, and he wondered if she could be a counselor as well, because Molly said she was brilliant with Brittany as well.

Brittany had something wrong with her that no one had been able to diagnose. She stuttered sometimes, and sometimes she lost her balance. She had a hard time carrying too much, as the muscles in her legs sometimes gave out. Matt continued to assign her the job of collecting the eggs, though, because he wanted her to be as strong as possible.

She'd only broken them once this summer, and Hunter smiled at the mere thought of the little girl. Matt's kids had never come to the farm with him, and Hunter found their presence here comforting. They made life at the farm even more appealing, and Hunter's gaze wandered in the direction Molly had gone.

He still hadn't kissed her, and he wondered what in the world he'd been waiting for. He didn't see her every day, for one thing. When they did get together, the amount of items they needed to talk about went on and on. Molly was detailed and organized, and she'd made starting the equine therapy center ridiculously easy for Hunter.

He realized that while he still held her hand and flirted with her, their relationship had almost become professional. Like he was the boss and she his secretary.

He frowned at the very thought of that. He did not want that kind of relationship with Molly Benson, and yet, he hadn't taken their romantic relationship to the next level.

"What are you afraid of?" he asked himself, a question Lucy would've pressed him to answer. He was afraid of making the wrong decision, for one. At work, here at the farm, and with Molly.

He was afraid he wouldn't be good enough for her, and that she'd eventually realize it when he'd fallen all the way in love with her again. He was worried about strapping her with a man who needed to talk to a therapist every week just to keep getting up and going to work.

He was terrified he wouldn't be able to support her when she needed it. Not financially, but emotionally. He was honestly scared out of his mind at becoming a father, though he did want children. A lot of them, actually.

With his fears flowing freely through his mind, he didn't see Gloria go in a different direction, and he didn't realize how close Matt had gotten until he said, "What brings you out to the farm tonight, Hunt?"

A smile touched his face. "Just needed a breather, I think. The city is…busy." Noisy, crowded, and intense too. It wore on Hunter's nerves and soul, and he much preferred the stillness and less frantic nature of the farm.

Matt nodded, climbed the fence, and stood next to him. "Things are coming along real nice, Hunt. Stables will be done in another month. Gloria is great with the horses, and she's been doing all that online training Molly suggested." He gave a long sigh that spoke more of contentment than frustration. "Listen, I wanted to talk to you about staying on here."

"Staying?" Hunter turned toward Matt and leaned his hip into the log there. "You never stay. Don't the kids go to school in Sugar Pond?"

Matt shook his head. "We can't go back there."

Hunter just waited, something Lucy would've done.

"She's an alcoholic," Matt finally said. "My wife. My *ex*-wife." He swallowed. "I—the kids deserve better than that, and it was up to me to protect them." He spoke in a quiet, haunted voice. "I took her to Salt Lake City, to a treatment program there. Sold the house. Came here. Everything we own is in a storage unit in town." He shook his head and finally tore his gaze from the pasture to look at Hunter.

"I'm really sorry, Matt," he said. "Of course you can stay on here. Dad won't care. We don't use the cabin when you're not here. The kids are welcome. In fact, Jane will be thrilled to have a girl closer to her age." He smiled at Matt, hoping the message that all would be well would get across.

"You're a good man, Hunter," Matt said. "It's been amazing watching you grow up."

Hunter didn't know what to say to that, so he didn't respond to it. "I'll tell Dad tonight. He really won't mind, but they'll be home soon, and I should let him know."

"Of course." Matt drew in a long breath and pushed it out. "Janice checked herself out of the program early," he said. "A couple of weeks ago. I don't know where she is. Keith isn't happy about staying here." This time, the sigh definitely carried frustration and heaviness. "I'm doing the best I can."

"That's all anyone can do." Hunter clapped him on the shoulder, and they shared a look before they both turned their attention back to the pasture. Gloria rode a horse there now, moving it from a walk to a trot and back.

"I'm sorry things are rough for you right now," Hunter said. "If there's anything I can do—anything, Matt—please tell me." He cleared his throat, trying to find the right words. "You've always been someone I look up to. I have plenty of money, and I know a lot of people in the city." He paused, unsure of how to continue. In the end, he just plowed on, praying he wouldn't offend the other cowboy. "A doctor for Brittany. A youth group for Keith. If you need someone to talk to...." He trailed off, because things had suddenly become really personal for him. "I have a great therapist," he concluded.

Matt glanced at him, but Hunter kept his eyes out on Gloria and the pretty paint horse she rode.

Hunter smiled at her and her skill. "A reservation at a fancy restaurant so you can take Gloria to dinner." He met Matt's eyes, and the flush crawling up the other man's neck wasn't hard to spot.

"Is it that obvious?" Matt asked.

Hunter shrugged one shoulder, glad he'd changed out of his office attire and into a more casual and comfortable T-shirt. "I don't know. I don't normally pay attention to stuff like that, but you guys have...something. Maybe it's the history you share."

"We dated for a year," Matt admitted. "A long, long time ago."

Hunter let a few seconds of silence pass. "And?"

"And what? I'm five months into a divorce. I'm not ready for a new relationship." He shook his head. "No. My kids aren't ready for that. They love their mother, and they miss her." Matt leaned against the top rung too. "*I* miss her," he added in a near-whisper.

Hunter nodded, silent because he had no idea what it felt like to get a divorce. He thought of Molly, and he wondered if she still missed her ex-husband. She'd told him very little about the guy, or why they'd gotten divorced, and Hunter hadn't asked.

His phone rang, and Hunter pulled it from his pocket to see Uncle Wes's name on the screen. "Excuse me, Matt. It's my uncle."

Matt waved to him, and Hunter swiped on the call as he walked away from the pasture. "Uncle Wes," he said in the happiest voice he could muster. He loved Uncle Wes, maybe the most out of all of his uncles. No, it was impossible for him to choose one he loved the most, as they each had played such an important role in Hunter's life.

"Hunt," Wes said. "Guess what?"

"What?"

"Michael, Easton, Opal, and I are twenty minutes from the city. Want to meet us at Hounds? The kids want chicken fingers, and I could use a burger without all those fancy toppings they keep putting on them in Coral Canyon." He chuckled, and Hunter joined in.

"I'd love that," he said. "I'm actually out at the farm, though, so I'm further away than twenty minutes."

"Oh," Uncle Wes said, clearly surprised at Hunter's location. "That's actually better. Is The Burger Babe still in business?"

"Of course," Hunter said, grinning. "It's the best burger joint in the whole country." They laughed together, and Wes said they could be there in thirty-five minutes. As The Burger Babe sat on the half-mile main street of Ivory Peaks, it would only take Hunter twenty to get there.

"I'm bringing Molly," Hunter said. "Is that all right?"

"I've got all three of my kids," Wes said. "Molly is no problem."

"Great," Hunter said. "We'll see you in a few." He ended the call and immediately dialed Molly.

"Hey, there," she said, a bit out of breath.

"Where are you?" he asked. "Want to go to dinner with my Uncle Wes and his kids?"

"They're in town?"

Hunter laughed, his heartbeat pounding though. "Apparently. They want to meet us at The Burger Babe in half an hour."

"Sure," Molly said. "I'm clear out in the hay loft, though. I'll be a few minutes coming in."

Hunter turned toward in the direction of the barns and buildings on the farm. "I'll be there in a minute. What are you doing?" He strode that way, hoping he'd catch her there. It was time she knew how he felt about her, and time for him to face his fears.

"Just putting a few things away." She grunted, and Hunter broke into a jog.

"Leave them for me," he said. "You don't need to put stuff away, Mols."

"I got it." She panted, though, and Hunter said he'd be there in a second and ended the call.

He arrived in the hay barn and found her coming down the ladder from the loft. She was so wonderful. Her beauty punched him right in the lungs as she turned around, and he kicked himself for getting so wrapped up inside his own life that he hadn't taken the next steps with her.

This was exactly like him forgetting to text.

She sighed and pushed her hair off her forehead as she smiled at him. "Whew. It's hot."

Hunter strode toward her and took her into his arms.

"Oh, okay." She giggled against his chest, her arms going around his back too. "This is nice, Hunt."

"I'm sorry," he said, pressing his eyes closed as he breathed in the scent of her hair. She carried strawberry there, along with alfalfa and wood. "I've been...distant."

"You've been busy," she said. "We've both been really busy."

He shook his head, his chest vibrating with the booming of his heart. He stepped back and looked her in the eyes. "I'm afraid," he admitted.

Molly searched his face. "Of what?"

"So many things," he said. "Of making the wrong decision for my career. Of saddling you with a husband who can't take care of you. Of even being a husband. Of falling in love with you. Of being a father." He shook his head, realizing he'd said so many things that could kill a relationship.

In fact, Molly's eyes had widened with every word he'd said.

"I don't want to be afraid," he whispered. "Remember how I said we could be ourselves with each other? That we didn't have to hide?"

She nodded, still searching his eyes for something.

"I've been hiding," he said. "Because I'm afraid you're going to wake up one day and realize I'm no good for you."

"Hunter." She took his face in both of her hands. "That's the most ridiculous thing I've ever heard."

"I still see Lucy every week."

"That's fine with me."

"I'm sometimes caught up in my own head."

She smiled gently at him. "You think I don't know that about you by now?"

"What if something happens, and you need me to be a strong emotional support and I can't do it?" His shoulders sank. "What if you—?"

"Hunter," she said quietly but powerfully. "I don't play the 'what if' game. We cross bridges when we get to them."

He dropped his gaze to the ground, then let it rebound to her mouth. "I'm falling in love with you all over again," he said. "It terrifies me, because I simply don't know if I can do or be all you'll need me to do or be."

Her fingers curled up around his left ear. "Hunter, you already are the man I need you to be."

"That can't be true," he whispered.

"I'm falling for you too," she said. "In fact, I might have already fallen. It's hard to know."

"Why's that?"

"Because you haven't kissed me yet, Hunt."

He met her eyes, the softness in hers encouraging. "I want to know more about your marriage," he said, continuing despite the hard edge that entered her gaze. "I want to know more about why it failed, so we can talk about what we'll do when things get hard. I don't want *us* to fail for a second time."

Molly swallowed and let one of her hands drop to his shoulder. "I don't want that either."

"I want to tell you about my birth mother, and why I'm scared out of my mind to be a father."

"Okay," she whispered.

"I want a lot of kids," he said, everything inside him spilling out.

"I want them too."

Hunter suddenly felt lighter than he had all summer. He didn't ask to kiss her, the way he'd done before. He simply lowered his head, closed his eyes, and pressed his lips to hers. The kiss was too strong in the beginning, and he knew it. He couldn't slow it or tame it though, because he still had so much inside of him that needed to come out.

She returned the somewhat rough kiss, though, and after a few seconds, he'd calmed enough to stroke his lips against hers in a more loving manner.

His blood heated, and his hands slipped up and into her hair. Every touch of her fingers along the back of his neck and his shoulders sent his cells vibrating.

Oh, how he liked this woman. He liked talking to her, and he liked listening to her, and he liked working with her.

He pulled away slightly, nearly breathless from that kiss. "I'm sorry I've been treating you like my secretary."

"You haven't been," she said, her voice definitely made of air. She closed the distance between them again, kissing him sweetly but with plenty of passion too. Hunter wanted to be present for this moment, so he pushed all the other thoughts out of his head and focused on kissing Molly Benson.

CHAPTER 16

Molly didn't want Hunter to stop kissing her. Ever. She never wanted to part from him, and as she kissed him back with as much passion as she dared to show, she felt herself fall in love with him all over again.

He was careful with her, and she loved that.

He took care of her, and while she could take care of herself, she didn't want to have to.

If the way he kissed her was any indication, he loved her, and Molly wanted him to know she felt the same.

Listening to him talk about his therapy as a reason he was afraid broke her heart, and she wished there was a way she could assure him that she didn't mind his flaws. His imperfections made him human, and Molly very much needed Hunter to be human so she felt worthy of his attention and love.

She loved the feel of his hair between her fingers, and

the taut muscles in his back. She liked the taste of his mouth and the shape of his lips against hers. She enjoyed the fire ignited along her scalp and neck and everywhere else he touched.

He broke the kiss, and Molly pulled in an audible breath, as if she'd just burst up from being underwater for a long time.

"Molly," Hunter whispered as he touched his mouth to her neck. She simply held onto him and reveled in the warmth of him in front of her, the touch of his hand on her lower back, the heat from his breath and lips against her collarbone.

The intimacy between them increased, and Molly needed to get control of herself and stop Hunter. "What time do we need to meet your uncle for dinner?" she murmured.

Hunter took the hint and straightened. His chest rose and fell faster than usual, and Molly watched him keep his head down for several long moments.

"Sorry," he finally said, turning away from her.

"For what?" The absence of his embrace sent a chill straight into her stomach, and Molly darted after him to catch his hand in hers.

"I got a little carried away." He flicked a glanced in her direction. "Sorry, it won't happen again."

Molly didn't know how to tell him she'd liked it. He paused in the doorway, the block of sunshine only a step away, and gazed out onto the farm. "I've kissed a lot of women, Molly."

A sting jabbed at her behind her heart. "Oh."

He looked at her, those eyes so dark and so dangerous and so filled with desire. "You can thank Uncle Wes for that tonight," he said with a half-smile. "You should know that you're still the standard for me."

"The standard?"

"I don't...feel...." He sighed and looked back out to the farm. "When I kiss other women, it's not like kissing you. When I kiss you, it's like I just can't get enough. I can't imagine wanting to kiss anyone but you, and I'm not going to lie—that scares me a little."

"It scares me a little too," Molly said. "Because I feel the same." She couldn't believe she stood in this barn, saying these things. She'd been so broken the day of her divorce, and she'd truly believed she'd never find someone who could love her the way a husband should.

The thought of having to tell Hunter about her ex-husband made her insides turn to mush, but the prize was so amazing that she'd do it. She wanted to be with him forever.

"I want more," Hunter said, sliding his hand along her waist and tucking her into his side. "But that doesn't mean I can have it yet."

"Yet," she said.

"Let's go to dinner," he said. "Nothing hard the rest of the night, okay? Just burgers and fries and fun with my cousins and my uncle."

"Okay," Molly agreed. "Are you still planning on coming to help me put together my new bookcase tomorrow?"

"That's tomorrow?"

"It's Saturday tomorrow," she said, smiling at him. Hunter could solve any crossword puzzle. He could lift a hay bale in each hand without even groaning. He shot x-rays into crystals and actually understood what the data meant when it came back. But he wasn't great with knowing what day of the week it was, or how much time had passed. He needed to be reminded of certain things over and over, and Molly found him very much like a second-grader in that regard.

"I didn't know Wes was coming to town," he said.

"Bring him along," Molly said. "It'll take less time, and then you two can do whatever you need to do." She took a step to get him to move forward too. They really were going to be late for dinner if they didn't leave soon. "I'm going to be in my classroom until lunchtime, and then Gloria's going to give me another horseback riding lesson."

"That's right," he said. "I remember now."

"Mm hm." Molly laughed with him, and while she had started to feel like her relationship with Hunter had turned clinical, that kiss had taken things in a brand new direction.

They pulled up to The Burger Babe, and Hunter nodded to an enormous black truck two or three spots away. "They beat us."

"That's because you kissed me forever in the barn," she teased.

He jerked his attention to her, and Molly leaned over the console and tipped her face up toward his. "I liked it, Hunter. Kiss me again real quick."

He did, barely matching his lips to hers before someone

rapped on the window behind him. He broke the connection and turned, laughing when he saw his uncle standing there. He opened the door and slid out of the truck, more loud laughter joining his.

His uncle clapped him on the back and the excited cries of children met Molly's ears. When she rounded the front of the truck, she found Hunter with a little girl in his arms and his other hand clutched in a little boy's.

Another child stood next to Wesley Hammond, who turned toward her. "Molly Benson." He engulfed her in a hug, lifting her right up off her feet. She squealed; he laughed and put her back down.

"Why'd you decide to come all the way here?" Hunter asked, taking the first step toward the entrance of the restaurant.

"Road trip," Michael said. "Dad loves 'em."

"I do love a good road trip," Wes said, and Molly smiled to herself. The man had defined road trip when he'd driven from right here in Ivory Peaks to all forty-eight contiguous states. He'd taken a cruise ship to Alaska and a plane to Hawaii, and Molly could only imagine the things he'd seen and experienced.

He'd turned sixty a couple of years ago, but he'd told everyone at the dinner she'd attended a month ago that he died his hair to keep the gray from taking over. He was dark like Hunter, and tall like Hunter, and extremely handsome like Hunter.

Molly felt like a dwarf in his presence, but when Hunter said, "Here, Easton, hold your daddy's hand. I want to hold

Molly's," she felt just as big and just as important as these Hammond men.

"Wes," someone said inside the restaurant, and more loud laughter followed. Hugging ensued, and they got seated ahead of a couple of other waiting parties. Glasses of soda appeared almost instantly, as if Wes had a list here of things he liked, and they were just brought over without him having to order them.

The chaos died down, but a basket of French fries and a tray of sliders arrived before a waitress did. Wes glanced up at the woman who'd brought them, his smile wide and genuine. "Thanks, Hillie."

"Anything for you, Wesley."

Molly watched her walk away, a measure of shock flowing through her for how obvious the middle-aged woman had been with her flirting. She met Hunter's eye, who quickly switched his gaze to his uncle.

"Wesley?" he asked. "Who's Hillie?"

Wes grabbed a couple of fries and bit off the tops of them. "She's an old friend."

"Sounds scandalous," Molly said pointedly.

"Yeah, Dad," Michael said, reaching for a fistful of fries too. "Scandalous."

Wes looked at his son, plenty of surprise on his face. "Listen to you. Do you even know what scandalous means?"

"It means something offensive or wrong," Michael said, shooting a glance at Hunter. Wes saw it; Molly did too.

"Someone has been giving my son crossword puzzles," Wes said.

Hunter held up both hands. "Someone told me to kiss as many girls as possible." He glanced at Molly. Wes did too.

"Yes, well, it's still good advice," Wes said, putting the other half of the French fries in his mouth. "That goes for you too, Mikey. Kiss lots of girls so you know what you like." He grinned at his son and then Molly. "I don't regret giving that advice."

Everyone laughed, including Molly, but when the sound died down this time, an awkward silence covered the table. Wes said, "Hillie's who I bought this place for," he said, almost under his breath.

Hunter opened his mouth, but he didn't say anything. Molly's shock cascaded through her in waves, because she didn't understand the life of a billionaire. She dropped her head and shot a glance at Hunter out of the corner of her eye.

A waitress appeared, and the mood evened. They put in their milkshake orders, and Wes started the food ordering with, "I'll have the Double Hammond, please."

Molly couldn't pick the menu up fast enough. Sure enough, right there at the top of the laminated page, with two stars next to it, sat the Double Hammond burger. Two all-beef patties, cheddar cheese, caramelized onions, lettuce, tomato, special sauce, and a fried egg.

The two stars indicated that it was a house special and a customer favorite. Molly scanned the rest of the burgers, and none of them had stars next to them.

There was a Hammond chef salad and a Hammond plate

of fries, which were covered with cheese and bacon and served with a side of ranch dressing.

Molly tilted the stiff page toward Hunter. "Did you know your last name is on several menu items?"

"I haven't been here in years," he said. When it was his turn to order, he also ordered the Double Hammond as well as the Hammond fries.

Molly decided to go all-in with the family, and she ordered the Hammond chef salad and her own plate of Hammond fries. "Is there some sort of Hammond drink too?" she asked, handing the waitress the menu.

"Oh, yes," she said. "I'll bring you one." She popped her gum and skipped away—really skipped—before Molly could ask what was in the Hammond drink.

She looked across the table to Wes, who simply raised both hands in a gesture of *Whatcha gonna do?*

"So lemme get this straight," Hunter said. "You bought this restaurant and gave it to Hillie, so now everything's named after you and when you come, you get treated like a celebrity."

Wes just grinned at his nephew. "Have you talked to Laura again?"

"Yes," Hunter said, and Molly's attention flew to him. He hadn't told her about another meeting with Laura.

He exchanged a glance with her, his anxiety obvious even before he shifted on the bench seat. "Just yesterday," he said. "She showed me the stock packages for family who work at HMC."

"Surely you get that whether you're the CEO or in Lab Six," Molly said, looking to Wes for confirmation.

He nodded, his gaze flicking between her and Hunter. "She's right," he said slowly. "How are you feeling, Hunter?"

"I'm not sure," he said. "I know she wants me to take it, and yesterday, she said her son has passed officially. He's the CFO at Myers and Sons, and he can't give it up."

"The grocery store?"

"Worldwide," Hunter said. "Neither of her daughters want to relocate, as neither of them are in the Denver area anymore." He hung his head and shook it. "I don't know. If I don't take it, it feels like someone who isn't a Hammond will get the seat for the first time in the history of HMC."

Molly folded her arms, her stomach as tight as her chest. It wasn't up to her what Hunter did for a profession, but she didn't think he'd be happy in the top floor corner office. Hunter already had demons to fight, and he deserved to be happy in his work.

"What about Jillian's kids?" Wes asked. "All of us in my daddy's line waited too long to have kids." He looked apologetic about it too. "Except for your dad, Hunt."

"I'm the only one right now," he said. "Your uncle Brian is still there. Why can't he move up to CEO?"

Wes picked up a glass of dark cola and took a sip. "Why can't Jillian?"

"Laura's only been doing it for thirteen years," Hunter said. "There's no minimum. Jillian or Brian could totally do it."

"They probably don't want to," Wes said. "Though they sure were ready to take control of HMC and get it back on their side of the family." He chuckled and shook his head. "Did she say anything about her brother or sister?"

Hunter shook his head. "Nothing."

Wes leaned back in the booth. "Uncle Brian has a couple of sons too. They've got to be at least a decade older than you." He wore interest in his eyes. "I wonder what they're doing." He smiled, and a completely unsaid conversation passed between him and Hunter.

"We have to help Molly in the morning," Hunter said. "Then we can get digging."

Molly stayed quiet, putting the pieces together. They were going to find out where the other Hammonds were, and why they either could or couldn't be the CEO of HMC.

Fine by her. She didn't want Hunter to take the job anyway, and she started praying that Hunt and Wes would find someone else who could—and would—take the job.

MOLLY HAD IGNORED HUNTER'S TEXT THE NIGHT before, so when he showed up with Wes the next morning, her nerves skittered a little bit. "Morning," she chirped from the doorway of her classroom. "Come on in. It's right over there." She indicated the long box she hadn't even cut the zip ties off of yet.

Hunter swept a kiss along her cheek as he passed, and Wes nodded to her. They opened the box and Wes took control of the instructions. With the three of them working, the bookcase bloomed to life within a half an hour. Molly never would've been able to put it together alone, and she smiled as she started moving books from her rickety cases and into the new one.

"Come on, now," she said. "Help me move all of these books. Then you boys can go."

Hunter and Wes did what she said, the conversation light and easy as they talked about the summer activities of Hunter's cousins in Coral Canyon. Before all the books had been moved, Wes's phone rang, and he said, "It's my wife. I'll wait in the truck, Hunt."

"Yes, sir," Hunter said, and Molly paused to watch the older man leave. She and Hunter had been alone for the drive back to the farm last night after dinner, but she hadn't brought up her opinions on his job.

His text screamed through her ears. *I know you don't want me to take the CEO job.*

She hadn't known how to respond, because if he knew, why did she need to affirm what he'd said?

"Are you upset with me?" Hunter asked in a quiet voice.

"No," Molly said, picking up another handful of *Magic Tree House* chapter books.

"You didn't respond to my text last night," he said.

"I didn't know how," she admitted. "I don't think you should take the job. You know that. What's there to say?"

"Why don't you think I should take the job?"

"Because, Hunter, I don't think it's the one you want."

"Sometimes we have to do things we don't want to do."

"Not something this big," she argued back. "People say that when they're talking about running on the treadmill or eating only salads. Cleaning the toilet. That kind of thing." She stopped working and watched him continue to move books from one shelf to another. "They don't take jobs as the Chief Executive Officer when they really want to work in a lab. Or on a farm."

Both of those jobs suited Hunter, and if Molly got to pick which of those, she'd put him back on his family farm with the horses, goats, and chickens.

"Can you stop?" she asked. "Just for a second. Please."

Hunter set down his armful of books and turned toward her. "I don't know what you want from me."

"I want you to choose based on what would make *you* happy, Hunter. Not what would make someone else happy." She'd done that far too often, and she did not want to watch him do the same. It never led anywhere good, in her experience.

His jaw jumped as he pressed his teeth together. "It's not that easy."

"Sure it is."

"For you," he said, his voice not loud or punchy, but just as forceful. "You don't have the Hammond name hanging around your neck. You have no idea what it's been like for me to carry that my whole life." His chest heaved. "I spent years choosing my mother when I didn't want to, just to make her happy. So don't stand there and lecture me about choosing something to make *me* happy."

Molly glared at him as his words sunk into her ears. She

wanted to hurl back the thought that she hadn't been lecturing him. They were having a *conversation,* and if they couldn't do that, it didn't matter how he made her feel when he kissed her.

Been there, done that, she thought.

The fight left her body, and she moved over to a tiny second-grade-sized chair and sat down. "I did not mean to lecture you," she said.

The tension lessened, and Hunter came to crouch in front of her. "Where is this coming from?" He put his hands on her knees, and Molly studied his long fingers.

"Tell me about your mother," she said. "And I'll tell you about my marriage."

CHAPTER 17

Hunter's throat felt so dry, but he swallowed and looked Molly straight in the eye when he said, "My mother abandoned me when I was six years old. Dropped me off at school; didn't pick me up."

Molly traced her fingers down the side of his face. He hadn't shaved that morning, and she let her hand drift across the beginning of his beard. "I knew she wasn't around. I thought your mom and dad were just divorced."

"They were," Hunter said. "My mom wanted me to come down to Florida all the time, but never for me. Never to show me a good time, take me to the beach, or so we could go to Disneyworld together. It was so she could impress her boyfriends with her stellar mothering skills. She's used me my whole life. I let her, too, because I wanted her to be happy."

Molly's eyes dropped to her lap, and Hunter hated that he'd lost his temper with her. He hadn't raised his voice, but he'd hated the contention between them. They'd only argued once or twice when they'd dated as teens, and it was over whether or not they should break-up.

"I know exactly what it's like to choose what someone else wants me to do just to make them happy," Hunter said. "Sometimes it has to be done."

Molly shook her head, a single tear sliding down her face. "Not for this. Family is different."

"How so?"

"This is your *job,*" she said. "It's not who you are. It's not—"

"It *is* who I am," Hunter said. "I was born a Hammond. It's *exactly* who I am."

Resignation filled her expression, and she swiped at her cheek to get rid of the tears. "I married a man named Tyrone Hensen, simply to make someone else happy."

"Who? Your mother?"

"Him," she said. "I did it for him. I did it for appearances. We'd been dating for a year, and I did love him." She turned her hands over and laced all ten of her fingers through each of his. "I did it to make his mother happy, and so I wouldn't have to tell my mother and father that I was unhappy. I tried to make it work, but there are some things that a person can't bend for."

She met his eye, and Hunter wanted her to speak in plain language. "You think you can bend and bend and bend, but Hunter, you can't. You'll break eventually."

"Is that what happened to you? You broke?"

"What happened to me was I made bad decision after

bad decision. I made excuses when my husband hit me. I made excuses when he cheated on me. I made excuses when he racked up debt on our credit cards."

A blush filled her face, and she ducked her head again. "I bent, and I bent, and I bent, because I wanted him to be happy. I wanted his parents to be happy. I wanted my parents to think I was happy. I didn't want to admit I'd made such an egregious mistake. In the end, though, I had to stand up for myself and demand something better than he could ever give me."

Hunter's fingers tightened until she started to pull away. He loosened his grip but held onto her hands. "I'm so sorry," he said. "He hit you?"

Molly looked up and into his eyes, hers wide and afraid. She nodded, just once.

Hunter released her hands then, dropped to kneeling, and gathered her close to his heart. "I will never do that, Mols."

"I know that." She wrapped her arms around his torso and held him tight. "I will not allow myself to be in that position again. I will not do something that will make me terribly unhappy just to make someone else happy. I certainly do not care what anyone else thinks of me or my relationships."

"Good for you," he whispered. "I wish I had half your strength."

Molly pulled back and took his face in her hands. "I just want you to be happy, Hunt. I know I can't do that—only you can—but I know a man's job plays a huge part in his happiness. Mine does, at least. I just don't think you'll be happy as CEO, and I don't want you to do something that will make you terribly unhappy just to make someone else happy."

Hunter leaned into her touch. "You do make me happy."

"But not at my expense," she said. "I don't have to do something that makes me miserable to make you happy."

Hunter cocked his head slightly. "True."

"You can do what you'd like, obviously," she said. "Sometimes an outside perspective is nice to have, though."

"Also true," Hunter said. His knees ached, and he stood. "I can't kneel like that. This carpet is like cement."

Molly grinned, and when he extended his hand to her, she put hers in it and stood too.

"Let's finish the books, sweetheart," he said. "Then Uncle Wes and I are going to do our best to find out what the other Hammonds are up to. Maybe it won't have to be me."

Molly nodded, and Hunter continued to move thin volumes from the old bookcase to the new one. His thoughts circled around and around one thing—the strength of character in Molly Benson.

He wanted to be like her; he wanted to stand up and say, "No, I don't want to be the CEO. I can't do what will make me unhappy just because my last name is Hammond."

He simply didn't know how.

As Molly plunked down the last stack of books, Hunter asked, "Would you pray for me, Molly?"

She faced him, those pretty eyes wide. "Right now?"

He nodded, his voice too tight to speak.

"All right." She cleared her throat. "You're much better at this than I am, though. So no judging." She flashed him a nervous smile.

"No judging," Hunter said, his voice like a croak.

She took his hands in hers and dropped her head. "Dear Lord," she whispered. "Hunter Hammond is a good man, with a very good head on his shoulders. He wants to do what is right for his family, his farm, and himself. He simply needs Thy light to show him the path he should take. If possible, please send that light into his life and mind. Help me to support him in whatever decision he makes, and...." She stalled, and the silence went on so long that Hunter cracked his eyes to see what was going on.

She looked up at him, her eyes glassy. "Help us to recognize the difference between compromise and sacrifice, and help us to accept Thy will." She took a breath, and when she said, "Amen," he said it with her.

"Thank you," he said, though he didn't feel any new light in his mind. He did want to do what was right, and he had lived according to that in the hopes that he'd make his father proud of him. In the process, he'd made himself proud of what he'd accomplished, and he wanted to hold on to that feeling.

"I should go," he said. "Uncle Wes is waiting for me."

"Sure," she said. "Go. Thank you so much for the help with the bookcase. Tell Wes thank you too."

Hunter smiled at her, unsure of this new energy between them. Was it good? Bad? Just different?

He leaned down and kissed her, and there was still plenty of chemistry in that touch. His feelings for her still vibrated through his whole body, and he still didn't want to ever kiss anyone but her.

He wanted to wake up next to her and call her with any news, good or bad. He wanted to hold her while they drifted to sleep, and he wanted to come home to her good cooking every single night.

He broke the kiss when he realized how 1950s his thoughts sounded. "See you this afternoon?" he asked, touching the tip of his nose to her cheek and sliding it down. "At the farm?"

"Yes," she said, but she didn't move to release him.

He finally stepped away from her, took a few steps backward, and waved before turning to leave her classroom. He hoped he wasn't walking away when he should've stayed. His stomach churned, because he hated leaving things as unsettled as they felt with Molly.

He reminded himself that she'd opened up to him about her marriage, and he'd told her about his mom. "A little bit," he said. "Not everything."

Outside, the hot sun beat down on the black asphalt, and Hunter shelved his concerns about Molly for now. He and Uncle Wes had some digging to do, and if there was something Hunter liked more than science experiments, it was hunting for information.

"Ready?" Uncle Wes asked as Hunter climbed into the truck.

"Yep. Let's hit it."

"Good," Uncle Wes said. "Because after I finished talking to Bree, I made a pretty interesting call to Jillian. We're meeting her for lunch." He grinned at Hunter. "First, though, we need to make a stop."

"Where?" Hunter asked as Wes backed out of the parking stall.

"You'll see."

A GATE GUARDED THE HOUSE WHERE JASON Hammond lived. Tall, black spires reached at least eight feet into the air, as if he'd had a lot of teenagers trying to climb the fence and break into the stone mansion behind it.

Uncle Wes stopped next to the intercom and pressed the button. No one answered. He tried again, and then a third time. Finally, someone said, "Who is it?"

"Wesley Hammond," Wes said. "I need to speak to Jason."

The gate started to rumble open, and Uncle Wes looked at Hunter. "Here we go." He drove through the gate and down a legit cobblestone path. The house sat just on the outskirts of downtown, in a neighborhood that was a couple of hundred years old. Maybe as old as the entire Denver area.

Bright green bushes lined the road, with plenty of flowers that looked like they'd just been planted. Towering cottonwoods lined the path, and the whole place felt like an oasis right there in the middle of the city.

If Hunter could live in a place like this, he might not dislike living in the city. He'd thought about putting a potted plant in his condo, but he could barely remember to turn off the lights before he went to work. No way he could remember to water a plant.

Wes pulled up to a wide set of steps and put the truck in park. They both looked up at the huge mansion before getting out of the vehicle. Neither of them spoke as they went up the steps, and the front door opened before they could knock or ring a bell.

A man stood there, and if the slope of his nose and the deep, midnight color of his eyes was any indication, he was a Hammond.

He stood just as tall as Hunter, and though he didn't wear jeans or cowboy boots, if he had, he probably could've passed for his older brother.

"Wes," he said in a pleasant voice, with a smile on his face. "What are you doin' here?" He took a few steps in his bare feet and embraced Wes. The two of them chuckled, and when Wes stepped back, he faced Hunter too.

"This is my nephew, Hunter," he said. "Hunt, my cousin, Jason."

"Nice to meet you, sir," Hunter said, extending his hand for Jason to shake.

His eyebrows went up, and he glanced at Wes as she shook Hunter's hand. "Sir? I like this one."

"He's quite respectful," Wes said with a grin. "He's twenty-five, and our dear cousin Laura wants him to be the new CEO at HMC."

Hunter watched the surprise roll across Jason's face. He wore a loose pair of white pants and what looked like a blue tunic. Everything was light and airy, and without shoes, he looked like he'd just finished a meditation session.

"Come in," Jason said. "It's far too hot to stand outside and talk." He led the way back inside, where blessed air conditioning filled the house. The ceiling rose at least three stories above Hunter, the inlays of gold reminding him that this Hammond had money—and a lot of it.

Hunter could have a house like this if he so chose. He didn't have to work at all, and he thought of the extra barns and stables going in out at the family farm, once again wondering if he should quit at HMC completely and focus on his true passion—the farm. Helping others, especially those who've served their country and community.

"Something to drink?" Jason asked.

"What do you do?" Hunter asked.

"Water for me," Wes said. "Wait. I'll take a diet cola if you've got one."

"I do." Jason lifted his hand and looked at Hunter. "I'm a stock broker."

Whatever Hunter had expected him to say, it wasn't that. He blinked at him, even more surprised when a woman wearing a pale teal dress crossed the lobby with a tray balanced on her palm, a single glass of dark brown liquid on it.

"Diet cola," she said, extending the tray toward Wes.

"Stock broker," Hunter said, watching Uncle Wes take a

sip of his cola, then watching the woman walk away. "You know, I'm not sure I believe that."

"Well, I'm a Hammond too," he said. "My father only had two sons, while Wes's here had five."

"Yes," Wes said. "Us Hammonds under Chris are at a *severe* disadvantage." He rolled his eyes, which caused Hunter to smile.

Jason grinned too, indicating they should follow him further into the house. He led them into a room to the left, where bookshelves lined the walls from floor to ceiling. Molly would love this place. Hunter didn't read many novels, and he loved it.

The knowledge contained in these books…he could feel the power of it streaming through the room. "Wow," he said.

"This is my father's collection," Jason said. "He and my mother had to relocate after her surgery, and I took over their house."

"Oh, so this isn't your place," Wes said. "Things make so much more sense now."

"Do they?" Jason laughed as he sat on a leather sofa. "I'm glad." He waited a moment as Wes and Hunter sat down. "I suppose you came to talk me into claiming a right to the CEO position at the family company." He lifted a cup of coffee to his lips, his eyes never leaving Wes's.

"That's right," Uncle Wes said, not even bothering to hide it. "See, Hunter's got a Master's degree in Bioinformatics, and he's needed in the lab." He leaned forward, putting his elbows on his knees. "You don't need the money, and if you're a broker, you can simply pass your clients to someone else in the firm for a few years."

Jason listened, his dark eyes hardening by the moment. "I'm not going to be the CEO."

"Why not?" Uncle Wes asked.

Jason turned away and put his coffee cup back on the saucer on the small table next to the couch. "Wes, we are quite different in age. You're what? Sixty?"

"Sixty-two," Uncle Wes said, his voice guarded now.

"I'm only thirty-seven," Jason said. "Twenty-five years can conceal a lot of secrets."

Hunter frowned, trying to read between the lines.

"I don't understand," Uncle Wes said.

"I live in this house simply to honor my parents, but I have no desire to work at HMC. I tried, for a year or two, and it is simply not for me." He looked at Hunter. "I understand your dilemma. I feel it inside me too. If one of us doesn't take the reins, who will? Someone outside the family? Then what becomes of the Hammond family company? Will the values be the same? Will the direction change?"

The man had just vocalized all of Hunter's jumbled thoughts.

Jason gave a small smile. "It is a sacrifice I cannot make." He looked at Uncle Wes. "Not only that, but I was told in no uncertain terms by the current CEO that there would never be a position I was worthy to fill at HMC."

"What?" Uncle Wes asked. "Why?"

Even Hunter leaned forward, but Jason's face gave away nothing.

"When I worked there, I worked with Kent in the financial department. I made some suggestions to how HMC invests and in what stock. I prepared a portfolio I thought would take us into the future with even more money."

Hunter exchanged a glance with Wes, his thoughts suddenly firing rapidly.

"Laura was not interested. She said there was a certain way we did things at HMC, and no changes were needed."

Uncle Wes sighed. "She's very traditional, that's all."

"She's stubborn, and short-sighted, and when I told her that, she fired me." He shook his head. "Even if I wanted to go back—which I don't—she would never allow me to be the CEO."

"What about Jillian?" Hunter asked.

"Jillian is very sick," Jason said. "I suspect that's why Laura wants to retire too."

Hunter felt like doors kept closing, and he couldn't get them to open again.

"I had no idea Jillian was sick," Uncle Wes said. "I just spoke to her this morning, and she didn't say anything."

"Her daughter just turned thirty," Jason said. "Maybe she'll do it."

Hunter didn't think so, but he supposed anything was possible. "I want to see the portfolio," he said.

Jason's eyebrows rose in surprise again. "I can email it to you."

That felt like a very final end to the conversation, and

Hunter stood, Uncle Wes only a half-beat behind him. “Thanks, Jason,” he said, shaking his cousin’s hand. Hunter merely nodded, his skin suddenly itching to get out of this house.

He made the escape quickly, and it wasn’t until he and Uncle Wes had put a couple of miles between themselves and the mansion that he said, “I don’t know, Uncle Wes. It feels like I’m going to have to do this.”

“It’s honestly not that bad,” Uncle Wes said. “You get to choose your own assistants, and I only slept in my office a couple of times.” He grinned at Hunter, who wished he had the heart to grin back.

He thought of how little he saw Molly now, and how hard it was to get out to the farm to see the progress on Pony Power.

If he took this job, those minutes and margins would be even smaller. As Uncle Wes drove around Denver, commenting on this thing or that park that he and his brothers had used to visit, Hunter only halfway listened.

It felt like no matter what he chose, someone was going to be upset with him, and he couldn’t bear to see Molly’s bright green eyes flashing with anger.

He also couldn’t imagine letting someone without the last name of Hammond run HMC.

What am I supposed to do? he begged the Lord.

The only answer he received was, *Don’t give up.*

He didn’t know what that meant. Give up on what?

CHAPTER 18

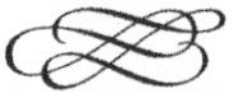

Molly stood at the door and smiled all of her new second graders out the door. The moment the last one left, she reached over and turned off the lights. She pulled the door closed and locked it.

At her desk, she sighed, every muscle in her body telling her she should've worked out that summer. At least walked around a lot more than she had. She'd worked a lot around Hunter's farm, mapping out where their barns and stables and paddocks would go for the new equine therapy facility. But that obviously wasn't the same type of work as teaching all day.

She opened her bottom desk drawer and took out the bag of peanut butter cups she'd put there last week. She rewarded herself with a specific candy each day during the first week of school, with making it through the first day always earning her her very favorite treat.

She unwrapped the miniature peanut butter cup and

peeled off the paper before sticking it in her mouth. Her eyes drifted closed and while her exhaustion was complete, she sure did enjoy this flavor combination of peanut butter and chocolate.

After she'd eaten a few sweet treats, she turned her phone over. Hunter had texted a few times, but Molly honestly wasn't sure she had the strength to read the messages. Their argument over his job felt like it had happened just yesterday, though it had been a few weeks now.

Things just hadn't been the same between them since, especially because he and Wes hadn't found anyone else to take the job.

It felt like time was marching forward, day by day, and soon enough, he'd be announcing his departure from Lab Six.

She still had prep to do for tomorrow, but before she began, she swiped on her phone to read Hunter's messages.

Hope you've had an amazing first day! he'd said, which caused her to smile at his thoughtfulness.

His next message read, *Can we go to dinner tonight? Or will you be too tired?*

Then: *I'm going to bring a whole bunch of pizza out to the farm. You'll be out there, right? Matt said you'd be coming out to meet with him and Gloria to go over the progress on the construction.*

Yes, she typed out to him. *I want chicken and bacon pizza with Alfredo sauce. Tons of cheese.*

Hunter didn't respond right away, and Molly got up to get her work done. There was always more to do, but Molly had learned how to do what needed to be done for the next day only. Otherwise, she'd spend hours and hours in her classroom after school.

A few hours later, she pulled up to the farmhouse she'd grown to love. Hunter's parents and siblings had returned from Coral Canyon, and she found his father sitting on the front steps with his daughter, showing her how to strip the bark from a stick.

They both looked up at her as she got out of the car, and Jane set down her knife and came bounding down the steps toward her. Molly smiled at the child and hugged her tight when she reached her. "How was school, you lovely girl?"

"I started sixth grade today," she said, stepping back. "Everyone seemed so big. Tall."

Molly beamed down at her. "You'll grow taller."

"Maybe," Jane said. "Mom is short."

"You can do anything a tall person can do," her father said from the steps.

"Yeah, except reach stuff," Jane grumbled. "Come see what we're doing."

Molly followed the girl and smiled at Hunter's father. "Hello, Gray."

"How was your first day, Molly?" He glanced at her and then focused on the wood in his hand again.

"Tiring," she said with a sigh. "I'll survive though. I keep telling myself that I've done this before. I'll get used to getting up early, and I'll remember how to scarf down lunch in only fifteen minutes."

Gray chuckled, and Molly joined him, though she'd spoken true. "Are you here for Pony Power?" he asked next.

"Yes," she said. "I'm supposed to have Matt walk me through how things are going with the construction."

Gray nodded, and when he didn't ask another question, Molly basked in the silence. It was so still and so peaceful out here. The wind moved through the trees in the distance, and she could hear it coming toward her.

The rustling grew degree by degree until the leaves on the trees in the front yard moved, and Molly let the breeze brush by her face. She took a deep breath of the fresh air that had already started to cool. The weather in the Rocky Mountains could be unpredictable at best. It could snow in September, and then the next day, be perfectly sunny and warm.

"Gray, do you think Hunter's going to take that CEO position?" Molly asked, the last word or two nearly choking her.

Several seconds of silence followed, and Molly was beginning to think she'd imagined herself asking the question when he said, "Yes."

She nodded, though her misery and desperation had exploded inside her.

"You don't want him to," Gray said, not really asking.

Molly shook her head, barely hearing him as he said something to Jane. He taught her for a few minutes, and Molly decided she couldn't stay.

"Excuse me," she said, standing up. "I need to go find

Matt and Gloria." That was true, but she really just wanted a moment to mourn for Hunter.

She'd barely made it around the side of the house before Gray caught up to her. "Molly," he said. "Wait a second."

She breathed in through her nose and took a moment before she turned back to him. He looked so much like Hunter, though his son was taller, darker, and broader.

"He feels like he has no other choice," Gray said.

"I know exactly what that feels like," she said, her chest collapsing on itself. "I will do my best to support him."

"I know you will," Gray said with a heavy smile. "I will too. That's all we can really do."

She nodded, said, "Excuse me," again and ducked away from him. She met Matt out by his cabin, and they went to find Gloria. She was working with a handsome black and white horse, and she quickly tethered him to a walking circle so she could go on the tour with Molly.

"So much has changed since I was here last," Molly said, looking around. "I guess it's been a couple of weeks." She'd been very busy preparing for the new school year, helping Ingrid and Kara move into their apartments for the new school year, and even going with Lyra and Mama to taste the wedding cake options.

"The biggest change is the row house," Gloria said, leading the trio that way. "It's finished inside now, and all they've got left to do is paint and seal the outside." She took Molly through it, and Molly marveled at the beautiful stalls, the fine craftsmanship on the doors, and the perfectly placed hooks and shelves for all the tack and feed.

"This is great," she said, looking around at everything and trying to take it all in at once.

"Matt did some tweaks on the design," Gloria said, a noticeable measure of pride in her voice. "We've both worked with plenty of horses in our day, and I have to say I agree with his changes."

"It's great," Molly said. Her inexperience with horses and barns and stables had been covered up by hiring a designer to work on the construction of the facilities needed for the therapy program. Pete Marshall had helped her several times, and she couldn't even see what had been changed.

Twenty minutes later, she'd seen everything, and they started the walk back to the farmhouse. "We're still on track for it to open next spring," she said. "We just need personnel now. Counselors, trainers, and maybe even an administrative position to keep the whole thing running smoothly."

Someone detailed and organized, who could make phone calls and greet wounded or scared kids with a smile and a piece of candy. *Someone like me,* she thought.

Molly pushed the thought out of her mind. She had a job she loved, and she barely knew how to ride a horse. Gloria had offered to teach her, but Molly had only taken a few lessons before things had gotten too hectic.

As she climbed the back steps to the deck, she heard Hunter's voice inside the farmhouse. "…no right to tell her that," he said, and he was not happy.

Matt looked at her over his shoulder, his eyes wide and

worried. Molly kept going, because she needed to face Hunter sooner or later. She supposed it was going to be sooner.

Gloria entered the farmhouse first, then Matt, then Molly, and she paused to take everything in. Elise stood at the edge of the counter, a wooden spoon in her hand. Gray and Hunter sat at the table, neither of them speaking. They both wore a grim look on their face, and Hunter's looked more like a tornado about to touch down.

"Pizza's here," he said, jumping to his feet. "Can we eat, Elise?"

"Let me call the kids." She went toward the front door while Gray stood and moved the pitcher of punch to the counter next to the pizza boxes. Paper plates and napkins had already been set out, and Molly strongly disliked how Hunter kept his back to her.

He hadn't said hello either, or even looked in her direction. Strong feelings moved through her, and she decided she wasn't going to let him ignore her. He couldn't hide from her.

She wouldn't hide from him.

As Tucker and Deacon came tearing into the house with loud voices, Molly moved past everyone to stand next to her boyfriend. She curled her fingers around his and said, "Hey, did you get my text about what kind of pizza I wanted?"

He'd never answered, and Molly hoped the simple question would lighten his mood.

He cut a look at her. "I got it."

"Thank you."

Jane came inside, and Chris rose from the couch where Molly hadn't even seen him and Bev. Hunter's grandmother didn't stand, and Molly didn't like the gray color of her skin. Alarm pulled through her, but no one else seemed to notice.

Gray said grace, and the kids attacked the cheese pizza. Molly took two slices of the chicken and bacon pie Hunter had ordered especially for her, and she took her paper plate over to the couch where Bev sat.

"How are you, ma'am?" she asked.

Bev gave her a weary smile. "I'm still kicking."

"Can I get you something to eat?"

"Oh, Chris is bringing me some of that all-meat kind." She reached out and patted Molly's knee. "You eat whatever you want, dear. You get to be my age, and it doesn't seem so important to eat salads for every meal."

Molly grinned at her. "Today, I ate half a protein bar and downed a Diet Coke for lunch." She giggled, glad when Bev did too. She took a big bite of her cheesy pizza just as Chris arrived with a plate for Bev, Hunter right behind him.

"Hey, Grandma." Hunter bent down and gave his grandmother a kiss on the top of the head. "Can I steal Molly from you?"

"You go right ahead, dear."

Hunter returned her smile and met Molly's eyes. He didn't look one second away from an eruption now, and Molly said good-night to Bev and Chris before going with Hunter out to the back deck.

He put his plate on the picnic table and sat down. She sat beside him, not quite sure what to say.

Hunter seemed to be mulling over his options too. He finally said, "I know my father told you I'm going to take the CEO job."

"I asked," Molly said. "It's not his fault."

"He had no right to tell you," Hunter said. "*I* was planning to tell you."

"Were you?"

"Of course I was."

Neither of them had touched their pizza, and Molly looked at her very favorite food in the whole world and couldn't imagine eating it. She couldn't look at Hunter, and though he sat right next to her, he felt worlds away.

"It's going to be okay," he said.

"If you say so."

"Molly."

"What, Hunter?"

He sighed. "It won't be forever, and I feel like it's the right thing to do."

She thought of the prayer she'd offered. She'd asked for God's light, so he'd know what to do, and perhaps he had been shown the path. She didn't have to like it though.

Her fears reared up, and she picked up her pizza and took a bite so she wouldn't have to say anything. She suddenly couldn't see a future with him in it. Even if they did stay together and get married, she'd hardly see him. He'd be so busy in that building, and Molly didn't want to start off their life together by herself. She didn't want to raise her children alone.

If Hunter became the CEO, he'd essentially be married to his job, and that meant he couldn't marry Molly.

"Please," he said. "Say something."

"There's nothing for me to say," she said.

"It's my family duty," he said. "One day, it might be one of our children's family duty."

She looked at him then, trying to see inside his head and understand his thought processes. "You still want to be with me?"

"Why wouldn't I?"

"Because you're not going to have time to breathe, let alone continue to build our relationship."

A cloud covered his face, and he turned back to his food too. "I don't think that's true."

"How many hours do you think a CEO works?" she challenged. "It's more than you work in Lab Six, and for a while there, I barely saw you."

He started to nod, his expression angry and his jaw tight. "I see now."

"See what?"

"You don't want me to take this job, because you don't want to be left behind."

"Yes," she said. "Exactly. Who would want to be left behind?"

"You want me to text and call and spend time with you."

"Yes," Molly said, not bothering to deny it. "Don't you want to talk to me and spend time with me?" Maybe he didn't, and Molly's insecurities rushed through her, staining her mind and making her throat and chest as tight as they could be.

"Who's going to raise all those kids you say you want?" she asked quietly. "Me? By myself? While you're up in that corner office, dealing with who knows what for who knows how long?"

"We're not even engaged," he said, his voice mostly made of a growl.

"I won't hold my breath then," Molly said, standing up. *He'd* brought up kids. *He'd* brought up the equine therapy program, and she'd been the one to put it all together while he worked in that high-rise downtown.

She felt so foolish. So...used.

She picked up her paper plate of half-eaten pizza. "Excuse me."

"Molly," he said, the growl and frustration gone now.

She paused, her back to him. He stood up and put one arm around her tentatively. "There's time for the job and for you."

She nodded, because she didn't want to fight. "I trust you, Hunter." She twisted and looked up at him. "I'm going to go, because I'm tired, and I have to teach again tomorrow."

"Okay." He dropped his hand, and Molly slipped away from him. She also didn't want to say anything she'd regret later, and she probably already had.

She couldn't go back into the house and face his family, so she scurried around the side of the house like a coward, got behind the wheel of her car, and hurried back to Saltine and Gypsy.

After feeding her pets, she grabbed a container of cubed cheese to make up for the pizza she hadn't eaten. Then Molly climbed into bed and cried into her cheddar.

CHAPTER 19

Hunter went back inside the farmhouse, where the conversation stopped upon his arrival. "She left," he said sourly. He sat down in the nearest chair and took a bite of pizza. It tasted like sawdust in his mouth, but he chewed anyway. He'd driven for an hour to get here tonight, and he couldn't stand the thought of making the drive back to the condo.

"She's not happy about you taking the job," Elise said.

"I know that," Hunter said, sending a glare down the table. "I'm not sure why, though."

"What did she say?" Dad asked.

"She said I wouldn't have time for her." Hunter didn't want to admit to the truthfulness of that. He barely had time to see her now, and he left the lab by six every evening. Now that school had started again, she'd be busier than ever. He wasn't complaining about her job.

The more he thought about her issues with him taking

the job, the more selfish she started to look. Hunter passed on dessert, told his parents to keep the leftover pizza, and didn't ask to stay in his old bedroom.

His father wouldn't let him leave without a tight hug. Afterward, he looked him straight in the eye and said, "You'll do the right thing, Hunter."

"I just want to make everyone happy," he said miserably, recalling the conversation he'd had with Molly about this very thing. "I want you to be proud of me. I want to do right by the Hammond name."

The real problem was that none of those things lined up with what *he* really wanted.

"Hunter," Dad said. "I *am* proud of you. I couldn't be prouder, in fact."

Hunter nodded, but he wasn't sure he believed his dad.

"You *have* done right by the Hammond name already," he said. "You're doing so much with what you've been given." He cocked one eyebrow. "And Hunter, you can't make anyone happy. That's not your job."

"Feels like it." He sighed, because he'd felt like this when thinking about his relationship with his mother too. "I need to go, Dad. It's a long drive back to the city."

Dad just nodded, sometimes his silence saying more than his words.

Hunter left the farmhouse, hoping the long drive would give his thoughts time to straighten out. They didn't, and he simply arrived on the twenty-third floor more exhausted than ever.

HUNTER KEPT HIS HEAD DOWN AND DID HIS WORK in Lab Six. He led the meetings he'd been assigned to lead, and he studied the reports coming out of the control room. He noted adjustments that could be made in the organic makeup of the drug he and his team were working on, and he ate sandwiches for lunch and ordered dinner to his condo in the evenings.

He made sure to text Molly whenever the thought occurred to him—and according to the alarm he'd set on his phone for seven p.m. Even just to ask her about her day in the classroom, if he couldn't think of anything else.

Nothing much happened in the lab that was too exciting, so he'd stopped talking about work. She didn't seem to want to hear about his job anyway.

She responded to his texts, but it felt like they were dancing on eggshells, and by the end of the week, Hunter's mood couldn't be worse.

Her house was closer to the city than the farm, and Hunter tossed his lab coat toward the hooks just inside the door of his condo and dialed her. He loosened his tie as the phone rang, and he'd just collapsed on the couch when she said, "Hunter, hello."

She didn't sound tired or upset. Quite the opposite, in fact. The sound of her voice sent a river of happiness through him, and Hunter didn't want to lose her. His throat tightened, and he swallowed, trying to find the right thing to say.

Did he love her?

He'd loved her as a teenager. He'd loved Abby as an adult. He loved his family, and Hunter knew what love felt like. He knew what it sounded like, and more importantly, thanks to his mother, he knew what it *didn't* look like and sound like.

"Are you there?" she asked. "Hello?"

"Yes," he said quickly so she wouldn't hang up. "Sorry, I just...what are you doing tonight? Would you—might you have time to come have dinner with me at my house?"

"Your house?" she asked, and he could envision her with her eyebrows up.

"Yeah," he said, looking around the condo. The whole place reminded him of a hospital room, though the lights splashed a yellow glow around the room instead of white. Nothing here said who lived here and that they took pride in living here.

"You've never been here," he said. "I can order dinner and it'll be here at the same time as you."

"Just a second," she said, and the sound of scuffling came through the line. She spoke to someone else on her end of the line, and Hunter suddenly didn't want to take her from whoever she was with.

"It's okay," he said. "Are you eating with your family?" He'd seen Molly's sisters and parents several times over the summer, as he still drove out to Ivory Peaks to attend church. Molly sat with him, and they'd exchanged pleasantries a few times after the service. She'd spent Sabbath afternoons with him at the farm, and Hunter didn't want to steal her from her family tonight.

"I'm with some work friends," she said. "It's okay. I can be there in a few minutes. We're actually on our way into the city."

"I don't want to interrupt you."

"I'd need a ride home," she said.

Hunter pressed his eyes closed, wondering why he was trying to get her to stay with her friends when he wanted her there with him. "I can give you a ride home."

"Okay," she said, and her voice softened. "Will you text me a reminder of where you live?"

"Yes." The call ended, and Hunter quickly typed out his address and sent it to Molly. He barely existed in this condo, so all he had to do to clean up was put his coffee mugs from the past few days in the dishwasher. The silence in the condo annoyed him, and he connected his phone to his Bluetooth speaker and set some classical music to play.

Lucy had encouraged him to listen to music without words. That way, his mind could churn through what it needed to, and he could find the answers he sought. Tonight, he busied himself on his phone to order dinner, and then he settled at the kitchen table and pulled a crossword puzzle in front of him.

Hunter wasn't sure how much time had passed before his phone chimed. He usually set an alarm whenever he did his puzzles, because he could get lost inside the clues and boxes.

"Mols," he answered, his mood much improved, though

his stomach told him he hadn't eaten yet. He got up from the table and strode toward the front door. "Are you here?"

"In the lobby," she said. "I have the food from Lola."

"I can come down." He opened the door. "I ordered a lot of food."

"I can make it," she said. "I just can't get the elevator to open. It needs a code?"

"Oh, right." Hunter had a card he scanned over the screen in the lobby. "It's two-three-seven-four."

"Okay." A moment passed, and she went, "Yep. I'll be up in a minute."

Hunter met her at the elevator door and took one of the bags from Lola. He had a hard time meeting her eyes, and when he did, she wasn't looking at him either. They flitted around each other, and Hunter hated that.

He hadn't felt this awkward in a long time, and he thought of something Lucy had told him once, years ago. *Address things head-on, Hunter. You'll be happier in the end.*

He didn't open his mouth on the walk down the hall, though. Lucy had also told him that he was the only one who controlled how he felt, and if he put off an awkward air, everyone could feel it.

Gathering his courage and confidence, he opened the door for Molly and smiled at her as she walked past him. Their eyes met for a moment, and that second of time sizzled. The chemistry and attraction between them hadn't lessened though they hadn't seen each other face-to-face for a few days.

She put the bag of food on the counter and started

unpacking it while Hunter closed and locked the door behind them. He joined her at the island and did the same with the food, laying it all out.

"Do you want to eat first? Or do you want a tour?" Hunter turned and opened a cupboard to take out plates. If he dined alone, he ate from whatever container the food came in. But on a Friday night, with his girlfriend, he could use plates and real silverware.

He slipped his hand in hers, moving slowly and gently. Her fingers made room for his, and he squeezed. "I've missed you."

Molly turned toward him, and he easily took her into his embrace. All of the awkwardness and unease inside him dried up, and Hunter let out a long sigh. "I've *really* missed you." He ran his hands through her hair, his desire sparking like static electricity. He wanted to kiss her, but he needed her to say something first.

How much she missed him would be nice.

"How was the first week of school?" he asked, glad she hadn't stepped away yet.

Molly tipped her head back, and Hunter gazed down at her. He stroked his fingers down the side of her face, a smile filling his soul. "You're beautiful."

She finally smiled then. "I missed you, too." She reached up and brushed her fingertips along his forehead where his hair was. "You're not wearing your cowboy hat."

"I do take a break from it every now and then," he teased. "Give my scalp a chance to see the light."

Molly grinned up at him. Her eyes drifted closed, and

Hunter read all the female signals fairly well, thanks to his kissing spree over the past ten years. He wanted to claim her mouth, but instead, he pressed his lips to hers gently, holding back his desire and pressing against his hormones.

This sweet kiss would communicate more than his hunger for her, and that was what he wanted her to feel in his touch.

His love for her.

He was right on the cusp of it, but he knew it bubbled and boiled and that soon he'd be swimming fully in love with Molly Benson.

She kissed him back with a slow, simple strokes, and Hunter pulled away after only a few seconds. He'd slid his hands up her throat to her face, and he held her there as he whispered, "I don't like it when we disagree."

"I don't either," she said.

He released her and stepped back. "I apologize for my mood on Monday evening. I was frustrated with my father for telling you, and I'm extremely frustrated at the situation in front of me."

She nodded and faced the food. "You texted all week, and you ordered from my favorite restaurant." She reached for the first container and opened it to reveal the garlic lemon green beans Hunter loved. "I think you're forgiven."

Hunter murmured, "Thank you, Molly."

"I'm sorry I've said anything about your job." She opened another container and got pork potstickers with soy ginger sauce. "You've always been driven in your work, and you're one of the most hardworking men I know. It's not up to me what you do with your life, and I apologize for butting in where I shouldn't have."

Hunter appreciated the apology, and he opened a couple of boxes to get to the main courses—honey-orange duck and the chicken pesto pasta. "This one is for you, sweetheart." He pushed the pasta toward her.

She sucked in a breath while Hunter reached for the aluminum bag that would have the garlic bread he adored. In his memory, Molly liked it too. He glanced at her to find her wiping at her face.

She twisted slightly away from him as she dished herself some pasta, and Hunter let her hide her emotion from him. Sometimes he needed a moment to compose himself, and he'd like it if she gave him that moment, so he gave it to her.

He opened another container to find the steak chimichurri and spiced potatoes, and one more to reveal the last main dish he'd ordered: turkey pot pie with roasted onions.

"You really did order a lot of food," she said.

Hunter loved to eat, and he hadn't been able to decide what to get. "We can order dessert later." He got out a bowl and put half the turkey pot pie in it, then started dishing some of everything else onto his plate. "Or we can walk down the street to The Corner. They have delicious bread pudding."

"I have a good raspberry bread pudding recipe," she said. "I should make it for you sometime."

"Yes, please." He smiled at her and took his food to the

table where he'd been doing his puzzles. "Something to drink? I think I have water and soda in the fridge. Maybe some lemonade." He hurried back into the kitchen and opened the fridge. "Nope. Just water and soda."

Molly crowded in beside him. "What kind of soda?"

He backed up a little so she could see. Her hand curled around his forearm, and Hunter's blood heated. He looked at her as she said, "I'll take that Dr. Pepper."

He reached for it and handed it to her, watching her for another sign that she wanted to be close to him. She smiled and took her plate and can of soda to the table. She sat across from him, and Hunter tamped down the urge to move over next to her and kiss her until he couldn't breathe.

Once they'd both settled at the table, Hunter picked up his fork and took his first bite. He wanted to continue their conversation, but he really didn't want to ruin this new peace they'd found between them.

They ate in silence for a few minutes, while Hunter gathered his bravery. "Molly," he finally said, and she glanced up at him. "I just wanted…I think my job is your business." He cleared his throat. "I mean, if we're really going to keep seeing each other, and we have long-term plans to be together, you should definitely have a say in what I do."

Her eyes rounded, but she quickly looked down at her half-empty plate. "You think so?"

"Well, I want to keep seeing you," he said. "I want to have a long-term plan with you." He put another bite of duck in his mouth and took his time chewing it. He'd given her time to say something, and she hadn't taken it.

Address it head-on.

"Molly," he said again, waiting for her to look up at him. "Be honest with me. Am I the only one who has a long-term plan for us?"

"Define long-term plan," she said.

"Marriage," he said. "Kids. A life we build together, with family vacations and Christmas traditions." He thought of Dad and Elise, and how they'd each compromised for the other. They each made their own happiness, but they talked about the things they didn't agree on. One didn't just bow out completely, and Hunter suspected that was what Molly had just done.

"When do you anticipate all of that happening?" she asked.

Hunter blinked, because he didn't have a timeline. "When we're both ready."

"Are you ready to get married?"

"To you?" he asked. "Yes." He nodded, because while the idea of marriage did terrify him slightly, if the woman at the altar with him was Molly Benson, he felt sure he could say "I do."

"How soon would you want children?"

"We're young," he said. "You tell me."

She didn't. Instead, she asked, "Would you want me to quit teaching to stay home and raise the kids?"

In his mind, yes, that was the life Hunter imagined. Molly at home with the kids while Hunter went to work.

Where that work was still hovered just out of sight, but Hunter knew not everything in life could be planned.

"That's up to you," he said. "I'd like to think we'd talk about it, and we'd come to a solution that worked for both of us, as well as our family."

Molly nodded and forked up another bite of pasta. "I'd be willing to consider a long-term plan for us," she finally said.

Hunter's heart flopped against his ribs, a wail starting in his ears. "Consider it?" How had he been so blind? He'd thought he'd been reading her signals pretty well, but maybe he'd been only seeing what he wanted to see.

"I have to be honest with you, Hunter." Molly set down her fork. "Because I don't think you're being realistic. I think you've got this fantasy in your head, and when real life manifests itself, you're going to be disappointed. Disappointed in me. Disappointed in our marriage. Disappointed that you've married me and that you've built the kind of life you don't really want."

Hunter stopped eating too and leaned back in his chair. He folded his arms, because he didn't need her to tell him what he wanted. He knew what he wanted. He'd spent years untangling his thoughts and emotions, and he already knew what was important to him.

"I know what real life is," he said.

She shook her head. "No, you don't. Not really. You've never had to scrimp and save and sacrifice for something."

"So this is about me being rich?" An old, familiar darkness entered his soul. He couldn't believe his money mattered to Molly.

"No." She shook her head. "I mean, kind of." She sighed and reached across the table as if he'd put his hands in hers. He didn't, and she pulled her hands back to her lap. "You didn't have to sacrifice to go to MIT. You're smart, and you got a scholarship."

"I worked dang hard at MIT," he said, the words carrying plenty of bite. She probably didn't know about the awards and merits he'd earned in college. He hadn't told her, because Hunter didn't need to brag.

"I know you did." She sighed. "But Hunt, you have to see what I'm saying. You didn't have to interview for jobs. You just had one waiting for you. You didn't have to save to start major construction at your family farm. You just did it, because you have a ton of money. You bought seventeen horses without even blinking an eye, for crying out loud."

Hunter couldn't argue with any of that, though he wanted to. He worked hard in the lab. He didn't buy those horses on a whim; he'd researched their origin first. Maybe he hadn't blinked when writing the check, but that didn't mean he hadn't done his due diligence with the animals.

Molly leaned forward, her bright eyes filled with earnestness. "I think your fantasy involves that farmhouse," she said. "Not a corner office. Not a high-rise condo with fancy woodwork everywhere, and the best appliances money can buy. It involves hay and goats, horses and cowboy hats. It has lots of little boys and girls running toward you when you come in from the farm, and a pretty wife waiting for you at the top of the steps, with your favorite meal on the table."

She paused, and Hunter knew she was giving him space to disagree.

"Eventually," Hunter said. "Yes. That's the dream."

She gave him a smile, but it didn't hold much happiness. "And I'm sure you'll get it. All Hammonds seem to get whatever they want. They dream big, and they achieve their dreams."

"Is there something wrong with that?"

"No." She shook her head and looked down. "No, there's not."

Hunter wasn't sure where she was driving. His experience with Abby had taught him that love didn't conquer all. She'd gone back to New York to fulfill her family duty; why couldn't he?

You're young, he thought. The whole future lay in front of him, and for the first time in months, he thought maybe it didn't include Molly Benson.

CHAPTER 20

Matt stepped out of his cabin and zipped his jacket all the way to his chin. The weather in the Rockies could be fickle, snowing one day and then nearly back to summer-like temperatures the next day.

Today, Mother Nature had decided to blow a cold wind across the farm, and Matt reached up to press his cowboy hat to his head. The kids had left for school ten minutes ago, and he enjoyed the silence in the cabin and around the land.

Elise took all the kids to school in the morning, and she worked out of an office nearby until kindergarten ended. She didn't do a lot for her landscaping and lawn care business in the winter, but she'd been considering expanding into snow removal. Matt didn't know what she did in her office, and he didn't much care.

She took his kids to school for him, and he picked everyone up in the afternoons. Gray would have all the animals fed by now, and Matt expected to see him jogging down the road at any moment.

Sure enough, the man went by, wearing long, black running pants, and a sweatshirt. He was as predictable as the sun rising and setting, and his habits actually made Matt smile.

He didn't like routine and consistency nearly as much as Gray Hammond, and Matt walked toward the newly constructed stables across the pasture from the row of cabins. Yesterday, he'd started his work in the office in the barn, going over the field rotation schedule for next spring. That way, he knew what to plow under this fall, and what to call in for the fertilizer and pest control crop-dusters.

Since school had started, he hadn't seen Molly out at the farm much. They'd pushed over the summer to get the construction done for the horses Hunter had purchased, and only one stable remained. The crew chief had promised Matt it would be done before October hit Colorado, and he glanced down the lane to see the skeletal frame of the unfinished stable.

Inside the biggest one, Matt breathed a sigh of relief to be out of the wind. He loved the design of this building, and he went down the main aisle, greeting the horses that came to see him.

He went around the back, behind their stalls and started opening the doors that would let the horses out into the paddock the stable bordered. With all ten of them out, he got to work on shoveling out their stalls and putting down fresh sawdust and straw.

He put new water in each stall and reopened the doors so the horses could come back in or stay out. That done, he went next door to the new hay barn, where he'd been organizing tack and making space for the new load of hay that would arrive that afternoon.

On his father's farm in Montana, buying hay could set the whole operation into the red. But the Hammond family farm didn't seem to have a budget. They didn't have to use the money the farm generated to live, and Matt envied them that.

When his father had passed, he'd inherited a healthy sum of money. Nothing like a million dollars, let alone the billions Gray Hammond possessed. Enough to make his life comfortable.

Matt had been working for someone else since his father's death, because he'd sold that farm and he'd needed to have a job where the daily tasks were well-defined by someone else. Then he could just get up in the morning, do the work, and go to bed at night.

He worked until lunch shifting around the hay and stacking it higher. He made a plan for how to rotate it, and he left notes for Gloria and Gray, the only other two people who worked the farm with him.

As if bidden by his thoughts, Gloria called his name as he finished his last note. "Right here," he called, throwing up his defensive walls. He could admit he was attracted to Gloria. He could, and he had.

He'd also told Hunter once that he wasn't ready to date

again, and that still remained true though another month had passed.

The beautiful blonde appeared from around the corner, wearing a pair of skin-tight jeans with plenty of dirt on them, a tight, red coat, and leather gloves. "I need you," she said. "We've got a cow caught in a fence."

Matt dropped the pencil and hurried after her. She'd obviously been out checking the herd, as a single horse waited right outside the barn.

"I'll get Shadow," he called.

"No time," she said. "Hop on with me."

Matt hadn't ridden a horse with another adult in a long time. He rode with Brittany all the time, but Gloria was quite a bit different than his daughter. She wasn't much wider, but she was taller, and wrapping his arms around her made his heart stutter and skip in a way it hadn't in a long, long time.

He held on as she spurred Knitted Cotton into a gallop. Her hair whipped behind her, and Matt put his head right next to hers to avoid it. She wasn't wearing a hat, and he suspected she'd lost it on the ride in.

They arrived at the tangled cow in only a few minutes, and Matt swung down to the ground first. Gloria followed, saying, "I tried to pull that line down, but I'm not strong enough."

Matt wasn't sure he was either, but he could try. "You grab onto her legs, so I don't get kicked."

Gloria got right in behind the cow and grabbed her hind legs. The cow lowed, clearly not happy with what was happening. The scent of blood hung in the air, but Matt ignored it as he positioned himself on the other side of the cow and bent to pull one line of barbed wire up and push the bottom one down.

"Three, two, one," he said, counting in quick succession. He put all of his strength into moving the lines that had been wired tight enough to prevent exactly what he was trying to do. He groaned with the effort, and said, "Just a little bit further."

His muscles strained, and a wave of heat moved through him. "Got it. Go. Go."

Gloria yipped at the cow, and it moved out of the fence. Matt released the lines and rubbed his gloved hands together, panting. The cow trotted off, still lowing like Matt and Gloria had done something horrible by saving it.

"Do we need to round it up and check her legs?"

Gloria sighed and turned to Matt. "Yep."

Matt wished he had his own horse. "Guess we should've roped it before we let 'er loose."

Gloria exhaled and smiled, something he'd been seeing more and more often lately. They hadn't talked much in the couple of months she'd been here. Gloria had always been a really private person, and Matt was still trying to figure out how to be a single father.

Now, though, everything seemed easy between them. "I'll lead, and you can ride," he said, starting back toward Cotton.

"I need to walk," she said. "I've been in the saddle for hours."

They both walked alongside the horse, Matt leading her by the reins. "After lunch, I'll go hunt down that cow and take care of her legs."

Gloria shook her head. "I'll do it."

"You're better at medical care than I am."

She gave him a smile, and Matt thought he saw a hint of interest in her eyes. "Can I ask you something?" she asked.

"Go ahead."

"You don't wear a wedding ring."

That wasn't actually a question, but Matt heard plenty of others stemming from the statement. "No," he said. "My wife and I divorced in March." He couldn't quite look at her.

"I'm sorry."

Matt took a deep breath. "I'm slowly moving on. Learning how to take care of the kids by myself." He glanced at her then. "She's an alcoholic, and I got full custody."

Gloria nodded, her head bent against the wind.

"What about you?" he asked. "Ever married?"

"No." She shook her head, and he wished he could see her full expression.

"Never met anyone?"

She looked up then, meeting his gaze. "Not that I wanted to marry. You know how some cowboys are."

Matt wasn't sure what she meant, but he agreed anyway. "Why—What happened in Montana to bring you here? I didn't think you'd ever leave Tailwind."

Gloria's face fell, and she looked away. Not down, again, but over toward the row of cabins where they both lived. "My father died," she said.

Confusion pulled at his eyebrows. "I'm sorry," he said. "You and your daddy…I know he meant a great deal to you." He'd raised Gloria alone after her mother had died when she was ten. She'd worked at Tailwind, a huge cattle ranch just outside of Sugar Pond, for her entire life.

"I'm still not sure why you're here," he said. "Surely your daddy left the ranch to you."

She didn't answer until they were almost back to the stable. "There was a will, but it didn't say what we all expected it to."

Matt really wanted to know what it had said, but he didn't want to pry. Gloria wouldn't appreciate it, and he liked talking to her. "Do you want to come to lunch with me? I'm making grilled cheese sandwiches to go with that chicken noodle soup Bev made yesterday. I take everything over to their place and eat with Chris and Bev."

She swung her attention toward him. "You do?"

He nodded. "They like it, and I like it, and…." He shrugged. "You're welcome every day, if you'd like."

"I'll get Cotton out in the paddock and come over," she said.

Matt smiled at her and touched the brim of his cowboy hat. "Sounds good." He left her in front of the stable and crossed the pasture back to his cabin. He'd bought a big bin as soon as he'd realized he'd have to haul ingredients from his cabin to the generational house where Chris and Bev lived.

He loaded bread, sliced cheese, butter, and garlic powder into the bin and started out the back door this time.

"Chris," he called as he opened the door. "Here for lunch." The scent of salt and something roasted hung in the air, and Matt's stomach rumbled for meat instead of a grilled cheese sandwich.

"Come in," Chris said, pushing hard to get himself out of the recliner. He wore a big smile as he greeted Matt. "Bev's got roast beef coming out."

"I was going to do sandwiches with the leftover soup," Matt said, taking the bin into the kitchen. He wasn't sure where Bev was, but she sometimes took a nap in the morning. Over the summer, he'd often find her in the small flower garden in front of the house, but it had been cleared already.

"Have you ever put roast beef on your grilled cheese?" Chris's eyes were still bright and alive, and Matt grinned at him.

"I haven't, but it sounds amazing."

"It is."

They worked together in the kitchen, warming soup and making sandwiches. When a knock sounded on the door, Matt quickly wiped his hands on his apron. "I invited Gloria." He hurried toward the door to let her in, while Chris called that he'd go get Bev.

Upon opening the front door, Gloria met his eyes and said, "Hey."

"Come on in." He stepped back to make room for her, and she passed him with a smile.

She gazed around the generational home. "Wow. This place is beautiful."

"Single level," he said. "Easy access. Your dad had a generational house, I think."

"He did," she said. "Never used it, though."

Matt wanted to say he would've had he lived longer, but he had enough tact not to. "We added roast beef to the sandwiches," he said, scooping one crusty, golden sandwich off the griddle. "Hope that's okay."

"I grew up on a cattle ranch," Gloria said. "We had beef for every meal."

He smiled at her and pushed the plated sandwich toward her. As he ladled soup into a bowl, Chris returned to the kitchen with his wife. Bev definitely looked like she'd just gotten out of bed, maybe for the first time that day.

Matt watched the two of them as Chris helped her into a chair and then said something to her in a quiet voice. He came into the kitchen, not quite able to shake the worry from his expression before Matt saw it.

His heart pounded hard for a moment, and he wanted to ask if Bev was okay. Something told him not to, and he handed the ready bowl of soup to Chris. "I'll do another," he said. He did, and once Gloria had it in her hand, she turned to join Bev at the table.

Matt put the other sandwiches on plates and took all three of them to the table too, while Chris dished up a couple more bowls of soup. When everyone had food at the table, Matt smiled around at everyone, his eyes lingering on Bev.

Her skin color pinked up as she ate, and soon enough, she was talking to Gloria like they were old friends. Gloria possessed plenty of charisma, and she could play a part really well. Matt liked being with her, and he didn't know what that meant for him.

They'd dated in the past, but she hadn't given any indication that she'd like to do that again. Matt had resisted the idea in the beginning as well, but today's events had his thoughts turning in a new direction.

"We better go find that cow," Gloria said once they'd all finished eating.

"Yep." Matt got up and started clearing the table. Gloria worked with him, and they loaded the dishes into the dishwasher.

"Leave the pots and pans," Chris called from the table. "I'll take care of them."

"All right," Matt said, and he quickly wiped the counter, loaded up the leftover bread and butter, his cheese and garlic powder, and he and Gloria stepped out the front door.

"That was fun," Gloria said. "Thanks for inviting me."

"Better than eating alone, right?"

"I don't mind eating alone sometimes."

"I seem to remember that about you." He slid her a smile, which she surprisingly returned. He sobered, something unsettling on his mind. "Do you…did you think Bev looked really ill?"

"Yes," Gloria said simply.

"Do you think I should say something to Gray?"

"You think he doesn't know?" Gloria studied him, her pretty eyes searching his.

"I don't know," he said. "I don't know how often he

comes to see them." Probably regularly, but maybe not right when Bev got up…at noon.

"If you're worried about it, and you think you should tell him, you probably should."

Matt just nodded, because he didn't want to overstep his bounds. At the same time, he knew Gray Hammond. They'd been working together for fifteen years, and he considered Gray one of his closest friends.

As they approached his cabin, he asked, "Would you come with me? To talk to him about his mother."

Gloria paused and looked at him again. He wasn't sure what was going on in her head, because she'd always been good at hiding how she really felt. Working on a busy cattle ranch, with dozens of rowdy men, she'd had to be.

"All right," she said. "Let me know when."

"Thanks, Gloria. Give me five minutes to put this stuff away, and I'll be right back to help you round up that cow." He started up the back steps. "Come on in out of the wind, if you'd like. I won't be long."

He didn't expect her to follow him, but she did, and Matt's nerves rattled around as he preceded her into his home. At the same time, her presence comforted him, and Matt wondered if he was ready to start thinking about allowing another woman into his life.

CHAPTER 21

Gray Hammond arrived at HMC just before lunchtime, his worry for his son propelling him all the way from the farm an hour away. He hadn't called Hunt and told him he was bringing lunch, and Gray wasn't terribly keen on going inside the building.

"You've been gone for years," he told himself. While the company provided excellent benefits and wages, surely a good majority of the people he'd known would be gone by now.

Gray reached for the sandwiches he'd stopped to get, and he got himself out of his truck and into the building. As he approached the receptionist desk, he recognized the man sitting there.

David Sanders stood, his eyes widening. "Mister Hammond?" he asked.

"It's just Gray," Gray said, remembering the days he'd strode by this desk, his power suit perfectly crisp, his shoes shiny, and his briefcase full of very important documents. Oh, what a different person he'd been then. "I'm hoping to see my son for lunch." He held up the bag of sandwiches. "He's assigned to Lab Six."

"Hunter, of course," David said, reaching for his keycard. "Let me get you in the elevator."

"I don't necessarily want to go in," Gray said, glancing toward the huge bank of elevators behind the desk. "I haven't told him I'm coming. Could you just find out when he has his lunch?"

David cocked his head to the side, and Gray knew what he was thinking. Why couldn't Gray just call his son and ask him to come outside for lunch?

"I know he's really busy on a project right now," Gray said, hoping that would explain enough. "He doesn't always have his phone. The lab supervisor is Helena Dunfield."

"Mm." David put down his keycard and picked up the phone. He dialed and spoke, and then pulled the receiver down from his chin. "She's checking right now. She thinks he and some others went into the diffractor room a while ago."

Gray nodded, glad his reason for not simply calling his son had panned out. Hunter hadn't been out to the farm much in the past month, and after he'd started therapy, Gray had learned how to tell when his son was pulling away.

He was definitely doing it right now, and Gray needed to tug him back into the center of the family. Hunter had no idea how central he was to the entire Hammond family, and after he'd spoken to Wes and Ames last night, Gray had planned this surprise luncheon today.

He feared Hunt was going to make decisions that would move him further from where he wanted to be, not closer. He was a brilliant man, with more intellect than Gray had ever seen. He had a dozen natural talents, and the things he didn't excel at, he worked hard to learn and master.

He'd been blissfully happy with Molly this summer, and about the time he'd decided to take the CEO job here, he'd started going quiet. Gray had asked him last night via text how things with Molly were going, and Hunter hadn't answered.

Silence and Hunter were never good, though they did like to play together.

"Okay," David said. "I'll let him know. Thank you, Helena."

Gray blinked and focused back on the receptionist. David gave him a smile. "Hunter is actually not in the lab today. He's on the twenty-fourth floor." David's eyebrows went up. "Would you like me to call the elevator?"

A war started inside Gray. He wasn't sure if he should go up to Laura's office or not. He'd had an office up on the twenty-fourth floor too, and he'd never once wanted to return to it. Something told him to go up, because he'd get to see his son in the CEO role. Maybe then the churning in Gray's gut would quiet.

"Sure," Gray said, pushing away from the desk. He followed David to the closest elevator and smiled his way inside the car that only went to the twenty-fourth floor. For

Hunt to get there, he'd have to ride from six down to the lobby, then in this very elevator up to twenty-four.

He arrived quickly, and when he stepped off, a woman stood who'd aged very well. "Myra," Gray said. "I can't believe you're still here." He laughed as she embraced him. "Have you seen Wes lately?"

"We went to dinner with his kids last time he was here." Myra stepped back, her smile genuine. "Only a couple of months ago."

"Of course." Gray still knew how to speak professionally, though he'd been feeding animals and raising children for the past thirteen years. "I heard my son was up here?"

"He's in with Laura," Myra said. "I sent her a text, as she's asked for no phone calls."

Gray looked down the hall, wondering what they could be talking about that required no interruptions. "You didn't need to do that. Surely they'll break for lunch." It was almost noon now. "I can just wait."

"Laura keeps an odd schedule," Myra said with a smile. Gray understood that code—his cousin probably ate breakfast at ten and lunch at two or three. Noon was not a milestone for her. Myra's phone chimed with a series of bells, and she leapt toward it. "Oh, that's her."

She picked up the phone and said, "They're on their way out now. You can go back if you'd like."

Gray gave her another smile and took the first step down the hall. He knew where the CEO's office was. He's spent hours in there with Wes, the two of them laboring, discussing, problem solving, and just talking as they worked here together.

Gray had loved working with his brother. He loved going to Coral Canyon in the summers and spending time with all of his brothers, as they'd all relocated up there. He wanted to move to Wyoming permanently too, and Elise did too. His parents were still here, though, and he still owned the farm.

At the same time, Gray knew his days in Ivory Peaks were numbered. Hunter was back, and his parents were older. Gray barely worked on the farm anymore, especially now that Hunt had kept Matt on full-time after their return from Coral Canyon.

"Gray," Laura said, coming out of her office first. "How good to see you." She wore a crisp skirt suit in dark red, making her sandy blonde hair even brighter. "I hope we didn't keep you waiting."

"Not at all," Gray said. "Had I known Hunt was up here, I'd have brought lunch for you too." He would have too. He held no ill will for Laura, though she'd definitely caused some issues for Hunter.

His son appeared in the doorway too, buttoning his suit coat before looking up at Gray. "Dad," he said, clear surprise in his voice. He glanced at Laura, as if she were a high school principal and Gray had been called in to discuss his disobedience. "What are you doing here?"

"I brought lunch." Gray lifted the bag of sandwiches again.

"The Salty Sub," Hunter said, a grin exploding onto his face. "They're my favorite."

"Use the conference room, Hunt," Laura said, and she retreated back into her office.

Gray nodded toward the conference room, and Hunter went inside first. Gray closed the door behind them and passed out the sandwiches. "I couldn't remember if you liked the London Wheel or the Salty Pig better. So I got both."

Hunter chuckled and started to unwrap both sandwiches. "I love them both. I'll eat half of each for lunch and finish the rest for dinner." He grinned at Gray and took a big bite of the sandwich with roast beef on it.

Gray's heart took courage, because Hunter seemed happy today. "How are you?" he asked, unwrapping his sandwich a little slower. He nudged a small bag of salt and vinegar chips toward his son.

Hunter nodded in an exaggerated way and finished chewing. "Good," he said. "I'm up here every Thursday now."

Gray took a bite of his sandwich, getting the honey roasted turkey beneath all the veggies he'd requested. He thought about what to say while he chewed and swallowed. "So full steam ahead on the job, then?"

Hunter nodded, his mood shifting right before Gray's eyes. "Only three months until I make the move permanently. I'm signing the paperwork next week, and it'll be public by Halloween."

Gray's chest pinched, and he couldn't say anything now.

His son was a grown adult. At twenty-five years old, Hunter could do whatever he wanted. He kept his eyes on his wrapper as he ate, his heart and mind combining to send up a plea to the Lord to help his son.

He'd said hundreds of such prayers over the years, and Gray saw no reason to stop now just because Hunter was an adult.

"Dad," Hunter said. "What did you come here to say?"

Gray looked up, realizing how quiet he'd become. "Nothing. Just wanted to see you."

"That's just not true," Hunter said quietly. He wadded up his wrapper and put it back in the bag. He met his dad's eyes. "You wouldn't have made the trip to ask me one question and eat a sandwich."

"Sure I would." Gray studied his son. He was so confident and so wonderful. "I feel like you've retreated from the family," he said, and Hunter started nodding.

"I've been really busy here," he said. "Trying to keep up with the work in the lab, taking stuff home from Laura." He hadn't mentioned Molly, and Gray hesitated to bring her up.

"I don't expect you to come out to the farm all the time," he said. "I don't know, Hunt. I just feel like you're pulling away, and I want you to know you can always come to me or Elise. We're here for you, and we love you."

"I know that, Dad."

"Good." He finished his sandwich, deciding as he did to learn everything he'd come here to learn. "Tell me the truth: You took this job, because you wanted to."

Hunter wiped his mouth with his napkin. "Yes," he said.

"It's actually been fun learning from Laura. I can do this, Dad."

"Of course you *can*, Hunt. It's not a question of whether you *can* or not. It's whether you *should* or not."

"You sound just like Molly."

"So you're still seeing her?"

Hunter shrugged. "We text and go to dinner every Friday. Does that count?"

"I don't know," Gray said. "Does it?"

Hunter rolled his eyes, his attitude salty today. Gray had put up with this when Hunt was a teenager, but he'd grown out of it quickly, and since then, they'd always enjoyed a great, mutually respectful relationship.

"She's working a lot," Hunter said. "I'm working a lot. We don't have the luxury of not having jobs, Dad."

"You don't need a job," Gray pointed out. "You're *choosing* to work here."

Hunter opened his mouth as if he'd argue, but he promptly closed it again.

Gray sighed, hating that after all these years, he still had no idea how to parent his son. "Listen, I know you don't want to hear it, but as your father, I need to say it."

"Go ahead," Hunter said, folding his arms.

"I'm worried about you. I love you so much, and I know you so well. I fear this is not the right place for you."

"Where would you place me?"

"The same place Uncle Wes would, and Uncle Ames. I spoke to both of them last night, and they were both quite surprised to hear you'd accepted the CEO job. I was surprised you hadn't told Wes, at the very least."

Hunter dropped his chin to his chest, clearly embarrassed. "I didn't know how."

"Because you knew what he'd say."

"Maybe."

Gray gave himself a few seconds to think and order his words properly. "Hunter, you have been blessed with a brilliant mind. I know you don't want to come straight to the farm, and I respect that. I know you'll end up there soon enough, and it'll be yours the moment you say you want it."

"I appreciate that, Dad."

"I know you love your science and your computers, and I fully support you working in Lab Six for as long as you feel like it's the right fit for you. I know it's important to you to help others, and the work in the lab feeds that." Gray took a breath, almost done. "I've been wondering how you're going to balance your job here with the equine therapy at the farm with your relationship with Molly. And that was just when you were working in the lab. It feels like a lot to me, and eventually something falls apart."

"Matt and Gloria are doing the majority of the equine therapy program," he said. "Molly too."

Gray nodded. "And you think seeing her once a week is where you want your relationship to be with her?"

"I don't know."

"Do you think that's where she wants it?"

"I don't know what she thinks."

He didn't know, because he hadn't asked her. Gray

wished he could shake his son and get him to wake up. "Hunter, you've loved that woman since you were fifteen years old. Stop and think about what you're doing. How many chances do you think you get?"

Anger entered his son's eyes, but Gray knew how to deal with an angry Hunter. It was the "I don't know" Hunter he hated. Or the one who said nothing.

"Dad, I really don't have time for a lecture."

"Okay." Gray stood up and gathered up his garbage. He took it to the trash can while Hunter rewrapped the sandwich halves he hadn't eaten. Amidst the movement and cleaning up, neither of them spoke.

Gray reached for the door handle and stepped out into the hall. He wasn't sure what he'd hoped would happen here today, but he felt like he'd failed.

"I'll ride down with you," Hunter said, and the two of them walked down the hall together.

"So good to see you, Myra," Gray said, employing his professional lawyer voice.

"Have a great afternoon, Gray."

He and Hunter got on the elevator, and the tension between them increased inside the enclosed area.

"What does Elise think?" Hunter asked.

"Your mother wants nothing but for you to be happy," Gray said.

"She doesn't think being CEO will do that." Hunter sighed. "No one does. What none of you get is that I don't either. I'm not doing this to achieve some level of happiness

I don't have yet. I'm doing it because I was asked to do it, and if I don't, there is no one else."

Gray just looked at his son, who glared back.

"I'm young," Hunter said. "I can do this for a couple of years, and then I can go back to the lab. Or out to the farm. Who knows? Who knows what life will bring?" His voice got louder, which wasn't typical of Hunter. "I have time, Dad. I don't need to get married and have a ton of kids right this second."

Gray nodded his agreement. "No, you don't. I just worry that if you don't hang onto Molly somehow, you'll lose her for a second time, and son, you might not get a third chance. A job is a job. Having the woman you love as your wife and the mother of your children makes your life worth living."

Hunter pressed his eyes closed and drew in a breath through his nose.

"One more thing," Gray said as the elevator started to slow. "You say you can do this for a couple of years and then move on. What I want to know is who you think will take your place in just two years? There's no one but you right now, and there will not be anyone else for at least another decade. At the very, very least."

The car dinged, and the doors slid open.

"Probably two decades," Gray said, reaching to put his hand over the door so it wouldn't slide closed. "Then you'll be forty-five, and looking for a wife the exact same way Uncle Wes did."

"It worked out for him."

Gray shook his head, because Hunter wasn't even listening. "Thanks for eating lunch with me, son. I love you." He stepped into Hunter and hugged him quickly, then got off the elevator and walked out of the building.

Buckled safely in his truck, Gray gripped the steering wheel and pressed his eyes closed. "Dear God, please bless my son. Hunter has already been through a lot in his young life, and he deserves a woman at his side who can love him and support him through all of his trials. He deserves to be that man for someone else. Please, please do not let him make a choice that will prevent him—or her—from having that. Please."

He wasn't sure if that woman was Molly Benson or not, but Gray knew the Lord did.

His phone rang, and the sound came through the radio speakers. Elise's name popped up on the screen, and Gray added one more "Please," before tapping to answer the call. "Hey, baby."

"Gray," Elise said. "Where are you? Could you stop by my office and get a folder for me? I accidentally left it there."

"Of course," Gray said. "I'm in the city, but I can stop on my way through town."

"The city?" Elise asked.

"Yeah." Gray sighed. "I came to visit with Hunt...."

CHAPTER 22

Molly waved goodbye to the last student running out the door, their oversized backpack bumping against their back. She pulled off her art apron and hung it by the door with a sigh, the week behind her now.

Finally.

Hunter usually called after school on Fridays, and they went to dinner together. They spent the whole evening together, and Molly had been telling herself that was enough for her for five weeks now.

She enjoyed talking to him and catching up on their week apart. He always ordered amazing food. He held Saltine, who adored Hunter, and he'd even brought a pouch of salmon for Gypsy last week. The cat had deigned to come down from the bookcase for as long as it took for Hunter to feed her the flaked fish bit by bit, then she'd gone right back to the top shelf and stared at him.

Kissing him still made her feel loved and cherished, and the fantasy in her head hadn't changed much. Molly knew what she wanted her marriage and relationship to be, and in the quietest of moments, she knew her reality with Hunter Hammond, should she marry him, wouldn't match the fantasy at all.

She skipped doing any prep for Monday, gathered her purse, shrugged into her coat, and left the elementary school. Several minutes later, she pulled into the driveway of her childhood home and called to her mother as she went through the front door.

"Molly." Mama poked her head out from the hallway. "What are you doing here, dear?" She came out and hugged Molly, thread stuck to her sweater.

"I need to make some cookies for tonight, and I thought you could keep me company." Molly grinned at her mother. "What are you working on?"

"Oh, Charlotte down the street has a daughter who really wants to be a purple people eater for Halloween." Mama looked down and picked the bright neon threads from her sweater. "I can spare a couple of hours." She smiled at Molly warmly. "How's school?"

"We've settled in nicely," Molly said. "I have such a great class this year." She'd needed it too, after last year's little devils. "I have a boy named Quinn."

"Wow," Mama said. "You don't hear that too often."

Molly shed her coat and draped it over the banister as she went past the steps. "He's the cutest little thing too.

Impossible to stay mad at, and he knows it." She laughed, and Mama giggled with her.

"What are the cookies for?"

"Hunter's uncle is in town," she said. "They're having a big dinner at the farmhouse, and I said I'd bring dessert." She opened a drawer in the kitchen and pulled out an apron. "I was going to make that Oreo mousse pie, but I don't have the energy." She gave her mom a quick smile. "There's always time and energy for chocolate chip caramel cookies, though."

"Always," Mama agreed, opening the pantry and retrieving the containers of flour and sugar. She continued to gather ingredients while Molly got down the recipe book from the small cupboard above the microwave.

"How is Kara doing?" Molly asked at the same time Mama asked, "How's Hunter?"

Molly focused on unwrapping the butter squares and putting them in a microwave-safe bowl.

"Kara's doing great," Mama said, filling the gap. "She doesn't like her Humanities class, but I think we all saw that coming."

"I did," Molly said. "She just has to get through those general ed classes, and she'll be fine."

Mama nodded and set a pot on the stove. "I'll do the caramel."

"Thanks, Mama." Molly put the butter in the microwave and set it for ten seconds. She didn't want it to be completely melted. She loved working in the kitchen with her mother, and strong memories flowed through her mind as she turned back to the recipe book to see how much sugar she needed.

"Ingrid's design professor asked her to teach a class next semester." Mama sounded so proud, and Molly knew why. Ingrid was a whiz when it came to fashion, and being asked to teach on a college level was a huge accomplishment.

"Wow," Molly said. "That's so great. She didn't tell me."

"She called this morning," Mama said. "I think she's planning to come home for Sunday dinner. You'll be there then, right?"

Before school had started, she and Hunter had spent the Sabbath at the farm, but for the past few weeks, Molly had been attending her family dinners on Sundays, the way she'd done before he'd returned to town.

"Yes," Molly said, measuring out the brown sugar.

"You can bring Hunter," Mama said.

"He goes out to the farm on Sundays," Molly said.

"Why don't you go with him anymore?"

"Uh." Molly twisted the tie on the brown sugar bag a little too hard. "He doesn't invite me? I don't know, Mama. We see each other on Fridays. That's the evening he's slotted me in."

To Mama's credit, she didn't respond right away. She poured a healthy amount of sugar into her pot and lit the flame beneath it. "Slotted you in?" she finally asked.

"Hunter Hammond is a very busy man," Molly said. "He's very good at compartmentalizing, and I get Friday night." He worked a lot, and she knew he spent the day in Laura's office on Thursdays. He ran errands and cleaned his house on Saturdays. Sundays were for family. He called his best friend in Cambridge on Mondays, and he saw Lucy, his therapist, every Tuesday.

Misery mixed within her as the butter and sugar creamed together, and Molly did her best to lace her tears behind a stoic mask. Mama didn't say anything while the mixer ran, but the moment it stopped, she asked, "What's going to happen with you two?"

"I'm going to break up with him," Molly said, shocked as the words came out of her mouth. She couldn't hold the tide of tears back then, and she focused on scraping down the sides of the bowl so she could add the eggs and vanilla.

"Molly." Her mother touched her shoulder, and Molly turned into her mother. She clutched her tightly while she cried. Thankfully, the tears dried up quickly, and she stepped back and reached for a paper towel.

Her makeup would be a mess, and she hated the over-hot feeling she got in her nasal passages and the back of her throat when she cried.

"It's fine," she said. "I just didn't realize that's what I was going to do until I said it."

"No?" Mama asked. "Why are you going to break up with him?"

"It's complicated," Molly said. "But honestly, Mama, I can't go along with someone who makes decisions that I know are going to make me terribly unhappy. I can compromise. I can discuss. I can accept a solution that's not exactly what I want. But I'm not going to bend, and bend, and bend until I break. Not again."

She shook her head. "I've been thinking about it a lot, and praying about it a lot, and I know that's the right decision for me." She glanced at her mother, who stirred the melting sugar on the stovetop without looking at it. She had her eyes fixed on Molly.

"I just keep coming back to—what was the point of my first marriage if I don't learn from it? Why did I have to go through that? To distrust myself and my every move?" She shook her head and cracked an egg into her creamed butter and sugar. "No. I learned from that experience that it's okay to compromise and sacrifice for the person you love." Her voice cracked, and she took a moment to put in another egg and measure her vanilla before continuing.

"But I can't go into this marriage knowing that all I'm going to get from him is Friday night. It's too far to bend. I'm already unhappy right now, and men usually act their best *before* the marriage."

Boy, did she know that all too well also.

"Maybe it'll be different once you're married," Mama said.

"If you knew how many times I told myself that while I was dating Tyrone...." Molly shook her head. "No. It won't. It actually gets worse, not better. Marriage is hard."

"I'm aware," Mama said, and Molly smiled as she paused the mixer again. She continued putting the cookie dough together, and her mother pushed the pot of salted caramel off the burner about the time she started scooping balls onto a sheet.

With those in the oven, Molly opened the fridge and took out a package of cheese. "I'm pretty sure I've gained ten pounds since school started." She opened the cheese and peeled off the top slice. "I can't stay away from this stuff."

Cheese was her weakness, and she loved the spiciness of pepper jack straight-up.

Mama smiled at her and cupped her face in one palm. "I'm very sorry about Hunter. I know how much you like him."

Molly's tears sprang to her eyes again. She didn't just like Hunter. She'd fallen in love with him all over again. She loved herself too, though, and she knew she simply deserved better than a man who could only fit her in for a few hours once a week.

LATER THAT DAY, SALTINE BARKED WHEN HUNTER rang the doorbell. Gypsy streaked out of the kitchen, and Molly picked up the tray of cookies and headed for the front door. She was dressed and ready, and after she opened the door, she said, "Hey, Hunt," and stepped onto the front porch with him.

"Let me," he said, taking the tray. "Are these those salted caramel chocolate chip cookies?" He looked at her with wide eyes full of hope, and she was reminded of the boy inside the man.

She smiled. "Yep."

"I love these." He started to peel back the plastic wrap. "Can I have one right now? I'm starving."

"You can have them all," she said. "You'll just have to be the one to explain why we didn't bring a dessert to your family potluck."

"Just one," he said, taking two cookies off the tray. A grin filled his whole face, and Molly couldn't remember the last time he'd looked so carefree. "Okay, two." He chuckled on the way to his truck, and he opened her door, the way he always did.

Molly second-guessed her decision to end things with him that evening. He was always such a gentleman with her, and he was twice as handsome in his blue jeans, black leather jacket with the yellow collar of his shirt peeking through, and his dark cowboy hat than he was in his suits and ties.

The conversation on the way to the farm was easy, and Molly talked about the art project she'd done that week, and what she was going to be for Halloween. Hunter told her about the visit from the head lab technician of a data analysis company in Texas that had come to Lab Six, and by the time they pulled up to the farm, they were caught up on each other's lives.

She hated the conversation, because it wasn't anything personal. It was a play-by-play of what had happened. Nothing about how she felt about her week, and nothing about what he was worried about at work.

She put a smile on her face as she mounted the steps at Hunter's side, because she didn't need to cause a scene at his family party. When he opened the door, light and sound spilled onto the porch, nearly knocking Molly backward.

Hunter likewise paused. "Oh, boy," he muttered. "Do we really want to do this?" He looked at her. "I quite enjoy our quiet Friday nights." With him looking at her like that, Molly would never break up with him. It was clear she was important to him.

Not important enough, she told herself. The feeling of selfishness came with the thought, and she'd been dealing with that every time it came too. She didn't feel like standing up for herself and what she wanted from a man and a marriage was selfish, though. She'd rather do that and be labeled selfish than regret yet another round of nuptials. There'd be no coming back from that.

"Hunter's here," someone said from within the house, and squeals of delight filled the air.

"Too late now," Molly said, but Hunter didn't hear her because of the small cousins running toward him.

"You better take this," he said, handing her the tray of cookies only moments before he scooped no less than three children into his arms. Molly smiled at everyone who came to greet Hunter, falling to the side as usual.

She didn't normally mind existing in Hunter's shadow, but tonight, she did. Tonight, it represented what the rest of her life would be like if she stayed with Hunter. Tonight, it served as a stark reminder of why she needed to break things off with him so they could both start to heal and move forward.

"Molly," Gray said, taking her by the elbow and guiding

her past the fray of cousins still mobbing Hunter. "Thanks for coming." He looked at her with something knowing in those dark eyes.

He took her into the back of the farmhouse, where two of his brothers stood around the long island with their wives. Elise, of course, scurried around the kitchen, setting dishes out, and putting serving utensils next to bowls and pans.

"Molly brought cookies," Gray announced, and Colton and Wes turned toward her. They walked over to her at the same time, and she hugged them simultaneously. More tears pressed against the backs of her eyes, and she held onto the strong shoulders of Hunter's uncles to try to contain them.

Colton released her first, and she had to step back. Neither Wes nor Colton backed up though. They studied her, and Molly couldn't hide her emotions fast enough.

"He's the biggest idiot," Colton said. "Honestly, Wes. He's going to lose her."

"Soon, by the looks of it," Wes said.

"Leave her alone," Bree, Wes's wife said, muscling through the two cowboys. "Come here, Molly." She put her arm around Molly's shoulders and guided her over to the table. "Dinner's almost ready, and you can sit right by me and Annie."

"Thanks," Molly said, taking her seat. She watched Gray, Colton, and Wes huddle up, and she really didn't like it.

"Hello," Chris called from the back door, and another round of noise reared up. They'd come to see Hunter's grandmother, who wasn't doing very well lately. Hunter had told Molly a couple of weeks ago that his grandmother had walking pneumonia and she wasn't getting any better, no matter what the doctors did for her.

His dad had called all of his brothers, and they'd arranged trips from Wyoming to come see their mother, just in case. Molly didn't want to think about Beverly Hammond dying, and she was sure Hunter didn't either. If she died, Hunter would be devastated, as he loved his grandparents so, so much. They'd helped to raise him, and he'd lived with them for many years, right here in this farmhouse.

Molly waited until most of the family had welcomed Chris and Bev, and then she took her turn. "Hello, you two," she said, hugging Bev first. "You look so pretty." She smiled at her, looking right into her dark eyes. "Hello, Chris."

"Hello, my dear." He hugged her too, and it was very easy after that to get lost among the Hammonds. With Wes's children, Colton and Annie, and Hunter's grandparents, there were sixteen people all told, including Molly.

Dinner began with a prayer, as usual for the Hammond household. The buffet took up the whole island, and Molly moved through the line behind Bree. She stuck close to the older woman, grateful for her presence at her side. Elise put her bottle of lemonade at the spot next to Molly, who looked up at her with questions in her eyes.

"Hunter can sit with his uncles," she said, her eagle eyes on the man in question. He was still in line with Wes in front of him and Colton behind, and Molly sensed an intervention coming.

She really didn't want that. *Coming here was a mistake,* she thought, if only because she didn't have great control of her emotions right now.

Nothing happened during dinner, and everyone exclaimed over the cookies once Elise put them out.

Finally, Hunter stood and reached for Molly. "We're gonna head out," he said. "I don't get to see her very often, and you guys have taken my whole night." He grinned around at everyone and a flurry of hugging and good-bying started.

Molly appreciated the quiet in a whole new way once she sat in Hunter's truck. He didn't say anything either, and it wasn't until he pulled into her driveway that she realized she was out of time.

"That was fun," she said.

He chuckled. "You're a good sport."

Molly smiled, but the gesture started to wobble on her face. "Hunter," she said, and it had the right amount of emotion in it to get him to look at her with alarm. She shook her head as a fresh round of tears arrived.

"I'm so sorry," she said, her voice pinched and a tad squeaky. "I think you're the most amazing person I've ever met, but you're on a path I can't go down."

"What are you talking about?"

He knew what she was talking about. They'd talked it to death already. "I'm not very happy with where we are right now," she said. "I don't see it changing for the better, and I'd like to be done."

"Done," he repeated.

"I'm so sorry," she whispered. "Thank you for a fun

night, and a...great summer." She needed to get out of this truck. "Good-bye."

She yanked at the door handle and practically leapt to the ground. She hurried up the sidewalk and through the front door, which she had miraculously not locked. If she had, she'd have stood on the porch with shaking hands, trying to get the key into the slim slot for the lock.

As it was, the door was closed behind her, and she fumbled to twist the lock before she'd even realized what she'd done.

Her mind may have been slow catching up to her heart, but only a moment later, they both knew what she'd done. She burst into tears at the same time her heart seemed to shatter, and she hurried away from the door so Hunter wouldn't be able to hear her in the off chance that he'd followed her.

Gypsy yowled, and Molly fed her through blurry, watery vision. She bypassed anything from the fridge tonight, and instead, gathered her fluffy, soft Saltine into her arms and retreated to bed with the pup, where she cried until she fell asleep from pure exhaustion.

CHAPTER 23

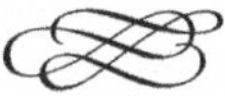

You're on a path I can't go down. Hunter couldn't get Molly's words or her tear-stained face out of his mind. Saturday evening, he put on basketball shorts and running shoes and went downstairs to the gym in his building. He ran. And ran. And ran.

On his way back upstairs, he suddenly understood why his father liked running. All Hunter could focus on was breathing. The pain in his calves. The hitch behind his lungs. Or maybe that was because the most physical activity he normally performed was horseback riding.

Sunday, he laid in bed and stared up at the ceiling, his alarm singing beside him. He didn't want to go to church, because then he'd see Molly. They'd been sitting together for months. What would people think when they didn't? What would her mother say to him? What would Pastor Benson think of him? What would his father say?

Hunter had managed to avoid the Hammond clan yesterday, but Uncle Colton and Uncle Wes were still in town. Not only that, but they'd both been texting him nearly non-stop, something he normally enjoyed. He loved his uncles, and he'd gone to them when he had problems in the past.

This felt like something he couldn't tell anyone about. At dinner on Friday night, Uncle Colton had even said he should get a ring on Molly's finger as soon as possible.

Hunter hadn't even been thinking about diamond rings. Not yet. His mind went round and round what isotope they could try in the lab, and the new budget proposal meeting Laura had scheduled for Thursday morning specifically so Hunter could attend.

His phone stopped playing the chime for him to get up, but it rang in the next moment. He rolled to pick up the device and saw Elise's name sitting there. He considered letting it go to voicemail. He could claim to be in the shower.

"Can't lie to the woman you consider a mother," he muttered, giving a tug to the power cord so it would come out. He tapped the green phone icon to connect the call. "Hey," he said.

"Hunter," she said pleasantly.

He laid back onto the pillow, deciding bed was a great place to spend the day. "What's goin' on?"

"You'll be at church, right?"

"Uh." He contemplated giving a fake cough. He couldn't do it. "Yeah." He sighed. "I'll be there. Why?"

"I know you don't get the emails, and Thea just sent out a plea for singers, especially men, in today's choir number."

"I can't—"

"If you do it, your father will," Elise said. "And Wes and Colton." She practically bit out the last syllable, and Hunter had the feeling all three men were standing right beside her, hanging on Hunter's decision.

A smile spread across his face. Of the four of them, he was the best singer, and it wouldn't be hard for him to stand up there and sing. Then he thought of having to look at Molly during the song.

If he showed up late and sat in the back, he wouldn't have to see her. He could duck out during the closing song and be out of the parking lot before she even stood up.

But if he went up front to sing...he'd have to look right at her to do it.

"I don't know, Elise," he mumbled.

"Seriously, Hunter," she said, her voice hushed now. "What will it take to get you to do it?"

A crazy thought entered his mind, and it would potentially blow something open that might not have been cracked yet. "You can keep everyone off my back about Molly Benson," he said. "Dad. Uncle Wes. Uncle Colton. All the uncles. I don't want texts about her, and I don't want to answer questions, and if there's even so much as a single breath that sounds like her name...." He let the threat hang there, because what could he honestly do?

"You make sure no one says a single thing about her today, and I'll sing the number."

Elise didn't respond right away. When she did, she asked, "Did something happen?"

"Yes," Hunter said. "She broke up with me on Friday night, and honestly, I wasn't going to go to church today. I was thinking I'd just lay in bed all day and do about fifteen crossword puzzles and never leave the condo again." He sighed miserably. "You want me to stand up in front of her and sing. I'll have to look her right in the eye. So I'm not doing it unless you can get everyone off my back. Not a single word."

"Oh, Hunter," she said. "I'm so sorry." She didn't commit to keeping everyone away or stopping the texting. "Your father and uncles love you, that's all."

"I know that," he said, pressing his eyes closed and wishing he could go back to sleep. When he slept, he didn't have to think. His heart didn't flop strangely in his chest. His thoughts didn't torture him.

"I'll call you back," she said, and just like that, she hung up.

Hunter groaned as he rolled into a seated position on the edge of his bed. Every muscle in his body hurt. "Why did I think running for an hour was a good idea?" He stood, but his back protested violently, and he fell back to the bed.

He finally managed to get in the shower, where the hot water helped loosen up some of his angry muscles. He shaved and brushed his teeth, swooped his hair up on the right, and dressed in his suit and tie.

Standing in front of the mirror in his bathroom, he barely recognized himself. He hadn't worn suits to school at MIT, and while he did wear a tie to work, he didn't have to pair it with a jacket.

"You will as CEO," he said to his reflection, his eyes finally finding themselves in the glass. That was the real change in him, and Hunter could only stare at the man he'd become.

Miserable.

He turned away from himself, because he'd been over it and over it, and there was no other way. He had to accept the CEO job. There was no one else, and he didn't *want* someone else to fill the seat.

"It should stay in the family," he said aloud as he sat on the corner of the bed to pull on his shoes. He'd been going out to the farm on Sundays after church, and he grabbed the backpack he took and checked to make sure the extra set of clothes inside was clean.

Set and ready, he went into the kitchen and pulled out a loaf of bread. While it toasted, he checked his work email. Laura had sent three messages, and he responded to them. He barely remembered buttering his toast, and he ate it almost as mindlessly.

Only when his phone rang again did he realize he'd been working on Sunday morning. This time, the screen said *Dad*, and Hunter looked up. If he didn't answer, his father would know why. If he did, he might have to talk about Molly.

He connected the call and put it on speaker. "Hey." He shoved another bite of toast in his mouth.

"Elise can't get your uncles to commit to leaving you alone about Molly," Dad said. "You might want to cut out the back."

Hunter sighed. "How am I supposed to do that, Dad?

Am I not coming to the farm today?" He suddenly wanted to be at the farm. It had been the one place he'd always belonged, no matter what. When his mother had left him, Dad had taken him to the farm. His grandparents had kept him for a few days while Dad figured everything out.

Whenever he got home from visiting Sheila in Florida, it was the simple act of feeding the goats that reminded him of who he was. He was Gray Hammond's son, not Sheila Hoopes's. It was Grandma who made sure he had the lemonade he loved. And Grandpa who taught him how to set a fencepost and how to saddle a horse.

Dad had been talking, but Hunter hadn't heard him. He clued in on, "...here. I'm just saying they want to talk to you about her. If you don't want that, you'll need to figure something out."

"I will," Hunter said. "Thanks for warning me."

"I love you so much, son," he said. "I'm sincerely sorry she broke up with you. I know how much you liked her."

"Yeah," Hunter said, because this felt like a conversation they'd had a decade earlier. "Thanks, Dad." He ended the call before his father could hear the emotion in his voice.

Hunter looked down at his toast and laid his head in his arms. "What am I supposed to do now?" he asked the Lord, not really believing he'd get an answer.

After all, he'd chosen the path he currently trod. He knew what he was supposed to do now. Get up and go to work every day. Run the family company. Be a Hammond.

WITH HALLOWEEN ALMOST UPON HIM, HUNTER centered the knot on his tie and reached for his jacket. He never went to work without the full package anymore, because Laura could call him up to the twenty-fourth floor at any moment. His team was frustrated with him, and Hunter couldn't fault them. He'd be upset if the guy who supposedly knew everything and was needed to run the experiments kept disappearing for days at a time.

He went down to the lobby, down the block, and up to the sixth floor. He pressed his palms against the front of his jacket as he entered Helena's office. "Good morning," he said crisply.

"Hunter." She smiled and stood to shake his hand. "I hate to see you leave."

He could only nod as he sat down in the chair opposite her desk. "HR says I can't keep doing both. Once the announcement is made, it'll be like a transfer."

She nodded, her curls bouncing with the movement. She reminded Hunter of a younger version of his grandmother. Dark, curly hair, pretty raven eyes, and a quick smile. "I got the email," she said, plucking a folder from her desk. She extended it toward him. "This is your transfer paperwork, just so everything is in line."

He took the folder but didn't open it. "Thank you."

"I really am going to miss you. Please do come down and see us anytime, and I might send some data up to you when no one down here can decipher it." She smiled, but Hunter knew she wasn't kidding.

"I'd love that," he said, standing. "I really am sorry. I didn't know all of this was going to happen."

"I know you didn't," she said, standing with him. "We'll just enjoy you while we can."

He nodded once and left her office. He shed his suit coat in favor of his lab coat and settled in front of his station. He tucked the folder under his keyboard and got to work.

Work was about the only thing Hunter could do these days to keep him from sinking into a deep depression or fighting the urge to smash his fist through the nearest object. He oscillated between hopelessness and anger so fast, sometimes even he got dizzy.

"Hunter," someone said, and he glanced up from his screen. Joel stood there, and he carried a personal-sized cake in his hands.

Hunter leaned back in his chair. "What's goin' on? It's not my birthday." He grinned at his friend.

Larry came over, and he had a candle he pushed down into the cake. "You've been here for five months," he said. "We have this big five month celebration in Lab Six, didn't you know?"

"We do?" Hunter asked with plenty of disbelief in his voice. About as much to match the sarcasm in Larry's.

Cassie put a stack of paper plates on Hunter's desk. "Yes," she said. "Here in Lab *Six,* we celebrate someone's *five*-month anniversary." She grinned at him and nudged his chair. "Now, get up. We want to sing to you."

Hunter chuckled as he did what she said. Somehow, they all knew he wouldn't be here for even six months, and even as he smiled at everyone in the lab who'd stood and faced him, a deep sense of sadness filled him. To think he'd been nervous about starting here, scared people would think he didn't belong, and terrified he wouldn't know what to do.

Cassie got up on a chair with Larry's help, and she raised her arm like she was about to lead the world' best choir. The team started a rousing song about five months in a job to the tune of *Row Your Boat*, and Hunter laughed through the whole thing.

Joel lit the candle and said, "Hurry up, or the smoke detectors will go off. Larry, you ready?"

"Ready." He held a big, blue, plastic bowl in his hands and carried a smile on his face.

Hunter stepped forward and blew out the single flame, and Larry quickly capped the cake with a plastic bowl. Hunter shook his head, because the smoke would get out sooner or later, but he supposed Larry and Joel knew what they were doing.

There was just the one cake, and everyone else went back to their tasks. Cassie, Larry, and Joel pulled up chairs while Hunter cut the cake into quarters. Once they each had a chunk, he grinned around at them. "Thank you," he said. "How did you guys find out?"

"You've been wearing a suit and going to the twenty-fourth floor for a month," Cassie said. "Call us crime scene investigators." She looked at Larry, and the two of them laughed.

"You're a Hammond," Joel said. "The smartest one I've known, and you're the only one your age. I told Helena the day you started you wouldn't be in the lab for longer than a year."

Hunter forked off a bite of cake but didn't put it in his mouth. "You did?"

"Absolutely," Joel said. "Your mind is like a computer, Hunt. You can handle a dozen tasks at the same time. You're a natural fit for CEO."

Hunter ate the cake, the rich chocolate making his taste buds rejoice. "No one in my family is happy I'm taking the job."

"Why not?" Larry asked.

"My girlfriend broke up with me because of it."

"Hunter," Cassie said sharply. "Why didn't you come to me? I would've told you what to do."

"What do I do?" he asked, not meeting her eye. Instead, he took another bite of cake.

"You march up to her front door with the biggest bunch of flowers you can find. Her favorite kind." She pointed around at the three men gathered at Hunter's desk. "It's not always red roses, by the way. Do some homework, you guys."

"Hey, my wife likes red roses," Joel said.

"I'm just saying," Cassie said. "You ring the doorbell, and you tell her you can't be the CEO unless she's beside you. *Beside*, Hunter. Not behind. Right at your side. That you *need* her to do this, and without her, you'll surely fail."

He listened to her and even nodded, but he wouldn't do what she'd advised. Molly didn't want to be at his side while he worked a hundred hours a week. She wanted him at her side in their home. She wanted him at her side when she brought home their baby and when she got home from work.

If he worked three times as much as a normal person, he really didn't have time for a wife or family. He could remember the hours his father kept, and Hunter had spent more time in this high-rise building in downtown Denver than he cared to admit. Dad had worked early mornings and late nights. He'd worked weekends and holidays. He'd brought Hunter when he couldn't take him to the farm or a friend's house, and Hunter once again envied his half-siblings who'd gotten a completely different version of their father.

Everything became ultra-clear in that moment. Molly was absolutely right. Dad was too. He really couldn't have everything, and it was time to stop hoping and praying and believing he could.

"Hunter." Helena came running into the office area. "Your father is on the phone. He's been trying to call you."

He stood up at the panic on his boss's face. "What is it?" he opened his top drawer and pulled out his phone, which he kept on silent. Dad had called six times.

Hunter didn't need to dial him back to know. A text flashed on the screen confirming the terror gathering into a tight knot in Hunter's stomach.

Dad: *911 - Hunter - call me. It's Grandma.*

CHAPTER 24

Wesley Hammond kissed his wife, wishing he'd had more years with her. So many more years. Bree completed him in a way he didn't understand and hadn't been able to predict, and he couldn't imagine life without her.

His dad now had to live without his version of Bree, and Wes had no idea how he was going to do it. The task of making it through even one day felt too hard for him, and his eyes burned.

"Come on, baby," Bree whispered. "We have to get ready to go out."

Wes didn't want to. He didn't want to leave his mother. He didn't want his children to grow up without their grandmother. He didn't want to have to watch his father try to be brave during the next few hours.

He turned away from Bree and faced his dad. He already had the mask cemented in place, and Wes's heart wept for him. He gripped Bree's hand and went around the casket to stand next to his father. "Hey, Dad."

Dad put his hand on Wes's arm and squeezed. "Will you say the family prayer, Wesley?"

"Of course," Wes said, though he didn't know how he was going to do that. Dad should've asked Ames, as the man never cried. Even now, standing in the room with the family and their deceased mother, he looked as rock-solid as always. His eyes shone with danger, and he didn't miss a single move anyone made. Ames would definitely be able to get through a prayer without crying.

Wes would not.

Gray and Hunter approached, and Gray would tap his watch and lift his eyebrows. Ever the taskmaster, Gray kept the family on track in all matters. He organized holiday events and sent birthday cards to every single niece or nephew, without fail. Wes's children adored their Uncle Gray, because he never forgot about them. Hunter was a massive plus in Gray's column too, as well as Elise. She always had candy or cookies for Wes's kids, and she loved them as much as she loved her own.

"Are we going to do the prayer soon?" Gray asked.

"I just asked Wesley."

Gray and Wes exchanged a look, and Gray turned around. "Everyone gather around, please. Wes is going to say the family prayer, and we'll need to follow the casket into the chapel."

The family circle tightened, and Wes reached for Hunter's hand. The boy meant so much to Wes, and he hated seeing the tears in his nephew's eyes. Worse was watching them stream down his face.

Elise came to Hunter's side and pressed into him, and that seemed to help him quiet his sobs. It certainly didn't help Wes, whose chest now heaved, and he hadn't even started yet.

He closed his eyes so he wouldn't have to see anyone else's reaction, and he bowed his head. There were no jokes today. No funny cowboy hats. No hugs with loud clapping on the back.

"Dear Lord," Wes started, and he couldn't quite continue. He swallowed and breathed and reached for Bree's hand. With her fingers between his, he could go on. Another breath, and he said, "We thank Thee for an opportunity to get together as a complete family unit. We love Thee with all our hearts, and we ask Thy spirit of comfort and peace to be with us in abundance today."

GRAY COULD LISTEN TO HIS BROTHER PRAY forever. Wes possessed a power and leadership that made others flock to him, Gray included. He'd always looked up to his oldest brother, and today was no different.

He had no idea how to comfort Hunter, and Elise had done her best.

Wes's prayer was so beautiful that Gray actually felt his heartbeat calm as Wes asked for the Lord's blessing on any in the family that needed that sense that all was well, that

He was in charge and He now encircled their mother in His loving arms.

Gray let his own tears fall silently down his face. He told himself he was allowed to cry at his own mother's funeral.

"Bless Dad with an outpouring of love, and bless each of us here to remember him in his time of need. In Jesus' name, Amen."

"Amen," Gray said, drawing in a deep breath and wiping his eyes quickly. He held the hand of each of his little boys, with Jane stuck to Tucker's side. Elise had told the children to do exactly as she said, and she'd instructed Deacon and Tucker to hold Gray's hands, and for Jane to never stray more than three feet from Tucker.

Elise could be commanding when she wanted to be, and Gray watched her look up at Hunter and wipe his tears and say something to him. He nodded, and she hugged him. It was odd seeing her be the strong one out of that pair, as Hunter was at least twice as big as Elise in every way.

"Please line up in order," Dad said. "Wes, Gray, Colton, Ames, Cy."

"Grandpa," June asked, her voice so tiny and so sweet. "Can I walk by you?"

"June," Ames barked. "Leave Grandpa alone."

"It's okay," Dad said, waving away Ames and his fury. He bent down and looked at little June. "You can walk right beside me, darling. Will you hold my hand and make sure I go where I'm supposed to?"

The four-year-old nodded, and she linked her hand into Dad's. He straightened and nodded to the funeral director.

He and another man began to wheel the casket toward the door.

Gray tugged on his boys' hands and they joined Hunter and Elise in the proper order. The walk down the hall seemed to take an eternity, and he hated more than anything else he'd done in his life walking into the chapel at the funeral home through the back door. He had to walk up the aisle to the front rows that had been reserved for the family, and everyone stared at them.

Dad sat right behind the casket, and Wes's family filled in the bench on his right.

"Go around to the left," Gray whispered to Hunter, and he led the family to the left side of the bench, sitting right next to his grandfather. Everyone else, including Dad's siblings and their children, and their children's children, filed in behind them. It seemed to take forever for the Hammond family to fill the benches, and then Pastor Benson stood up and positioned himself behind the mic.

The man had obviously been crying too, and that only made Gray's breath freeze in his chest, as if someone had taken their giant boot and stomped on his lungs.

"Welcome, everyone," Pastor Benson said smoothly. "What a beautiful, solemn occasion. I can feel the intense love this family has for Beverly Hammond." He looked down and shuffled his notes. "We'll start our program today with a life sketch by Colton Hammond, son of Beverly and Christopher Hammond. After Colton, we'll have a musical number by Ava and Ella Hammond, two of Beverly's granddaughters."

He looked up and out into the crowd. "We'll go to that point." He sat back down, and behind Gray, Colton stood up and made his way up onto the dais to speak into the mic.

One look at his younger brother's face, and Gray was beyond relieved his name had not been in his mother's final letter, at least not for a major part in the funeral. She'd assigned all the talks right there in her notes to her sons, and Gray's part was to feed everyone and make sure she was buried on the farm, not in the town cemetery.

That had been trickier than Gray had anticipated, because there were laws about where bodies could be buried. Gray had managed to ensure his mother's wishes would be honored, and he and Elise had enough food to feed the entire town of Ivory Peaks at the church, and they'd spoken to Margie Benson about helping to get it all set up while the family was at the cemetery.

Colton looked up, his dark eyes bright, and Gray thought, *Bless him, Lord.*

Colton Hammond had loved his mother with a love that couldn't be described. As he looked at the rows and rows of family members, he wondered if his mother could see them too. His eyes caught Annie's, and her slight nod gave him the courage to say what he needed to say.

"Beverly Trudy Clarke Hammond was born right here in Colorado," he said, his voice steady and clear. "As a little girl, she loved to watch the sun rise, and she used to get into trouble for leaving the house before dawn." He smiled, thinking he'd gotten the best job at the funeral.

"In fact, Mother used to get into a lot of trouble. She once brought bubble gum to school and got it stuck in her hair. When her mom came to get her, she threatened to cut her hair clean off because of it. Thankfully, my grandmother was good with a pair of scissors, and Mom didn't have to lose much hair.

"Later, though, Mom climbed onto the Ridgeway Bridge and jumped into the river below." He chuckled and shook his head. "She 'accidentally' told two boys she'd go to the same prom with them. She forgot to fill her radiator with antifreeze and broke down on the side of the road." He cleared his throat.

"The man who rescued her became her husband about six months later, and Bev became a Hammond on February eleventh, during the biggest snowstorm the Rocky Mountains has ever seen. She and Dad couldn't leave the reception venue to go on their honeymoon. Dad decided they couldn't stay in a ballroom, and he drove them to a local hotel, nearly crashing the car a dozen different times." He grinned out at the crowd. "Of course, the more Mom told that story, the more times Dad almost killed them."

Everyone twittered, and Colton consulted his notes again. "Mom and Dad wanted a big family, and they tried hard to get a girl." His throat closed, because he loved his brothers with every bit of his heart. "Instead, they got five big, loud, strapping, complaining, dedicated sons." He took a moment to look every one of his brothers right in the eyes.

Wes looked one breath away from collapse, and that surprised Colton. He was always the most put together; the strongest.

Right now, though, it looked like Gray had taken that role. Cy hadn't looked up once, and he didn't now either, and Colton knew he'd need to make sure his brother went to counseling every week for a while. Ames held his head high, his jaw so tight, Colton thought it might break by the end of the funeral.

"We put our mother through several disasters," he continued. "I think she prayed daily for her own sanity while we were teenagers, and then once we became adults, she'd beg the Lord to send us a good woman so she could be a grandmother." His throat clogged again, and he swallowed to get the lump to go away. "Gray was her favorite son, because for many, many years, he was the only one who had made Mom's deepest wish come true. He gave her Hunter, and—"

Colton couldn't go on. He'd looked at Hunter, and that was a huge mistake. The man cried openly, and Colton wanted to wrap him in a tight hug and hold him until all the pain went away. He'd tried to do that for the boy when he was a child, and it felt like this was too big, too all-encompassing for anyone to ever make right.

Colton reached up and wiped his eyes. "Mom and Hunter were cut from the same cloth. She loved him with everything inside her, and he did the same for her. Everyone knows she made sure he had the lemonade he loved, and for the longest time, Hunter had a special desk where Mom kept his crossword puzzles for him.

"She did that for everyone important to her. If Mom found out someone loved to bake, she'd put together a recipe book for them. When Gray married Elise, she set up a sewing studio for her. When Matt told Mom he missed his kids, she put together care packages for them and mailed them to Montana. When my daughters got married, Mom sent cards and gift baskets filled with fruit and chocolate."

Colton had so much more he could say, but he felt like he needed to wrap this up. He looked down at his notes, his vision blurring with tears. He had no idea how to finish or what to say next, and panic reared within him.

AMES HAMMOND WATCHED HIS BROTHER AT THE pulpit, and there was definitely something wrong. He sat on the end of the row, and without hesitating, he got to his feet and started toward Colton. He had no idea what he'd say once he got up there, and he certainly didn't want any eyes on him. It was bad enough that he had to dedicate the gravesite, but his father said it was a simple prayer. Ames knew how to pray, but his emotions had been so tangled since his mother's death that he still hadn't ordered the words properly.

Colton turned toward him as he walked the last few steps. "Where were you?" he whispered, and Colton held up a whole sheaf of papers, his eyes wild.

Ames put his hand on Colton's and looked him in the eye. "Deep breath," he murmured. They breathed in together, and Colton started to calm. Ames had never thought of his older brother as one who'd panic. Everything Colton did seemed flawless, and he, as the middle brother, was the glue that kept the family together.

Ames suddenly knew what to say. He nudged Colton a foot or two to the side and looked at the crowd. "Mom taught Colton that he was the glue for the family. See, he's the middle brother, sandwiched right between two perfect older brothers and then two rebellious twins. She used to tell him that the Good Lord sent him straight to her, to help her keep the family united." He looked at Colton and smiled. "He's always done it too, and I think he's struggling a bit to figure out how to keep doing it without Mom in his corner. He used to use her as a reason why we all needed to get along. He'd say, 'Come on, you guys. Mom just wants us all to get along for one afternoon. It's Mother's Day.'"

His own throat closed, but panic wasn't anywhere nearby. He faced the crowd again, his love for Colton as bright as it ever had been. "Now he'll have to figure out how to unite us without Mom, and I suppose y'all better start praying he can find a way to do it."

Several people laughed quietly, and Ames smiled too. "We love our mother with our whole hearts, all of us boys. She loved and accepted us for who we were, and she did the same for our wives and children. She was an exceptional woman." He reached up and pressed one hand to his heart, glad each of his brothers automatically did the same, even Colton.

With that, Ames nodded and gestured for Colton to go in front of him. He did, and the two of them left the dais so Cy's twins could perform their musical number.

"Thank you," Colton said when they reached their bench. "I just froze up there."

Ames could only nod as he retook his spot on the end of the bench. His one-year-old, Jilly, climbed into his lap, her thumb in her mouth. He cuddled her, needing the love of a precious child to calm him. His pulse continued to sprint through a beautiful musical number about springtime and the Savior, and Ames pressed his eyes closed and prayed he could stuff this sadness and nervousness behind the wall of anger.

Anger he knew how to manage. Anger he could control. Anger he understood.

If he could just stay angry enough until the funeral, burial, and family luncheon ended, then he could cry behind closed doors. His sons started to whisper on the bench next to him as the pastor got up and said Wes would be the final speaker, and Ames turned his attention to them as they continued to argue.

"Knock it off," he growled. Sophia reached over and took the coloring book from Lars. She indicated he should go sit on her other side, and she scooted over to separate the twins. She met Ames's eyes, and his gratitude for her doubled.

She lifted her arm around Chris and patted Ames's

shoulder, a gorgeous smile on her face. It wobbled, and Ames knew she'd miss his mother as much as he would. His eyes burned, and he seized onto the warmth and used it to strengthen his anger.

As he turned back toward the front, everything got cemented back into its rightful place, where he could deal with it later.

Cy Hammond watched his girls sing for their grandmother, and it made his heart fill with love. Over and over and over. When they returned to the bench, he took them both into his arms and whispered how amazing they were.

The Lord had given him and Ames a set of twins each. Ames had boys; Cy girls. Ava sat on his lap while Ella took the spot on the bench next to him.

Cy was in a bad way, but his heart had been lifted by the spirit of song, and he glanced over at Patsy. She met his eye, worry in hers, and he gave her a fast smile. She bent to pick up something Wade had just thrown on the floor, and Cy reached for the two-year-old too. He pulled the boy on his lap and pointed up to the front. "See Uncle Wes? We have to be quiet so we can hear him."

Wes read a poem that was their mother's favorite, and he talked about everyday life with her. "She asked me no less than fifty times if I was seeing anyone," he said, a big smile on his face. "I think she about died when I finally told her I was dating Bree. In fact, she was rendered speechless, and anyone who knows Mom knows how hard that is to do."

Cy smiled, and the rest of the funeral felt more like a celebration instead of a tragedy. When Gray had called and said Mom had died, Cy hadn't been able to move. He'd stood in his office in the motorcycle shop, numb from head to toe. His secretary had found him there, and her voice had unfrozen him.

Since then, it felt like every cell in his body buzzed and raced and zipped through his blood. Only now did he start to feel slightly calmer.

The service ended, and once again, the family paraded after the casket. They gathered on the sidewalk outside while the casket was loaded into the back of the hearse, and then the funeral director said, "Family should follow first, and then guests. We'll begin the graveside service in thirty minutes."

Thirty minutes, Cy thought. Maybe he could breathe normally for thirty minutes. His role in the funeral was to speak at the luncheon. Her letter specifically stated that it didn't need to be long, but that Mom wanted each of her sons to contribute to the events of the day.

Cy still wasn't sure what to say at the luncheon, but Gray had arranged for it to happen at the church, and Cy figured the Lord would be there to guide him.

Cy's girls stayed close to him, and he led them toward their truck. "Climb in, guys." He turned to help Patsy with Wade, and he lifted the child into the car seat strapped in the back. “Tommy, you ride up front like on the way here.” His five-year-old did as he said, and when Cy got behind the wheel, he started the truck and paused.

He met Patsy’s eyes, and then each girl’s in the rearview mirror. “I love you guys,” he said. “Each of you, so much. Your mother loves you, and we’re glad each of you are in our family.” He reached across Tommy and took Patsy’s hand in his.

“Love you, Daddy,” Ella said, and Ava echoed it.

“Love you, Dad,” Tommy said, and from right behind him, Wade said, “Wuv, da, da, da.”

Cy started to laugh, and that caused everyone else to do the same. As he turned on his lights and eased into the procession behind Colton, Cy took a moment to press his eyes closed and whisper, “Thank you, Dear Lord, for this family of mine.”

For his small, core family of six, and for the large extended Hammond family of at least sixty. For his brothers. They were crazy, yes. Loud and obnoxious too. But they were his, and he was theirs, and he loved them powerfully.

CHAPTER 25

Molly stood on the sidewalk, her hands tucked in her pockets, as Beverly Hammond's casket got loaded into the back of the hearse. She stood close to her mother and father, not daring to get too near Hunter.

He hadn't seen her, and she didn't want him to. He was already in enough distress, and she didn't need to add to it with her presence at his grandmother's funeral. Seeing him cry made her heart break right in half, and she wished she could be the one at his side, holding him up and whispering things to keep him strong.

She watched Elise do that, and then they walked with Gray and the littles, as Hunter called them, over to a minivan.

"Are you going to the cemetery?" Mama asked.

Molly shook her head. "No, I'll go to the church and start getting things ready." She gave her mother a quick smile, holding back the tide of tears. They weren't all for Bev, though she'd known her well enough to weep over. "I spoke to Elise, and she gave me some instructions."

"We'll be along in a few minutes," Mama said, turning with Daddy to talk to the Housers, long-time members of their church.

Molly hadn't seen Hunter in three weeks, since she'd broken up with him. If he came to church, he sat behind her and slipped out before she could stand at the conclusion of the sermon and sweep the back of the chapel. She missed him so much and seeing him today reminded her of how much she loved him and wanted to support him.

But he'd been announced as the next Chief Executive Officer of Hammond Manufacturing Company two days ago, and it sure felt like he'd taken another dozen steps down a path where she couldn't follow.

The suit he wore today looked like it belonged on a CEO, and Molly finally turned away from him. She drew in a deep breath of the crisp mountain air and started toward her sedan. The plain, four-door, navy blue car epitomized everything about Molly's life.

Mundane and boring. Predictable. Sensible.

She couldn't help who she was or what made her comfortable, and she'd never felt like she had to apologize for being herself. Now, as she unlocked the car and got behind the wheel, she wondered why she'd ever thought she could be with a man like Hunter Hammond. The man was extraordinary, and while some said opposites attract, that didn't mean the couple ended up together.

At the church, Molly shed her coat and hung it outside the kitchen. She tied an apron around her waist and looked at the bags and boxes of food covering every available inch of counter space.

She started removing the items from the bags and lining them up. It was simple work, and it comforted her. Her mind felt less frenzied as she put bagged salads together and grouped the bottles of dressings nearby.

Long, covered aluminum trays sat on the stove, and Molly heated the three ovens in the kitchen to two hundred and fifty degrees and slid the meat and mashed potatoes inside to keep warm.

She went into the attached gymnasium, where her father and two deacons from their church had set up the tables and chairs earlier that day. Three tables had been pushed end to end to make the buffet, and Molly began bringing out paper plates, plastic cutlery, a huge bowl for the salad, the bottles of dressing, and serving spoons for the hot food.

She found a basket for the bread and started untwisting the ties on the bags. The back door opened, and Mama and Dad came in, talking in low voices. Molly flashed them a smile, glad when Ingrid and Kara bustled in from the cold too. Lyra hadn't made the trip from Utah, and Molly missed her, the hole she'd left in their family so large in that single moment of time.

"I've got things set up out in the gym," Molly said. "Just cutting the bread now."

"Did you get the drinks?" Mama stepped over to one of the fridges and opened it. "Ingrid, everything in here." She opened the oven next. "Okay, good. This is warming." She looked at Kara and nodded to the other fridge across the kitchen. "There's barbecue sauce in that one. A couple of other sauces. Those go out on the tables too, please."

Dad left the kitchen, and Molly glanced at his back as she sliced through another roll. Mama and Ingrid mixed punch in a huge drink dispenser and then filled individual pitchers with it before taking them out to the tables.

"Butter," Mama said on one of her trips back into the kitchen.

Molly had just finished the bread and nodded to where it sat on the counter. "I'll take these out and come help."

Her mother's skin carried a hint of grayness, and Molly wondered when she'd eaten last. She took the rolls out to the buffet, glancing around at the few people who'd started to arrive. She didn't want to see Hunter, but she couldn't help scanning for him anyway.

None of the Hammond sons were there, and Molly ducked back into the kitchen, relief pouring through her. Mama stood at the counter, one palm pressed against it, her eyes closed.

Alarm rang through Molly. "Mama?" She hurried across the kitchen to her, noticing she'd gotten down a stack of small plates but she hadn't started unwrapping butter cubes yet. "What's wrong?"

"I have a terrible headache," Mama said, opening her eyes. She smiled softly. "I'm okay. I just need to take some pills. They're in my purse. Would you?"

"Let me get you a roll too," Molly said, already turning

away. She hurried back into the gym, snatched a roll, and returned to the kitchen. She collected the pills and poured her mother a glass of punch from the leftover liquid in the drink dispenser. "Here. Eat. Take these."

Her mother swallowed the pills and took a bite of the roll, still smiling. "Thank you, Mols."

"Let me help you to Daddy's office," Molly said, linking her hand under her mother's arm.

"I'm okay."

"No," Molly said firmly. "You're gray and exhausted. You need to eat that whole roll, and you need to rest for a few minutes. Ingrid, Kara, and I can handle this."

Kara came into the kitchen and looked at them. "What's going on?"

"Mama needs help getting to Dad's office." Molly turned toward her. "Is everything set out there?"

"Dad's helping Cy with the mic right now." Kara came toward their mother, the same alarm on her face. "Come on, Mama."

"Get the hot food out," Mama said over her shoulder, and Molly nodded at her. She opened a drawer and found hot pads. She started tossing them on the counter, and when Ingrid returned from setting out the pitchers, Molly indicated them.

"Put those on the buffet for me, would you? I'm going to bring out the trays." She opened the oven and pulled the first of several long trays out of the oven. With two filled with meat and two with potatoes on the table, Molly surveyed the buffet.

"Butter," she murmured, the chatter and number of people in the gym swelling by the moment. She and her sisters put cubes of butter on plates, and they spread out to put them on each table. Along with the pitcher of punch, and the salt and pepper shakers, the plate of butter completed the necessary items on each table.

Molly had just finished putting her last plate on the front table when Cy Hammond stepped to the microphone. "Ladies and gentlemen," he said, his voice so like Hunter's it made Molly's whole chest vibrate.

She kept her head down as she headed for the back of the gym. With any luck, she could escape to the kitchen and send out Ingrid or Kara when something needed to be replaced. With her heart pounding, she made it through the doorway and into the kitchen, where her breath whooshed out of her mouth.

"Anything else?" Ingrid asked, looking up from her phone.

"I think we're set."

"What happened with Mama?" Kara asked.

Molly filled them in, and they agreed to talk to Dad after the luncheon ended. As far as Molly knew, Mama's cancer was in remission, but she had to take care of herself if she expected to have the energy and health she wanted. "She just didn't eat this morning."

"She'd started to perk up a little when I left her," Kara said.

Ingrid turned her phone toward Molly, who peered at the texts. Her eyes scanned, her brain trying to make sense of the conversation she'd come into mid-sentence. She glanced to the name at the top of the screen. "Who is Mister Plaid Shirt?"

"It's this man in my floriculture class," Ingrid said with a flirty smile. "He's the only male, so he's naturally quite popular." She hit all the consonant sounds really hard. "He asked me to dinner last week, and it was magical." She sighed as she smiled down at the phone. "Kissed me on the first date."

"Ingrid," Kara said with a giggle. "What does he look like?" The three of them crowded around her phone while Ingrid pulled up her gallery and showed them a couple of pictures. A man with light hair smiled at them, his teeth straight and white, his eyes a brilliant shade of blue.

She flipped to a picture of the two of them, and Molly said, "You guys are adorable together. He's handsome, Ingrid. What's his real name?"

"Hans Sellers," she said. "Isn't that a great name?"

"Oh, boy," Kara said, rolling her eyes. "She's really smitten."

"Ingrid Sellers," Ingrid said, a long sigh coming from her mouth.

Molly giggled and stepped back. "I'm happy you like him so much, Ingrid." She moved over to the doorway and peered out. "But what about you not getting married until you're thirty-five?"

"Well, plans aren't set in stone." Ingrid joined her in the doorway.

Cy still stood at the microphone. "...used to say that

work would do our souls good." He smiled around at everyone. "Anyway, I learned a lot from my mother, but the thing I learned best was how to love." He smiled around the gym, and Molly felt the love he spoke of way down deep in her chest.

She couldn't help looking for Hunter, and he sat at a table near the front, his father on one side and his grandfather on the other. He held his youngest brother on his lap, and one of his uncle's little girls as well.

Molly watched him while Cy said one of his uncles would say the prayer over the food, then they'd be eating from the buffet at the back of the gym. An older gentleman stood up, and he did belong to the Hammonds, though he wasn't nearly as dark as Hunter and all of the men in his family.

Molly folded her arms and bowed her head, studying the pattern on the tile at her feet, adding her own prayer for peace and comfort for this good family.

SEVERAL DAYS LATER, MOLLY'S PHONE RANG AS SHE pulled into the parking lot at school. Matt's name sat on the screen, and her heart beat out a couple of extra thumps. She quickly tapped the icon to open the call. "Matt, hi," she said.

"Good morning, Molly," he said, and she calmed slightly. "I was wondering what you're doing this weekend. Chris and I have lunch quite often, and he asked about you."

Molly turned into a parking spot and put her car in park. "He did?"

"He said Bev spoke of you often, and he found something she'd set aside for you."

"Oh." Molly stared out the window at the stormy sky, wondering what in the world Bev Hammond would've set aside for her. She thought quickly through her schedule for the weekend as Matt continued to say he and Gloria ate lunch with Chris almost every day.

"I can come tomorrow or Sunday," she said, hoping with every fiber of her being he'd say tomorrow. Hunter surely went to the family farm on the Sabbath. "Tomorrow would probably be best," she said. "My mother's been feeling a little under the weather, and I'm cooking on Sunday for my family."

"I'm sorry about your mother," Matt said. "Is she okay?"

"Yes," Molly said, swallowing. She'd gone in for another round of tests just yesterday, and hopefully they'd all hear the results very soon. "She's just...run down." Molly didn't know how else to describe it. Mama wasn't sick with a virus or anything like that. She was just exhausted, and Molly had seen her this tired when she'd gone through her chemotherapy treatments.

She really didn't want to watch her mother go through that again, and she pressed her eyes closed as she said a quick prayer.

"Tomorrow's fine," Matt said, breaking into her thoughts. "Gloria's right here, and she says if you wear the right shoes, she'll give you another lesson." He chuckled, and Molly joined in with a giggle.

"She's got a deal," Molly said. The call ended, and she faced the day with a better mood than she'd had a few minutes ago.

The following day, she showed up at the farm wearing blue jeans, a sweater, cowgirl boots, and a coat. She pulled a knitted hat over her ears as she got out of her car, and she smiled at Gloria when she came out of the barn.

"Molly," she said. "I haven't seen you in a while."

"Yes." Molly didn't know what else to say, and she gave Gloria a quick hug that felt more awkward than friendly. She got the distinct impression that Gloria didn't let too many people get too close to her, so when Matt joined them and she gave him a warm smile, it was practically the temperature of lava.

The wind rustled through the trees on the far side of the pasture from where they stood, the rushing of it as it moved almost like the sound of a river. Molly loved the woods, the mountains, and the trees. She loved nature, and she smiled at Matt and Gloria as her nerves settled.

"I guess I'll just say it," she said. "You two know Hunter and I broke up, right?"

Matt blinked but Gloria nodded.

"Okay," Molly said, drawing in a deep breath. "I just don't want it to be weird. I don't need to be re-set up with him or anything."

"That's not what this is," Matt said, his eyes wide. "At

all." He exchanged a glance with Gloria. "We would never do that to you, Molly."

She nodded, glad she'd said something. "Okay. Thanks." She smiled at them again, lunging at Matt and hugging him. "Thank you for inviting me out here." It felt good to have his arms around her, though there were no romantic feelings between them. She stepped back and inhaled as she looked at the completed stables and barns.

"This place is so amazing," she said. "How are the horses coming along? Will you guys open in the spring like we planned?"

"That is another reason we asked you to come out here," Gloria said slowly. "We can't run this program without you, Molly."

"Oh, Hunter—"

"Hunter put you in charge of it," Matt said. "Gloria and I can work with the horses and counselors, but we need you to handle the children."

Molly looked back and forth between them, her indecision raging. Could she really drive out to this farm every day? Hunter's farm?

He won't even know, she thought. "How often does Hunter come out here?"

"Only Sundays," Matt said. "I swear, Molly."

She nodded. He'd be CEO soon, and he was probably already keeping those hours. His advancement had been announced, and the beginning of the new year only lay a couple of months away.

"Okay," she said. "Fine. I can do it." She put a smile on her face that felt like it stretched too far. "But I think it's too cold for a lesson today. Can we just eat lunch in a warm house?"

Matt chuckled and ducked his head. Gloria grinned and said, "Yes, I agree. Let's go."

Molly went with them to a single-story house behind the farmhouse, falling easily into the small talk. She enjoyed her time with them, and she clutched the tiny crystal apple Chris said Bev had bought for her at a craft fair the previous summer when she hugged him after they'd eaten.

On her way back home, Molly tried not to let the horrible reality of her real life press in on her and ruin the past couple of hours, but it did anyway.

She walked into her house alone. She fed her dog and cat and faced the empty space. Everything was so quiet, with nothing to do, and Molly slouched onto the couch with tears in her eyes.

She hoped this hopeless, lonely feeling would pass quickly, and she opened her mouth and prayed for exactly that.

CHAPTER 26

Hunter twisted in his chair and looked out the windows. Snow fell outside in a wicked way, and it reminded him of his time in Massachusetts. That, or the fact that he currently listened to Will detail his plans for the upcoming new year.

"With the new funding," Will said. "We'll be able to take on twenty percent more veterans in the first quarter alone."

"That's great," Hunter said. "You've been doing an amazing job out there, Will."

"Are you still planning to come for Thanksgiving?"

Hunter thought of Cambridge, and he did miss the city. He loved to walk along the Charles River, even in the winter, and he often found himself trawling up and down the pedestrian mall here in downtown Denver, his thoughts half a continent away.

Or just over in the next town, at an elementary school. Every strawberry blonde he saw made his heartbeat quicken, and every time his phone made any noise at all, his adrenaline spiked.

"Yes," Hunter said, making his decision. "I'm still planning on coming for Thanksgiving. You're sure your parents can put up with me?" He grinned at his joke, because Will's mother had once told Hunter she preferred him to her own son, because Hunter just said, "Yes, ma'am," and "No, ma'am," instead of challenging everything she said.

Will's affinity for arguing made him an excellent problem solver, though, and he and Hunter had gotten along extraordinarily well. Hunter had never been as nervous as he'd been when he'd moved to Cambridge.

He'd signed a lease for an apartment with four bedrooms and six men. He'd had a private room, and right next door had been Will. Their second year at MIT, they'd found a house and shared that, just the two of them. Hunter still owned the house, and Will managed that too. Now, he rented it to an MIT student in need for hardly anything, because Hunter didn't need the money.

Even Dad didn't know about the house in Cambridge, other than that Hunter had bought it to live there. He'd never asked if Hunter had sold it or kept it, and Hunter hadn't volunteered the information.

Will finished laughing and said, "You better bring some of those caramel chocolate chip cookies. She'll probably leave my dad for you then."

Hunter belted out a laugh too, but deep inside, all of his organs writhed. Those caramel chocolate chip cookies could only be made by Molly. He'd felt like this before, and he'd quelled the loneliness and depression by going out with other girls. Lots and lots of other girls.

Hunter wouldn't do that this time, he knew. He was older now. More mature. He didn't need to experiment to find the type of woman he liked. He knew.

He also knew he couldn't have everything he wanted. Life didn't work that way, and Hunter had started to accept that reality.

"See you soon," Hunter said, finishing up their conversation and letting his phone drop to his lap. He stared out at the weather, feeling the same cold and numbness inside him. He hated feeling this way, this sort of film of nothingness, where he could get through anything because no matter what, he never felt too bad.

His intercom beeped, and a woman said, "Mister Hammond?"

He sighed as he turned back to the expansive desk. When he'd first moved to this office on the twenty-fourth floor, he'd wondered how he'd ever fill a desk this big. Now, it held all kinds of things, and Hunter knew what each folder and file held. He knew why Elise had told him to put plants in the office, and he glanced at the family picture they'd had taken at his grandmother's funeral.

He hated the picture, because he looked like someone had smashed tomatoes in his eyes. He'd cried so much that day, and Hunter hated the extremes in his emotions. He'd once told his uncles it was all or nothing, and that had definitely been the case lately.

Candace started talking before he could reach the button

and tell her he was listening. "Your one-fifteen is here, and the food is on the way up."

Hunter pressed the button and said, "Thank you, Candace. Can you hold them and send everything and everyone in at once?"

"Of course, sir."

Sir. Hunter hated being called sir. He was only twenty-five-years-old, and his assistant was easily a decade older than him. Myra was still working for Laura, but once she retired on January first, Hunter would get the same assistant his Uncle Wes had had for years.

The CEO had two people who made sure he had everything he needed, and Candace had moved over from legal to work with Myra and Hunter. He liked her quite a lot, as she always had everything ready for him the moment he stepped off the elevator in the morning.

Hunter stood and paced toward the far wall of his office. Though this room was huge, he often felt caged here. He tried not to think that he'd only been in the office for two weeks, but he did anyway. He and Molly had been separated for almost five weeks now, and he still hadn't found the courage to gather her favorite flowers and knock on her front door.

He didn't need her to do this job. He could do the job without her.

It was actually living that was unbearable.

He walked from one side of the room to the other, taking time to feel every stride, each pull in his muscles as he moved. Lucy had taught him to focus on specific parts of his body, feeling them in isolation to help keep his thoughts from scattering.

He pressed his fingers together, feeling each pressure point, and he paused in front of the windows again and took a long, deep breath.

As if on cue, a smart rap landed on the door, and Hunter turned to see his huge mahogany door slowly creeping open. "Sir, everything's ready." Candace entered, carrying a couple of white paper bags in her hands. Behind her walked Ruby Cameron and Sylvia Quinn, the two women who headed up the legal department at HMC.

"Ruby," Hunter said, putting a smile on his face. He stepped around his desk and extended his hand toward her. She hadn't taken Dad's job when he'd left the family company years ago, but she had it now. Hunter knew what her schedule was like, as he'd lived it as a child.

She smiled and shook his hand. She stepped to the side so Hunter could shake Sylvia's hand as well. "You cut your hair," he said, admiring it. Laura had taught him to always lead with a compliment, and to always know something personal about the people he was with. He'd already started his files, and he'd gone over Ruby's and Sylvia's that morning.

"I like it. Did you color it too?"

Sylvia smiled at him, and it settled into something personal not professional. "Yes," she said. "It's darker now."

"Yes," Hunter said. "Quite a bit darker." He'd need to put that in his file. Part of him felt devious, keeping files on people, but Laura told him it was no crime to make people feel at ease and like they meant more to you than the numbers they were bringing.

Legal didn't have numbers for him today, but Ruby wanted to review the two cases in litigation right now, and as they'd last longer than Laura, Hunter had started working on them with the team.

"Let's see," Candace said, pulling containers from the paper bags. "Hunter, here's your steak sandwich." She set it on a clear spot on his desk. "Ladies, pull that shelf out and pull up a chair."

Hunter's desk had a shelf that pulled out of the front of it to make it into a table, so he didn't have to use a conference room or house a table in his office. Ruby pulled out the shelf, and Candace set down another container with, "Berries and nuts salad, extra poppyseed dressing."

Hunter rounded his desk and reached for a napkin in the stack Candace had already dropped. The plastic silverware lay there too, and he took a fork while Ruby inched her chair closer to his desk.

Sylvia sat too, and Candace gave her the ham and cheese panini she'd ordered, then set her own salad on the corner of the desk. She always stayed during the meetings to take notes and keep track of things Hunter needed to do following the discussion.

"Ruby, how's Mark?" Her husband owned a guitar shop here in Denver, and Hunter had been considering learning the instrument. In the end, he hadn't, because he barely had time to breathe, sleep, and eat, so taking up a hobby didn't seem wise.

Ruby let out a sigh. "He needs to relocate the store, but he's having trouble finding an appropriate spot."

"Why does he need to relocate?" Hunter opened his container, his mouth watering at the sight of the steak and slaw and sourdough bread. He glanced at Ruby, who stirred her dressing into her salad.

"One of those marijuana candy stores opened up right next door," she said. "Lots of people milling about, with plenty of smoke. He comes home half-stoned almost every day."

"You're kidding," Hunter said, somewhat shocked. He lived downtown, and while marijuana was legal in Colorado, he hadn't seen much of it.

"The shop's been broken into several times." Ruby forked up a bite of salad and held it in front of her. "He just needs a new place, but his location is good right now, and he's been there so long, his rent is dirt cheap."

Hunter listened, wondering if he could help in some way. He didn't know much about retail locations, but surely there would be an open retail space or a neighborhood that would benefit from a guitar shop.

"Why don't you talk to Beth in internal systems?" he asked. "Her husband does all the real estate for us, and he might know of somewhere that's dying for a guitar shop."

"I'm not sure we can buy a place," Ruby said, though her eyes held an interested glint now.

"Robert might not know much about commercial real estate, but he'll know someone who does." Hunter took a bite of his sandwich, his eyebrows raised. After swallowing, he said, "It's worth asking."

"Yeah," Ruby said, finally slipping from professional to personal. "Thanks."

He survived the meeting, and another. He made it through another day, and then another. He'd started marking time by counting how many times he walked back and forth from his building to HMC, the short half-block distance between the lobbies not enough to get his restless energy out.

He didn't run again, though, because that had been torture. Instead, Hunter filled every waking moment with something—work, phone calls, cleaning his office or condo, walking around downtown, or therapy.

"Shoot," he said, jumping up from his desk. "Therapy." He swiped his phone from the desk, and hurried toward his office door. "I'm late," he said to Candace as she looked up. "Will you call Lucy and let her know I'm on my way?"

"Hunter." She stood, and the fact that she'd used his first name got him to slow down. "Your appointment with Lucy isn't until five today."

He turned back, his brow furrowed. "It's always at four."

"Right." Candace smiled at him. "But she had an emergency this morning, and she called and pushed you back an hour." She came around the front of the desk and perched on the front of it. "Did you really think I'd let you be late for an appointment?"

Relief ran through Hunter, and he smiled too. "No, of course not." He hooked his thumb over his shoulder. "I'm going to go anyway. I've got my files." He lifted his briefcase like he owed Candace an explanation.

"Okay," she said. "I'm sneaking out after you too. Remember my son has his fencing tournament tonight?"

"Yes," Hunter said. "Have a good evening." He gave her a quick smile and turned to leave. He nodded to everyone on his way out of the building, just like he always did. He hated the formality, and Hunter bypassed his lobby, though he now had time to take his briefcase upstairs before his appointment.

He wandered down the street, which was starting to fill with businessmen and women on their way home from their very important jobs. The noise on the street increased, and Hunter stood there in the sea of people, watching them walk and talk, either to each other or on their phones.

They all wore black or blue, with long, wool coats to keep the November chill off their skin.

He'd never felt so alone.

"WHAT DO YOU MEAN?" LUCY ASKED, AND HUNTER sighed.

"Can I take off my shoes?" he asked, reverting back to when he was thirteen years old and had first started coming to see Lucy.

She gave him a smile and waved her pen, just like she had the first time he'd asked if he could take off his shoes during his therapy session.

Hunter kicked them off and lay down on the couch. "I don't know what I mean. Aren't you supposed to tell me what I mean?"

Lucy gave a light laugh that only lasted a couple of seconds. She wouldn't tell him what he meant. She never had before, and in fact, she'd ask him an annoying question if he didn't talk.

He exhaled out until he felt like the front of his lungs would stick to the back, and then he inhaled again. "I think I'm trying to figure out if having a high-pressure job means I can never have a wife and family."

"Is that what you think?"

"I've never seen anyone do it."

"Does that make it true, though?"

"Or they try, and then they end up divorced. I know what that's like for children, and I don't want to put my kids through that." Uncle Wes flashed through his mind. He'd basically lived two lives. One where he was the philanthropist who founded a pharmaceutical company and then ran HMC for years and years. Only when he quit did he move on to wife and family. Dad had done the same thing. Uncle Colton too.

Uncle Ames and Cy both had pretty big jobs, with huge companies they ran. But a motorcycle shop and a police dog academy weren't the same as running the family company. The scale was much smaller, for one, and they were only risking their own money, not the livelihoods of hundreds and hundreds of people. Maybe thousands. With a family name to uphold.

"You do want children, though."

"Yes," Hunter said.

"What did your grandfather do?"

"He ran HMC," Hunter said, his mind racing now. He sat up. "He ran HMC, and my grandma was right there with him. They had five kids while he ran HMC." He *had* seen someone who'd worked the job and managed a family at the same time.

He needed to go visit Grandpa, and he wished Grandma was still alive so he could ask her how she had liked her husband working a hundred hours a week. Maybe Grandpa hadn't worked that much. Maybe Hunter worked too much.

He simply didn't know what to do with his time if he wasn't working.

If you had Molly, you'd know what to do with your time, he thought.

Lucy had asked him something, but Hunter hadn't heard her through his thoughts. He bent over and started re-lacing his shoes. "I have to go, Lucy."

"Tell me where you're going," she said, standing up.

Hunter heard the concern in her voice, and he looked up. "I'm going to go visit my grandpa. Ask him how he did it." He finished tying his shoes and stood too. He stepped toward Lucy and hugged her. "Thank you, Lucy. You always find a path in my mind I haven't been able to see."

"You do all the work, Hunt, just like always."

He stepped back and ducked his head. "How's Georgie?"

"Not going by Georgie anymore," she said with a smile.

"He's fourteen now, and he's declared it's 'just George'." She laughed and shook her head.

Hunter smiled at her. "I get that." He paused and cocked his head. "You work a lot, right, Lucy?"

"A fair bit," she admitted.

"How do *you* do it?"

Lucy blinked, and Hunter held up his hand. "Never mind. Too personal. I get it. I'm still learning that boundary."

"It's okay," Lucy said. "We're friends, Hunter. It's a hard line. Between us, and between how much I work and when I need to be done." She set her notebook on her desk and turned back to him. "Let me tell you something my father told me, a long time ago. He worked a lot, but not in suits and office buildings. He had two jobs to support our family, and he'd come home for fifteen minutes to change his clothes and grab a sandwich before he went to his night job."

She flashed a smile that contained a tiny bit of trepidation. Hunter shrugged into his coat, but he listened intently.

"He said that he paused on the front step of our house every time he got home. He'd shed anything upsetting, troublesome, or hard that had happened at work. Right there on the stoop. He never brought it home. Never. When he left the next day, he said, 'Lucy, the troubles were always waiting, right where I'd left them. I'd pick them up and take them with me. Work on them while I was gone. Drop them when I got home.'" She smiled again. "That's what I try to do. Set strict hours for myself and take nothing home. It's worked for Allen and I. It may not work for everyone."

Hunter couldn't even imagine his father doing that. Sometimes things happened that required immediate attention. Could he simply say he wasn't available if a crisis didn't happen during his designated work hours?

He didn't want to spend his life apologizing to his wife and kids when he had to "run to work real quick." He already knew nothing at HMC was done quickly.

"Good luck, Hunter," Lucy said. "We'll talk about how things go with your grandfather next week?"

"Yeah," Hunter said, distracted as he turned toward the door. The drive out to the farm passed quickly, and Hunter dang near rammed his truck into the front porch when he saw a familiar sedan in his rearview mirror.

"Molly." He slammed on the brakes and twisted around, watching the taillights on a dark blue sedan as they left the farm. Part of him wanted to race after her and tell her he'd quit in the morning.

When he got out of the truck, though, his dad said, "Hunter," and laughed as he came down the steps. "What brings you to the farm in the middle of the week?"

What a great question. Hunter turned and met Dad's eye, then looked back down the lane. The car had rounded the corner, and he couldn't see it anymore.

He couldn't see which way to go in his life. He turned toward his father and hurried forward, stepping right into his arms. Hunter had always been able to go to his father and feel like he belonged, and though he was an adult who'd been living on his own for years now, he hadn't outgrown the need for a hug from the one person who'd always loved him the most.

"Oh, my boy," Dad whispered. "Come in and tell me and your momma all about it."

CHAPTER 27

Molly held up her hand for Allison to give high-five. The little girl did, and then grabbed Molly around the middle, giving her a hug too. Molly giggled with her and said, "Have a good Thanksgiving."

Bryce got a hug too. Spencer always took a handshake, and she watched him walk down the hall when everyone else was running toward their holiday break. That little boy was going to be President of the United States one day, and Molly shook her head with a smile.

Hug, high-five, or handshake. She said good-bye to every child in her class until the very last one had gone.

With a happy sigh, Molly stood. She had a lot to be grateful for, and she'd been writing down one thing each day in November. Today, her entry would definitely have something about these fudge-striped cookies her room mother had left after their class party.

She smiled and picked up a cookie, biting it in half as she sat at her desk. She'd do the bare minimum for next Monday, and then she could enjoy the Thanksgiving holiday with her family.

Lyra would arrive from Utah tomorrow, and Molly had plans to spend the day in Mama's kitchen as they put together pies and peeled potatoes, sliced bread for the stuffing and shopped for the last-minute things Molly had forgotten she needed.

It happened every year, no matter how many notes to herself Molly made. Last year, she'd forgotten cornstarch for the pies. This year, she already had it in the box she'd been putting things in all week.

"Bye," she said to Sarah, the teacher across the hall, as she closed and locked her classroom door. Everyone smiled and said good-bye today, as they'd all have the next five days off.

Molly went home and scooped Saltine into her arms. "Hey, buddy," she said into his neck. He tried to lick her face, and she shook her head and set him down, laughing. "No licking."

Gypsy growled low in her throat, the sound almost like a purr. Molly knew better, and she glanced over at the gray feline. "I'm coming," she said, dropping her purse on the table just inside the laundry room. One glance at the food bowls there showed the cat still had plenty of food. "You didn't even eat today."

She continued down the hall, the cat prancing in front of her. She came to a complete and sudden halt upon entering the kitchen. “Gypsy.” Frustration filled her at the sight in front of her. The croutons Molly had put in her food box had clearly enticed the cat, as the shredded bag bore the brand name Mickelson’s, her favorite brand of the garlic butter croutons.

From there, Gypsy had clearly gone nuts, as even the small bottle of pumpkin pie spice lay on the floor at her feet.

Her first instinct was to grab the cat and squeeze it really, really tightly. Her second was complete resignation, and she sighed as she bent to pick up a fragment of the crouton bag. “You idiot cat,” she said as Gypsy meowed and hopped onto the back of the couch.

“Yes, I’m talking to you,” she said. “Now I have to go buy more croutons, and Ingrid is going to be here in an hour.” She didn’t need the croutons for dinner that evening, though, and Molly straightened and typed into her notes that she needed to get more of them for tomorrow’s trip to the store.

The Wednesday before Thanksgiving would be busy at the supermarket, but Molly was used to it. She’d get up and go early, and hopefully, she and Mama wouldn’t have to go back for anything.

All of her tests had come back negative, and the doctor had determined she’d had a touch of the flu. She’d rested, stayed home from church for a while, and let her husband and Molly pick up the chores around the house for a couple of weeks. She felt great now, at least according to her texts, and Molly had no reason to doubt her.

She picked up the errant bottles of spices and the packet

of Ranch dressing mix Gypsy had managed to get out of the box and put them back where they belonged. She swept, getting all the most delicious buttery crumbs from the croutons off the floor.

"You left the best part," she called to the cat on top of the bookcase. Gypsy just let her eyes squint closed, and Molly thought seriously about rehoming her for the first time.

She quickly washed up and started dinner. Ingrid and Hans had only been dating about a month, maybe a bit longer, but her sister liked him so much. She claimed they saw one another every single day, and she'd asked Molly how long it took to fall in love with a man.

Ingrid had always done things faster than Molly, and she'd always known what she wanted. Molly would be the first member of the Benson family to meet Hans, and one glance at the clock told her they'd be here in twenty minutes.

The rice wouldn't be done in time, and Molly turned up the oven with the meatballs already in it. She'd just finished making the gourmet vegetables, and they too had to go in the oven. She could slide them in on the bottom rack if she had to, but she'd prefer they get their own bake in the proper place.

With everything bubbling and boiling, she quickly wiped up the counter and her dining room table, trying to remember the last time she'd used it. She'd been eating at Mama's or on the couch, if she were being honest. Sometimes out of a container in her car, if she didn't want to come in and get glared at by Gypsy.

The cat had a way of making her feel guilty for eating without sharing, and Molly sometimes needed a break from the staring. She tossed the disinfectant wipes into the trash can and turned back to the kitchen. What else needed to be done so she could entertain her sister and her boyfriend?

Her heart thumped painfully beneath her breastbone, but she thought it too late to root out her feelings for Hunter and somehow get to a place where seeing Ingrid with Hans wouldn't hurt her.

Of course it was going to hurt to see Ingrid laughing and flirting and oh-so-happy with her boyfriend. Molly needed it to hurt, actually. She'd learned that just because something hurt, that didn't mean it should be avoided.

She wanted to meet the man Ingrid was falling for, and she wanted to support her sister. After checking the rice one more time, she opened the oven and pulled out the meatballs. There would be a few minutes of greetings and introductions and small talk before she'd serve dinner, and the veggies could finish then.

She scooped the meatballs into the mushroom sauce she'd made and covered the pot with a lid. She'd just set the baking sheet in the sink when the doorbell rang.

Molly glanced around the kitchen one more time, finally looking at herself. "Shoot," she muttered. She'd forgotten to change. She still wore her school T-shirt, with a giant cartoon tiger on the front of it.

"Just a second," she called, but she hesitated as she

turned toward the hall. Was she really going to make her sister wait outside on the porch in the cold while she changed her clothes? Of course not.

She hurried through the living room to the door and opened it. Ingrid stood there, her hands tucked into the pockets of her stylish coat. "Hey." Molly grinned at her and stepped back. "Come in." She looked past her sister to the driveway, but she didn't see anything but Ingrid's sporty red car. "Where's Hans?"

Her gaze flew back to Ingrid's, hoping with everything inside her that she and Hans hadn't broken up. "What happened?"

"He's still at work," she said with a smile. "They got slammed with a couple of big orders." Ingrid stepped inside, and Molly started to relax. "He'll be here soon."

"We should've just ordered pizza and requested him as the driver."

Ingrid laughed as she peeled off her coat. "You live outside his delivery jurisdiction anyway." She faced the house and sighed. "I love your place. I'm so ready to be done with roommates."

Molly stepped past her and led the way into the kitchen. "No, you want to switch out your female roommates for a male one." She glanced over her shoulder, throwing Ingrid a knowing smile. "A single *male* one."

"Maybe," Ingrid said coyly as she pulled out a barstool and sat. "Have you talked to Lyra?"

"No, why?" Molly opened the fridge and pulled out a couple of cans of soda. "Diet or Cherry?"

"Diet," Ingrid said. "Lyra told Mama she wanted to move up the wedding."

Molly popped the top of her cola and frowned. "To when?"

"Christmas," Ingrid said, tapping the top of her soda can.

"Oh, my word," Molly said. "Mama can't handle that. She hasn't even been working on the wedding this month, because of her health."

"They didn't tell Lyra."

"I'll tell her then," Molly said, something protective rising up inside her. "She can't do that to Mama."

"I think Mama tried to tell her, but you know how headstrong Lyra can be."

Molly nodded, already tapping out a message to her younger sister. A minute later, she said, "Done. She just needs to chill." She practically tossed her phone on the counter, slowing at the last moment so she didn't break it.

A few minutes later, the veggies were done and Molly had changed into a festive red and black sweater. When the doorbell rang, Ingrid shrieked, and Molly giggled at her as she went to answer the door.

The handsome blonde man Molly had seen on Ingrid's phone stood on the stoop, and he smiled with the strength of the sun. Molly felt his spirit and his charm, and it was no wonder Ingrid had fallen for him in a single month.

He reminded her so much of Hunter, and she found herself smiling back with the same power. "You must be Ingrid's Hans," she said.

"I am," he said, his grin turning up a notch. "I sure like

it when it's said like that." He came in when she stepped back. "Do you think you could help me convince her to make it official?"

Molly closed the door and turned back to Hans. "What do you mean?"

"Hans," Ingrid said behind them, but he didn't turn or flinch.

His smile stayed steady, and the only movement he made was to lift his hand in the universal sign of *just a minute, please*.

"I asked her to marry me, and she said it's crazy to get engaged so quickly." Hans's brilliant blue eyes sparkled like sapphires.

Molly could only gape at him. "What did she say?"

"She said she needed to think about it." Hans leaned even closer and spoke in a hushed voice. "Really, I think she just wants a bit more time to go by so no one knows I proposed on day twenty-nine."

Molly couldn't believe it either. At the same time, she could see Ingrid and Hans together, and when he turned and greeted her, Molly saw the love on his face. She witnessed it on Ingrid's too, and she basked in the excitement and warmth the couple put off.

Feeling like her lungs might crack, Molly went into the kitchen, where Hans had just finished kissing Ingrid hello. "Your coat," she said. "I'll take it."

He removed it and handed it to her. She took it into the living room and tossed it over the back of the couch, where Ingrid had put hers. "You should do it," she said, turning back to them.

"Do what?" Ingrid asked, glancing from Molly to Hans.

"Say yes," Molly said, taking a step forward. "Marry him. It's obvious you love him, and he loves you, and who cares how long you've known him?" She looked between the two of them, her heart racing now. "Say yes."

With wide eyes, Ingrid looked at Hans and swatted his chest. "You told her."

Hans laughed and laced his fingers through Ingrid's before she could really hit him. "Of course I told her. She's your sister, and you said she had to approve."

Molly met Ingrid's eyes. They'd closed slightly, and she actually ducked her head now. "She does."

"Why?" Molly asked. "I would support whoever you chose to marry."

"Your opinion means a lot to me." Ingrid stepped forward and hugged Molly. "Do you really think I should say yes?" she whispered.

Molly held onto Ingrid tightly, hoping to use the pressure to keep her voice from breaking. "Yes," she whispered back. "Don't miss this. Don't let him go." She squeezed her eyes shut, because she didn't want to cry. Not tonight.

She hugged Ingrid until her sister stepped back, and Molly wiped quickly to rid herself of any errant tears. "I approve," she declared. "Now tell the man yes."

Ingrid turned back to Hans and lifted both hands as if to say *what are you gonna do?* "I guess it's a yes."

Hans whooped and scooped Ingrid right up off her feet.

The two of them laughed, and Molly placed one hand over her heart as she experienced their happiness.

"Wow, if I'd known it was going to be that easy, I'd have come over last week," Hans said, setting Ingrid back on her feet. He engulfed Molly in a hug too, and she laughed with him too. "Thank you, Molly."

The merriment stayed high as Molly served dinner. She learned Hans was a few years older than Ingrid, that he managed a pizza place close to campus, and that he would graduate at the same time as her.

Molly enjoyed the conversation, and she said, "You better call Mama first thing in the morning," as Ingrid and Hans started putting on their coats to leave.

"We will," Ingrid said, flashing another smile at Molly. "Thanks, Mols."

She waved to them from inside the house, barely keeping Saltine from following them. Once she closed the door, she sighed, utterly exhausted now that the adrenaline was starting to ebb.

She left the dishes and went down the hall to her bedroom, simply ready to be done thinking for the day. She spent a few minutes removing her makeup and tying up her hair. She changed into pajamas and sank to her knees beside the bed.

"Lord," she prayed. "Did I let Hunter go too soon? Did I make a mistake?" She paused, trying to hear an answer. Sometimes she felt something reverberating through her bloodstream, and she'd have her answer.

She wasn't sure if she'd made a mistake or given up too

soon, but she knew she loved Hunter, and perhaps love was enough to sustain them through tough times. Perhaps love could see them through his years as CEO.

"How do I fix this?" she asked next, pausing once again to listen. Her mind started to whir as she grasped for ideas for how she could get Hunter back into her life…this time, for good.

MOLLY RETURNED TO SCHOOL THE NEXT WEEK, and she went out to the Hammond family farm in the middle of the week. She could work on the children's program from her house, but she liked to sit in the heated office with Matt and Gloria and run her ideas by them.

She'd designed a flyer over the Thanksgiving holiday, and her next step was to build a website. She'd secured the domain name, and while she'd never built a website, she had confidence in herself that she could do it.

She had it on her list to talk with Matt and Gloria about, because perhaps one of them had experience with web design.

She strongly suspected Hunter did, but she still hadn't figured out how to talk to him. She'd thought she could simply text him an update about Pony Power and see if he responded. Matt said he hadn't asked about it at all, and Molly assumed he'd simply forgotten how excited he'd been about starting the equine therapy facility.

It was a lot of work, and he certainly wouldn't have time

to do it. He didn't need to do it, though. He'd asked her to head it up.

He hadn't asked her to stop working on it, so Molly continued to devote a few hours to Pony Power each week.

Thursday morning, she woke to fifteen inches of fresh snow and a notice that school had been cancelled for the day. Relief filled her, because her sedan didn't handle the snow very well, and she'd barely made it home from the farm last night.

She stayed in her pajamas and padded into the kitchen to make hot chocolate. She curled into the couch with Saltine and a plate of toast, her mug of hot chocolate on the table next to her. "Game shows or a movie?" she asked the little dog.

Gypsy meowed from the kitchen, but Molly ignored her. "Movie," she said. She'd loved watching game shows as a child and teenager, but they weren't as fun anymore. She'd always wanted to go on *The Price is Right* and spin the big wheel, but she'd barely left the state of Colorado.

She told herself she was still young, and then she heard Hunter say it in her mind too. He'd told her that once, when they'd been arguing about his job and how he'd balance it with a family.

Something banged outside, and Molly startled. Saltine barked, his voice almost a howl. That was his way of saying he was scared but trying to be tough, and Molly shushed him. She got up and peeked through the blinds, hoping it was just the wind blowing through the neighborhood. A big, icy chunk of snow falling from a roof. Something easy and innocent.

A huge gray truck sat on the street in front of her house.

A gasp flew from her mouth, and Molly let the blinds fall back into place. She blinked, her pulse pounding as her stomach swooped, and reached to pull the string to open the blinds.

Hunter had gotten out of the truck. He faced her house, the expression on his face completely unreadable. He looked down the street as if waiting for someone else, and Molly followed his gaze.

Another truck pulled up with a logo on the side of it, indicating they did snow removal. Molly pressed one hand to her heart as the driver got out and Hunter spoke to him, indicating that yes, they needed to clear her driveway and sidewalk.

He shook the man's hand and turned as another car arrived. This one had a bouquet painted on the door, with a great big heart on the roof of the car. Hunter rounded his vehicle to step into the street, as the sidewalks were covered in snow, and she lost sight of him as he went behind his truck.

The car pulled down the street and parked in front of the next house, and Hunter picked up a shovel and got to work. Molly couldn't move. She couldn't go heat more water and milk for those out there working to clear the snow away.

She just watched as Hunter and the other two men he'd hired dug out her driveway and sidewalk. She stepped to the side as they started up the walk to her front porch, and she even held her breath for a moment, as if they'd hear her breathing in and out through the walls.

She heard their voices talking, and she dared to peek through the blinds again. The snow removal truck eased away, and the floral car pulled into the now cleared driveway. A white van did too, and a woman got out and went to the back of the vehicle.

Hunter approached both of them, and they each said a few things before he faced the house again. He drew a deep breath, and Molly recognized the nerves on his handsome face. He fought through them, and he took a step toward her front door.

CHAPTER 28

Hunter had no idea what he was doing. Every time he blinked, his vision turned as white as the landscape blanketing the greater Denver area. He managed to take one step and then another, and before he knew it, he stood at the door.

Knock or ring the bell? Saltine wasn't barking yet.

Would she be awake? They'd canceled school.

Behind him, the two women he'd asked to meet him there pressed in closer, as the temperature wasn't anywhere near warm. It wasn't even near cold. It was downright frigid.

Hunter reached out and pressed the doorbell, thinking finally that it was a softer way of announcing his arrival.

A few moments later, Molly opened the door, her eyes wide as she stared at Hunter.

He turned and took the first bouquet from Tessa, his new friend at Romantic Roses. He flashed her a quick smile and focused on Molly again. "Mols," he said, the familiar nickname clogging in his throat. He cleared it away and ducked his head, embarrassed and nervous.

He looked at the pretty pink petals of the tulips. Ingrid said she loved tulips. That gave him enough courage to look up and into those brilliant green eyes again.

"I'm in love with you," he said, shaking his head as if he wished he weren't. He extended the flowers toward her, and surprisingly, she took them.

He took another bouquet from Tessa. These were daffodils, and they had beautiful centers in white, apricot, and yellow. All in the yellow and orange color family, their beauty made him smile. He held it out toward Molly, thinking of the conversation he'd had with her mother yesterday.

"Your mama said you love daffodils, and I have to admit they're beautiful." She took those flowers too, and he added, "I apologize for being so rigid in my decisions. I hope you'll forgive me, and that we can try again."

He took the next bouquet, his fingers shaking with cold. He was going to have to tip these women more than he'd anticipated. These were deep, red roses. "I can't keep trying to live without you," he said, his voice quiet. "I love you. I need you. I hate that I can't call you at the end of the day. I hate that I can't text you at lunchtime and say I hope you're having a good day. I hate that I went out to the farm and saw your car leaving and nearly broke down."

He drew in a breath. "Please, please forgive me."

"I broke up with you, Hunter," she said as she took the roses from him. "Why are you apologizing?"

"Because you broke up with me, because I went down a path you couldn't."

"Has that changed?"

Hunter took the last flower arrangement, a pretty bouquet of calla lilies. "Not entirely, but the way I'm approaching it has changed drastically. I'd love to just talk to you about it."

"He wants to share breakfast with you too," Kenna said, and Hunter turned toward her too.

"Right," Hunter said. "Your dad said you love the stuffed French toast from Kitchen 979, and I managed to get Kenna to bring it to you."

"Come in," Molly said, stepping back to make room for him.

Relief filled Hunter, and he stepped into the warmth of the house. Kenna followed him, bringing the large white pastry box with their breakfast in it. Tessa entered last, closing the door behind them and sealing the cold out.

She busied herself with vases and setting up the flower arrangements while Kenna unpacked the food, plates, and utensils.

Hunter couldn't look away from Molly the whole time, and she seemed to look everywhere but at him. "Thank you," Hunter told Tessa and Kenna, walking with them toward the front door. "Thanks so much."

The two women left, and Hunter closed the door and locked it before facing Molly. He pressed his back into the door. "I talked to my grandfather," he said. "He says you've been coming out there, and that if there's any way I can get you back, I should."

Molly simply leaned into the counter and looked at him.

Hunter cleared his throat. "He and my grandma had five kids while he was CEO. He said it's as simple as I want it to be. It's as simple as me choosing you and my family above the job." He hadn't been doing that, and Hunter would need to work hard to find the right balance. He wasn't great at balancing things, and he hadn't known that until very recently.

"Now that I know what I need to work on, I know we can make this work."

"You really think so?" Molly asked, looking down and tucking her hair behind her ear. She stooped and picked up her little white dog.

Hunter walked toward her, every step making his heart beat faster. "I really think so," he said. "With my whole heart. It's not about us being on two different paths. We're different people, and we're always going to be on different paths. But what if they're parallel paths? What if you're right next to me, and I can simply reach out and hold your hand from the path I'm on?"

"Because we want the same things and are going to the same place," she said.

"Right," he said. "Your dad gave a sermon on that when we were kids. I called him and asked him to send me a copy." Hunter paused a few feet from her and reached into his back pocket.

Molly reached out and covered his hands with hers.

Though her hand was much smaller than his, he stilled at the simple touch. "I know what he says." She gave him a smile. "Especially if it's a sermon from when we were younger. He used to recite them around the house until he had them memorized. I had no choice but to memorize them too."

Hunter dropped the single sheet of paper he'd printed and took her hand in both of his. "I will not abandon you to raise the children alone," he said. "I will be there for you, and for our family. I know I can do it."

Molly searched his face, and Hunter didn't have any evidence to back up what he'd just claimed. He expected her to ask him how, but she didn't. Tears filled her eyes, and Hunter reached up and brushed them away.

"What are you thinking?" he asked, desperate to know how much further he had to go.

"I'm thinking that we're young," she said. "And we have time to start a family. We have time for you to be CEO for five years—or more. I don't know." She gently tugged her hand away from him. "I've been thinking that I made a mistake and that I need to fix things with you, because I love you."

Hunter's smile filled his face. "Molly Benson, you're my first love." She looked up at him, her smile matching his. "I've never stopped loving you, even when I was away, even when I fell in love with someone else. I think God doesn't always put two people that are perfect for each other together so early in their lives, but I one hundred percent believe He does sometimes." He leaned toward her. "That's us, sweetheart. Me and you. He gave me you when I needed you as a teenager, and he put you right back in my life this summer, because He knew I was too bone-headed to get the hint the first time."

"I've broken up with you both times," Molly said, a quick sob leaking out of her mouth. "If you're a bonehead, what does that make me?"

"Cautious," Hunter said without missing a beat. "Which you have every right to be." He stepped closer and slowly gathered her into his arms, beyond pleased when she let him. "I will not hurt you. I will be the husband and father you want me to be. I'm not going to be perfect, but I swear to you, Molly, all you'll need to do is sit me down and tell me what you want, and I will do it."

She shook her head. "That's not how marriage is, Hunt. We should talk about things and compromise. It's not all about me."

Hunter swallowed, because she was just so good. "Okay," he said. "Let's do that. I'd like to have a few months to prove to you that I can do this and pay attention to you. To find the balance. I'm guessing you'd like that too, but you'll want things to happen quickly. Where's the compromise in that?"

Molly laughed, and Hunter chuckled with her. When they sobered and their eyes met, Hunter leaned down and kissed her. The feelings moving through him reminded him of pure peace, because this woman loved him, flaws and all. This woman would forgive him when he messed up. He could be himself with her, and he didn't have to hide anything.

"I can't keep trying to live without you," he whispered, sliding his lips down her neck. "I can work and work and work, but that's not living."

Molly took his face in her hands and looked straight into his eyes. "You're my first love too, Hunter. When our paths diverge or start to stray from that parallel alignment, promise me we'll work on getting them back where they belong—together."

"I promise," he said.

She nodded and turned toward the breakfast setup. "Okay," she said. "I'm starving, and this is getting cold. Should we eat?"

"Sure," he said, waiting for her to take a seat at the bar. He sat next to her. "I have so much stuff to tell you."

"Yeah?" she asked, picking up a fork. "What kind of *stuff*?"

He thought of his therapy sessions over the past couple of weeks, his trip to Cambridge for Thanksgiving, and the talks with his father and grandfather. "So much." He poured syrup over his French toast. "But first, you never did say how long you're willing to give me to achieve the balance between home and work...."

EIGHT MONTHS LATER:

Molly swung down out of the saddle, still a bit shocked she could do so without stumbling. She'd actually fallen trying to get off a horse in the past, but she rode so often now, it was almost like breathing.

"How's it going, Amy?" she called to a girl in the walking ring with one of Molly's favorite horses, Cinnamon Sugar. She had a creamy white coat with sprinkles of brown and black, as if someone had dusted her with cinnamon sugar. The horse possessed a gentle spirit, which was perfect for someone like Amy.

"Good," the twelve-year-old called to Molly.

She went over to the fence and put one foot on the bottom rung as she watched Amy walk with Cinnamon Sugar.

"Can you get her to stop?" Molly asked as they came around the ring toward her.

Amy made a clucking noise with her mouth, and the horse stopped. She beamed at Molly, who smiled back. "You're getting so good with her."

"Thanks," Amy said. "You're here because I have to go in for my session, right?"

Molly nodded, waiting for Amy's outburst. She'd come to Pony Power for help with her anger. She'd been in two behavioral units last year, because she threatened other children and had no way to deal with her explosive anger.

Amy's face fell, and she stepped over to Cinnamon Sugar. "I have to go now," she said to the horse. "Thank you for walking so good for me."

Cinnamon just hung her head there, and Amy stroked her hand down her nose. She turned back to Molly. "All right. Let me put her away."

Molly nodded, because the kids were actually required to do as much as they could with the horses, including getting them out for their therapy with them and putting them away.

Travis came out of the barn to help Amy with the horse, but he didn't touch anything he didn't have to. Molly listened to the construction going on way over by the trees, and she looked to the big domed building that had started to take shape in the past three weeks. They needed an indoor arena to continue to offer equine therapy during the icy winter months in the Rocky Mountains, and Molly wanted all of the kids here to continue to get the help they needed, snow or shine.

Once Amy had put Cinnamon Sugar away properly, she

put her hand in Molly's. She smiled at the girl who was almost the same height as her. "How's your dad?"

"He's still dating that woman," Amy said sourly.

Molly just nodded. She wasn't the therapist, and she didn't get into their treatments and therapies. She knew their family situations, and she tried to stick to asking about their parents.

"But we're going to my grandma's house in Pennsylvania next week, just the two of us."

"That's great," Molly said, delivering Amy to one of the cabins where their counselors worked. "If I don't see you, have fun in Pennsylvania."

Amy smiled and went up the steps and inside the cabin. Molly sighed and turned back to the pasture. Pony Power was still a skeletal operation, with only four counselors they employed full-time. That limited the number of patients they could have, and Molly needed to find more qualified people to assist with the therapy. They had plenty of horses, but they didn't all get to work.

Matt and Gloria had no problem keeping up with their care and training, and Molly was grateful for that. She looked up into the cloudless blue sky, the sun nearly directly overhead. Hunter would be leaving the office soon, as he'd committed to only working half-days during the summer so he could be out at the farm in the afternoons. A full month into the summer, and he hadn't missed a single day.

He was really good at balancing work and their relationship, and she was ready for him to propose already.

They'd talked everything to death, and Molly thought if

he didn't ask her to marry him soon, she was going to miss her chance for a winter wedding. Mama had stopped asking if she'd gotten a diamond that day about two weeks ago, and Molly huffed with frustration.

Ingrid and Hans would be married next weekend, and Lyra had tied the knot two days after the semester ended in April, just the way she'd originally planned. If Molly could get Hunter to propose, and she got married in December or January, her mother would've pulled off three weddings in only nine months.

Molly had already told Hunter she didn't need or want anything big. He'd agreed, and then he'd taken both of her hands in his and said, "Molly, baby. I'd run away with you and get married just the two of us if I thought I could get away with it." He'd smiled, and she could still see it dancing on his mouth and in his eyes.

"But Elise would fillet me alive, and everyone at work would be devastated if they couldn't come."

"You're a Hammond," she'd said, and he'd nodded. That was all there was to say. The Hammond name was *everywhere* in Denver, and Molly would be kidding herself if she thought her wedding to Hunter wouldn't be the event of the year.

"Can we keep the dinner to close family and friends only, at least?" she'd asked.

He'd assured her that they could, but the man hadn't asked her to marry him yet. She headed over to his grandfather's house, because she ate lunch with him, Matt, and Gloria every day. Well, every day all four of them were available. Sometimes it was just her and Matt and Chris. Sometimes just her and Gloria and Chris. Sometimes just her and Chris. Once, Chris had gone to town for a doctor's appointment, and Molly had eaten with Matt and Gloria in the generational house.

Today, she heard voices through the open windows as she approached the house. She almost tripped on the single step from sidewalk to porch when she heard someone say, "Shh, she's here."

Molly lifted her hand to knock. "Matt?" She opened the door with her other hand. "Chris?"

She stepped inside the house, and though she'd just heard someone say something, she couldn't see anyone. "Hello?"

Hunter stepped out of the hallway, a wide smile on his face.

Surprise hit Molly hard in the chest. "Hey," she said. "How did you get on the farm without me seeing your truck?"

"I have my ways," he said, and knowing him, he'd have dug a tunnel from the downtown building to the farm. Or flown in on a helicopter.

He reached her, his arms going around her easily. He smelled like fresh earth, leather, and musk, and she pulled back. "You've been here all morning. I can smell the leather on you." She searched his face, and he didn't deny it.

"I rode Talksalot out to the clearing," he admitted. "Before that, Dad and I went fishing."

Molly cocked her head. "You took the day off."

"I figured the day I get engaged should only have all the things I love best in it."

Before Molly could comprehend what he'd said, he reached for something on the nearby dining room table and dropped to both knees. "Molly Benson, I've loved you for as long as I can remember. I want to take our first love and make it into a forever love. Will you be my wife?" He held up the ring box, and then chuckled. "Oops. Gotta open that." He did, the familiar spring-loaded snap filling the house.

Molly's throat seemed stuck together, especially when she looked down at the massive diamond in the box. "Hunter," she gasped. Her eyes found his again. "Yes," she said, nodding. A smile covered her face. "Yes. Yes!"

Hunter laughed as she started to giggle, and she slid the ring on her finger. He gathered her to him, though he still knelt on the ground. He wrapped those strong arms around her and pressed his cheek to her chest. Molly laughed and said, "Stand up and kiss me, cowboy."

He did, taking her face in his hands first. "I love you, Molly."

"I love you too, Hunter." She kissed him, and applause filled the house. Molly broke the kiss as his parents and the littles came out of the hall, followed by his grandfather. Matt and Gloria had been hiding in the pantry, and Molly shook her head as they opened the door and spilled out.

Her parents rose from behind the couch, and Molly started to cry. Ingrid came in through the back door and said, "I got it, Hunt. Look." She handed him her phone, and Molly heard the playback of the proposal.

"You guys," she said, looking around at the people she loved so very much.

Mama grabbed onto her and hugged her. "He is perfect for you, Mols. I have no qualms about him at all."

"Thank you, Mama," Molly said, and she stepped into her father's powerful embrace next. "You'll walk me down the aisle, right, Dad?"

"Of course, peanut." He grinned at her, and she turned to Gray and Elise Hammond. They both hugged her, Elise holding her especially tight for several extra moments.

"I'm going to take good care of him," Molly promised her.

Elise nodded and glanced at Gray. "You come to me if you need any help dealing with him. I know all of their weaknesses." They laughed together, and Elise added, "Besides, I'm not worried about you taking care of him. I told him he better treat you like a queen, and he's promised he will."

"I will," Hunter said, appearing at Elise's side. "Look, Mom." He held up a sparkly tiara and reached out to settle it on Molly's head. "She's my queen." He beamed at Elise, who he'd been calling Mom more and more lately, and then Molly.

"Kiss," Ingrid said. "I think the video ended before Hunter got up and did that."

Heat filled Molly's face, though she'd already kissed him in front of all of these people. Hunter didn't seem to have any qualms about it, and he kissed Molly again, a slow, sensual kiss that prompted ahh's from the women and whooping from the men—and only increased the fire running through her body.

Molly broke the kiss with a giggle, which quickly silenced as she leaned her forehead against Hunter's. "You and me," she whispered. "I love you."

"Me and you," he said back. "Love you too."

Keep reading for the first two chapters of **HIS SECOND CHANCE**, which features Matt and Gloria!

SNEAK PEEK! HIS SECOND CHANCE
CHAPTER ONE

Matthew Whettstein finished with his tie and went down the hall to the kitchen. Britt and Keith both sat at the tiny table pushed into a corner, each with a bowl of oatmeal in front of them. "How is it?" he asked his kids.

"Good," Keith said, getting up. He too wore his best Sunday suit, but his tie sat askew at his collar. Britt gave Matt a thumbs-up, her mouth full of her lunch.

Matt hated that he'd made oatmeal for lunch, but it was easy, and they had a long day ahead of them still. Not only that, but he'd been out in the fresh snow, fighting the tractor and then the barn doors for far too long.

If they didn't leave in the next five minutes, they'd be late to the wedding.

Matt did not want to be late for Hunter Hammond's marriage ceremony. He loved the kid—now a twenty-six-year-old man, Matt supposed—as if he were his own, and he'd been working for the Hammond's on their family farm for over fifteen years.

"Finish up, Britt," he said, turning to his son. "Let me fix your tie, bud."

Keith held still and let him do it, but he wore an edge in his eyes. Matt smiled at him anyway, because with a fifteen-year-old, it was either smile or snap. "It's crooked. I'm pretty sure Hunter was dating Molly when he was fifteen, and look at them now." Matt got the offending knot in just the right place and ran his hands down his son's shoulders.

He'd definitely put on some muscle since they'd moved to Ivory Peaks eighteen months ago. Keith had been working the farm too, earning money and learning the ins and outs of horse care from one of the best—Gloria Munson.

Matt thought he was a pretty decent groomsman too, and his pride in his work had only increased since he'd made the move permanent.

Keith loved working with the horses, though he'd never said so. Matt could just tell by the way the boy got up in the morning and took care of them before school, rain or shine. He could sometimes be found leaning against a fence, talking to a horse. He led them all to their therapy appointments, and he'd even agreed to participate in the equine therapy program that Hunter and his soon-to-be-wife, Molly, had started last year.

Pony Power had opened her doors to children with a variety of needs in May of this year, but Matt, Gloria, Molly, and Hunter had been working on the program for almost a year before that. He loved watching the kids come and go on the farm, and he loved that his two children had been getting the help they needed too.

Behind him, a crash sounded, and Matt spun to find Britt on the floor, her bowl still skittering toward his boots. "You okay?" He stepped over the dish to his daughter, gently putting his hands under her arms and lifting her up.

Tears filled her precious blue eyes, and Matt hugged her, wishing with everything in him that he could take her weaknesses and illnesses from her. He couldn't, and most days, he'd accepted that. Sometimes, though, the ache in his father heart brought about a sense of injustice and sadness. He'd taken her to a half-dozen doctors, and none of them could give him an official diagnosis. With her stuttering and her poor muscle control, one had hypothesized she'd had a stroke at some point in her life.

Another had said her symptoms sometimes came from mental retardation, usually caused when the brain went without oxygen for too long. Another thought perhaps fetal alcohol syndrome. The real problem was, Brittany had not suffered any of those things, at least not that Matt knew of. No strokes. No time underwater or without oxygen. Her mother hadn't drunk while she was pregnant.

"You're okay," he whispered to his daughter, pressing his eyes closed for only a moment. "Did your legs just give out?"

She nodded against his shoulder, being very brave and only sniffling. She suddenly pushed away from him, her eyes wide and afraid. "Is my ha-ha-hair okay, Dad-dad-daddy?"

She reached up to touch her pretty hair, which Elise and Jane had come to braid that morning.

Jane was Hunter's half-sister, and she was only a couple of years older than Brittany. His daughter loved Jane with her whole heart and soul, and they'd been planning on matching hairstyles for the wedding for months now. Elise, Jane's mother, could plait hair into any number of braids, and she'd done one down to Britt's ear on each side, then pulled them back into a ponytail on the back of her head. The rest of her hair fell in soft curls to her shoulders, and Britt had stood in front of the mirror for ten minutes after Elise and Jane had left the cabin.

"It's still perfect, baby," he whispered, smoothing down a couple of errant curls. He touched his nose to hers, choking on his emotions. "You're beautiful." He lowered her to the ground and kept a firm grip on her forearm until she found her balance.

Just like that, she was back to her cheerful and positive self, and Matt wondered how she did it. He wanted to retreat down the hall and punch something while he growled about how unfair life was. After the anger subsided, he'd fall to his knees and beg God to help him with his daughter.

For a while there, Matt had begged God to cure Brittany, but after several months of pleading without any change in her condition, Matt realized he'd been asking for the wrong thing.

He didn't need Brittany to be cured; he needed to learn how to help her, take care of her, and protect her.

That was when Matt had decided he couldn't stay with his ex-wife. The road since then had been mostly uphill, with plenty of ruts and potholes, but Matt felt like he, Keith, and Brittany were almost to the top of their personal mountain.

"Ready?" he asked the kids. "We better get going. It snowed eight inches out there, and we've got to get to the gardens by one."

"I've got Britt," Keith said quietly, stepping around Matt in the small kitchen and taking his sister's hand. "You're bringing the saddle, right?"

"Stars and lights," Matt said, something his father used to say whenever he was surprised or scared. "I forgot." He jogged down the short hall to his bedroom, where the stained and polished saddle waited over the armchair. He gazed at it for a moment, then hefted it onto his shoulder and rejoined his children in the kitchen. "Got it. Let's go."

Matt had already cleared a path to his truck, and he'd already driven it that morning. They got to the vehicle, and Matt put the saddle in the backseat with Britt. "You keep an eye on that, now, okay?" He grinned at her as she pulled her seatbelt across her lap and clicked it into place.

He got in the front with Keith, and since he'd only been home for about forty-five minutes, the truck still held some heat. He got it fired up and the heater blowing again, and they set out for the Royal Chinese Gardens, which lay on the outskirts of Denver.

The drive took a while, but at least the snow plows had been out to clear the roads. Matt sang along with the radio, grinning at Britt as she added her sweet voice to the country songs she knew. Keith rolled his eyes a time or two, but Matt saw him tapping his foot to at least three tunes.

The gardens touted masterfully carved hedges, rare plants and trees from China, and the biggest flowering blossom festival in the state. All of that happened in the springtime, though, and as it as the middle of January, and everything existed under two feet of snow, Matt didn't think they'd be seeing any flowers today.

How wrong he was. The parking lot gate had blue and white flowers laced through it, telling people they'd reached the right destination if they were looking for the Hammond wedding.

Matt should've known. The Hammonds had more money than most people could comprehend, but they weren't stuck-up or pretentious. They were, however, public figures, and as such, there was an image to uphold. As he parked in an empty spot, Matt saw no less than three people with cameras, each doing something different, though he wasn't sure what.

"Come on." He got out, and while the temperature could steal a man's breath, he didn't mind it. He hailed from Montana, and he'd been working his father's farm for decades in weather much colder than this.

He retrieved the saddle from the backseat and listened to Keith tell Britt there might be icy spots on the sidewalk, so she needed to hold onto him tightly. She promised she would, and Matt led the way toward the huge, light, airy dome in the center of the gardens.

Molly had wanted a winter wedding, but she knew it would still have to take place indoors. She and Hunter had wanted to be married before Christmas, but the holidays had turned out to be a popular time for nuptials, and the Chinese Gardens had been booked. She'd taken the next available Saturday, and Matt had wondered what all the fuss was about.

Now, he knew. As he walked down the cleared and salted sidewalk, he understood why Molly had wanted this venue. Why she'd brought the pictures to the lunches she came to out at the farm, and why she and Gloria had poured over them for so long and so often.

Tall, alabaster pillars lined the walkway on both sides, a delicate white rope hanging down in a smile between them. Pink, red, orange, and yellow flowers ran the length of the supports, and on every other one, a large picture of Molly and Hunter had been nailed right at adult eye-level.

He couldn't help smiling at the photos. Molly and Hunter were some of his best friends, and he loved them both so much.

His breath steamed in front of him, and the saddle grew heavy. He finally reached the dome and opened the door so his children could enter before him.

"There you are." A woman rushed toward him as if she'd been lying in wait to accost him the moment he arrived. "Thank heavens. Bring that saddle right up front." She spun on her heel and marched away from him, moving fast for someone in a skirt so tight around the knees.

Matt nearly rolled his eyes, but he followed Jessa

Thompson, the wedding planner. He couldn't even imagine what she'd have done had he forgotten the saddle.

"Find us a seat," he called over his shoulder to the kids. "Maybe up here by Elise." He passed her, and she got up to look behind him.

He continued all the way to the altar, where he and Jessa positioned the saddle in the exact right spot. "I knew it would fit," he said, pride in every syllable. He gazed at the saddle, which Jessa started decorating with flowers.

"The wedding starts in twenty minutes," she said, giving him a dirty look. "I thought you were never going to show up."

"I told you what time I'd be here," he said. "It takes five minutes to lace flowers through the leather." He knew, because he'd done it himself, and if he could get his thick fingers to tuck stems through the straps he'd purposefully created and looped to hold them, anyone could.

"Still."

Still what? he wanted to ask, but he didn't. He turned away from Jessa and retreated back to the first couple of rows. All of the Hammonds had already arrived, and Matt had a hard time telling some of Hunter's uncles apart. He did have a set of identical twins in there, so Matt didn't feel too badly about it.

He shook hands with Chris, Hunter's grandfather, and sat down next to him. "How are you?" he asked quietly. Quiet enough that no one nearby would overhear. He had a special relationship with the man, almost like Chris could channel the spirit of his father.

"It's been a busy morning already," Chris said with a smile. "Spilled juice all down the front of one of the flower girl's dresses, and then Ames got in a car accident on the way here."

"You're kidding." Matt stood up and looked around. "He's here, though, right?"

"He's here. He was driving over with Colton, so they didn't have any kids with them, thankfully."

Matt sat back down and looked at Chris. The man had eyes the color of fresh dirt, and he wore his eighty-four years of age really well. His dark hair was always trimmed, and Matt had learned that Elise had been doing that for him for years. Today, he wore an impressive suit—probably one very much like the ones he used to wear as CEO of the Hammond family company.

Hunter was the CEO now, and Matt had seen him in plenty of similar-looking suits, as he sometimes came straight to the farm from the office.

Matt would rather die a slow death than wear a suit to work each day. Just wearing one to church each week, sans jacket, was a chore for him. He always unknotted his tie and unbuttoned that top button the moment he hit the driver's seat following the sermon, and he hoped he didn't choke today. After all, the wedding would be a lot longer than a Sabbath-day sermon.

"Matthew," a man said, and Matt turned toward the pastor himself.

"Hello, Pastor Benson." Matt stood up again, a smile dancing across his face. "Is she ready?"

"She seems to be." Pastor Benson shook his hand, his smile warm and his eyes filled with kindness. "She's actually asked me to find you. She wants you to come to the bride's room for a minute."

"Really?" Matt glanced around as if someone would tell him the pastor was lying.

"Do you see Gloria?" Pastor Benson asked. "She's supposed to go back too."

"I haven't seen her." Matt turned to survey the rows and rows of chairs, which had started to fill since he'd arrived. Jessa flitted from this item to that one, and the noise inside the dome increased as more and more people streamed through the doors in the back.

Matt swallowed at the sheer size of this place. It must hold five hundred people, and he suddenly very much wanted to escape.

"There she is," he said, a measure of relief filling him when he spotted Gloria's soft, wavy hair and freckled face. "I'll grab her, and we'll go back."

"Thank you," Pastor Benson said. "I need to get set up at the altar." He smiled and walked that way. Matt had listened to Molly detail how her father would walk her down the aisle first, then perform the ceremony. He supposed Pastor Benson did need to get some things organized before he went to join the wedding party.

Matt paused next to Elise and said, "Molly asked for me and Gloria to come back for a minute. Are you okay with the kids?" He looked at Keith, who nodded.

"We're fine, Dad."

"They're fine," Elise assured him.

He nodded at her, his gratitude for the woman reaching new heights. When she'd first come to Ivory Peaks, Matt had wondered what Gray Hammond had been thinking. She wasn't a city slicker, but she didn't understand farm life. Elise had learned, one day at a time, and she'd been fearless.

Matt admired that, and as he walked toward Gloria, he couldn't help admiring her too. Physically, she was downright gorgeous, with strong arms and shoulders that still looked feminine. Today, she wore a bright blue dress that hugged her curves and fell to her knee, along with a pair of black heels that put her closer to Matt's height. Maybe only a couple of inches shorter, in fact.

Since she'd arrived in Ivory Peaks, he hadn't been in a place to do much more than work with Gloria on the farm. They'd talked about their lives back in Montana, as she'd been born and raised in the nearby small town. They'd even dated for a while in Sugar Pond, and looking at her now, Matt wondered if he could have a second chance with the woman.

His heart boomed in a weird way, something it hadn't done in a long, long time. He nearly tripped over his own feet as he tried to figure out what was different now that hadn't been yesterday.

Maybe you're ready, he thought. He'd come to Ivory Peaks only a few months after his divorce, and he hadn't been thinking about getting a new girlfriend or wife.

Maybe now you are.

"Gloria," he said, his voice actually breaking as if he were the fifteen-year-old talking to the girl he had a crush on.

She turned from one of Hunter's aunts and looked at him. Her eyes slid right down to his polished and pristine cowboy boots and back to his face. Something glinted there, and Matt cocked his head.

"You look nice," she said, and for Gloria that was a huge compliment. She was task-oriented, always greeting him with something more like, "We have eight stalls to shovel this morning, and then I'm going to need your help with moving that stubborn bull out to the second pasture."

Matt was sure she'd never complimented him before. "Thank you," he managed to say, though he reached for his tie to adjust it. "You look amazing, as always." He glanced at Bree, who smiled at him. "Uh, Pastor Benson said Molly wanted to see us for a moment."

Gloria's eyebrows went up. "Oh. Okay."

For some reason, he offered her his arm, and for a reason wildly unbeknownst to him, she took it. Warmth spread through him, and his pulse increased until he could feel it fluttering in the vein in his neck. "I'm not sure why," he managed to say as they stepped away from Bree. "I was just tasked with finding you and taking you back."

"Let's go see what she wants," Gloria said in a soft voice he'd only heard her use a few times. Whispers from the past streamed through his mind, and Matt fantasized about a new future with Gloria. One where she didn't tell him he was blind to see his failing farm for what it was, and one where he didn't tell her she needed to grow up and realize the world was bigger than Sugar Pond.

Maybe she could forgive him for the things he'd said two decades ago.

Maybe he could ask her to dinner, and maybe she'd say yes.

A smile lit his soul as they left behind the burgeoning crowd and entered a private hallway. Gloria actually stepped closer to him, and Matt glanced at her as he tucked her arm into his body.

He wasn't sure if he was ready to move past his first failed marriage, but something in the back of his mind said, *Yes, you are, Matthew. It's time.*

SNEAK PEEK! HIS SECOND CHANCE
CHAPTER TWO

Despite not being overly feminine or girly, Gloria Munson sure did love a good wedding. The Hammonds knew how to throw a party too, as she well knew from her time on the family farm. Every birthday, every holiday, every weekend it seemed, food and family could be found at the farmhouse where Gray Hammond lived with his wife and family.

Hunter Hammond came to the farm often enough for Gloria to know him well, and his almost-wife, Molly, came even more often than that. If Gloria had to put a label on Molly, she'd call the woman her best friend.

They worked together closely, along with Matt, on Pony Power, and besides Gloria, no one liked to see the horses and children in the program more than Molly.

"Did she say what she wanted?" Gloria asked, trying to tame the thrashing of her heart.

"If she did, I didn't get the message," Matt said, his body so warm next to her forearm and hand. She had no idea why she'd linked her arm through his, only that it had felt natural and easy in the moment. Not only that, but he looked so dashing in his full, three-piece suit, and perhaps she'd imagined the two of them about to attend a high-society ball.

She did read a lot of historical romance novels, after all. She hadn't made it to the point where she'd bought any Regency dresses or anything. Gloria barely liked to wear a dress to church. In Montana, she'd been known to go in her jeans and cowgirl hat, but once she'd lost her father, the ranch, and every shred of dignity she had, Gloria had left the state in her rearview mirror.

In Colorado, she'd been reinventing herself one day at a time. Rebuilding her sanity one horse at a time. Restocking her savings one dollar at a time.

She probably had enough to splurge on a ballgown now, should she really want one. Gloria thought of the bright orange Post-it notes she'd scattered around her cabin. One on the bathroom mirror, one on the refrigerator, one above the front door.

Your own ranch.

Gloria wanted her own ranch with every fiber of her being. She'd thought she was set to inherit the one she'd worked with her father for so long, but that hadn't worked out.

"Here we are," Matt said, drawing her back to the hallway in the grand dome surrounded by snow-covered gardens. Gloria had found the landscape just as beautiful with flowers and vines wafting in the wind, the snow heaped on the sides of the sidewalk, and a cold, blue chill in the air as she had when she'd visited the Royal Chinese Gardens last spring.

He reached up and knocked on the door, and not two seconds later, a woman pulled it open. Her face softened as she took in Matt and Gloria, and Ingrid said, "Come on in," as she stepped back and opened the door. "Matt's here."

Matt swallowed visibly, and Gloria understood why. Every single person in the room was female, all of Molly's sisters, her mother, her cousins, and even some friends. Gloria's life centered on the family ranch on the outskirts of Ivory Peaks, and she didn't know every person Molly associated with.

"Matt," Molly said, swishing forward in an enormous wedding gown. She radiated sunlight and joy, her smile broad on her perfectly made up face. "I just have something for the two of you." She twisted but didn't try to turn in the dress. She'd probably fall down with a train that long and bushy. "Kara? Did you have those little boxes?"

"I have them," another woman said, and she too belonged to Molly. This sister had never been to the ranch, so she must be Lyra. She'd been living in Utah and going to school, and she'd gotten married this past spring.

She handed a pair of dark blue jewelry boxes to Molly, who extended them toward Matt and Gloria, her smile on double-high now. "Open them."

"You didn't have to get me a gift," Gloria said, removing

her hand from Matt's arm and reaching for the box. "In fact, I'm pretty sure people bring the bride and groom gifts." She met Molly's eye and smiled.

"I want you to wear these during the wedding," she said.

Gloria looked down at her box, and then at Matt. He gestured for her to go first, so she cracked the lid. A pair of gorgeous, dazzling diamond earrings sat nestled among black silk, and Gloria sucked in a breath. "Molly." She looked up at the woman. "I can't accept these."

"Yes, you can." Molly reached for the box and took it back. "You didn't even wear earrings, and I knew you wouldn't. You *need* these." She took them out and handed them to Gloria. "There's a mirror right over there if you need one." She turned expectantly to Matt.

"Here goes nothing," he said. "But my ears aren't even pierced." He grinned at Molly, who giggled, and opened his box.

Gloria caught sight of the shock on his face first and looked down into his jewelry box second. Cufflinks.

"These are amazing," he said, taking them out of the box. He stepped into Molly and hugged her tight, and Gloria wished she'd done that. She wasn't particularly touchy-feely, though she did feel things deeply. She just didn't know how to express them. Once, her grandmother had said she was stoic and strong-willed, because she'd been raised by a single father who knew how to communicate with horses and cattle better than humans.

Gloria had often found herself doing that too. She could murmur the secrets of her heart to a horse, and it would simply close its eyes halfway as if in bliss and listen.

Matt turned to Gloria. "Help me put these on?" He wore hope and delight in his eyes, and Gloria nearly dropped her earrings at the sight of the boyish smile on his face. Her heart thumped in her chest as she handed her earrings to Molly to hold and reached to help Matt with his cufflinks.

He extended the first toward her, and her fingers touched his to take it from him. Sparks shot up her arm, and she steadfastly refused to look at him again. If she did, she had no idea what might happen. She'd probably spontaneously combust or something.

"I'm not sure…." She threaded the link through and popped out the back. "Oh. Got it." She smiled at him, her stomach swooping. At least she hadn't burst into flames. He didn't smile though, and she'd seen that look in his eyes before. Desire swam in those half-blue, half-gray depths, and she felt it move through he too.

She shifted her feet, which hurt in the heels, and she took the second cufflink. With that one in place, the cute little horse sparkling just like her earrings, she stepped back. She needed a lungful of air that wasn't scented like Matt's cologne and the woodsy, clean smell of his skin.

Her fingers twitched when she looked up and saw he had a lock of hair that had fallen onto his forehead. Before, when they'd dated, she'd swoop that back into place, lean into him, and kiss him.

Before, when Gloria had confidence and the whole world in front of her.

Now, she took another step back and bumped into Ingrid. "Sorry," she murmured. Molly handed her the earrings, and Gloria walked over to the mirror. It had been a long time since she'd dressed up with jewelry. She'd sold anything of any value before leaving Montana, and she certainly didn't need diamonds to teach a horse how to stay close to the rail.

With the gems in her ears, Gloria let her hands fall back to her sides. A distinct feeling cascaded over her, and she could only stare at her reflection. She felt beautiful, and Gloria never felt like that.

"They're lovely," Molly's mother said, and Gloria turned toward her.

Swallowing, she said, "Thank you." She turned and went back to Molly, whose sisters were now pinning her flower crown in place. "We should go, Matt." She stopped next to Molly, trying to figure out which words to use.

"They complete that outfit," Molly said, holding very still. "You were gorgeous before, but now you're over the top." She grinned. "You're going to have so many men asking you to dance. Hunter has practically everyone from HMC here. There's a very good looking lab technician named Larry...." Her eyes sparkled with mischief, and Gloria shook her head though she smiled.

She sort of lunged at Molly and hugged her tight. So tight, Molly grunted. "Thank you." Gloria released her and walked past Matt, not able to look him in the eyes. Behind her, he said something to Molly, and before she knew it, he'd caught up to her.

He didn't offer his arm again, and they'd already started down the hall anyway. "Those earrings are stunning," he said.

"It's too much," she said. "I shouldn't have taken them."

"You know the Hammonds are billionaires, right?" he asked.

Gloria's step slowed, and she cut a look at Matt out of the corner of her eye. "I mean, I haven't asked, and I haven't seen their bank accounts."

"Every one of them," he said. "Hunter, all of his siblings, though they don't know it yet. His dad. All the uncles. The grandfather. Billions." He smiled in a soft, friendly way. "They can afford a pair of earrings."

Gloria wanted to argue with him that principles had to be maintained. At the same time, she didn't want to argue with him.

His fingers brushed hers, and Gloria pulled in a breath. On the next step, she inched a little closer to him, and this time his hand caught right on hers. He fumbled slightly but quickly aligned their fingers.

"Is this okay?" he asked, his voice a near-whisper as they approached the end of the hall. Beyond that doorway, the grand hall would arch above them, and they'd attend the wedding.

Gloria couldn't get her voice to work, so she simply nodded.

Matt squeezed her hand, and she wondered how she could tell him everything that had happened in the past twenty years. *One piece at a time,* she thought.

He increased his step and jumped in front of her right as they reached the doorway. "Are you staying for the whole thing?"

She had no choice but to look into those eyes. His curiosity lived there, shrouding something else she couldn't identify.

"The wedding, the dinner, the dance?" he asked. "All of it?"

"I was planning on it."

He took a step closer and looked down at the narrow space between their bodies. She had no choice but to breathe in the sexy, male scent of him, and while her brain screamed at her to back up, her feet didn't move a single centimeter.

"Are you really going to dance with anyone who asks?"

Gloria emitted a light scoff. "No one's going to ask."

"*I'm* asking," he said. "Right now." He took her other hand in his and met her gaze. "I don't want you to dance with anyone but me tonight."

She had no idea what to say. He wore his confidence well, and he always had. Well, he'd been a bit different than she remembered when they'd first reunited in Ivory Peaks. She'd learned he was only four months out of a marriage, and he'd seemed softer. Still strong and hardworking, but not so filled with bluster and laughter.

Months had passed since then. Over a year. Slowly, she'd watched him heal into a new version of himself, and surprisingly, Gloria had done the same. Her attraction to Matt had never really left her; it had only been lying dormant.

Until now.

"What do you think?" he whispered. "Will you dance with me—and only me—at this wedding?"

Coming soon!

His First Love (Book 1): She broke up with him a decade ago. He's back in town after finishing a degree at MIT, ready to start his job at the family company. Can Hunter and Molly find their way through their pasts to build a future together?

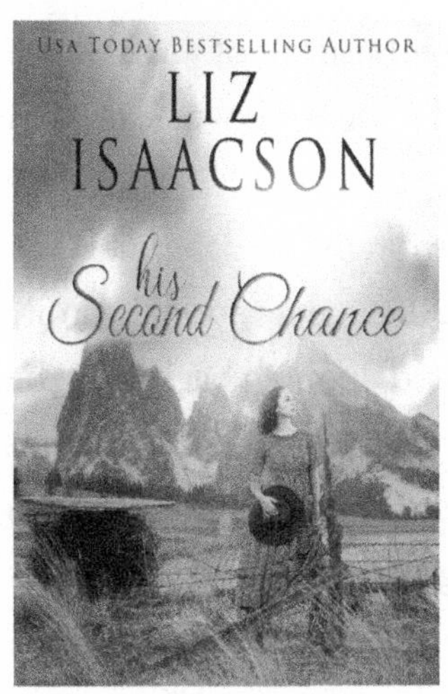

His Second Chance (Book 2): They broke up over twenty years ago. She's lost everything when she shows up at the farm in Ivory Peaks where he works. Can Matt and Gloria heal from their pasts to find a future happily-ever-after with each other?

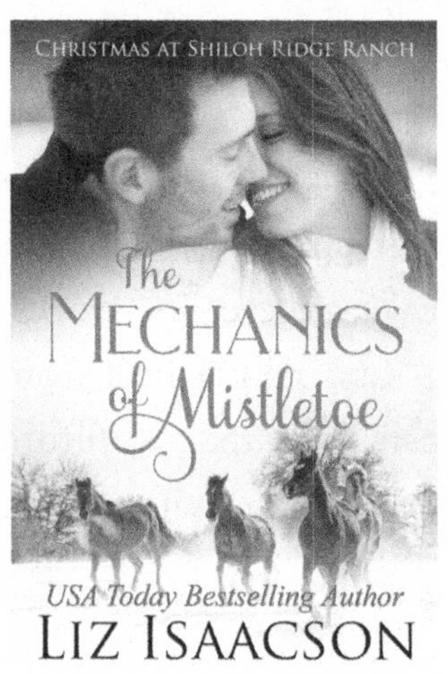

The Mechanics of Mistletoe (Book 1): Bear Glover can be a grizzly or a teddy, and he's always thought he'd be just fine working his generational family ranch and going back to the ancient homestead alone. But his crush on Samantha Benton won't go away. She's a genius with a wrench on Bear's tractors...and his heart. Can he tame his wild side and get the girl, or will he be left brokenhearted this Christmas season?

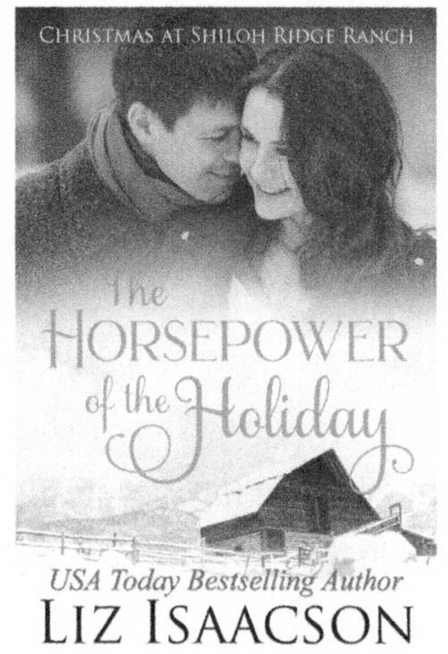

The Horsepower of the Holiday (Book 2): Ranger Glover has worked at Shiloh Ridge Ranch his entire life. The cowboys do everything from horseback there, but when he goes to town to trade in some trucks, somehow Oakley Hatch persuades him to take some ATVs back to the ranch. (Bear is NOT happy.)

She's a former race car driver who's got Ranger all revved up... Can he remember who he is and get Oakley to slow down enough to fall in love, or will there simply be too much horsepower in the holiday this year for a real relationship?

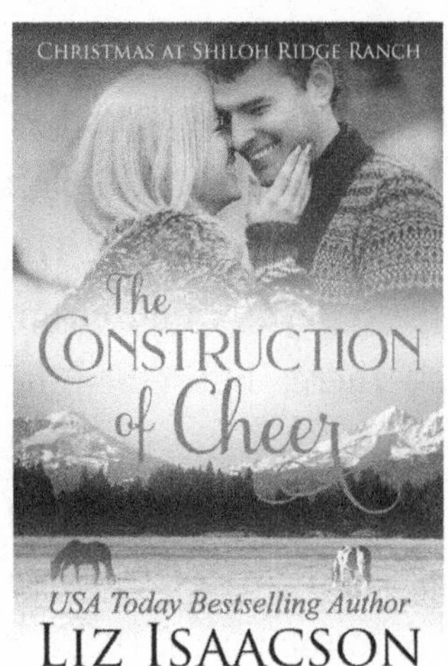

The Construction of Cheer (Book 3): Bishop Glover is the youngest brother, and he usually keeps his head down and gets the job done. When Montana Martin shows up at Shiloh Ridge Ranch looking for work, he finds himself inventing construction projects that need doing just to keep her coming around. (Again, Bear is NOT happy.) She wants to build her own construction firm, but she ends up carving a place for herself inside Bishop's heart. Can he convince her *he's* all she needs this Christmas season, or will her cheer rest solely on the success of her business?

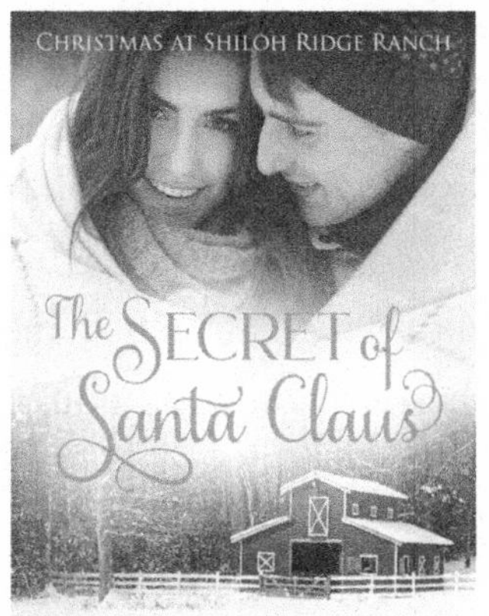

The Secret of Santa (Book 4): He's a fun-loving cowboy with a heart of gold. She's the woman who keeps putting him on hold. Can Ace and Holly Ann make a relationship work this Christmas?

The Harmony of Holly (Book 5): He's as prickly as his name, but the new woman in town has caught his eye. Can Cactus shelve his temper and shed his cowboy hermit skin fast enough to make a relationship with Willa work?

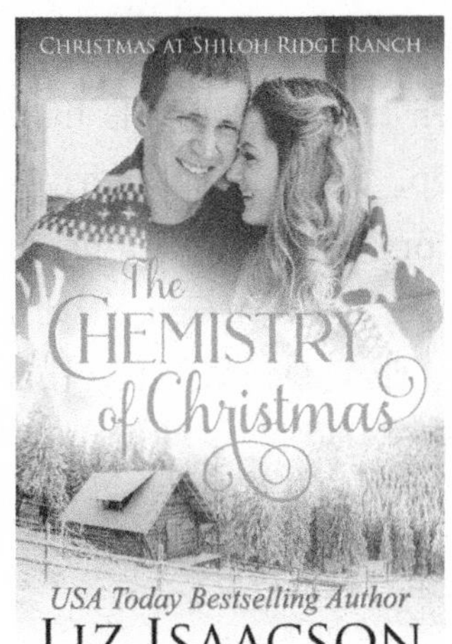

The Chemistry of Christmas (Book 6): He's the black sheep of the family, and she's a chemist who understands formulas, not emotions. Can Preacher and Charlie take their quirks and turn them into a strong relationship this Christmas?

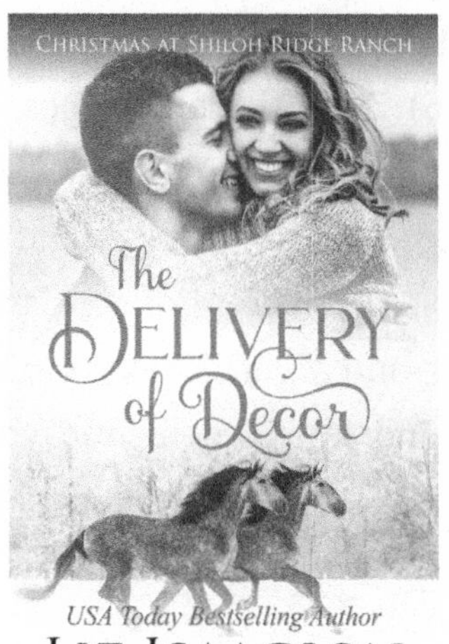

The Delivery of Decor (Book 7): When he falls, he falls hard and deep. She literally drives away from every relationship she's ever had. Can Ward somehow get Dot to stay this Christmas?

Rhett's Make-Believe Marriage (Book 1): She needs a husband to be credible as a matchmaker. He wants to help a neighbor. Will their fake marriage take them out of the friend zone?

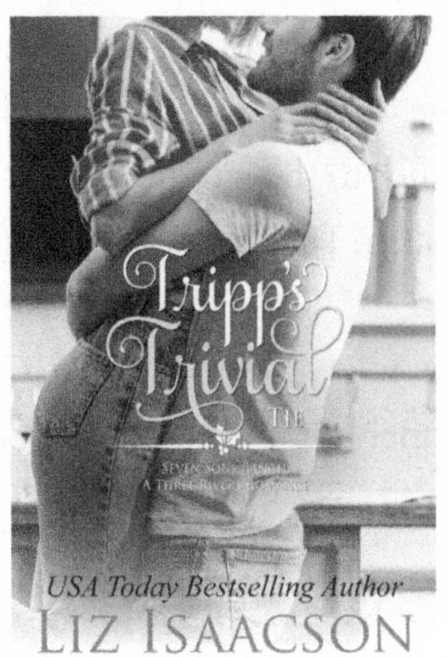

Tripp's Trivial Tie (Book 2): She needs a husband to keep her son. He's wanted to take their relationship to the next level, but she's always pushing him away. Will their trivial tie take them all the way to happily-ever-after?

Liam's Invented I-Do (Book 3): She's desperate to save her ranch. He wants to help her any way he can. Will their invented I-Do open doors that have previously been closed and lead to a happily-ever-after for both of them?

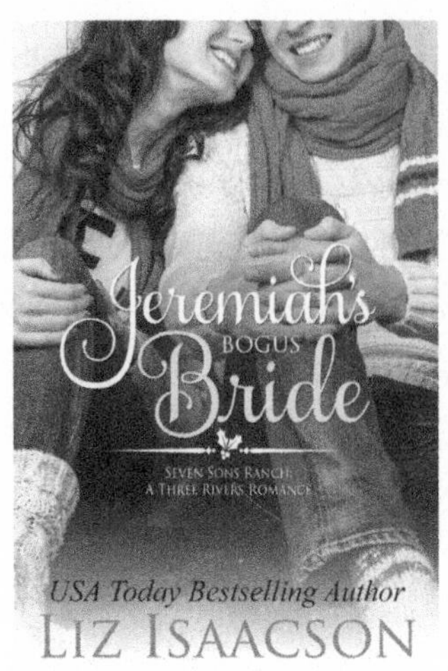

Jeremiah's Bogus Bride (Book 4): He wants to prove to his brothers that he's not broken. She just wants him. Will a fake marriage heal him or push her further away?

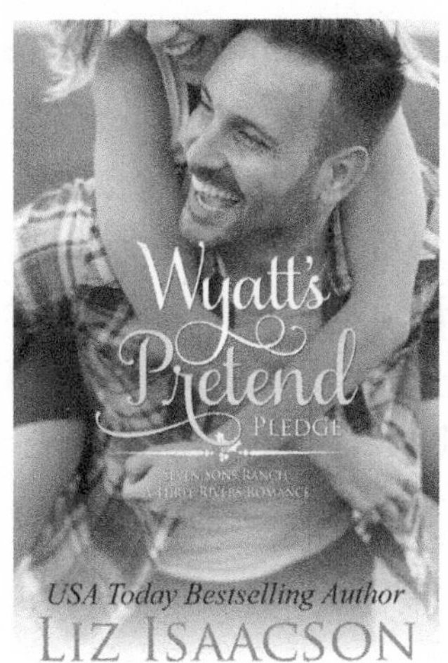

Wyatt's Pretend Pledge (Book 5): To get her inheritance, she needs a husband. He's wanted to fly with her for ages. Can their pretend pledge turn into something real?

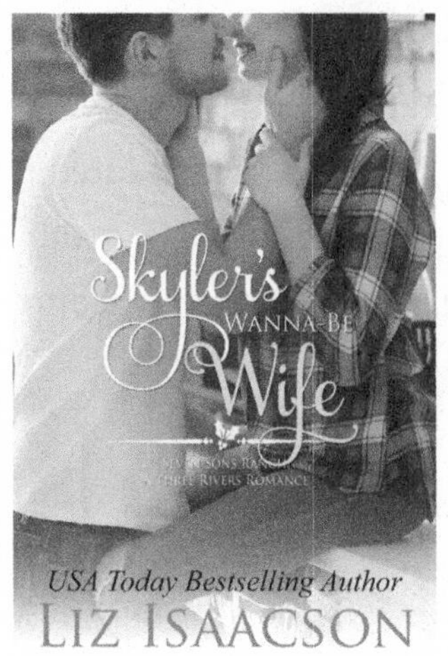

Skyler's Wanna-Be Wife (Book 6): She needs a new last name to stay in school. He's willing to help a fellow student. Can this wanna-be wife show the playboy that some things should be taken seriously?

Micah's Mock Matrimony (Book 7): They were just actors auditioning for a play. The marriage was just for the audition – until a clerical error results in a legal marriage. Can these two ex-lovers negotiate this new ground between them and achieve new roles in each other's lives?

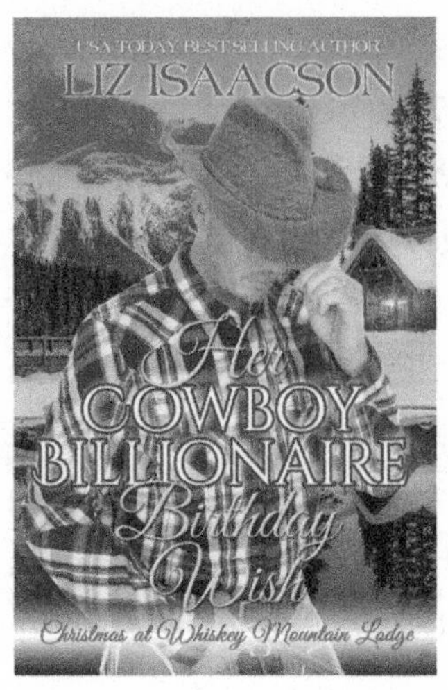

Her Cowboy Billionaire Birthday Wish (Book 1): All the maid at Whiskey Mountain Lodge wants for her birthday is a handsome cowboy billionaire. And Colton can make that wish come true—if only he hadn't escaped to Coral Canyon after being left at the altar...

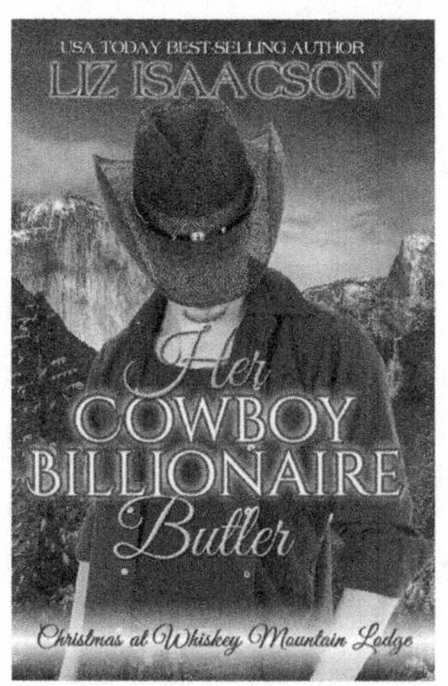

Her Cowboy Billionaire Butler (Book 2): She broke up with him to date another man...who broke her heart. He's a former CEO with nothing to do who can't get her out of his head. Can Wes and Bree find a way toward happily-ever-after at Whiskey Mountain Lodge?

Her Cowboy Billionaire Best Friend’s Brother (Book 3): She's best friends with the single dad cowboy's brother and has watched two friends find love with the sexy new cowboys in town. When Gray Hammond comes to Whiskey Mountain Lodge with his son, will Elise finally get her own happily-ever-after with one of the Hammond brothers?

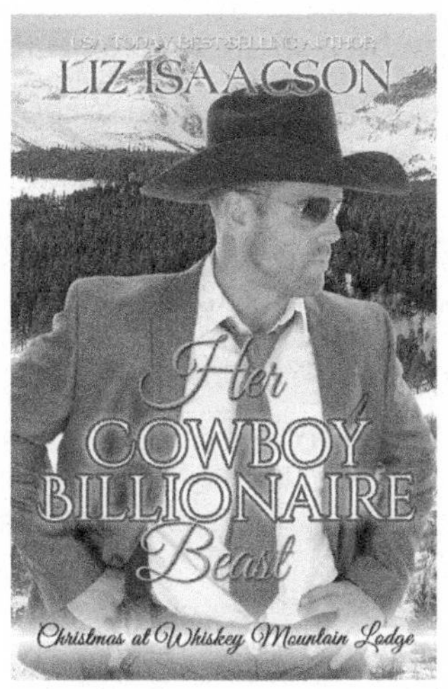

Her Cowboy Billionaire Beast (Book 4): A cowboy billionaire beast, his new manager, and the Christmas traditions that soften his heart and bring them together.

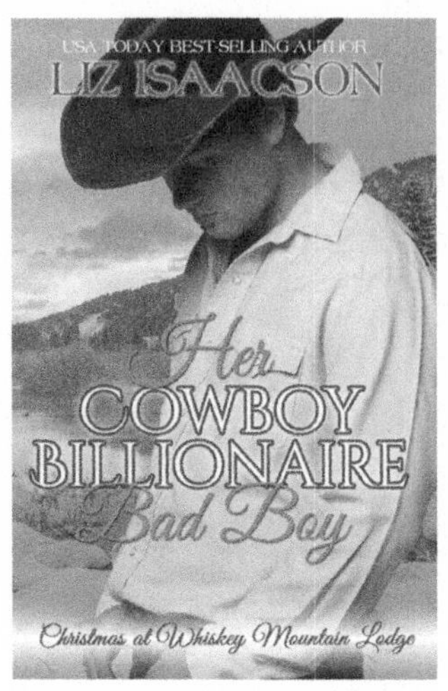

Her Cowboy Billionaire Bad Boy (Book 5): A cowboy billionaire cop who's a stickler for rules, the woman he pulls over when he's not even on duty, and the personal mandates he has to break to keep her in his life...

BOOKS IN THE CHRISTMAS IN CORAL CANYON ROMANCE SERIES

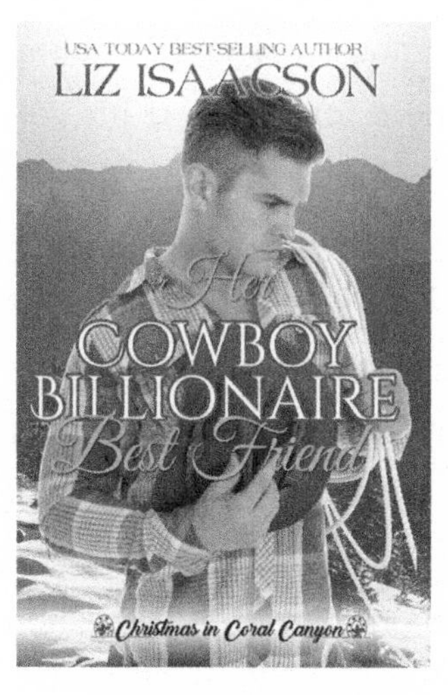

Her Cowboy Billionaire Best Friend (Book 1): Graham Whittaker returns to Coral Canyon a few days after Christmas—after the death of his father. He takes over the energy company his dad built from the ground up and buys a high-end lodge to live in—only a mile from the home of his once-best friend, Laney McAllister. They were best friends once, but Laney's always entertained feelings for him, and spending so much time with him while they make Christmas memories puts her heart in danger of getting broken again…

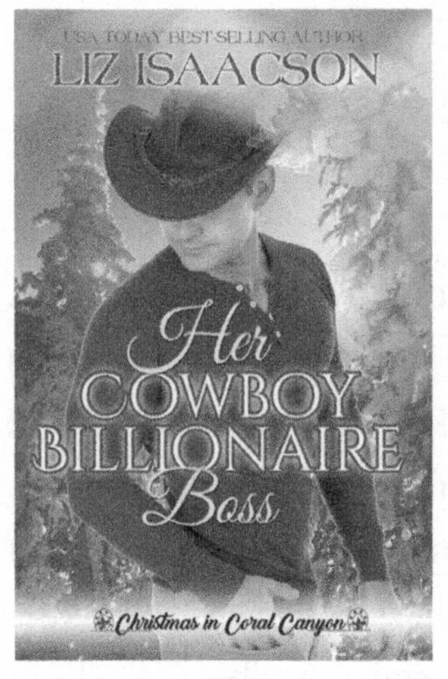

Her Cowboy Billionaire Boss (Book 2): Since the death of his wife a few years ago, Eli Whittaker has been running from one job to another, unable to find somewhere for him and his son to settle. Meg Palmer is Stockton's nanny, and she comes with her boss, Eli, to the lodge, her long-time crush on the man no different in Wyoming than it was on the beach. When she confesses her feelings for him and gets nothing in return, she's crushed, embarrassed, and unsure if she can stay in Coral Canyon for Christmas. Then Eli starts to show some feelings for her too...

Her Cowboy Billionaire Boyfriend (Book 3): Andrew Whittaker is the public face for the Whittaker Brothers' family energy company, and with his older brother's robot about to be announced, he needs a press secretary to help him get everything ready and tour the state to make the announcements. When he's hit by a protest sign being carried by the company's biggest opponent, Rebecca Collings, he learns with a few clicks that she has the background they need. He offers her the job of press secretary when she thought she was going to be arrested, and not only because the spark between them in so hot Andrew can't see straight.

Can Becca and Andrew work together and keep their relationship a secret? Or will hearts break in this classic romance retelling reminiscent of *Two Weeks Notice*?

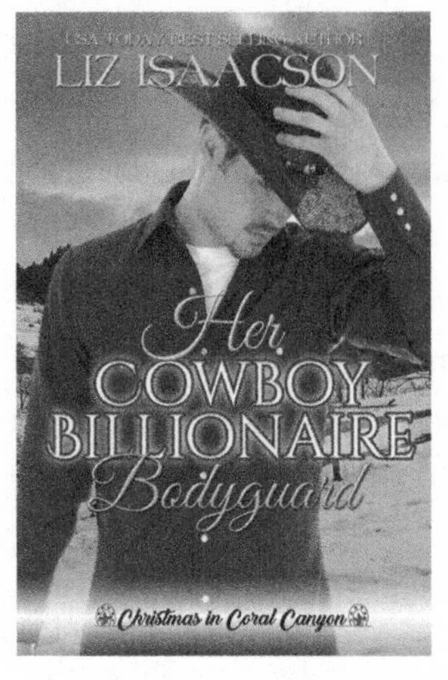

Her Cowboy Billionaire Bodyguard (Book 4): Beau Whittaker has watched his brothers find love one by one, but every attempt he's made has ended in disaster. Lily Everett has been in the spotlight since childhood and has half a dozen platinum records with her two sisters. She's taking a break from the brutal music industry and hiding out in Wyoming while her ex-husband continues to cause trouble for her. When she hears of Beau Whittaker and what he offers his clients, she wants to meet him. Beau is instantly attracted to Lily, but he tried a relationship with his last client that left a scar that still hasn't healed...

Can Lily use the spirit of Christmas to discover what matters most? Will Beau open his heart to the possibility of love with someone so different from him?

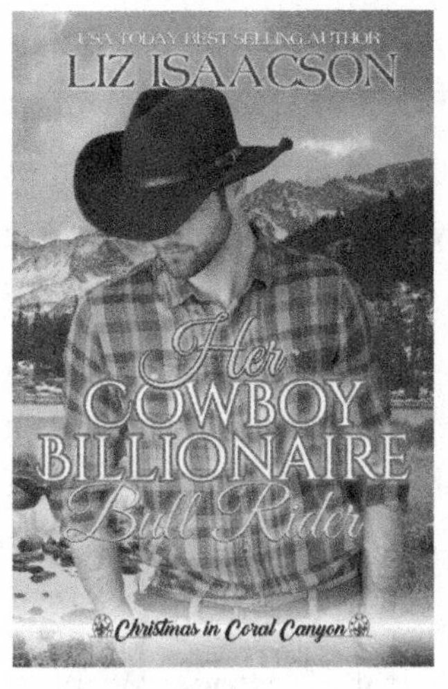

Her Cowboy Billionaire Bull Rider (Book 5): Todd Christopherson has just retired from the professional rodeo circuit and returned to his hometown of Coral Canyon. Problem is, he's got no family there anymore, no land, and no job. Not that he needs a job--he's got plenty of money from his illustrious career riding bulls.

Then Todd gets thrown during a routine horseback ride up the canyon, and his only support as he recovers physically is the beautiful Violet Everett. She's no nurse, but she does the best she can for the handsome cowboy. **Will she lose her heart to the billionaire bull rider? Can Todd trust that God led him to Coral Canyon...and Vi?**

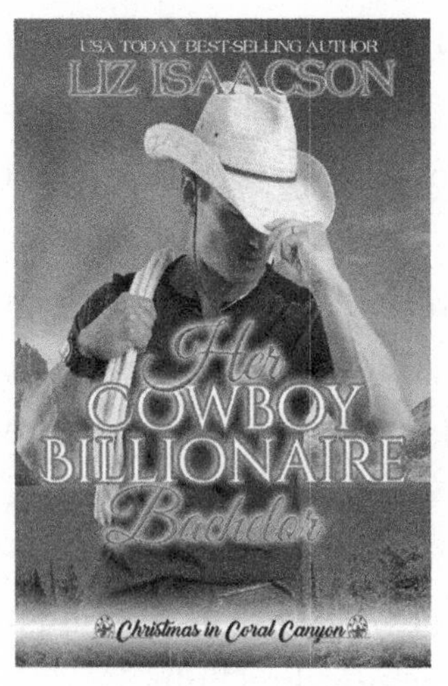

Her Cowboy Billionaire Bachelor (Book 6): Rose Everett isn't sure what to do with her life now that her country music career is on hold. After all, with both of her sisters in Coral Canyon, and one about to have a baby, they're not making albums anymore.

Liam Murphy has been working for Doctors Without Borders, but he's back in the US now, and looking to start a new clinic in Coral Canyon, where he spent his summers.

When Rose wins a date with Liam in a bachelor auction, their relationship blooms and grows quickly. **Can Liam and Rose find a solution to their problems that doesn't involve one of them leaving Coral Canyon with a broken heart?**

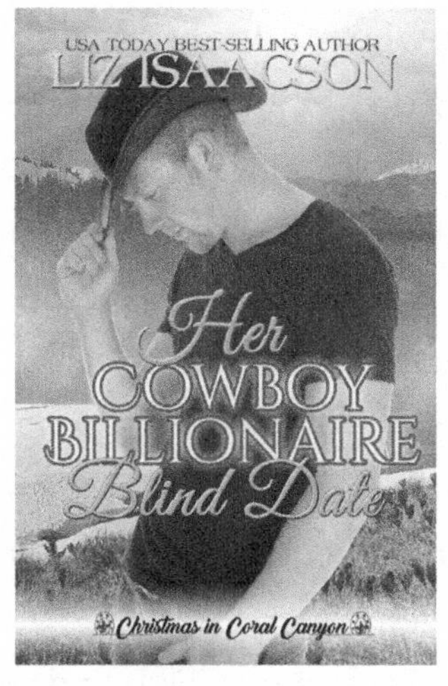

Her Cowboy Billionaire Blind Date (Book 7): Her sons want her to be happy, but she's too old to be set up on a blind date...isn't she?

Amanda Whittaker has been looking for a second chance at love since the death of her husband several years ago. Finley Barber is a cowboy in every sense of the word. Born and raised on a racehorse farm in Kentucky, he's since moved to Dog Valley and started his own breeding stable for champion horses. He hasn't dated in years, and everything about Amanda makes him nervous.

Will Amanda take the leap of faith required to be with Finn? Or will he become just another boyfriend who doesn't make the cut?

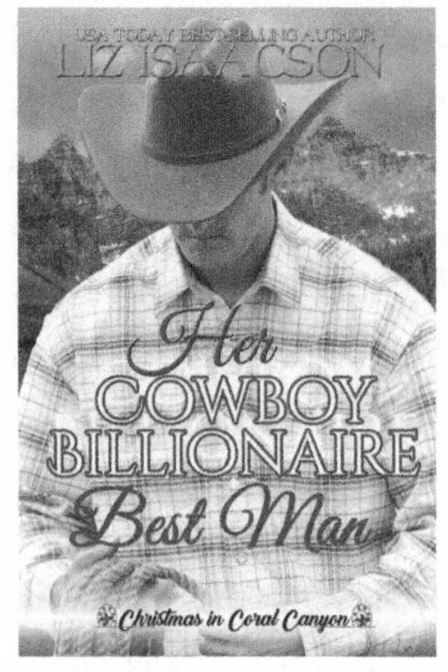

Her Cowboy Billionaire Best Man (Book 8): When Celia Abbott-Armstrong runs into a gorgeous cowboy at her best friend's wedding, she decides she's ready to start dating again.

But the cowboy is Zach Zuckerman, and the Zuckermans and Abbotts have been at war for generations.

Can Zach and Celia find a way to reconcile their family's differences so they can have a future together?

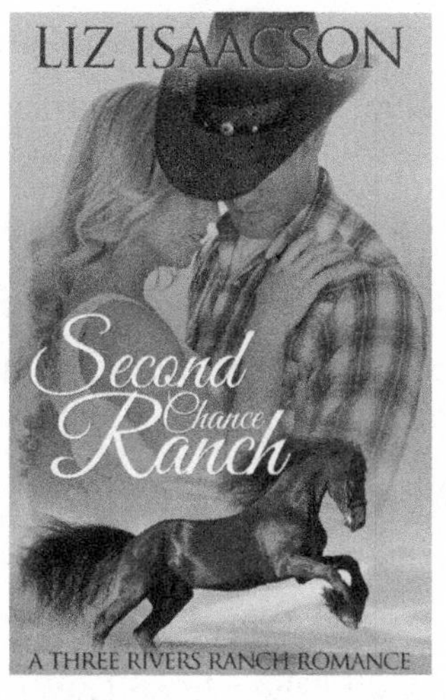

Second Chance Ranch: A Three Rivers Ranch Romance (Book 1): After his deployment, injured and discharged Major Squire Ackerman returns to Three Rivers Ranch, wanting to forgive Kelly for ignoring him a decade ago. He'd like to provide the stable life she needs, but with old wounds opening and a ranch on the brink of financial collapse, it will take patience and faith to make their second chance possible.

Third Time's the Charm: A Three Rivers Ranch Romance (Book 2): First Lieutenant Peter Marshall has a truckload of debt and no way to provide for a family, but Chelsea helps him see past all the obstacles, all the scars. With so many unknowns, can Pete and Chelsea develop the love, acceptance, and faith needed to find their happily ever after?

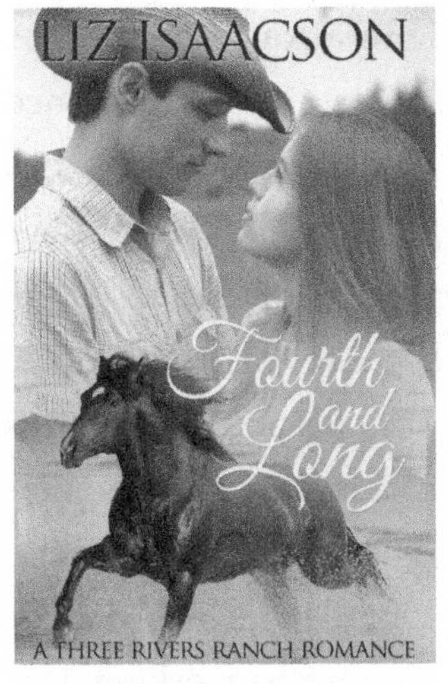

Fourth and Long: A Three Rivers Ranch Romance (Book 3): Commander Brett Murphy goes to Three Rivers Ranch to find some rest and relaxation with his Army buddies. Having his ex-wife show up with a seven-year-old she claims is his son is anything but the R&R he craves. Kate needs to make amends, and Brett needs to find forgiveness, but are they too late to find their happily ever after?

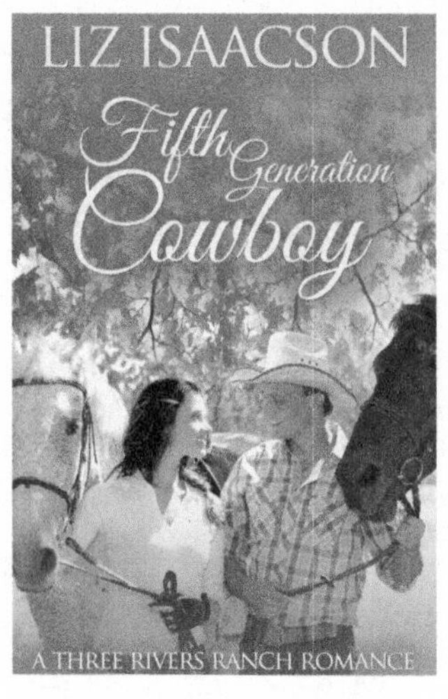

Fifth Generation Cowboy: A Three Rivers Ranch Romance (Book 4): Tom Lovell has watched his friends find their true happiness on Three Rivers Ranch, but everywhere he looks, he only sees friends. Rose Reyes has been bringing her daughter out to the ranch for equine therapy for months, but it doesn't seem to be working. Her challenges with Mari are just as frustrating as ever. Could Tom be exactly what Rose needs? Can he remove his friendship blinders and find love with someone who's been right in front of him all this time?

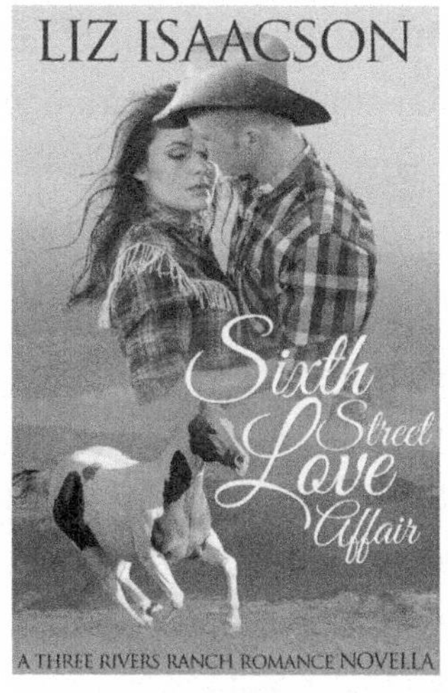

Sixth Street Love Affair: A Three Rivers Ranch Romance (Book 5): After losing his wife a few years back, Garth Ahlstrom thinks he's ready for a second chance at love. But Juliette Thompson has a secret that could destroy their budding relationship. Can they find the strength, patience, and faith to make things work?

The Seventh Sergeant: A Three Rivers Ranch Romance (Book 6): Life has finally started to settle down for Sergeant Reese Sanders after his devastating injury overseas. Discharged from the Army and now with a good job at Courage Reins, he's finally found happiness—until a horrific fall puts him right back where he was years ago: Injured and depressed. Carly Watters, Reese's new veteran care coordinator, dislikes small towns almost as much as she loathes cowboys. But she finds herself faced with both when she gets assigned to Reese's case. Do they have the humility and faith to make their relationship more than professional?

Eight Second Ride: A Three Rivers Ranch Romance (Book 7): Ethan Greene loves his work at Three Rivers Ranch, but he can't seem to find the right woman to settle down with. When sassy yet vulnerable Brynn Bowman shows up at the ranch to recruit him back to the rodeo circuit, he takes a different approach with the barrel racing champion. His patience and newfound faith pay off when a friendship--and more--starts with Brynn. But she wants out of the rodeo circuit right when Ethan wants to rejoin. Can they find the path God wants them to take and still stay together?

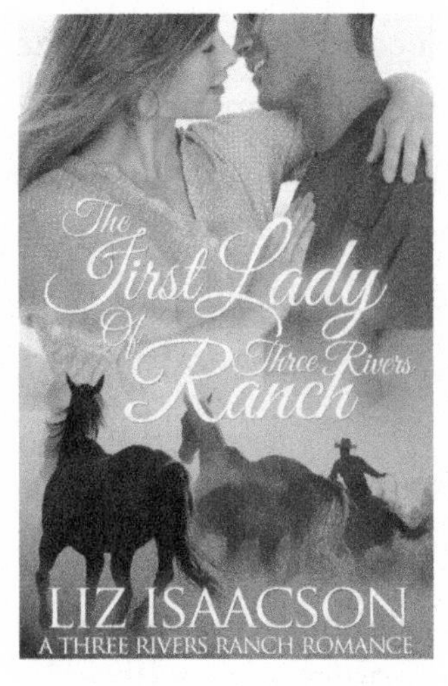

The First Lady of Three Rivers Ranch: A Three Rivers Ranch Romance (Book 8): Heidi Duffin has been dreaming about opening her own bakery since she was thirteen years old. She scrimped and saved for years to afford baking and pastry school in San Francisco. And now she only has one year left before she's a certified pastry chef. Frank Ackerman's father has recently retired, and he's taken over the largest cattle ranch in the Texas Panhandle. A horseman through and through, he's also nearing thirty-one and looking for someone to bring love and joy to a homestead that's been dominated by men for a decade. But when he convinces Heidi to come clean the cowboy cabins, she changes all that. But the siren's call of a bakery is still loud in Heidi's ears, even if she's also seeing a future with Frank. Can she rely on her faith in ways she's never had to before or will their relationship end when summer does?

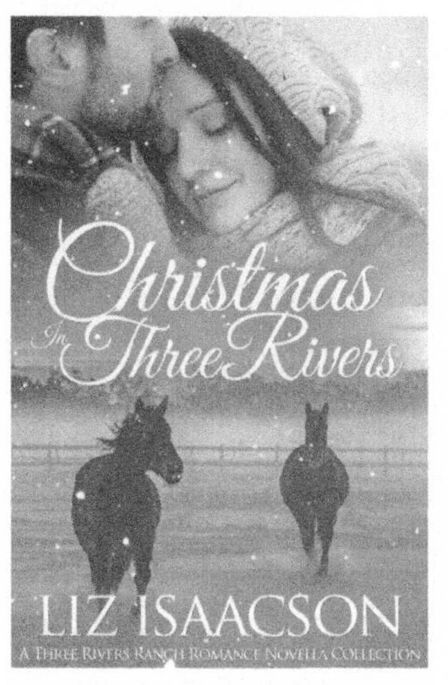

Christmas in Three Rivers: A Three Rivers Ranch Romance (Book 9): Isn't Christmas the best time to fall in love? The cowboys of Three Rivers Ranch think so. Join four of them as they journey toward their path to happily ever after in four, all-new novellas in the Amazon #1 Bestselling Three Rivers Ranch Romance series.

THE NINTH INNING: The Christmas season has never felt like such a burden to boutique owner Andrea Larsen. But with Mama gone and the holidays upon her, Andy finds herself wishing she hadn't been so quick to judge her former boyfriend, cowboy Lawrence Collins. Well, Lawrence hasn't forgotten about Andy either, and he devises a plan to get her out to the ranch so they can reconnect. Do they have the faith and humility to patch things up and start a new relationship?

TEN DAYS IN TOWN: Sandy Keller is tired of the dating scene in Three Rivers. Though she owns the pancake house, she's looking for a fresh start, which means an escape from the town where she grew up. When her older brother's best friend, Tad Jorgensen, comes to town for the holidays, it is a balm to his weary soul. A helicopter tour guide who experienced a near-death experience, he's looking to start over too--but in Three Rivers. Can Sandy and Tad navigate their troubles to find the path God wants them to take--and discover true love--in only ten days?

ELEVEN YEAR REUNION: Pastry chef extraordinaire, Grace Lewis has moved to Three Rivers to help Heidi Ackerman open a bakery in Three Rivers. Grace relishes the idea of starting over in a town where no one knows about her failed cupcakery. She doesn't expect to run into her old high school boyfriend, Jonathan Carver. A carpenter working at Three Rivers Ranch, Jon's in town against his will. But with Grace now on the scene, Jon's thinking life in Three Rivers is suddenly looking up. But with her focus on baking and his disdain for small towns, can they make their eleven year reunion stick?

THE TWELFTH TOWN: Newscaster Taryn Tucker has had enough of life on-screen. She's bounced from town to town before arriving in Three Rivers, completely alone and completely anonymous--just the way she now likes it. She takes a job cleaning at Three Rivers Ranch, hoping for a chance to figure out who she is and where God wants her. When she meets happy-go-lucky cowhand Kenny Stockton, she doesn't expect sparks to fly. Kenny's always been "the best friend" for his female friends, but the pull between him and Taryn can't be denied. Will they have the courage and faith necessary to make their opposite worlds mesh?

Lucky Number Thirteen: A Three Rivers Ranch Romance (Book 10): Tanner Wolf, a rodeo champion ten times over, is excited to be riding in Three Rivers for the first time since he left his philandering ways and found religion. Seeing his old friends Ethan and Brynn is therapuetic--until a terrible accident lands him in the hospital. With his rodeo career over, Tanner thinks maybe he'll stay in town--and it's not just because his nurse, Summer Hamblin, is the prettiest woman he's ever met. But Summer's the queen of first dates, and as she looks for a way to make a relationship with the transient rodeo star work Summer's not sure she has the fortitude to go on a second date. Can they find love among the tragedy?

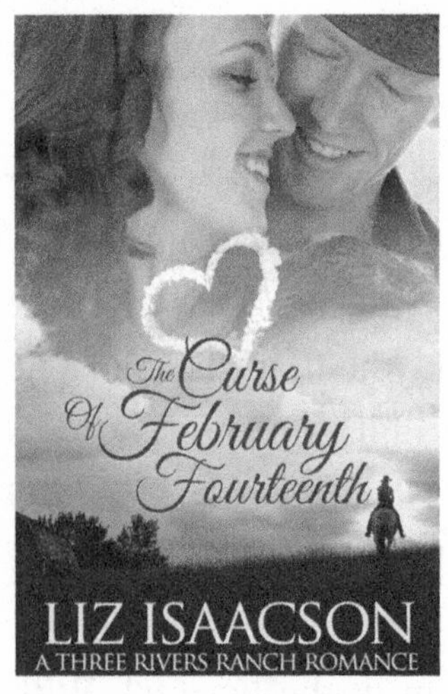

The Curse of February Fourteenth: A Three Rivers Ranch Romance (Book 11): Cal Hodgkins, cowboy veterinarian at Bowman's Breeds, isn't planning to meet anyone at the masked dance in small-town Three Rivers. He just wants to get his bachelor friends off his back and sit on the sidelines to drink his punch. But when he sees a woman dressed in gorgeous butterfly wings and cowgirl boots with blue stitching, he's smitten. Too bad she runs away from the dance before he can get her name, leaving only her boot behind...

Fifteen Minutes of Fame: A Three Rivers Ranch Romance (Book 12): Navy Richards is thirty-five years of tired—tired of dating the same men, working a demanding job, and getting her heart broken over and over again. Her aunt has always spoken highly of the matchmaker in Three Rivers, Texas, so she takes a six-month sabbatical from her high-stress job as a pediatric nurse, hops on a bus, and meets with the matchmaker. Then she meets Gavin Redd. He's handsome, he's hardworking, and he's a cowboy. But is he an Aquarius too? Navy's not making a move until she knows for sure…

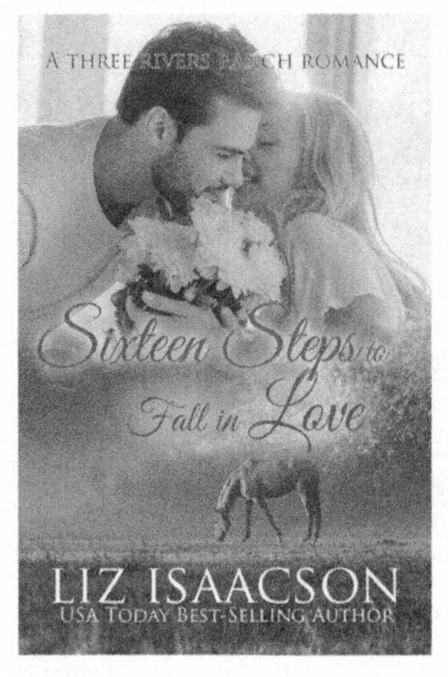

Sixteen Steps to Fall in Love: A Three Rivers Ranch Romance (Book 13): A chance encounter at a dog park sheds new light on the tall, talented Boone that Nicole can't ignore. As they get to know each other better and start to dig into each other's past, Nicole is the one who wants to run. This time from her growing admiration and attachment to Boone. From her aging parents. From herself.

But Boone feels the attraction between them too, and he decides he's tired of running and ready to make Three Rivers his permanent home. **Can Boone and Nicole use their faith to overcome their differences and find a happily-ever-after together?**

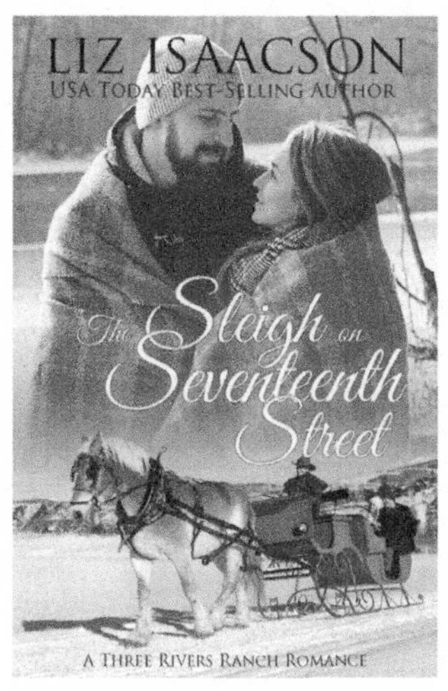

The Sleigh on Seventeenth Street: A Three Rivers Ranch Romance (Book 14): A cowboy with skills as an electrician tries a relationship with a down-on-her luck plumber. Can Dylan and Camila make water and electricity play nicely together this Christmas season? Or will they get shocked as they try to make their relationship work?

BOOKS IN THE LAST CHANCE RANCH ROMANCE SERIES

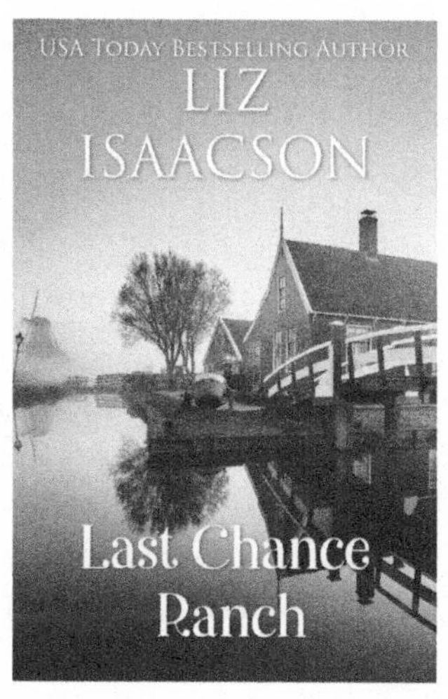

Last Chance Ranch (Book 1): A cowgirl down on her luck hires a man who's good with horses and under the hood of a car. Can Hudson fine tune Scarlett's heart as they work together? Or will things backfire and make everything worse at Last Chance Ranch?

Last Chance Cowboy (Book 2): A billionaire cowboy without a home meets a woman who secretly makes food videos to pay her debts...Can Carson and Adele do more than fight in the kitchens at Last Chance Ranch?

Last Chance Wedding (Book 3): A female carpenter needs a husband just for a few days... Can Jeri and Sawyer navigate the minefield of a pretend marriage before their feelings become real?

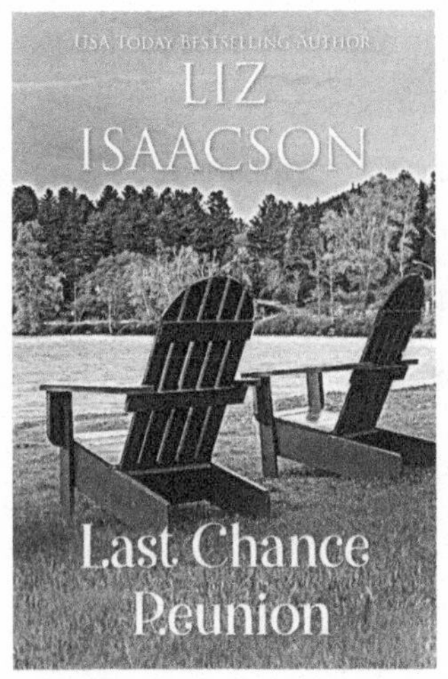

Last Chance Reunion (Book 4): An Army cowboy, the woman he dated years ago, and their last chance at Last Chance Ranch... Can Dave and Sissy put aside hurt feelings and make their second chance romance work?

Last Chance Lake (Book 5): A former dairy farmer and the marketing director on the ranch have to work together to make the cow cuddling program a success. But can Karla let Cache into her life? Or will she keep all her secrets from him - and keep *him* a secret too?

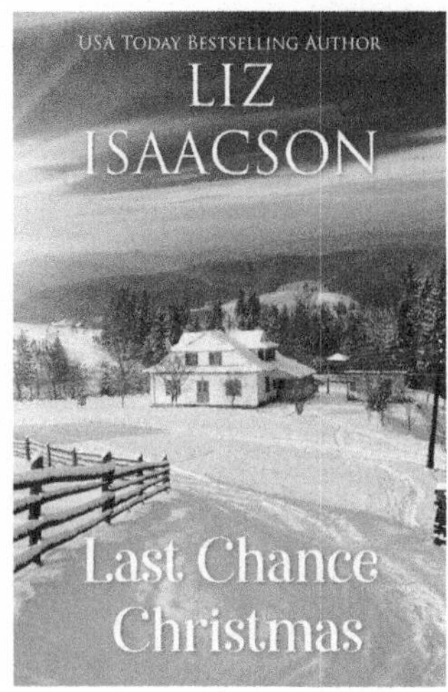

Last Chance Christmas (Book 6): She's tired of having her heart broken by cowboys. He waited too long to ask her out. Can Lance fix things quickly, or will Amber leave Last Chance Ranch before he can tell her how he feels?

BOOKS IN THE STEEPLE RIDGE ROMANCE SERIES:

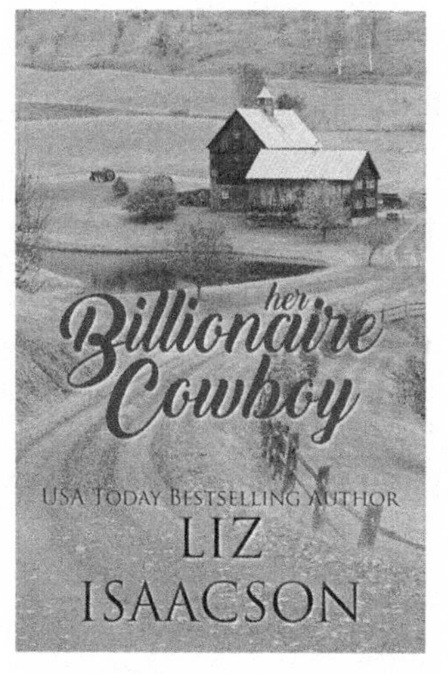

Her Billionaire Cowboy (Book 1): Tucker Jenkins has had enough of tall buildings, traffic, and has traded in his technology firm in New York City for Steeple Ridge Horse Farm in rural Vermont. Missy Marino has worked at the farm since she was a teen, and she's always dreamed of owning it. But her ex-husband left her with a truckload of debt, making her fantasies of owning the farm unfulfilled. Tucker didn't come to the country to find a new wife, but he supposes a woman could help him start over in Steeple Ridge. Will Tucker and Missy be able to navigate the shaky ground between them to find a new beginning?

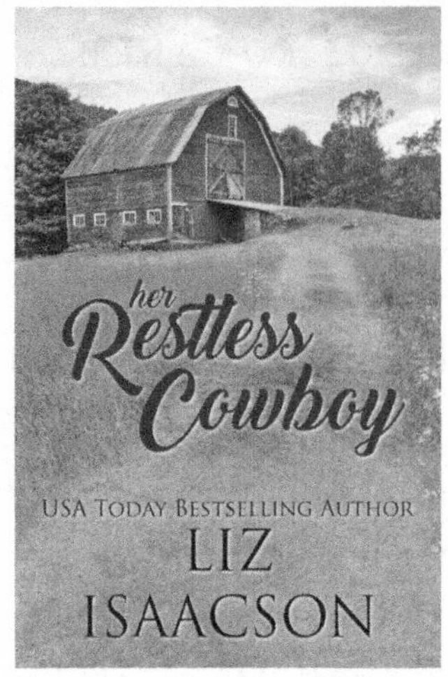

Her Restless Cowboy: A Butters Brothers Novel, Steeple Ridge Romance (Book 2): Ben Buttars is the youngest of the four Buttars brothers who come to Steeple Ridge Farm, and he finally feels like he's landed somewhere he can make a life for himself. Reagan Cantwell is a decade older than Ben and the recreational direction for the town of Island Park. Though Ben is young, he knows what he wants—and that's Rae. Can she figure out how to put what matters most in her life—family and faith—above her job before she loses Ben?

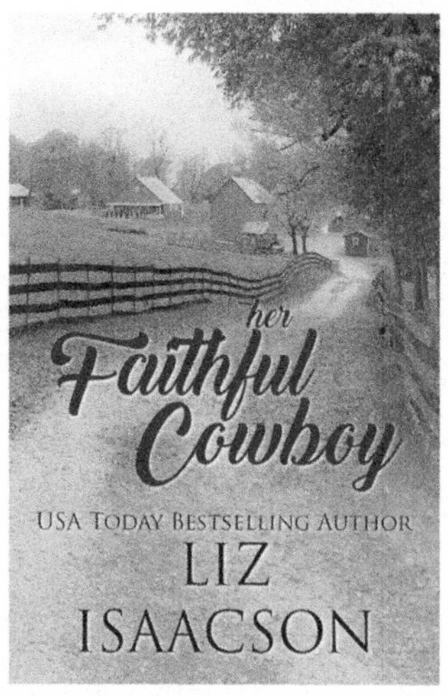

Her Faithful Cowboy: A Butters Brothers Novel, Steeple Ridge Romance (Book 3): Sam Buttars has spent the last decade making sure he and his brothers stay together. They've been at Steeple Ridge for a while now, but with the youngest married and happy, the siren's call to return to his parents' farm in Wyoming is loud in Sam's ears. He'd just go if it weren't for beautiful Bonnie Sherman, who roped his heart the first time he saw her. Do Sam and Bonnie have the faith to find comfort in each other instead of in the people who've already passed?

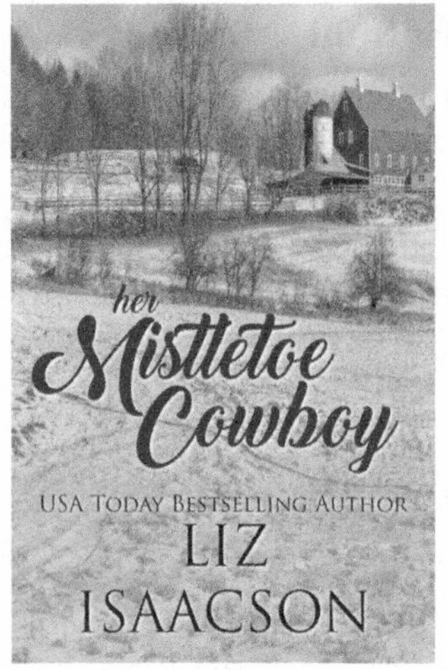

Her Mistletoe Cowboy: A Butters Brothers Novel, Steeple Ridge Romance (Book 4): Logan Buttars has always been good-natured and happy-go-lucky. After watching two of his brothers settle down, he recognizes a void in his life he didn't know about. Veterinarian Layla Guyman has appreciated Logan's friendship and easy way with animals when he comes into the clinic to get the service dogs. But with his future at Steeple Ridge in the balance, she's not sure a relationship with him is worth the risk. Can she rely on her faith and employ patience to tame Logan's wild heart?

Her Patient Cowboy: A Butters Brothers Novel, Steeple Ridge Romance (Book 5): Darren Buttars is cool, collected, and quiet—and utterly devastated when his girlfriend of nine months, Farrah Irvine, breaks up with him because he wanted her to ride her horse in a parade. But Farrah doesn't ride anymore, a fact she made very clear to Darren. She returned to her childhood home with so much baggage, she doesn't know where to start with the unpacking. Darren's the only Buttars brother who isn't married, and he wants to make Island Park his permanent home—with Farrah. Can they find their way through the heartache to achieve a happily-ever-after together?

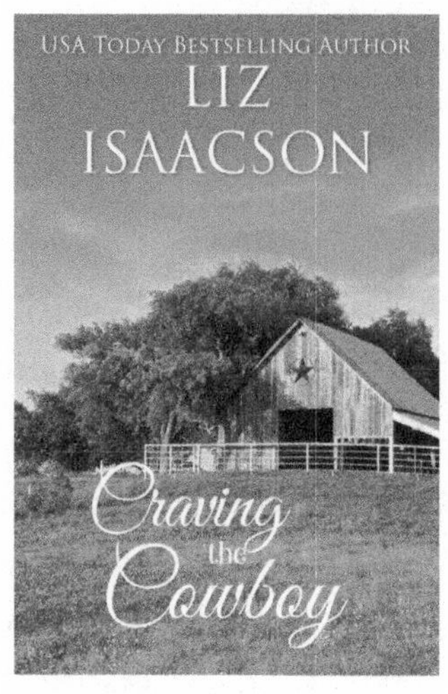

Craving the Cowboy (Book 1): Dwayne Carver is set to inherit his family's ranch in the heart of Texas Hill Country, and in order to keep up with his ranch duties and fulfill his dreams of owning a horse farm, he hires top trainer Felicity Lightburne. They get along great, and she can envision herself on this new farm—at least until her mother falls ill and she has to return to help her. Can Dwayne and Felicity work through their differences to find their happily-ever-after?

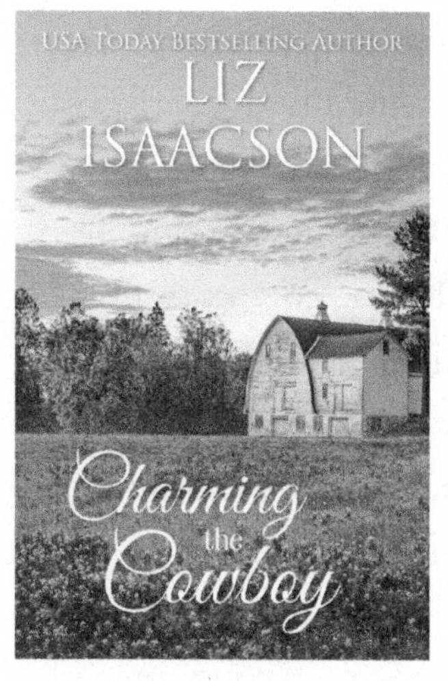

Charming the Cowboy (Book 2): Third grade teacher Heather Carver has had her eye on Levi Rhodes for a couple of years now, but he seems to be blind to her attempts to charm him. When she breaks her arm while on his horse ranch, Heather infiltrates Levi's life in ways he's never thought of, and his strict anti-female stance slips. Will Heather heal his emotional scars and he care for her physical ones so they can have a real relationship?

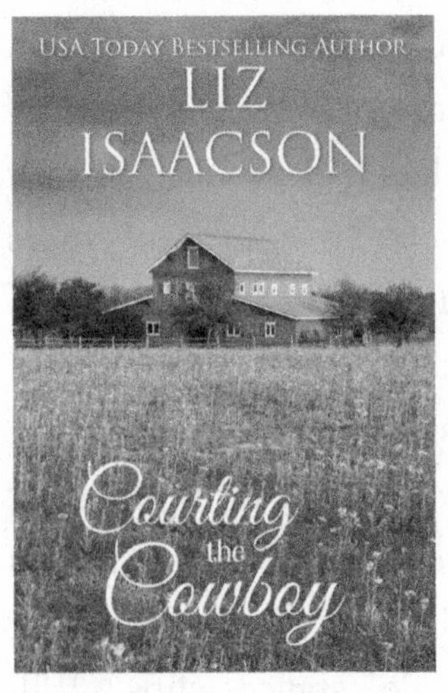

Courting the Cowboy (Book 3): Frustrated with the cowboy-only dating scene in Grape Seed Falls, May Sotheby joins Texas-Faithful.com, hoping to find her soul mate without having to relocate--or deal with cowboy hats and boots. She has no idea that Kurt Pemberton, foreman at Grape Seed Ranch, is the man she starts communicating with... Will May be able to follow her heart and get Kurt to forgive her so they can be together?

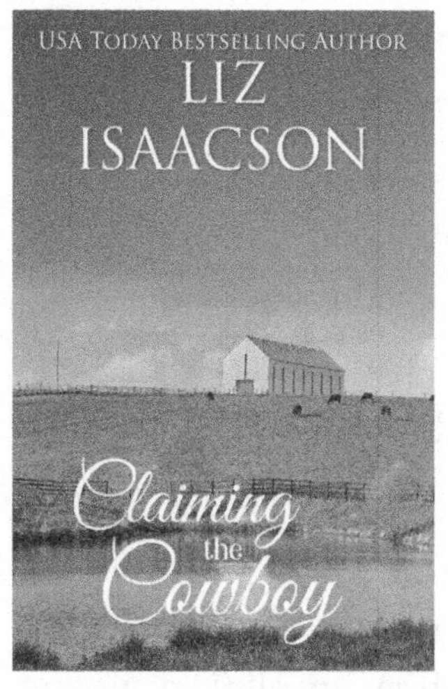

Claiming the Cowboy, Royal Brothers Book 1 (Grape Seed Falls Romance Book 4): Unwilling to be tied down, farrier Robin Cook has managed to pack her entire life into a two-hundred-and-eighty square-foot house, and that includes her Yorkie. Cowboy and co-foreman, Shane Royal has had his heart set on Robin for three years, even though she flat-out turned him down the last time he asked her to dinner. But she's back at Grape Seed Ranch for five weeks as she works her horseshoeing magic, and he's still interested, despite a bitter life lesson that left a bad taste for marriage in his mouth.

Robin's interested in him too. But can she find room for Shane in her tiny house--and can he take a chance on her with his tired heart?

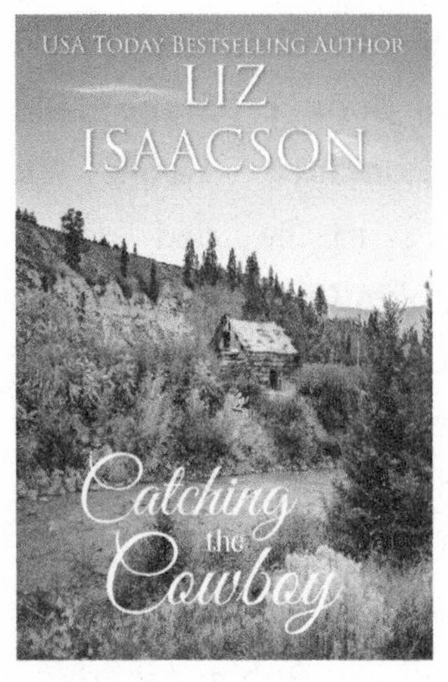

Catching the Cowboy, Royal Brothers Book 2 (Grape Seed Falls Romance Book 5): Dylan Royal is good at two things: whistling and caring for cattle. When his cows are being attacked by an unknown wild animal, he calls Texas Parks & Wildlife for help. He wasn't expecting a beautiful mammologist to show up, all flirty and fun and everything Dylan didn't know he wanted in his life.

Hazel Brewster has gone on more first dates than anyone in Grape Seed Falls, and she thinks maybe Dylan deserves a second... Can they find their way through wild animals, huge life changes, and their emotional pasts to find their forever future?

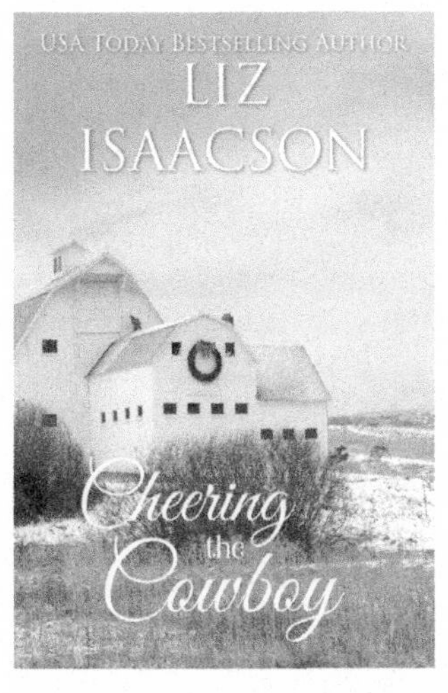

Cheering the Cowboy, Royal Brothers Book 3 (Grape Seed Falls Romance Book 6): Austin Royal loves his life on his new ranch with his brothers. But he doesn't love that Shayleigh Hatch came with the property, nor that he has to take the blame for the fact that he now owns her childhood ranch. They rarely have a conversation that doesn't leave him furious and frustrated--and yet he's still attracted to Shay in a strange, new way.

Shay inexplicably likes him too, which utterly confuses and angers her. As they work to make this Christmas the best the Triple Towers Ranch has ever seen, can they also navigate through their rocky relationship to smoother waters?

PRAISE FOR LIZ ISAACSON

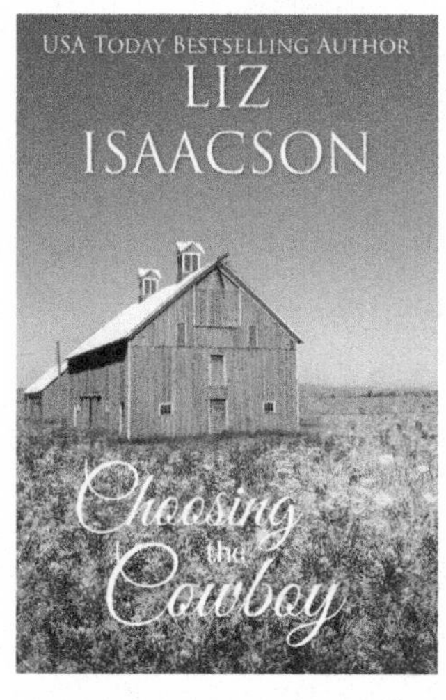

Choosing the Cowboy (Book 7): With financial trouble and personal issues around every corner, can Maggie Duffin and Chase Carver rely on their faith to find their happily-ever-after?

A spinoff from the #1 bestselling Three Rivers Ranch Romance novels, also by USA Today bestselling author Liz Isaacson.

BOOKS IN THE HORSESHOE HOME RANCH ROMANCE SERIES:

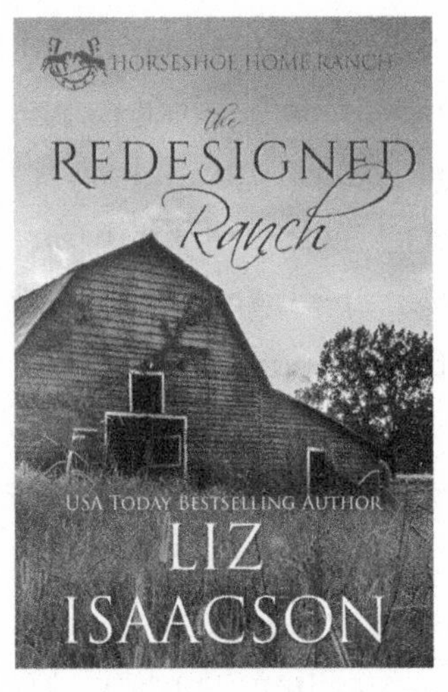

The Redesigned Ranch (Book 1): Jace Lovell only has one thing left after his fiancé abandons him at the altar: his job at Horseshoe Home Ranch. Belle Edmunds is back in Gold Valley and she's desperate to build a portfolio that she can use to start her own firm in Montana. Jace isn't anywhere near forgiving his fiancé, and he's not sure he's ready for a new relationship with someone as fiery and beautiful as Belle. Can she employ her patience while he figures out how to forgive so they can find their own brand of happily-ever-after?

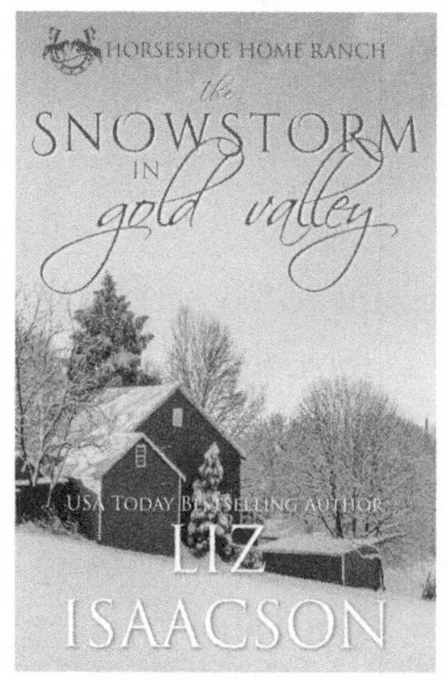

The Snowstorm in Gold Valley (Book 2): Professional snowboarder Sterling Maughan has sequestered himself in his family's cabin in the exclusive mountain community above Gold Valley, Montana after a devastating fall that ended his career. Norah Watson cleans Sterling's cabin and the more time they spend together, the more Sterling is interested in all things Norah. As his body heals, so does his faith. Will Norah be able to trust Sterling so they can have a chance at true love?

The Cabin on Bear Mountain (Book 3): Landon Edmunds has been a cowboy his whole life. An accident five years ago ended his successful rodeo career, and now he's looking to start a horse ranch--and he's looking outside of Montana. Which would be great if God hadn't brought Megan Palmer back to Gold Valley right when Landon is looking to leave. Megan and Landon work together well, and as sparks fly, she's sure God brought her back to Gold Valley so she could find her happily ever after. Through serious discussion and prayer, can Landon and Megan find their future together?

Be sure to check out the spinoff series, the Brush Creek Brides romances after you read FALLING FOR HIS BEST FRIEND. Start with A WEDDING FOR THE WIDOWER.

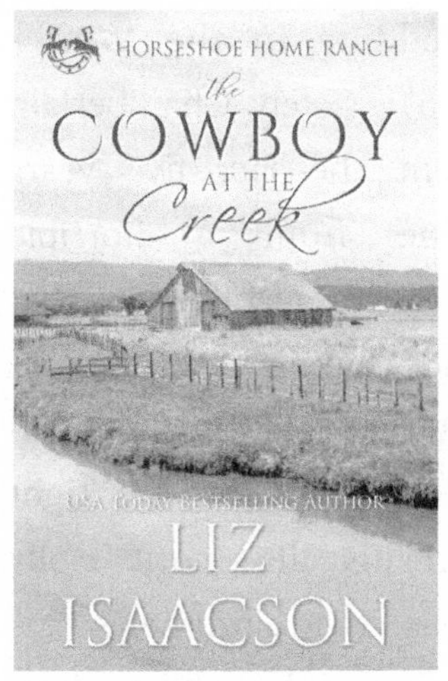

The Cowboy at the Creek (Book 4): Twelve years ago, Owen Carr left Gold Valley—and his long-time girlfriend—in favor of a country music career in Nashville. Married and divorced, Natalie teaches ballet at the dance studio in Gold Valley, but she never auditioned for the professional company the way she dreamed of doing. With Owen back, she realizes all the opportunities she missed out on when he left all those years ago—including a future with him. Can they mend broken bridges in order to have a second chance at love?

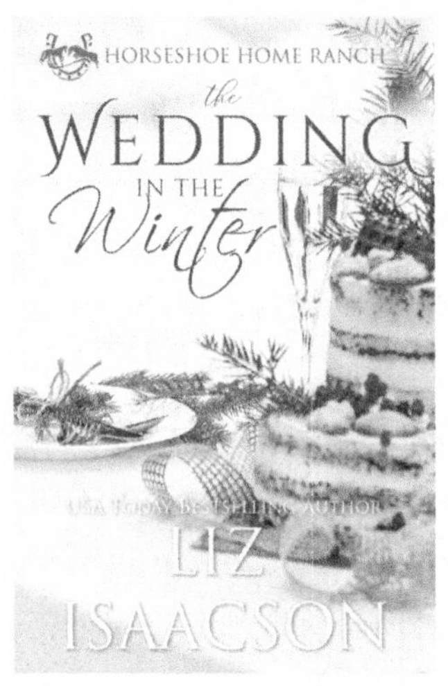

The Wedding in the Winter (Book 5): Caleb Chamberlain has spent the last five years recovering from a horrible breakup, his alcoholism that stemmed from it, and the car accident that left him hospitalized. He's finally on the right track in his life—until Holly Gray, his twin brother's ex-fiance mistakes him for Nathan. Holly's back in Gold Valley to get the required veterinarian hours to apply for her graduate program. When the herd at Horseshoe Home comes down with pneumonia, Caleb and Holly are forced to work together in close quarters. Holly's over Nathan, but she hasn't forgiven him—or the woman she believes broke up their relationship. Can Caleb and Holly navigate such a rough past to find their happily-ever-after?

The Long Way Home (Book 6): Ty Barker has been dancing through the last thirty years of his life--and he's suddenly realized he's alone. River Lee Whitely is back in Gold Valley with her two little girls after a divorce that's left deep scars. She has a job at Silver Creek that requires her to be able to ride a horse, and she nearly tramples Ty at her first lesson. That's just fine by him, because River Lee is the girl Ty has never gotten over. Ty realizes River Lee needs time to settle into her new job, her new home, her new life as a single parent, but going slow has never been his style. But for River Lee, can Ty take the necessary steps to keep her in his life?

Christmas at the Ranch (Book 7): Archer Bailey has already lost one job to Emersyn Enders, so he deliberately doesn't tell her about the cowhand job up at Horseshoe Home Ranch. Emery's temporary job is ending, but her obligations to her physically disabled sister aren't. As Archer and Emery work together, its clear that the sparks flying between them aren't all from their friendly competition over a job. Will Emery and Archer be able to navigate the ranch, their close quarters, and their individual circumstances to find love this holiday season?

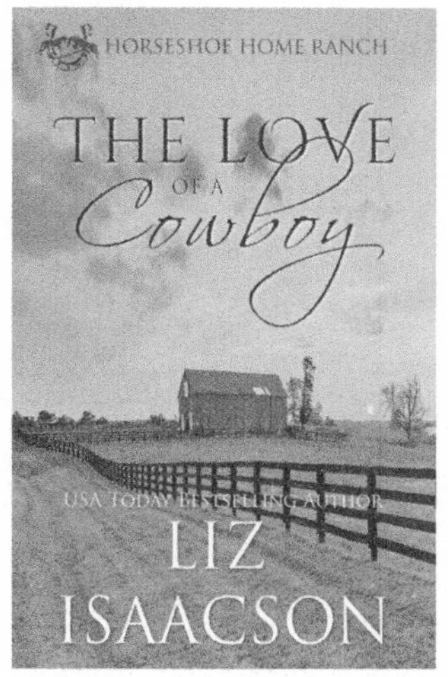

The Love of a Cowboy (Book 8): Cowboy Elliott Hawthorne has just lost his best friend and cabin mate to the worst thing imaginable—marriage. When his brother calls about an accident with their father, Elliott rushes down to Gold Valley from the ranch only to be met with the most beautiful woman he's ever seen. His father's new physical therapist, London Marsh, likes the handsome face and gentle spirit she sees in Elliott too. Can Elliott and London navigate difficult family situations to find a happily-ever-after?

BOOKS IN THE BRUSH CREEK BRIDES ROMANCE SERIES:

Brush Creek Cowboy: Brush Creek Cowboys Romance (Book 1): Former rodeo champion and cowboy Walker Thompson trains horses at Brush Creek Horse Ranch, where he lives a simple life in his cabin with his ten-year-old son. A widower of six years, he's worked with Tess Wagner, a widow who came to Brush Creek to escape the turmoil of her life to give her seven-year-old son a slower pace of life. But Tess's breast cancer is back…

Walker will have to decide if he'd rather spend even a short time with Tess than not have her in his life at all. Tess wants to feel God's love and power, but can she discover and accept God's will in order to find her happy ending?

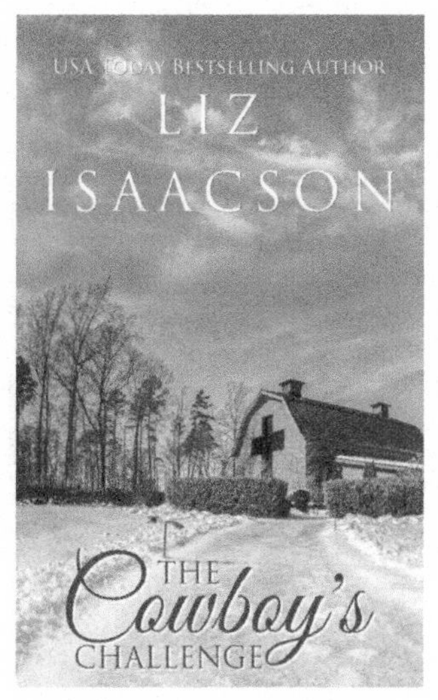

The Cowboy's Challenge: Brush Creek Brides Romance (Book 2): Cowboy and professional roper Justin Jackman has found solitude at Brush Creek Horse Ranch, preferring his time with the animals he trains over dating. With two failed engagements in his past, he's not really interested in getting his heart stomped on again. But when flirty and fun Renee Martin picks him up at a church ice cream bar--on a bet, no less--he finds himself more than just a little interested. His Gen-X attitudes are attractive to her; her Millennial behaviors drive him nuts. Can Justin look past their differences and take a chance on another engagement?

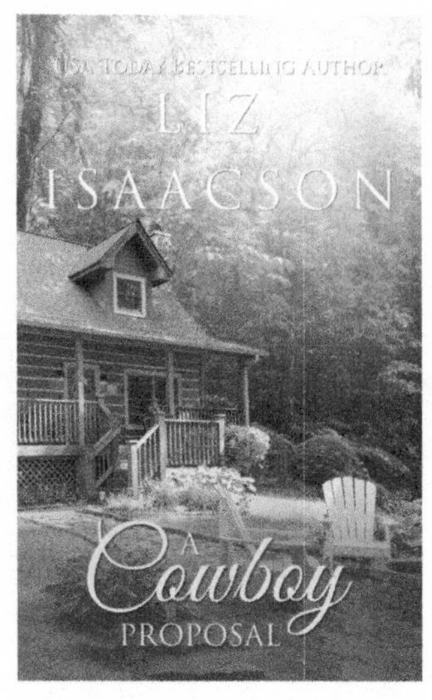

A Cowboy Proposal: Brush Creek Brides Romance (Book 3): Ted Caldwell has been a retired bronc rider for years, and he thought he was perfectly happy training horses to buck at Brush Creek Ranch. He was wrong. When he meets April Nox, who comes to the ranch to hide her pregnancy from all her friends back in Jackson Hole, Ted realizes he has a huge family-shaped hole in his life. April is embarrassed, heart-broken, and trying to find her extinguished faith. She's never ridden a horse and wants nothing to do with a cowboy ever again. Can Ted and April create a family of happiness and love from a tragedy?

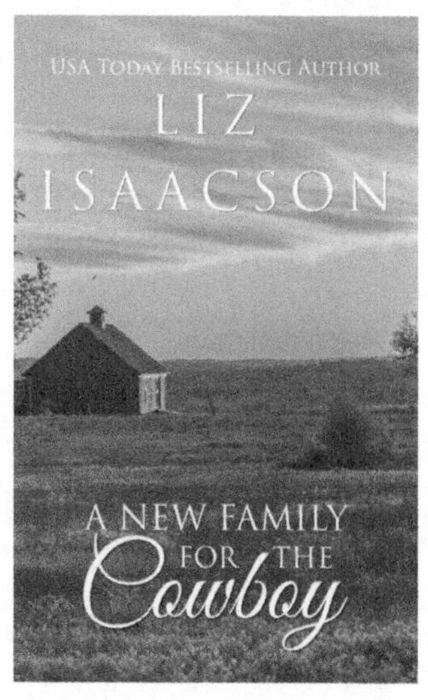

A New Family for the Cowboy: Brush Creek Brides Romance (Book 4): Blake Gibbons oversees all the agriculture at Brush Creek Horse Ranch, sometimes moonlighting as a general contractor. When he meets Erin Shields, new in town, at her aunt's bakery, he's instantly smitten. Erin moved to Brush Creek after a divorce that left her penniless, homeless, and a single mother of three children under age eight. She's nowhere near ready to start dating again, but the longer Blake hangs around the bakery, the more she starts to like him. Can Blake and Erin find a way to blend their lifestyles and become a family?

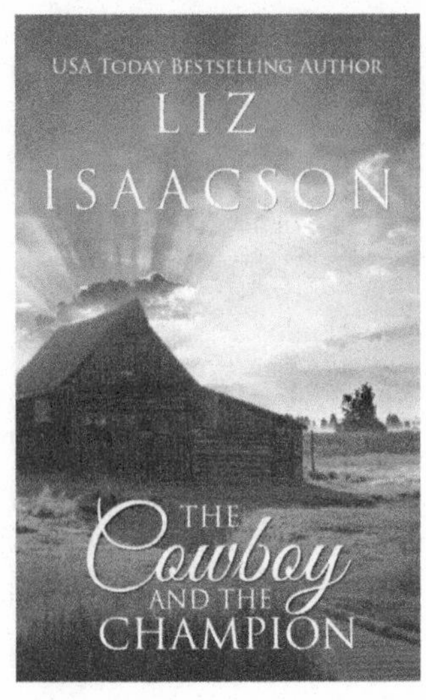

The Cowboy and the Champion: Brush Creek Brides Romance (Book 5): Emmett Graves has always had a positive outlook on life. He adores training horses to become barrel racing champions during the day and cuddling with his cat at night. Fresh off her professional rodeo retirement, Molly Brady comes to Brush Creek Horse Ranch as Emmett's protege. He's not thrilled, and she's allergic to cats. Oh, and she'd like to stay cowboy-free, thank you very much. But Emmett's about as cowboy as they come.... Can Emmett and Molly work together without falling in love?

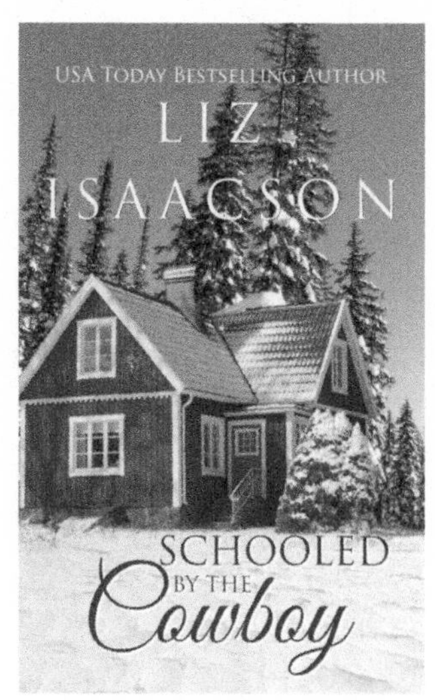

Schooled by the Cowboy: Brush Creek Brides Romance (Book 6): Grant Ford spends his days training cattle—when he's not camped out at the elementary school hoping to catch a glimpse of his ex-girlfriend. When principal Shannon Sharpe confronts him and asks him to stay away from the school, the spark between them is instant and hot. Shannon's expecting a transfer very soon, but she also needs a summer outdoor coordinator—and Grant fits the bill. Just because he's handsome and everything Shannon's ever wanted in a cowboy husband means nothing. Will Grant and Shannon be able to survive the summer or will the Utah heat be too much for them to handle?

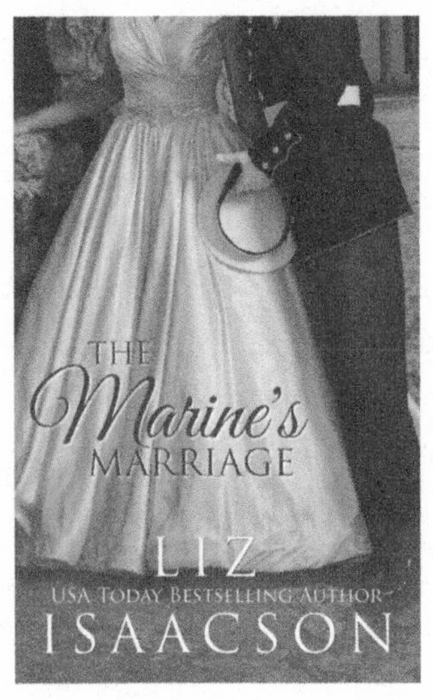

The Marine's Marriage: A Fuller Family Novel - Brush Creek Brides Romance (Book 1): Tate Benson can't believe he's come to Nowhere, Utah, to fix up a house that hasn't been inhabited in years. But he has. Because he's retired from the Marines and looking to start a life as a police officer in small-town Brush Creek. Wren Fuller has her hands full most days running her family's company. When Tate calls and demands a maid for that morning, she decides to have the calls forwarded to her cell and go help him out. She didn't know he was moving in next door, and she's completely unprepared for his handsomeness, his kind heart, and his wounded soul.Can Tate and Wren weather a relationship when they're also next-door neighbors?

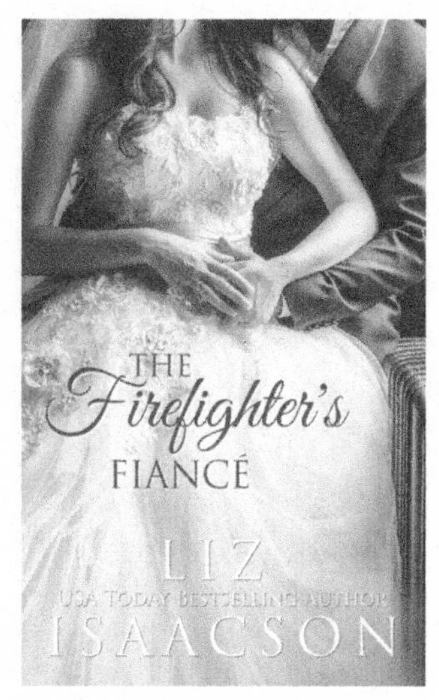

The Firefighter's Fiancé: A Fuller Family Novel - Brush Creek Brides Romance (Book 2): Cora Wesley comes to Brush Creek, hoping to get some in-the-wild firefighting training as she prepares to put in her application to be a hotshot. When she meets Brennan Fuller, the spark between them is hot and instant. As they get to know each other, her deadline is constantly looming over them, and Brennan starts to wonder if he can break ranks in the family business. He's okay mowing lawns and hanging out with his brothers, but he dreams of being able to go to college and become a landscape architect, but he's just not sure it can be done. Will Cora and Brennan be able to endure their trials to find true love?

The Trooper's Treasure: A Fuller Family Novel - Brush Creek Brides Romance (Book 3): Dawn Fuller has made some mistakes in her life, and she's not proud of the way McDermott Boyd found her off the road one day last year. She's spent a hard year wrestling with her choices and trying to fix them, glad for McDermott's acceptance and friendship. He lost his wife years ago, done his best with his daughter, and now he's ready to move on. Can McDermott help Dawn find a way past her former mistakes and down a path that leads to love, family, and happiness?

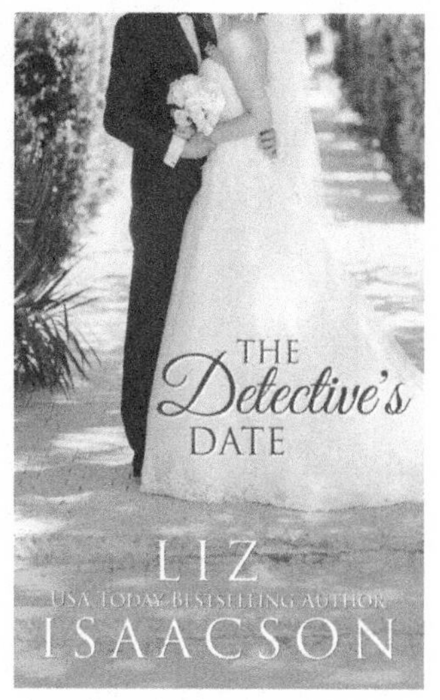

The Detective's Date: A Fuller Family Novel - Brush Creek Brides Romance (Book 4): Dahlia Reid is one of the best detectives Brush Creek and the surrounding towns has ever had. She's given up on the idea of marriage—and pleasing her mother—and has dedicated herself fully to her job. Which is great, since one of the most perplexing cases of her career has come to town. Kyler Fuller thinks he's finally ready to move past the woman who ghosted him years ago. He's cut his hair, and he's ready to start dating. Too bad every woman he's been out with is about as interesting as a lamppost—until Dahlia. He finds her beautiful, her quick wit a breath of fresh air, and her intelligence sexy. Can Kyler and Dahlia use their faith to find a way through the obstacles threatening to keep them apart?

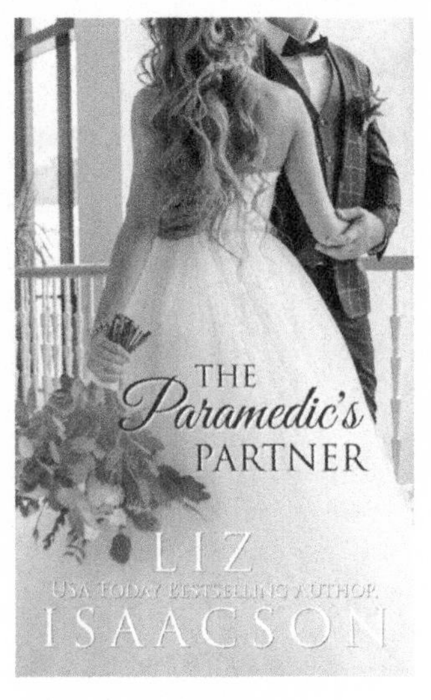

The Paramedic's Partner: A Fuller Family Novel - Brush Creek Brides Romance (Book 5): Jazzy Fuller has always been overshadowed by her prettier, more popular twin, Fabiana. Fabi meets paramedic Max Robinson at the park and sets a date with him only to come down with the flu. So she convinces Jazzy to cut her hair and take her place on the date. And the spark between Jazzy and Max is hot and instant...if only he knew she wasn't her sister, Fabi.

Max drives the ambulance for the town of Brush Creek with is partner Ed Moon, and neither of them have been all that lucky in love. Until Max suggests to who he thinks is Fabi that they should double with Ed and Jazzy. They do, and Fabi is smitten with the steady, strong Ed Moon. As each twin falls further and further in love with their respective paramedic, it becomes obvious they'll need to come clean about the switcheroo sooner rather than later...or risk losing their hearts.

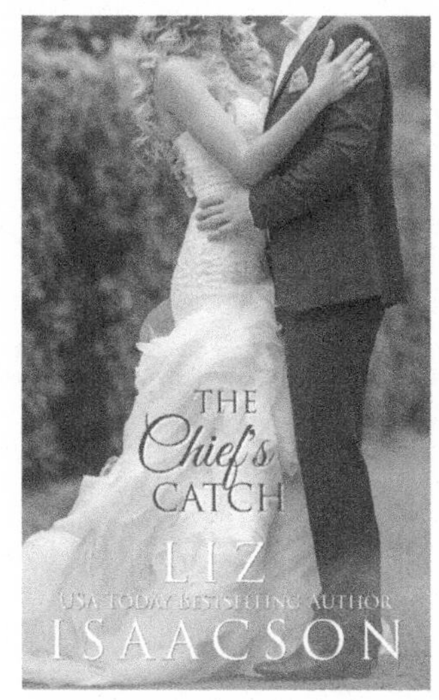

The Chief's Catch: A Fuller Family Novel - Brush Creek Brides Romance (Book 6): Berlin Fuller has struck out with the dating scene in Brush Creek more times than she cares to admit. When she makes a deal with her friends that they can choose the next man she goes out with, she didn't dream they'd pick surly Cole Fairbanks, the new Chief of Police.

His friends call him the Beast and challenge him to complete ten dates that summer or give up his bonus check. When Berlin approaches him, stuttering about the deal with her friends and claiming they don't actually have to go out, he's intrigued. As the summer passes, Cole finds himself burning both ends of the candle to keep up with his job and his new relationship. When he unleashes the Beast one time too many, Berlin will have to decide if she can tame him or if she should walk away.

ABOUT LIZ

Liz Isaacson writes inspirational romance, usually set in Texas, or Montana, or anywhere else horses and cowboys exist. She lives in Utah, where she writes full-time, drives her daughter to her acting classes, and eats a lot of peanut butter M&Ms while writing. Find her on her website at lizisaacson.com.

Made in United States
Orlando, FL
17 January 2022

13605571R00286